Praise for I

"The best book I'

Lora Leigh on *Tall, Dark and Deadly*

"O'Clare [writes] page-turners filled with well-developed characters, and sparkling, sharp-witted dialogue…and attraction so strong you can feel it!"

—*Romantic Times BOOKreviews*

"Gripping." —*A Romance Review*

"Ms. O'Clare has written a gritty, dangerous, and sexy story. The action starts on the first page and doesn't let up until the last. *Tall, Dark and Deadly* is a page-turner packed with sensuality and suspense. You won't want to miss this one."

—*Fallen Angel Reviews*

"Intriguing [and] highly stimulating…a fantastic blend of mystery and suspense."

—*All About Murder*

"The passion and steamy sensuality are great, as are the action and emotion."

—*Romance Reviews Today*

St. Martin's Paperbacks Titles By

LORIE O'CLARE

Tall, Dark and Deadly

Long, Lean and Lethal

Strong, Sleek and Sinful

Play Dirty

Get Lucky

Get Lucky

Lorie O'Clare

St. Martin's Paperbacks

This is a work of fiction. All of the characters, organizations, and events portrayed in this novel are either products of the author's imagination or are used fictitiously.

GET LUCKY

For information address St. Martin's Press, 175 Fifth Avenue, New York, NY 10010.

ISBN: 978-0-312-37216-3

Printed in the United States of America

St. Martin's Paperbacks edition / April 2011

St. Martin's Paperbacks are published by St. Martin's Press, 175 Fifth Avenue, New York, NY 10010.

10 9 8 7 6 5 4 3 2 1

Chapter One

Marc King stood in front of the roaring fire, sipped coffee, and stared at the snow falling outside the large window. Several college girls pushed their way into the lodge, giggling and stomping snow off their boots. They spotted him, smiled, and whispered to one another as they hurried across the large lobby area. A bit young but definite prospects. He was going to enjoy his time here.

"Mr. King." The lady behind the counter grinned a toothy smile when he turned and approached her. "If you continue providing such enticing eye candy to all the ladies as they enter the ski lodge, we're going to have to put you on payroll," she said when he reached the counter.

"Does the job pay well?" he asked, deciding he liked how her dark eyes sparkled when she smiled.

"It depends on what you consider good pay," she returned, her quick candor as appealing as her ready smile.

"I'm not cheap."

"I'm sure you aren't." She shifted her attention to her computer, her slender fingers flying over the keyboard. "But not all payments come in the form of cash."

"Sometimes being paid in forms other than cash makes the job all the more appealing."

"Damn shame you consider looking good a job." Her thick black hair tumbled past her shoulders almost to her ass. And when she turned from the counter, reaching into a drawer and pulling out a card key, then slipping it into a small envelope, he thought it was a damn fine ass.

Marc focused on her name tag, instead of the enticing swell of her breasts, when she turned around.

"Now you're making a job sound as if it is something unappealing." He shifted his attention from her name tag to her face. "London, do you not like your job?"

"Now Mr. King."

"Call me Marc."

She nodded. "Marc, some jobs are done out of necessity and not for enjoyment."

"But others are done because you can't live without doing them."

Her smile faded, although only for a moment. "You're in room two-ten." She pointed to her right. "If you go around the corner here you'll see the elevator. Do you have any luggage we can bring up for you?"

He held up his duffel. "I travel light."

Her dark brows lowered over her black eyes. "You have everything you need to stay here for a month in that duffel?"

Marc smiled, admitting he must appear odd. "I don't own winter clothes. I plan on doing some shopping while I'm here."

She puckered her lips, red lips that were full and round and moist. "Good looking and he likes to shop." Goddamn. London was absolutely the most gorgeous creature he'd ever laid eyes on.

Marc leaned against the counter, "Come shop with me."

London stiffened, holding the card key in its envelope in mid-air. Marc was staring into her eyes, which was the only reason he saw turbulence instantly swarm in them. In the next moment, whatever emotion had spawned to life inside her disappeared. She cleared her throat.

"Enjoy your stay at Elk Ski Lodge," she said, her tone changing and sounding pleasant and professional. Either she worried about crossing a line between employee and guest or he'd said something that triggered an emotion in her that she was trying to conceal.

"I have a feeling I will," he told her, winking and even more impressed when she didn't blush or grin bashfully. Instead, surprisingly, London winked back.

Marc returned to his car, enduring the blizzard blowing outside when he opted to take the wide sidewalk that someone must have been shoveling or snowblowing every ten minutes, since it was relatively clear. He grabbed his laptop and the single suitcase he didn't mention to London then returned through a service door into the lodge. He glanced toward the large dining area while waiting for the elevator. The lodge accommodated quite a few people and was one reason why he'd chosen this ski resort when he decided on some serious downtime.

Being alone didn't appeal to him and he'd heard how Elk Ski Lodge was one of the more popular ski resorts, known for being pricey and catering to those who didn't mind throwing lots of money away to enjoy what Mother Nature offered for free. The holidays were over, and those who could afford it were skiing to work off those excess pounds after eating too much over the holidays.

Marc wasn't here to burn off calories, although he was definitely entertaining the idea of trying his hand with that hot little desk clerk. Building up a sweat with her a time or two would make this the perfect vacation. Other than finding a hot piece of ass to warm the cold winter nights, the idea of being where no one knew who he was or what he did for a living appealed to him very much.

Marc was proud of the family business his father had started after retiring from LAPD. King Fugitive Apprehension, more commonly known as KFA, was one of the most successful bounty hunter businesses in the world. And Marc knew he'd done his share to help build that reputation. He didn't mind at all giving his father credit for making the business successful with all his years of being a detective behind him. But Marc held his own.

The elevator beeped just as two women, possibly five or ten years older than Marc, hurried to join him. He held the door, allowing them to enter, then followed, turning just as London walked down the hall in front of him. She glanced his way, before the elevator doors closed. Her black eyes were so compelling. He held on to the image of them after the doors closed.

"Are you and Harold going on the tour or to the disco tonight?" a platinum blonde with fake breasts and tanned leathery skin asked her friend. She gave Marc a quick once-over when he looked at her.

"He wants to go on the tour." Her companion was a redhead. One of them wore enough perfume to douse the entire elevator.

Marc smiled and nodded to both of them when the elevator opened on his floor.

"If men like that will be at the disco, I don't care where our husbands go." Both women laughed as the elevator doors closed behind him.

Marc found his room and unloaded his luggage, then took a look at the literature by the phone. He found information on the events taking place at the lodge, and there was a disco dance, complete with a live DJ and promises of an incredible light show, planned for that evening. If married women like the ones in the elevator would be on the prowl, he'd be smart to find something else to do. Glancing down the list, he read the details for a walking tour.

"In this weather?" Marc dropped the brochure on the bed and walked over to the window, pulling back the thick curtain and staring at the white wonderland outside. "My blood isn't thick enough for this."

He was here to get away from life, though. And he didn't plan on hiding out in his room and sitting at his laptop. After taking time to set it up and get online, Marc glanced at the list of activities again. He stared at the name of the tour guide listed after the description. London Brooke. There couldn't be two women named London working here, could there?

Marc grabbed his keys and wallet and stuffed the card key for his room in his back pocket. It was time to go shopping. He needed warmer clothes.

London closed out her drawer and pulled off her name tag. Leaving the front desk in care of the night shift, she headed to the back storage room where she changed out of her uniform shirt, tugging a sweatshirt over her head.

"London?" Meryl Angelino tapped her knuckles on the door and stuck her head around, her red mop of hair damp and tousled. "Looks like we're canceling the tour tonight."

"What?" London grabbed her down ski jacket and slipped her vest over her sweatshirt before hugging her jacket to her chest as she followed Meryl out of the storage room.

"You'd think you'd be happy for a night off. I don't know anyone who works hours like you do."

"It's not hard to do when you don't have a life." London tucked her coat under her arm and stared out the lobby window with Meryl.

"You're a bad liar." Meryl wasn't an ugly woman, but her red curls were impossible and she did little to try to control them. Little Orphan Annie didn't have it as bad. When Meryl grinned, though, her green eyes were full of life and energy. There was an inner beauty about her that was enviable. A man would go after Meryl for more than a piece of ass. She wasn't cursed with a body that made men forget to think with the head on their shoulders.

"I'm not lying. When would I have time to have a social life?"

Meryl shook her head. "Someday I'm going to get you to tell me what you're running from."

"I'm not running from anything. Life is great!" She smiled and meant it. Never again would she have to run from a soul. She was settled and working hard, earning legitimate money, which made life even better. "So how many signed up for the tour?" she asked, changing the subject. Her past was where it belonged, and no one in Aspen, Colorado, had a clue about it. It was going to stay that way.

"Five," Meryl said, glancing at the clipboard in her hand.

London looked over Meryl's shoulder, smelling her strawberry-scented shampoo. "Five isn't that bad."

Meryl made a face. "The weather is getting worse. You know we can't take tourists out in a storm like this. They're worse than children. And the last thing we need is to lose one of them."

London didn't know a lot about children, but she didn't need an explanation of the analogy. Meryl came from a family so large she was never alone, even when she wanted to be. It was an enviable life, but London wouldn't bitch just because her dad had knocked her mom up and the two of them were forced to allow a kid to tag along during their escapades. Today her life was good enough to make up for the many years she'd slept alone in a car or a shabby motel room while her parents ran con after con until they were chased out of one town and headed to the next.

"Okay. Fine." She hated having to regroup, and now she would have to figure out what to do with her evening. Today her life was structured and she always knew what she would be doing the next day, even the next week. Interrupting that pattern annoyed the tar out of her. "So we stay here in the lobby until these five show up and let them know it's canceled."

"Want me to do that?" Already Meryl was handing her the clipboard.

London laughed, accepting it. "Go. I'll wait. No point in both of us standing here."

"You're a gem." Meryl gave her a quick hug. "Oh, Mom wanted to make sure you'd be at Sunday dinner."

"I'll be there." The Angelinos didn't approve of anyone being alone, and London didn't mind the large family gatherings, for the most part.

"Good enough." Already Meryl hurried across the lobby. "I'm going to get out of here before I get stuck. Be sure and call me if you can't get out."

"I will." London stared at the list of those who'd signed up for the tour. One name stood out over the others. Marc King. Maybe it was for the best that the tour was canceled. She didn't need to be stuck in a blizzard with a man like him.

Plenty of men checked in at the lodge, some of them single and some pretending they were single. There were plenty who believed they were God's gift to all women. But Marc King *was* God's gift to women. His powerful, chiseled features would put Adonis to shame. Marc's hair was short, which London preferred on men. The day-old growth that was just enough to darken his jawline added to his bad-boy appearance. His shoulders were broad. His chest was thick and muscular. Every inch of him appeared to be a fine-tuned machine. Yet a machine to what means? His larger-than-life persona was more than just an aura. Marc King was well over six feet tall. Everything about him spelled trouble. From his easy flirtatious nature to the way he had watched her while she checked him in.

London couldn't stop the image that appeared in her mind of him standing in the elevator. There were two women behind him, eyeballing that tight, firm ass of his. But the way he focused on her, those compelling light blue eyes, damn near made her trip over her own feet. Marc King had looked at her as if he knew every one of her dark secrets. It was like he understood her better than she did. It was an incredibly unnerving sensation, especially when she felt challenged to know why he was the one person who so easily broke through the protective wall that prevented anyone from seeing her dark, branded soul.

It was a very good thing the tour was canceled tonight. A man like him would melt the snow around him. London didn't need to be around a man who somehow managed to dismantle her so easily. For over twenty years she'd trained and perfected her outer shell, learning how to smile at the world as if she didn't have a care.

When he'd checked in and told her to come shopping with him, London had almost agreed. It was definitely a blessing that the weather had taken a turn for the worse.

Nonetheless, a mixture of disappointment and relief hit her half an hour later when everyone showed up for the tour but Marc. She explained to the guests why they were canceling, assured them the tour would probably be on for tomorrow evening, then headed to the front desk.

"Mind putting this on the peg in the back room?" she asked Todd, the night clerk and auditor for the lodge.

"No problem." Todd, who was a skinny college kid from

New York with the accent to prove it, grabbed the clipboard and the phone when it rang as he walked by. "Elk Ski Lodge," he answered, his voice dropping a notch. "Hello, Mr. King, yes, Marc. What can I do for you?"

London hated how her insides quickened just knowing Todd was speaking with Mr. Eye Candy.

"That sucks, man. I know how you feel. It took me forever to learn how to drive in this stuff. But honestly, we don't really have anyone to call to come get you."

London placed her hands on the counter, unable to walk away from the conversation. She raised her eyebrows in a question as Todd looked at her.

"One of our guests is caught in a snowdrift. He can't get his car out," Todd whispered, explaining the call to her.

"Have him call a tow truck. Does he need a number?"

"He's already called a wrecker," Todd explained. "It's going to be at least an hour and a half before anyone can get to him. He wants someone from here to come get him."

London stared at Todd, feeling her fingers press into the counter, her body refusing to move when her brain screamed to walk away. It was a damn shame Marc was stuck. But it happened. She would bet he had a newer car and could sit out the wait in the comfort of his heated vehicle.

"Yes, Mr. King, I mean Marc," Todd was saying. "I was explaining to our daytime clerk what the situation is." His expression sobered before Todd looked at London, puzzled.

What? she mouthed, ordering herself to wave good-bye and leave him to his conversation. She wasn't listening to herself very well.

"He wants to speak to you," Todd said, handing her the receiver, and shrugging at the same time.

She took it, moving to the side of the counter closer to

the phone, and rested her elbow against the counter. For some reason she didn't want Todd staring at her while she spoke with a guest. Although Marc King wasn't just any guest. Something about him turned her insides to jelly, and she shouldn't be allowing that to happen.

"This is London," she said, hoping Todd didn't notice how her voice came out no more than a breathy whisper.

"London Brooke."

"Yes, that's me."

His voice was a deep purr, like a mountain lion or some other dangerous predator. "Aren't you doing a tour tonight?"

She exhaled, rubbing her free hand against her jeans. The only reason he wanted to speak to her was because he'd signed up for the tour.

"Well, I was. It's been canceled for this evening. You're welcome to sign up for it tomorrow night. The weather isn't conducive for a walk into the mountains tonight."

"I'd have to agree with you there," he said. When he chuckled, her heart skipped a beat. Never in her life had she heard such a cheerful laugh sound like a dangerous prediction. "Does that mean you're off the clock?"

"Yes."

"I don't suppose you would help a man in need."

Images flashed before her eyes, when she imagined what kind of help she could offer him.

"Do you think you could come get me?" he asked before she could say anything.

"Oh." London experienced a sliding sensation, as if she'd been teetering at a steep incline and finally slipped over the edge. She braced herself, sucking in a breath. Tell him anything. Say whatever was necessary to get out of helping him or being alone with him for any amount of time. Lie through her teeth; create some story. Whatever it took. "I guess so. Where are you?" She shoved her insane thinking out of her head. Marc King was just a man.

"This should get you Employee of the Month," Todd told her when he took the receiver and hung it up.

London barely heard him. She nodded and grunted absently as she walked across the lobby and down the hall toward the employee entrance. What kind of idiot was she? He might be just a man but this was how women were mugged, raped, or worse. Marc King might be the sexiest man London had ever seen, but she didn't know a thing about him. Stuffing the piece of paper where she'd written down Marc's cell phone number into her jeans pocket, she stood inside the door and pulled her jacket on over her sleeveless vest. London fought the urge to make a pit stop in the bathroom, check her hair, make sure she looked good.

"Oh no, you don't," she grumbled under her breath, forcing herself instead to head out into the cold.

Employees didn't rate covered parking, and it took almost twenty minutes to let her car warm up while scrapping ice off the windows. Snow continued falling in torrents, but fortunately she'd purchased a newer Jeep shortly after moving to Aspen. Learning to drive using four-wheel drive, especially on roads as they were now, took a bit more time. After three years of enduring Colorado winters, London wouldn't say she was a pro, but she'd learned a few tricks. One of them being staying off the roads when it was impossible to see beyond the beam of the headlights.

"You haven't listened to anything else you've told yourself not to do," she mumbled under her breath, sitting behind her wheel and warming up as she stared at the windshield wipers beating back and forth across her windshield. "You should call him, apologize. He can sit and wait for the professionals to come haul his ass out. They'll bring him here." And at this rate she'd still be here when he arrived.

As she dug out Marc's cell phone number, from her front jeans pocket, her cell phone rang in her purse.

"Well hell," she grumbled, straightening and grabbing her phone out of her purse, which was on her passenger seat. The number wasn't familiar. It rang a second time as she tried again to get under her down jacket and into her jeans pocket to pull out the piece of paper with Marc's number on it.

Her phone rang a third time. It was the same number written on the paper. Had Todd given Marc her number? Lodge employees didn't give out personal information about each other. Three years and she'd never seen that rule broken. Which confirmed how valid her initial reaction was. Marc King wasn't like other men. She didn't waste her time imagining what he'd said to Todd to get her number.

"Hello," she said, aware of how breathy her voice sounded.

"I wanted to check on you."

"Oh. I just dug out my car and cleared my windows."

"Okay. I'm not going anywhere. The wrecker service just called me back to let me know it could be another couple hours. I'll probably be no more than a large lump of snow when you get here," he added, laughing easily.

London shifted her car into gear. "Hang tight. I'll come rescue you before you're completely buried."

"Where I come from, a man is supposed to rescue a lady."

"Obviously you aren't where you come from."

"You're right about that," he agreed, again laughing.

The raw baritone triggered something deep inside her.

It was more than sexual. Her instincts, developed and tuned differently than most, were warning her. Was it simply that this incredibly tall, muscular, gorgeous man had what it would take to seduce her? Or was her gut warning predicting that Marc could pull her into another type of danger?

Suddenly, she was anything but cold. A heat she hadn't experienced in a really long time crept throughout her insides, swelling and creating a throbbing between her legs.

"I honestly feel like a complete idiot for getting stuck like this."

"Is your car damaged?" she asked, leaving the cleared parking lot that had coils in the pavement that kept it warm so snow would melt easier on it.

"I'm fine. Thanks for asking."

London grinned, squinting against the hard-blowing snow and accelerating slowly onto the highway. "I'm glad you're fine. And don't feel bad for going off the road. It's hell out here."

"My car is insured, although not replaceable. But I don't think it's damaged as much as just stuck." There was a slight pause. He spoke again before London could think of what to say. "But if you're driving I should get off the phone with you."

"Probably a good idea. Hang tight." She hung up the phone and hoped she knew exactly where he was.

Almost an hour later she crawled to a stop, hitting her flashers as her headlights beamed on a vintage Mustang that was damn near buried in the snow. Pulling her cell back out of her purse, she returned the call to the number that had called her last.

"Are you in there?" she asked when he answered on the first ring.

"Is that you out there?"

"Your rescue team is here."

"Team of one, I hope." His deep baritone purred into her ear.

London's heart didn't jolt as hard this time. Marc had a natural charm and charisma about him that would break a girl's heart before he'd even given thought to spending time with her. Her defenses were sliding into place. That wouldn't happen to her.

London smiled, taking in the Mustang and how it had slid off the road. She imagined if it weren't made of solid metal, the way cars used to be made, it probably would have been totaled. As it was, she wouldn't be surprised if there wasn't a dent. Marc hadn't driven into hard-packed snow. "Let's hope you're still grateful you only have one person helping you after we get you out of there," she said, shaking her head as she imagined him going way too fast to get his car lodged the way it was. "Can you open your car door?"

"Probably."

The silence through the phone let her know he'd turned off the car. But when he grunted, obviously pushing against his car door, London's heart picked up a beat. God. Even his grunt was sexy. She really needed to get a grip. All this was about was being a Good Samaritan. In no way could she allow anything about this man to fog her brain to where she lost her control around him. More than likely he spoke to every person the way he did to her, she told herself.

"Crap," Marc hissed in her ear.

"What?" she asked.

When he didn't answer, she strained to see through the white cloud of snow outside while pressing the phone harder to her ear. "Marc, are you there?" she asked. "Marc?"

He wasn't answering and she couldn't tell if he'd managed his way out of the car or not. The driver's-side door was on the other side, although she could barely see the passenger side, with snow already trying to freeze to her windshield in spite of her windshield wipers being cranked.

"Shit," she hissed, hanging up her phone and placing it back in her purse. She pulled out her gloves, slipped them on, zipped up her jacket, and pulled up her hood.

The wind blew hard and fierce, and she was immediately blinded by snow when she got out of her Jeep. London forced the door closed and stomped over the uneven ground, aware of how slippery it was. Holding her arms out to balance herself, she walked along level ground as far as she could until she had to start down the incline into the ditch alongside the road where Marc and his car were.

"Marc?" she yelled, and grew more worried when she didn't hear him answer her, although it was hard to hear her own voice with the wind whistling fiercely around her.

London took another step, then slid the rest of the way down the incline until she slapped her gloved hands against the side of his car.

"Are you okay?" she yelled, straining to see through blowing snow as she kept her hands on his car and worked her way to the driver's side.

"Fine. Although I feel like an ass," Marc muttered, sounding very close.

She almost stepped on him. Marc sat on the ground, his long, thick legs stretched out in front of him. London stared down at him and couldn't help grinning. His light blue eyes danced with amusement and a thick thigh-length bright blue coat brought out their color even more. It was unzipped. He didn't wear gloves. And his short brown hair was soaked and trying to form curls around his face.

"Comfortable?" she asked, knowing if she offered him a hand he'd pull her down on top of him before she'd have the strength to help him to his feet. "You should probably close your car door before there is as much snow in there as there is out here."

"I've lost my phone." He pushed himself to his feet, holding on to his car door for leverage. "I pushed open the door and then slid on my ass. The phone flew out of my hand."

She glanced at the ground around him. Even if they did find the phone, the snow was wet and it was probably ruined. He seemed pretty upset about it, and she imagined it was a pretty expensive phone. She began a methodical search, squatting down and trying to imagine where it might have slid after leaving his hand.

"It's probably ruined," Marc offered, echoing her thoughts. "And we're both going to be soaked and freezing at this rate." He closed his car door, then squatted next to where he'd fallen. He ran his bare hand through the snow. "Go back and get in your car and stay warm. I'll search for it for a few and then join you. I really appreciate your driving out here."

"You're going to give yourself frostbite at this rate."

"I've done worse to myself," he told her, his face and neck red from the cold, making his blue eyes even brighter when he grinned at her. "Go back to your car."

"You aren't in any position to be giving orders." She squatted next to him and dug into the snow, searching with her gloved hands as she worked through the snow. "Why don't you go sit in my Jeep. You aren't even dressed properly to be out here."

"What are you talking about? I spent all afternoon shopping for winter clothes."

"Then someone needs to teach you how to wear them. Zip up your coat before you freeze your . . ." She met his gaze and watched his eyes darken as he stared at her. God, he was gorgeous. "Before you freeze your 'you know what' off."

"We don't want that to happen."

London looked away first, refusing to blush or put any meaning behind his comment. Instead, she focused on her task and quit nagging him about how he was dressed or whether he should stay or go to her Jeep. It wasn't her problem if he gave himself frostbite. She was on a rescue mission, and the cold, rendering him harmless by freezing his balls off, might be to her advantage. If he was too cold to flirt with her on their return trip to the lodge, quite possibly London would get him to his room and then get out of there without doing anything she would most definitely regret.

"I think I found it." Marc pulled his bare hand out of a small snowdrift next to him and held up something for her to see. "Yup. Got it. Let's get out of here." He stood, rubbing the phone on his jeans, "Thanks for helping me look, and for coming out here and rescuing my crazy ass."

"You're definitely giving that impression," she said, shaking her head at him as she studied how red his bare skin was. "I swear you're going to be hurting from your skin being exposed to this bitter wind for this long. You really don't know much about cold weather, do you?"

"We don't get a lot of snow in L.A." He reached for her, placing his hand on her back as if she were the one who needed assistance working her way around his car to her Jeep. "But I'm a quick learner. I'll zip up next time," he offered, as his hand moved, pulling her hair under her hood and causing a slight pinch against her scalp.

When Marc looked at his car, London remained next to him, all too aware of his hand on her, but stared at his half-buried car, as he did.

"That's a nice-looking Mustang," she offered, guessing his thoughts. "I'm sure it's fine."

"I hate leaving it on the side of the road alone," he said, his voice softer, almost compassionate.

She glanced up at him, but didn't say anything. He wasn't shaking, or reacting at all to the cold. She imagined cuddling into his large body and how hot it would be. Then giving herself a firm, mental scolding, she forced her attention to his Mustang. It was a metallic red, looked to be in mint condition, with two black stripes going down the middle. It was an all-male, rough-and-ready type of muscle car. Fast and dangerous—probably just like its owner.

"Okay. Let's go."

When Marc slid his hand up her back to her shoulder, the pressure she'd endured earlier deep inside her suddenly swelled to dangerous levels. She hit a slick spot and he tightened his grip, pulling her against him as he wrapped his muscular arm around the back of her shoulders. Pulling her against him didn't help matters at all. Even with his thick down coat covering his large torso, London could feel every inch of hard, packed muscle brush against her. It was almost impossible to see from the blowing snow, but if she could, there wasn't any doubt in her mind she'd be able to watch snow melt underneath them as they walked to her Jeep. The heat roaring to life inside her was intense enough to ignite into flame.

London's Jeep seemed a lot smaller with Marc sitting shotgun. Even after he scooted his seat back as far as it went, his long legs still appeared cramped. She peeled off her gloves and pushed her hood off her head.

"I owe you big-time for this," he told her, watching her when she managed to turn her Jeep around on the road and started back to the lodge. "Did I keep you from any plans you had this evening? I hope you contacted anyone who might be waiting for you at home."

London would have guessed every line out of his mouth to be smooth and polished. He was doing a lousy job of fishing to find out if she was single.

She reminded herself that, in spite of being larger than life and sexy enough she wanted to cry from the need building inside her, Marc was just a man. He had no more power than what she allowed him to have. "I was scheduled to work this evening," she reminded him.

"I have to repay you somehow."

"Don't drive in snowstorms anymore."

Marc laughed. "Have you had supper?"

"I'm not sure the kitchen will still be open by the time we get you to the lodge." She glanced at the clock on her dash, surprised it was as late as it was. "And I'm positive you won't get delivery on an evening like this."

"You're kidding."

"I could probably arrange to have something made for you in the kitchen," she offered, keeping her eyes on the road although she was acutely aware of him watching her.

"Then I'd be even further in your debt."

"No, you're not. I'm just doing my job."

"I'd like to think you wouldn't travel out on a night like this for just anyone."

A silence grew between them as she fought for something to say. It crossed her mind to simply tell him to back off. London could handle Mr. Perfect, though.

"You asked me to come get you," she said, not wanting the silence to linger too long. It would only show him the accuracy of his implication that there might be a mutual attraction between them.

"And it made getting stuck in the snow worth it because now I'm alone with you."

She ignored her pit-pattering heart and reminded herself she could handle him. All she needed to do was get the conversation onto safer ground.

"I'm not reading you wrong, am I?"

"What?"

When she glanced at him, Marc switched his phone to

his other hand and stroked her hair behind her shoulder. "You want me as much as I want you."

"Fooling around with guests is against policy," London informed him and wondered if he was more than she could handle.

Yes, she could. He might be the sexiest man alive, but then it dawned on her that knowledge was her advantage. She knew that about him. He knew nothing about her.

Chapter Two

Marc's hands and face burned like a motherfucker when he and London pulled into the parking lot behind the lodge. His fingers were numb, which sucked, since he was sure London's thick black hair was as smooth as silk, but at the moment he couldn't feel a thing, other than shooting pain as his body thawed.

He knew a bit more about frostbite than he'd let on to London, but admitting his knowledge of cold weather would make him look even more the idiot for being out in it so ill prepared. There wasn't any way he could let his phone fall into the wrong hands, though. Which was another thing he couldn't let London know.

When he'd left home, he hadn't known for sure how long he'd be gone, or where he was headed. He hadn't lied to London. He didn't have a wardrobe full of winter clothes. But he owned a winter coat and long underwear and gloves. A good bounty hunter was always prepared to hunt wherever necessary. His father would have chewed his ass a lot worse than London had if he'd been out in a winter storm without proper clothing. Focusing on weather, and not whoever he was hunting, inevitably ended up with

Marc losing the hunt. Marc's dad always caught his man, or woman. So far, Marc had the same reputation. No way would the old man be able to say he was one up on Marc.

Marc knew he was competitive. The best bounty hunter in the world was his father, so Marc would be as good as, if not better than, Greg King. His father had been shot the year before after making a hasty decision to head into the heat of the fire without discussing it with Marc first. It was actions like this that made Marc think he needed to stay on with KFA and not branch out on his own. His father needed him.

The only way he would remain on top of his act, though, was to clear the L.A. smog out of his head. He wouldn't be gone too long. If a difficult case came up, Marc would head home. When he'd left home, he never would have guessed he'd end up at a ski lodge during the middle of a blizzard. But he was here, and would be close-knit with everyone in the lodge if he couldn't get out due to the weather. It was imperative he keep a low profile and not let someone like London wonder why someone from L.A. would have winter clothes and know how to stay warm in a snowstorm. He didn't want her wondering anything about him, except maybe how he was in bed.

"Did you want me to see about getting you food from the kitchen?"

He didn't want London dropping him off and leaving. She would be the perfect distraction while he was here. It wasn't just that he wanted to see her naked underneath him. Marc liked her personality. She was sharp, thought on her feet, and had a quick wit. Besides that, the way she hesitated when he confronted her about wanting him told him more than her lame excuse about violating policy.

"I'd really appreciate it." He climbed out of her Jeep on his side and met her when she closed her door. "And thank you for the ride."

"You're welcome." There was a glow in those onyx eyes that did something to his insides he couldn't quite label. "You should probably go get out of those wet clothes."

Marc pulled the employees' door open for her and allowed her to enter first. "Room two-ten," he reminded her.

London turned around, pushing all that long, thick black hair of hers over her shoulder. "I remember what room you're in, but I wasn't planning on coming up."

"I thought you said Room Service would be closed by now. Are you going to bribe someone into bringing my food to me? I'd much rather you ordered for two and brought it up yourself." When he saw her hesitate, he moved closer, slipped his arm around her narrow shoulders, and walked alongside her down the quiet hallway. "Actually, you're right. I'm being selfish."

"I'm glad you understand," she began.

"I'll go change my clothes and then meet you down here. Should I just find you in the dining room?"

There was a T in the hallway and they turned toward the elevator. One look over his shoulder confirmed the dining room was closed. He wondered if there was anyone still in the kitchen.

"Go put something warm on," she encouraged. "I'll meet you in the lobby."

A few minutes later, Marc let himself into his dark, quiet room.

His fingers tingled as if they were asleep, and he definitely would need waterproof boots very soon. His feet were burning, and so were his cheeks. All the pain and suffering he had endured was worth it, though, to spend time getting to know London. She hadn't pulled away when he'd put his arm around her. London wanted him, too. Now he simply needed to plot a way to get her into his bed.

Marc cursed under his breath when he confirmed his phone no longer worked. He stared at the hotel room phone when it began ringing.

"Hello?" he said, his mind racing when he couldn't think of anyone who knew he was here. Although it could just be the front desk.

"Hi, Marc," London's sultry voice breathed into his ear. "It looks like the best I can offer at this hour are cold sandwiches. Do you prefer ham or roast beef?"

"Yes to both," he said, untangling the cord and backing up until he sat on the edge of his bed.

Her melodic laughter caused his insides to tighten. London had a voice hot enough for phone sex.

"All right," she agreed. "Cheddar, Swiss?"

"Pile it on there, darling. I'm a starving man. Make yourself a sandwich, too, and charge it to my room."

"Whatever you wish." She sounded incredibly cheerful.

"I'll remember you said that." He grinned at the silence that followed. She wasn't shooting him down, and rendering her speechless didn't bother him at all. "Do I have time for a shower?"

"Sure. I'll make you a plate and have it ready for you when you come down."

"Don't leave before I come down."

Again that silence. "Promise?" he pressed.

"Okay," she offered, the one word barely a whisper.

If she wanted to play hard to get, Marc didn't have a problem with that. He saw the interest in her eyes. The way they glowed when he caught her watching him earlier offered him all the information he needed for now. It wasn't as if he wanted a relationship. Women like London wouldn't jump at an affair, which also added to her list of appealing qualities. He'd never been into cougars or sluts who would put out for anyone. Maybe Marc preferred the hunt. It put more substance into a meaningless affair.

A hot shower did wonders. Marc slipped into new jeans and a heavy sweater he'd purchased that afternoon, then returned to sit on the bed next to the hotel phone. He needed to touch base with his family, let them know where he was and that his cell phone was down. Marc punched the pillows, leaned back and got comfortable and placed the call to his home out in L.A., noting the hour difference and that they would probably be done with dinner and possibly even down by the beach enjoying the cooler evening temperatures.

"KFA!" his father bellowed into the phone.

"Dad. It's Marc." He didn't comment on his father answering his personal cell phone the way he would answer his work phone. His parents could use a vacation, too.

"What number are you calling me from?" Greg King's deep baritone suddenly sounded tense. None of them used phones other than their own, which had scramblers installed to protect them, and their clients.

"That's why I'm calling you. I ran my Mustang into a snowdrift earlier tonight, and when I got out my phone fell in the snow. It's out of commission."

"What about your car? And a hotel room phone?"

Marc didn't usually give much thought to how different their phone conversations were from other families. It was second nature to look over his shoulder, double-check any new environment he entered, and not say a word about where he was, or what he was doing, over an insecure line.

"I'll know more after the tow truck brings it to the lodge. We're in a doozy of a blizzard right now."

"How did you get to the lodge?" Greg didn't ask where the lodge was.

"One of the employees here was nice enough to come get me so I wouldn't have to sit it out inside my car for several hours waiting to be pulled out of the snow."

His father chuckled for the first time, whatever it was that had distracted him when he answered easing away as he understood what his son had just gone through. "I'll remember never to let you drive next time we're in snow."

"Not this kind of snow." Marc wouldn't argue with him there. "I'll see about ordering another phone or grabbing one in town once I'm able to get there. But in the meantime, if you need me, you'll have to call the lodge." He didn't have to offer the number. It would be on his father's caller ID.

"Well, I hope you're enjoying your vacation," Greg said. "Let me know when you get a new cell."

"Will do, and it's been okay so far. I checked in this morning, so I'll keep you posted." He didn't see any reason to mention London. Marc leaned forward, swinging his legs off the bed. "How are things going there?"

"You aren't secure," his dad reminded him. "Enjoy your vacation and you can catch up when you get home. There's nothing you can do out there anyway."

"Nothing I can do out here?" If there was a tough case, Marc would have to cut his vacation short.

"We'll talk later."

"I'll let you know when I have a new cell phone." That wouldn't mean he'd be secure and Marc knew it. Marc and his family used scramblers they installed in their cells to prevent anyone from overhearing their conversations.

"Better call your insurance company, too."

"Yup." Marc got a good deal on the vintage Mustang he'd bought before the holidays. "Hopefully it's not hurt, just stuck."

"Let me know."

Marc took a moment to talk to his mom, promised to stay in touch, and hung up the phone. He knew the rest of his family felt the stress from their last case. Although they'd handled many jobs for bonding companies in the

L.A. area, bringing in criminals who skipped out on court dates or didn't show up to meet parole officers and then tried skipping the state, none of those cases held the same appeal as the big ones they landed every now and then.

It hadn't quite been a year since they'd returned from Mexico, having gone down there to find their mother's boss. He'd been killed, and that was when they swapped out their bounty-hunting hats, which were illegal in that country anyway, and started doing some snooping around. They weren't private investigators but that didn't mean from time to time a bit of investigation wasn't warranted. Marc was proud of KFA's skills and reputation. He and his family had ended up taking out a world-renowned assassin and disrupting the warped game he was playing. The only problem, though, was when the assassin was killed they weren't able to learn who else might be playing this incredibly brutal and warped game of kidnapping citizens with certain unique skills and turning them into killers.

If his father had discussed his plan to infiltrate the house of the man they were hunting, Marty Byrd, with Marc, prior to allowing himself to get captured, and then later shot, maybe they would have gathered more intel. Marc wasn't so proud to believe the case would have gone a lot better if he'd been more informed. His father was one hell of a bounty hunter. But they were all capable of making mistakes and it was Marc's job to be there for his dad.

Marc admitted the wear and tear of that case was part of the reason he needed time away from KFA for a while, but not if a serious case came their way. Clearing his head, taking a look at life from an angle other than a bounty hunter's, would make him better at what he did. Marc loved being a bounty hunter. It was in his blood. He and his brother, Jake, had followed their dad into the line of work without looking back. There was something about hunting another man, or woman, that fulfilled a part of him that otherwise was an empty void inside. Even here, on downtime, Marc knew he wouldn't be able to go too long without resuming a hunt. Although he wouldn't have run into London Brooke if he hadn't come here. She had no idea how much her presence would make this a great, rejuvenating vacation.

Marc stacked the brochures that were in his room in a pile and placed them next to the phone. He dropped his nonworking cell on his bed and headed out to find his new conquest.

The elevator was crowded. He could have taken the stairs but decided against it. The last thing he'd admit to anyone, especially London, was that his feet burned like a son of a bitch and the rest of him didn't feel a lot better. She'd been right about him being underdressed. He would have to admit he'd never known cold the way it was outside in that storm.

Everyone piled out of the elevator, hurrying in the direction of the disco. Marc followed the crowd and watched them head through the main lobby to another hallway. Doors opened and the thumping sound of music accompanied by laughter and happy partiers filled the lobby until the doors swung shut behind everyone.

"Mr. King?" A thin guy behind the front desk held up a plate. "I believe this is for you."

"Marc." Calling him Mr. King made Marc think the clerk was asking for Marc's dad. "And thanks. Where is London?"

"I'm not sure. Probably headed out. She isn't working tonight."

Marc pulled the cellophane back from the plate and picked up half of one of the sandwiches. He took a bite. It was cold, as if it had been refrigerated. He glanced down at the bread pressed into several layers of meats and cheeses.

It didn't look like she'd just thrown together a sandwich for him. It had been made earlier today and stored in a refrigerator. Marc took another bite. Beggars couldn't be choosers.

Marc turned to Todd, which was what the guy behind the counter's name tag said. He'd turned to help someone else. Several other couples strolled into the lobby, but London wasn't anywhere in sight. Marc took another bite of his sandwich, holding the chilled plate, and headed down the opposite hallway. He peered out the door they'd entered and stared at her green Jeep, which was already half-covered with snow that stubbornly continued falling. He closed the door quickly, willing the cold to go away, and continued at his sandwich as he searched for her.

A partially closed door had a sign on it that said: EMPLOYEES ONLY. Marc heard London talking beyond the door and paused, knowing he shouldn't eavesdrop but taking a moment to listen before making his presence known. If it was a private conversation, he would give her privacy and move on to wait for her.

"I haven't made it home yet. . . . No, I didn't get stuck." London paced into view but didn't look his way as she spoke to someone on her phone. "One of the guests got stuck in the snow. I picked him up and brought him back here."

London's hair fell to her waist. She walked away from him, running her fingers through it. Marc watched in awe as it streamed down her back like raw silk. It glowed under the light and appeared not to have a tangle in it. What he wouldn't do to run his fingers through it, learn its texture and how hard he could tug before she moaned with pleasure.

"Marc King," she said, pulling him out of his fantasy. "Yeah, I know." Her laughter was melodic.

Marc ached to know what the person had said on the

other end of the line that London agreed with. He sensed they were talking about him and whatever it was made London laugh.

"I can't imagine what it would be." London stopped walking, standing with her back to him. "Yeah, go ahead and take it. I really appreciate it. It's a thick package?" London shook her head. "No. Trust me, I don't have any family who would send me anything." She laughed again, although the ring of happiness wasn't in it this time. "Sounds good. I appreciate it, Meryl. See you tomorrow."

Marc took a few steps backward and walked up to the door, this time pushing it open. "There you are," he said, and held up the plate. "Thank you for supper."

"You're welcome." She stared at her phone in her hand, looking distracted.

"Something wrong?" Marc swore there was something haunted in her gaze when she looked up at him. It disappeared quickly. "You weren't hiding from me, were you?" he asked, not wanting her to know he'd lingered outside the door and listened to her conversation.

"No." The pleasant smile she planted on her face looked like the one she had used when she stood behind the counter, professional and without emotion. "Not at all," she assured him. "It's just . . ." She paused; then making a face, she waved her hand in the air. "It's nothing. My friend found a package at my door and I can't imagine who would send me anything."

"Family maybe?"

"No. It wouldn't be from family."

She either didn't have family or didn't get along with them. Marc doubted she'd tell him if he pressed. He reminded himself he wasn't after lasting friendship with London. If she offered anything about herself, great. If not, no worries.

"I guess you have a surprise waiting for you then."

"Surprises are seldom pleasant," she murmured.

"True," he admitted, watching her.

She shifted her attention to his partially eaten sandwich, then edged past him. "Shall we find a place for you to sit and eat your sandwich?"

There were more layers to London than Marc had initially guessed. They sat in an alcove on the third floor of the lodge. It was at the end of the hallway and to the side of the elevators, just out of sight. A love seat and coffee table were surrounded by windows, which made it a bit chilly. He imagined in the daytime there was probably one hell of a view. Right now though, the black glass was cold and lowered the temperature easily ten degrees colder than the hallway.

"How long have you worked here?" Marc munched on half of the second sandwich while London nibbled on the other half. It was all the food she would accept, and although she was thin, he'd bet she could put away a meal if she set her mind to it. She didn't strike him as the type who worried about her weight and dieting.

"Three years." She sucked her index finger into her mouth, licking mayonnaise off it. London didn't appear to be performing the act to lure him in, but damn, it looked hot as hell.

"What made you take a job at a ski lodge?" He wanted to keep her talking, find something she would open up and discuss with him. So far it had been questions and short answers.

"There was a job opening," she offered, her smile distant. She appeared distracted. "It's a great ski lodge, the best in the state if you ask me."

"And why is that?" He didn't know anything about any of the other ski lodges, but it was as good a time as any to learn.

"This is the most beautiful part of the state. Anyone

will tell you that." She beamed as if she had something to do with making the mountains surrounding them appear as they did. "I know you just got here, but when you get a chance check out the architecture of this building. It used to be a mansion owned by a recluse millionaire. The story is downstairs on a plaque in the lobby. When the organization that bought it changed it into a ski lodge, they added on all these additions where all the rooms are."

"Fascinating," he said, downing the remainder of his sandwich. He enjoyed listening to her.

"But of course what really makes this the best ski lodge in the state is our award-winning customer service." She beamed at him.

He could imagine what she might win awards at, but saying as much would sound lewd. It would also probably scare her away. Marc hadn't seen the real London yet. He wasn't sure why she hid behind a mask, but her body language and tone of her voice suggested she'd yet to open up to him. God. He loved a challenge.

"I'm not interested in customer service, but in the lady when she isn't behind the counter," he let her know, taking the plate that had held the sandwiches off the couch from between them and placing it on the coffee table.

When he reached for her hair, anxious to feel if it was as silky as it looked, London grabbed his wrist. She had a firmer grip than he'd guessed she would.

"You said earlier I was as interested in you as you were in me," she said, her voice suddenly soft. "You saw body language, which is what most people see. That doesn't mean attraction. It means I saw a good-looking man and appreciated his qualities."

"It's mutual, sweetheart." Although she had a grip, Marc twisted his wrist out of her grasp and locked his fingers between hers. "You are one hell of a beautiful woman."

She didn't blush, which meant she'd heard the compliment many times before. Marc wasn't surprised or offended.

"Are you saying you're interested in only the surface, but not what's inside?"

He definitely wanted to be inside her. "Your personal life is your business. I'm not trying to create some false image here. This is my vacation. I'm here for some much-needed downtime. I'd like to be with you while I'm here."

"I see." She nodded once, as if trying to decide whether she would accept his terms or not.

Marc didn't see a problem in trying to convince her. Taking her jaw in one hand, he untangled their fingers and put his other hand on the side of her head. Her hair was like silk. When she tilted her head back, her gaze smoldered. But it was her lips, so soft and moist when he pressed his against hers, that tilted his world to the side.

She opened for him, and the invitation hardened every inch of his body. Marc dragged his fingers through her hair and wrapped his arms around her. When he dipped inside her mouth, her tongue met his with hunger he hadn't anticipated. A sense of vertigo attacked his system when he devoured her.

Marc wasn't sure what he'd expected out of their first kiss. He wasn't a fool, nor a pompous ass. Sure, he'd imagined her in various positions, crying out his name. His fantasies were blurry, the details not ironed out. But he hadn't expected her to taste so incredibly good. He wasn't prepared for her to be as aggressive in kissing him, as if she'd waited for this moment all day.

When he encouraged her to lean back and submit to him, soft strands of silky hair tickled his arms. Her slender body tucked against his. The way she molded against him and returned the kiss stole every thought from his brain. He'd never considered himself a master of seduction and doubted it was his skills that turned her into such a willing and eager partner. But they kissed as if they'd done it a million times, with none of the awkwardness or hesitation that so often accompanied that first kiss.

Marc moved his mouth to her cheek and then began a trail down her neck. He gripped her waist, feeling her round, perky breasts pressing against his chest. If he didn't get control of himself, he'd push his hands up her shirt and cup those soft, full mounds of flesh.

It took more strength than he thought he had at the moment, but Marc straightened. He was rewarded by a beautiful flush in London's cheeks and slightly swollen, parted lips. Her tonguc darted over them at the same time she fluttered her lashes and slowly looked up at him. London wasn't short, but she wasn't the tallest woman he'd been with, either. It didn't seem to bother her when she tilted her head and focused on him. He saw quiet confidence and extreme satisfaction. London didn't do what she didn't want to do, and he had a feeling she had few regrets.

"I'm going to head home now," she whispered, and cleared her voice.

"You're driving home in this shit?"

London stepped out of his arms and tugged at her sweatshirt. Her nipples were hard underneath. "I've done it many times." She offered him a small laugh. "You get accustomed to driving in snow when you live here."

"How far is your home from here?" He knew Aspen was a good twenty-minute drive. He'd done it earlier today, and that was when it wasn't snowing or dark.

London picked the plate off the coffee table and walked away from him. He caught up with her at the elevator. "Come to my room. You call the shots," he promised. "But it's not safe to drive home in this weather. I don't care how many times you've done it."

London shook her head. "There is no way I'm staying the night here. I work here, remember?"

"I can be very sneaky," he offered, grinning.

She grinned, too, and shoved her thick, smooth black hair behind her shoulder. "I'm not sure that is saying good things about you."

The elevator doors opened with a *ding* and an older couple stepped out, nodding and smiling at both of them. Marc stood to the side and placed his hand on London's shoulder when he escorted her into the elevator after the couple walked around the corner.

"That isn't what I meant," he said. "I didn't mean for it to sound bad."

"Yeah, it did. Images of you climbing out of married women's bedroom windows came to mind." She was relaxed, a natural, when the conversation was light and easy.

"I meant I wouldn't do anything to compromise your job here. I'm not a coldhearted bastard."

"I'm sure you aren't." London reached forward and pushed the button for the main floor. "I risked coming up here with you."

"You would have gotten in trouble for sitting and eating with me?"

"No," she said slowly. "But if anyone saw me coming or going from your room I would never live it down. It's not something I plan on ever making a habit of doing."

"Good." He knew the rule. Three strikes and he was out. Marc wouldn't push his luck and finished riding down with her in silence. At least he knew she didn't make a habit of sleeping with any guest who appealed to her. For some reason, that made him want her more.

Granted, having tasted her mouth, he was anxious to taste the rest of her. Marc followed her to the small room where he'd found her earlier on the phone. London picked up her coat and gloves where she'd left them on a table.

"I'll walk you to your car," he suggested.

London shook her head slowly, making a face that showed her exasperation. "You aren't wearing your coat. At this rate, you'll end up nursing a fierce case of frostbite before you've been here a week."

That was his third strike and he hadn't seen it coming. But she had him there. If he stood outside in this storm while she warmed up her car, he'd be shaking so furiously he wouldn't be able to move his arms to give her a hug.

"Mr. King?" Todd, the desk clerk, appeared in the doorway of the break room, his attention shifting from Marc to London. "I'm sorry. I mean Marc. I tried calling your room a couple times. The tow truck is here with your car. They are out in the parking lot right now."

"Thanks, man." Marc offered him an easy smile, ignoring the question in the night clerk's eyes. He backed out of the break room, waiting for Todd to reluctantly leave them alone and return to the lobby. "I need to run to my room and get my coat. Don't leave before I can say good-bye."

By morning, the snow had quit falling. Marc's hair was still damp as he surveyed his car and determined there was no damage. Damn good streak of luck. Glancing across the parking lot to where London's green Jeep was parked, he wondered if he'd be as lucky with her.

He made a detour to the gift shop and picked up a pale pink silk rose and placed it in front of London on the counter. "So do you work here every day all day?" he asked, keeping his voice low and ignoring her wary look as she stared at the rose.

"Eight to six, Monday through Friday," she said, sliding the rose off the counter and tucking it neatly out of sight. "How's your Mustang?" she asked when another guest approached the counter.

London didn't wait for his answer but helped the other guest. Another employee, a redhead with curls and a healthy glow that made her look as if she'd just come in from playing in the snow, walked behind the counter and smiled at him.

"Have you been helped?" she asked.

"Yes," He returned her easy smile and leaned against the counter, taking in the busy lobby. It appeared a group was getting ready to head out to ski, the chatter about the fresh snowfall varying from excitement to others sounding nervous.

"Here's that package you told me to pick up for you," the redhead told London. "It was leaning against your front door."

Marc shifted his attention to the women. London and the other woman moved to the far corner behind the counter, whispering between themselves as London accepted a small, flat package that looked as if it had been a rough ride reaching her house.

"Aren't you going to open it?" the woman asked.

"Fine." London sounded exasperated but grinned at her co-worker as she slid her finger under the glued seal and opened the package. She slid several pieces of paper out and studied them.

Marc swore all color drained from her face.

Whatever reaction she had to the contents she concealed quickly as she slid everything back into the package. "I'll be darned," she said, offering that polite smile and laughter that didn't reach her eyes. London wore a better mask than some of the hardened criminals he'd dealt with in the past. "It's from my family. Thanks for saving it from the storm," she said, patting her friend's shoulder. "I'll be right back," she added, and headed down the hallway to the employees' break room.

If he made a show of following her, he would piss her off. London didn't appear thrilled about whatever it was she got in the mail. Since she didn't want her co-worker to know about it, he doubted it would be something London would share with him.

He would make the best of his day, take advantage of the blue skies and forecast predicting no snow for the next twenty-four hours. The first thing he needed to do was take care of his cell phone. Leaving London to her job, he decided he would be in the lobby when she was ready to get off work.

Marc let himself into his room to grab his broken phone, impressed Housekeeping had already been there and his bed was neatly made and fresh towels were piled in the bathroom. It was a really nice room, spacious, with room to entertain and work, depending on the guest's agenda. A love seat similar to the one he'd sat on with London last night was in one corner, with an upright chair next to it and a small oval coffee table finishing off the intimate setting. On the other side of the room was a decent-sized desk, where he'd set up his laptop. The big-screen TV could be seen from anywhere in the room, and the king-sized bed wasn't crowded into the room as that sized bed often was in hotel rooms. There was a Jacuzzi in the bathroom that he'd love to soak in with London. If she held on to her rule about not coming to his room that wouldn't happen.

Marc wondered if it would be worth the money to get a room in Aspen. They could spend the night there until she was comfortable enough to have him over to her house. She also didn't mention working weekends. Maybe they could make a day of it. Oftentimes people who worked all day never took time to see the sights in their own town. He paused in the middle of the room when he realized the direction of his thoughts. He was laying out a plan to spend quality time with her, get to know her better; that wasn't the deal. He'd be smart to keep the game plan focused around getting her naked. Good physical sex, fun times, and no one got hurt. Long days spent together walking and talking risked other emotions surfacing.

As he lectured himself he took in the contents of his room. "Where's my phone?" He stared at the freshly made bed, the clean, uncluttered nightstand. "I left it on my bed last night."

He remembered it clearly. Before going downstairs last night for his sandwich, he'd tossed the phone on his bed. Had it been there when he'd come upstairs last night and crashed? His thoughts had been full of London and it had been late. He'd entered his room, pulled back the covers, and stretched out with the remote until he'd fallen asleep. He would have noticed if his phone hadn't been on his bed, though, wouldn't he?

Marc got down on his hands and knees, working his large frame to the floor until he could lift the blankets and peer underneath. The bed stood on a wooden base, which meant there was less than a foot of space under the bed before there was wood. He didn't see his phone. Nonetheless, he moved to the other side of the bed and repeated the process. No phone.

"Well, crap. They don't just disappear." He scowled at his desk, walked over to his laptop, fingered the neatly stacked brochures. Just for good measure, he went through his suitcase and then laptop case as well as his duffel bag. "Apparently this one disappears."

An unsettling feeling gripped his gut as he fisted his hands against his hips and stared again at the room, willing the phone to appear. There were numbers on that phone that could incriminate some people if they fell into the wrong hands. An expensive scrambler was installed in his cell phone. He couldn't imagine it falling into the wrong hands out here in Aspen, Colorado. But at the same time, cell phones didn't just vanish.

In spite of water damage, someone with the right knowledge might be able to pull information off it. Marc didn't consider himself paranoid, just cautious. Which was why he'd played in the snow last night until he found it. Now it was gone.

After searching his room one more time, even taking time to look in places he knew it wouldn't be, Marc sat at his desk and picked up the room phone.

"Front desk," London purred into the phone. "What can I do for you, Mr. King?"

"You make it sound as if you're talking to my father."

Her professional laugh had a nice sound to it and Marc smiled, in spite of the tension growing in his gut.

"We're supposed to address all guests formally," she explained. "What's up?"

She didn't sound worried he'd called to bother her while she was working, which spoke volumes. London figured him to be a man who respected boundaries. And he was.

"My cell phone is missing," he said without preamble. "Who cleaned my room?"

"That's not good. Hold on." She didn't put him on hold but hummed in his ear as she made him wait. "Sally cleaned your room. She finished thirty minutes ago. More than likely she is still on your floor. But Marc, she is bonded and has been here longer than I have. No one has ever complained about her," London added, lowering her voice as she finished speaking. "Are you sure you left it in your room? Maybe it's in your coat pocket."

"I'll check." He put the phone down, positive he hadn't left his cell phone there but willing to check just to cover all bases. "Nope," he said when he picked up the receiver and once again reclined in the chair and faced his laptop. "I left it on my bed before I came down last night for my sandwich and now it's gone. I've torn this room apart, London. It's not here."

"Why would someone take a broken phone?" London asked. "I'm really sorry. We have forms down here if you want to file a complaint," she added.

Something told him advertising that his phone was missing wasn't a good idea. "No. It would have been easier to have my SIM card, but I can call my provider when I buy a new phone. What are you doing tonight?" he asked, changing the subject. The sooner he got into town and contacted his provider, rendering his broken phone useless, the better.

"Working. The walking tour is tonight."

"Sign me up. I'll see you tonight."

"Okay. Sorry about your phone. I'll talk to Sally."

"Don't bother. It sounds like she's got a solid reputation and I don't want Housekeeping holding a grudge against me."

London laughed. "It would suck to sleep on dirty sheets."

"There's promise in that comment," he teased.

This time London's laughter sounded more sincere. "Try not to get stuck driving into town," she scolded.

"I know who to call if I do."

London didn't usually watch the clock while at work. She liked her job for the most part. It wasn't the same thing every day, and with such a large resort there were always issues to handle with the many guests. And this time of year the place was almost full. She hurried down the third floor, staring at the small couch where she and Marc ate sandwiches the night before. If only Marc being part of the tour tonight was the only thought distracting her from work.

After dropping towels off for one couple, then helping another guest get his laptop online, she tried not thinking about Marc as she headed to the service elevator. It made banging sounds and jerked a few times as she took it to the first floor, but London barely noticed. The contents of the package Meryl had brought to her this morning still had her stomach tied in knots.

There was no return address. But after she saw the contents she understood why. They were pictures of her mom and dad, but not the type of snapshots most family members sent to each other. London doubted her parents sent these pictures. Each shot was engraved in her brain, and they appeared like a slide show in her mind.

One picture was of her mother, standing at a counter with a gun poised at a person facing her. She wore a scarf on her head, but London knew it was her mom. The picture looked like it had been taken from a security camera. The next shot, of London's father, appeared to be taken in the same building. He was hurrying out the door with large bags under his arms. The concerned, focused look on his face was captured by the camera.

There were a handful of other pictures, a couple of her parents driving in a car. One was of her mother lying out naked, sunbathing on a beach. There was even a shot of London's father with another woman, someone she didn't recognize. They weren't touching each other but standing very close and appearing to be having a very private conversation.

The pictures that had been sent to London were odd in themselves. But it was the note, typed and not signed, that terrified the crap out of her.

Say good-bye to your mother and father. You're never going to see them again.

It had taken over an hour to quit shaking after reading the cryptic message, and even then London remained jumpy. The elevator dinged before the doors opened onto the first floor and London jolted out of her thoughts. She stepped out of the elevator, studying the group of people walking together ahead of her down the hall. They turned to head for the dining room and one couple glanced her way. It took a moment to return their smiles.

"Get a grip," London hissed to herself, speaking under her breath as she hurried down the hall.

Most guests recognized her and smiled, since she'd checked a lot of them in. There were other employees who worked the front desk and it was hard to remember the faces of all their guests, but that didn't mean they didn't remember hers. People smiled at her all the time when she walked around the lodge. It was her job to be a friendly face and return the smile, not to suspect and worry about anyone who gave her a moment's attention.

The note didn't make any sense. And for the life of her she couldn't figure out the pictures. Her mother's hair was different colors in several of the shots, but that didn't mean necessarily they were taken over any particular length of time. When London was growing up her mother often changed the color of her hair from one week to the next. It wasn't until London was a teenager that she figured out her mother did it because she and London's father were always wanted for one crime or another.

If it weren't the cops looking for them, it would be bookies or a member of the Mafia in whatever town they might be in. London figured her parents were always on the run because they were really bad at pulling off cons or committing whatever crime they did in whatever town they were in. She couldn't even count how many times they'd moved while she was growing up, sometimes not staying in a town longer than a week. It never made sense that Jonnie and Ruby Brooke were never arrested.

Apparently, now they'd reached the end of their line.

Not only did someone have their number and was quite possibly closing in, but that person also knew London was their daughter and where she was. She tripped over her feet when it occurred to her it might be smart to pack up and move, relocate, so whoever was planning on taking out her parents wouldn't come after her, too.

Not that she'd committed any crime. London had never so much as shoplifted a candy bar. She didn't cheat on her taxes. She'd never put down the wrong amount of hours she worked on a time card. It was an odd thing. Definitely not something she'd ever bragged about to a soul, but London was honest to a fault. She prided herself on not even lying. It wasn't as if all of her honesty and her crime-free life would make up for her parents' many misdeeds. London knew no matter how she led her life, it wouldn't erase her parents' sins. Somehow leading her life the way she did made her feel better about herself. It helped her live with her head held high, with the ability to smile and feel good about each new day when she opened her eyes in the morning knowing that in spite of coming from two terrible crooks, London Brooke was a good person.

She sidestepped into the employees' break room and glanced at the clock. She never kept an eye on the time while at work. There wasn't reason to, especially when she never had anything planned after work. Today she watched that damn clock as if it might suddenly do tricks.

It was 3:00 P.M., two hours away until she would see Marc. London reached for her coat that hung on the hook on the wall and patted it. The package Meryl gave her this morning was still in her inside pocket. She might be waiting anxiously to see Marc again, but it wasn't as if she could talk to him about the pictures and the note. Showing him the pictures would require way too much backstory. There was no way she would tell him her life story. No one knew anything about her past.

Which meant there was no one she could talk to about this. She dragged her fingers through her hair, combing out the strands as she blew out a frustrated sigh. She didn't have a clue what to do.

Suddenly she was mad. Fuck whoever it was who had sent her these pictures. They had a lot of nerve messing with her life. She was happy, content, and not guilty of a goddamn thing. If her parents had fucked up, that was their problem. Hell, she didn't even know how to reach them and couldn't remember when she'd last talked to either of them. For all she knew, her parents might not even know where she was. London doubted they cared.

She stalked out of the employees' break room, deciding that the best thing to do was burn the pictures and pretend they were never sent. Some stranger with an agenda wouldn't ruin her life. She marched right into Marc, bouncing off his steel chest and shrieking in surprise.

"I didn't mean to startle you," he said, grabbing her arms to stabilize her when she would have stumbled backward. "You look frustrated. Having a bad day?"

London didn't want Marc seeing her frustrated. She didn't want him seeing her as anything other than happy, relaxed, and pretty. His comment pissed her off further and she jerked out of his grasp, then rubbed her arms, willing herself to calm down before she said something stupid and gave herself away.

"Wow, you got back a lot sooner than I thought you would." She fought for a cheerful smile and willed those pictures out of her head permanently. If only Meryl hadn't stopped by her house. Maybe then the pictures would have been ruined by drifting snow and she never would have seen them or the morbid message.

"The roads were clear today." He searched her face as if seeing that something was distracting her. Marc seemed able to see past her mask she wore so well for the entire world. "I got a new phone."

He held it up for her to see, grinning easily. His eyes were the color of the sky. His short brown hair looked like it would be curly if he let it grow out. As it was, it bordered his broad cheekbones. She dropped her attention to a hairline scar on his jawbone. It wasn't that noticeable. Yet somehow since she could see it, the small wound that had never healed right gave him more of a roguish appearance. He was so tall, so incredibly muscular, and better looking than any other man she'd ever met.

There's no such thing as perfect, she reminded herself.

"Have you shopped for a phone recently?" he continued, his gaze drifting over her face as he spoke. "I actually had fun. I didn't expect replacing my right arm to be such a pleasant experience."

"I'm glad," she said, forcing her attention to the phone in his hand, and knowing he was joking. His fingers were long and strong looking. Remembering him tangling them in her hair seemed to make the hallway get warmer.

"This one is already loaded with a couple of games. I decided on one that takes quality pictures over the MP three player." He held it up before she could say anything and pushed a button on it. The phone flashed in her face. "Gotcha," he said, his grin broadening.

She blinked, shocked he just took her picture. Why in the hell would he do that? She had to look like shit. Her heart started racing and again her anger peaked. Just as quickly she forced herself to calm down. Why should she care? Tourists had taken her picture before. Granted, most of them asked. Marc wasn't her usual tourist, though. The quick seesaw of emotions almost made her dizzy.

Marc continued searching her face as he rambled on about his phone. She got the eeriest sensation the chatter about his phone was a front while he focused on her, searching for proof she was distraught about something. London gave herself a mental shake. Marc didn't have an agenda, other than getting her naked. She forced her paranoid thoughts out of her head.

"Does it make phone calls?"

"Damn. I forgot to ask." He brushed his finger down her cheek, a quick gesture that ended before she could say anything about him touching her like that where someone might see. "I'll let you get back to work. See you in a couple hours."

Marc had to admit the walking tour was fun. They were a large group, over twenty. London and another guide, Meryl, the curly-haired redhead, wore battery-packed microphones wrapped around their ears so everyone could hear them. They told anecdotes and stories of the Old West as they walked the group through a pretty easy hike. He wasn't the only one feeling the lack of exercise and actually breaking a sweat on their return to the ski lodge. Others around him sounded winded as they chatted among themselves.

"As you look at these mountains, you see their beauty and a great place to vacation," London said into her microphone. "However, in 1879 prospectors endured the elements and made it to this area. They determined the area contained large deposits of silver ore. That was the beginning of Aspen, Colorado. They saw these mountains as a major investment."

Marc didn't try finding a spot alongside London. He brought up the rear and could hear her melodic, cheerful voice as she continued sharing Aspen history.

"Over the next fourteen years, Aspen's fortunes rose as it eventually produced one-sixth of the nation's silver and one-sixteenth of the world's silver."

"A lady like you would look better in gold than in silver," a man next to London said too loudly.

If he thought his comment would garner laughter from the rest of the group, he was mistaken. Everyone ignored him. A much younger man, twenty years old at the most, eased in alongside London and whispered something to her. Her laughter could be heard through the microphone. Marc wouldn't be surprised if someone as sexy as London wasn't hit on by male guests on a daily basis. Her dark blue jeans hugged her perfectly shaped ass, and the down coat she wore hid the shape of her upper body but hugged her narrow waist. The sunset glowed off the mountains and glistened in her long straight black hair. She definitely competed with their surroundings as being the most beautiful sight out here.

London appeared to handle the men's attention with professional ease, stepping around them without making it obvious she avoided their advances. Marc didn't want to be one of the many who struggled for a moment of her time. Instead he focused on the glory of the mountains. He'd never seen anything like it.

There were other hikes he could sign up for to do some serious hiking into those glorious mountains. Instead, they'd taken a pretty level path between two of the mountains and around a large gully that included several breathtaking waterfalls. There wasn't anything that compared to the beauty around him. Marc stared in awe at his surroundings, swearing he'd drifted into some alternate universe that was a frozen winter wonderland.

London and Meryl stopped the group and turned to face them. The men surrounding London seemed to fight for who would stand next to her as she continued speaking.

"In 1881 the first Aspen newspaper was published. That year the first school opened here, too," London explained. "A volunteer fire station and our first hotel opened. During that time the remaining Ute Indians were moved out of Colorado and into Utah."

"I'm glad they left you here," the older burly man said, again speaking too loudly so everyone could hear him.

He had a clear view through the group when the jerk tried stroking London's long black hair. Something inside Marc clenched, causing him to fist his hands before he realized his reaction to the asshole fondling her. London dodged the man's efforts.

This time a few around them laughed at the asshole's feeble attempt at humor. London met Marc's gaze. She wasn't laughing. She stared at him and her expression turned imploring. She wanted his help, his protection. It was a gut feeling and one he didn't bother trying to analyze. London looked away first, turning around and picking up pace toward the ski lodge, which was now in view.

Marc worked his way through the amiable group as they kept moving, managing not to offend anyone until he reached London's side.

The men around her didn't give him the time of day. They probably assumed he'd joined her group of admirers. It was the one man who'd try touching her who gave Marc an assessing once-over. The look on the man's face made Marc think he didn't appreciate competition in winning over the pretty tour guide's attention. The man turned his back to Marc and again tried touching London.

"I know many of you are here for the skiing." London spoke into her microphone as she grabbed the burly man's hand. Then letting it go, she walked away from him and closer to Marc as she continued smiling and speaking into her microphone. "What you might not know is skiing is relatively a new sport in our country. Although skiing started as a public sport and activity here in Aspen in 1936, it wasn't until after World War Two that the first lifts were built and skiing became a form of revenue that helped keep Aspen alive."

"We offer all levels of skiing classes," Meryl continued

when they neared the lodge. If she picked up where London left off to allow her co-worker time to move again and dodge the burly man, it wasn't apparent. Meryl continued with a friendly tone and gestured to the lodge. "Be sure and stop in at the bar," Meryl said, her bouncy red curls hanging around her face as she grinned. "Our bartenders are full of more folklore of the area."

"This one here is my date," the burly man next to London announced. "The rest of you can fend for yourself."

London skillfully dodged his groping hands. "I'm afraid *you're* going to have to fend for yourself," she told the burly man, causing the other men around her to break into laughter.

She wore her professional smile, which she held on to as they entered the lobby. The group spread out, filling the large room. Marc followed London to the front desk, where she pulled off her microphone. When she almost slammed it down on the counter it became obvious she was anything but happy.

London stormed off to the employees' break room, slamming the door behind her. Marc made it to the door at the same time the burly man did.

"Hey, man," Marc said easily. "I don't think she's in the mood for company."

"Then you better head on your way." The smell of alcohol lingered in the air when the guy spoke. "This one is mine tonight."

"She is not yours tonight, or any other night, for that matter," Marc informed him, and watched the man's expression transform.

At first Marc thought him drunk, but when he snarled at Marc a warning light flashed inside. There was almost something sinister about the guy. Although he was at least several inches shorter than Marc, he sized him up. His expression remained dark and hateful when he glared.

"So that's how it is," the man said under his breath. "You better watch your back, my friend."

"I'm not sure we're friends, and trust me, I always do." Marc gave him an easy smile and moved so he blocked the break room door until the burly guy strode off. Then turning, Marc rapped on the door with the back of his hand. London didn't answer, so he pushed it open. "Are you okay?" he asked gently.

Meryl appeared next to him when he stepped into the break room. London looked up at both of them, her gaze almost frantic when she shoved a flat package full of papers into her coat.

"Seriously, girl, what happened out there?" There was concern in Meryl's voice.

"I'm fine. And nothing," London snapped. "Please, both of you. Leave me alone."

Marc backed out, closing the employees' break room door behind him. Meryl faced him in the hallway, giving him an appraising look.

"Are you two going out?" She was cute, in an Orphan Annie sort of way, but it was the natural glow in her eyes, something Marc had learned to pick up on in his line of work and assessing people, that showed him Meryl was probably a concerned friend.

"I wouldn't say that exactly." He and London hadn't been on a date, and other than when he'd kissed her senseless, they hadn't had much alone time at all. "We haven't even known each other a week," he offered, but guessed Meryl would know that. "I think that guy pissed her off, though, and I should have been more attentive on the tour. I could have gotten rid of him for her."

"I'm sure you could have." Meryl's gaze swept up and down him as she rocked up on her feet, giving him an easy smile. "I think she's more upset about that package she got."

If he admitted not knowing about the package, Meryl might not tell him anything else about it. "Why do you think that?" he asked.

"I think it's from her family. And with London, I don't know, it's like she didn't exist before three years ago. Try and ask her about her family, or her past. She's a pro at not answering."

Chapter Three

London couldn't believe she was doing this. Standing at the end of her dining-room table, she surveyed her work. The white tablecloth, flowers in the middle of the table, her best china and silverware. She had to admit it looked damn good. Why was she going all out like this just because she'd been tricked into having Marc over for dinner?

Maybe not exactly tricked. She returned to her kitchen, running her hands down her apron and making sure nothing had splattered onto her dress before returning to her stove. The roast was done. Potatoes stood in the pot on the back of the stove waiting to be scooped onto the platter. Rolls were in their basket with a cloth over them. She stirred the gravy. If he hadn't asked her out for Friday night, she wouldn't be going through all this work.

When he did ask her out she had to give him her spiel about not dating guests. He offered to take her to another town. She'd hesitated. Marc pointed out if he just came by to her house, it really wouldn't be a date. That had been Wednesday.

Between then and now she'd learned what his favorite

dish was. Of course he'd be a meat-and-potatoes man. Then she'd started plotting the evening. Now she stood in one of her nicest dresses, with the best table setting she owned set out on her table that up until this morning she'd used to stack anything she didn't want to put away or didn't know where to put.

"The wine," she told herself, remembering it was supposed to breathe for an hour.

When she started her menu of pot roast and potatoes it didn't seem that it would be all that much work. Then she told herself Marc coming over was just a good excuse to do some deep cleaning of her house that she hadn't gotten around to, since she wasn't ever here. He might not have even noticed she took off a few hours early in order to make sure everything was in order when he came over at eight. Marc had signed up for another of the tours, something he'd been doing almost every day since taking their walking tour.

He managed to come around at least once a day when no one else was around and steal a kiss or at the least compliment her on her looks. Marc wasn't tacky, pushy, or annoying. It amazed her how when any other guest started coming on to her too strong Marc always seemed to be nearby. He was perfect at getting every annoying weasel to leave her alone. In fact, it was damn hard to fault Marc at all on anything he did.

The gravy wasn't clumping. Everything was perfect. London glanced at the clock. Two minutes before eight. Something told her Marc would be on time. She spotted the vase she'd set up on her windowsill over her kitchen sink and studied the four silk flowers, each a different color. Marc had snuck those flowers to her throughout the week. Would it be tacky for him to learn she'd saved them and, in fact, put them on display in a vase?

She damn near jumped out of her skin when someone

knocked at her door. "Definitely on time," she said, scrambling out of her apron and frantically folding it and stuffing it in the bottom drawer in her kitchen. "I guess the flowers stay."

Marc didn't know if he liked London's flushed expression with very little makeup or the incredibly stunning, figure-hugging dress she wore without shoes better. London sighed, smiled, and pulled her front door open farther.

"I knew you'd be on time," she informed him, inviting him into her home.

"I almost wasn't when I decided to buy these and couldn't find the florist. My GPS decided to have a brain fart." Marc held out the bouquet of flowers, red roses with some other flowers stuck into the arrangement. "I didn't know if you had a vase or not."

He didn't usually feel awkward, even on first dates. And he reminded himself this wasn't a date. London had been very strict about the terms surrounding him coming over for dinner. When her expression transformed as she accepted the flowers and she lifted her gaze to his, not saying anything for a moment, he knew he'd made the right choice.

"Marc, they're absolutely beautiful," she whispered, burying her nose in them as she turned and walked barefoot across her living room. "Everything is ready. Come on in."

He glanced at his car parked out on the street and at the houses across the street before closing the door. London lived in a stable-looking neighborhood, very middle-class, with each home, including hers, appearing neat and well cared for. Her sidewalk and porch had been cleared of snow, and he wondered if she shoveled it or if she had a service tend to the deed. Marc closed the door and secured the dead bolt, done out of force of habit, before turning and taking in her living room.

"Something smells incredibly good." His stomach seconded the notion, growling when he breathed in the rich aroma of home-cooked food. They ate at home as a family when they could. His mother insisted on it at least once a week since she'd returned home and reunited with their father. Those were memorable, happy times, and sitting down with London for a good meal sounded just as appealing.

"Come on in. I'm not waiting on you. You can help put food on the table." There was laughter in her tone.

Marc glanced at the dark living room, light flooding into it from the adjoining dining room. There were a few prints on the walls, comfortable-looking furniture, and a round braided carpet that almost reached the walls and showed off the wooden floor underneath at its edges. As comfortable-looking as the room was, it wasn't personalized. London either didn't spend a lot of time in this room or simply worked so much she hadn't gotten around to putting anything personal in there. He noticed there wasn't a TV in the room and there weren't any pictures of family or friends. He remembered Meryl's comment about London refusing to discuss her past. There was proof of that here, with no hint of anything about the woman other than what he already knew.

"If I knew we were eating buffet-style, I would have brought food instead of flowers," he said, studying the place settings in the dining room as he found his way into her kitchen.

London grinned at him over her shoulder, stirring something on the stove. "I like the flowers."

He spotted them on her windowsill next to another vase that held all the silk roses he'd bought for her at the gift shop throughout the week. A wave of intense satisfaction rushed through him, and he returned his attention to London. He would have to remember flowers went a long way with this woman. She hadn't thrown away any of the flowers he'd given her.

"So what do you want me to do?" he asked, the smells of whatever she'd made almost making him drool.

"You could pour wine." She nodded to a bottle on the counter. "The glasses are already on the table."

He took to his task, his stomach growling again when she brought in a pot roast, nicely arranged on a formal serving platter with potatoes and carrots surrounding it.

"That looks good enough to be on a cover of some kind of cooking magazine."

London shrugged, placing it on the table and returning to the kitchen. "I don't cook that often and it was kind of fun."

"I'm glad my idea of eating appealed to you." He watched her walk away, enjoying the hell out of how her dress hugged her figure, showing off her narrow waist and incredible ass. The dress ended above her knees, and her legs were shapely, not muscular but toned and long. "If this tastes even half as good as it smells, I'll be in heaven."

He hadn't poured the second glass of wine when she returned with biscuits. "Well, I hope you like it," she said, tugging on her dress before sliding into her chair.

Marc hurried to finish pouring the wine and placed the bottle next to his plate as he joined her at the table. "Allow me to serve you," he said, deciding he should take on at least one more task. London had gone to a lot of work to prepare this meal for them. "It's the least I can do."

The food was incredible, the company even better. Marc found himself leaning back, laughing along with London as she told a story about a guest who'd stayed at the ski lodge earlier the previous year.

"By the time he'd checked out I swear he'd stayed in over twenty rooms," she said, swirling the wine in her glass as she shook her head and continued laughing. "We never did figure out why he complained about each room and insisted on being moved."

"There are some unique characters in this world," Marc said, and reached to pour both of them more wine.

"The only bad part about a great meal at home is cleaning up afterward." London sipped at her wine and slid back from the table. "I guess we can let the dishes soak until later."

"Nope. I know my manners. You cooked the food; I'll clean up. Sit there and tell me more stories," Marc encouraged, taking her plate and his and heading to the kitchen.

London twisted in her chair, looking at him as if he'd grown a third eye. "You're seriously going to wash all the dishes?" she asked.

"Yup." With a glance he saw there wasn't a garbage disposal, turned and found the trash can, then scraped the remaining food off both plates into it. "And you're going to sit and keep me company. So what did you do before you worked at the Elk Ski Lodge?"

He caught her shrugging before she twisted in her chair again when he entered the dining room and grabbed the platter with the roast and remaining vegetables on it. They'd put a good dent into all of the food, but there would be leftovers. Since he didn't want her changing the subject, he took the platter into the kitchen, set it on the counter, and returned for the roll basket.

"I've been at the lodge for three years. There were a few jobs before that after I finished high school."

"How old are you?" he asked, realizing he didn't know.

"Aren't guys not supposed to ask ladies that?" she asked, grinning broadly.

"I think that rule doesn't fall into place until we're over forty." He rinsed the plates and stacked them next to her sink. "Let me guess. Twenty-seven? Twenty-eight?"

London leaned back in her chair, laughing, and drank

more of her wine. If she was getting tipsy, he liked her this way. "I'm mortally offended," she said, still laughing. "I'm twenty-five. Your turn. Age and job description please, sir."

"Twenty-seven and I own part of a family business." Now it was his turn to change the subject. "Where is the dish soap?"

"You really don't need to wash the dishes." She stood, moving toward him with a lazy stroll.

"Is there something else you'd rather do?" he asked, reaching for her with wet hands.

She giggled, making an effort to dodge him. Her dress looked pretty nice, and since it was possibly "dry-clean only" he used that as his excuse to drag his damp fingers through her hair, capturing her face and lowering his mouth to hers.

London didn't relax against him as easily as she did the last time he kissed her, but she tasted so good Marc didn't care. Gripping the side of her head, he tilted her so he could devour her better. She tasted of their dinner and the wine. But it was the heat that greeted him, slowly drifting to his brain, that made him slow the kiss and pull her closer. London groaned and he dragged his fingers through all that thick, tangle-free silk down her back until he clasped her rear end.

More than anything he wanted to explore every inch of her. He was acutely aware of the zipper down her spine and forced himself to instead caress her smooth, round ass as he continued feasting on her mouth. If he moved too quickly she'd make him stop. He wasn't sure how he knew that, but he didn't doubt it for a moment.

"You really don't want your dishes washed," he murmured into her mouth, knowing he could stop now, but if he held her in his arms much longer he'd be carrying her in search of her bedroom.

"Huh," she gasped, letting her head fall back and her eyes remain closed when he raised his head. The slight grin on her face added to the vision of beauty Marc stared down at. "Soap is in the cabinet under the sink," she said, holding her position.

"You are wicked," he accused, letting his gaze drop to the view of her breasts with the material of her dress stretched over them.

London relaxed even more in his arms. If he let her go, she'd fall backward; not that he would ever let her go. Marc blinked, suddenly realizing this wasn't casual sex or friends with benefits. They'd known each other a week. He'd booked his room at the lodge for a month. If this was how he felt about her right now, where would they be when it was time for him to leave?

He was a selfish bastard. Marc would take what London offered and worry later about where it might lead them. He wanted London too much to start analyzing something as serious as a relationship.

"I tell you what," he said, squeezing her ass and pulling her dress up until he felt the edge of the material in his hands. That was enough to open her eyes. "I'm going to wash your dishes and then I want more of this," he said, lowering his head and nibbling at her lower lip.

"You drive a hard bargain," she informed him. When she straightened, London appeared a lot more sober than she had a moment before. "And we'll see. No promises."

London couldn't remember when she last had more fun washing and drying dishes. Marc jumped into the task, making her feel obligated to get out a hand towel and dry.

"You see," he told her. "I learned at a young age washing the dishes was the much better task than drying them. My brother and I had to do this every night. It was our chore; that was before we got a dishwasher."

"Oh yeah? Sounds like you were so tortured." She enjoyed hearing about his childhood and trying to imagine what it would be like being in a family where there were actually chores given. Any time her parents told her to do something, they'd forgotten they'd told her before she found time to do it. Although for the most part, her parents ignored her. She kept whatever house they were living in clean because they didn't. They were always too busy plotting their next venture, or business deal, as they liked to call it.

"Most definitely," he told her, grinning and showing how little he was tortured. "Washing is the easier half of the task. When you dry, you have to not only dry the dish but also put it away. Usually the dish towel is too wet to keep drying dishes and so you have to get another one. Yet another part of one task. When you wash, that is all you do. This is the easier half of the job."

"Sounds like you put a lot of thought into the matter," she said, laughing.

"Yup. I was all about making sure Jake did more of the chores. I lived to see to that fact."

"So you were the oldest?"

"Yup. And definitely the better of the King men," he told her, suggesting there might be a competition between the two of them. "Jake is a player."

"And you're not a player?" She twisted her damp dish towel and aimed it at him. "I think I'll be the judge of that."

Marc shifted his attention from her face to her towel. "I'd think twice before doing that," he said, his voice lowering into a challenge.

London let the towel go, releasing it with one hand and aiming low. The towel slapped against Marc's waist before he ducked backward, his blue eyes suddenly glowing as his mouth twisted into an ornery grin. London's heart skipped a beat and started pumping too quickly in her chest. She reloaded as fast as she could, aiming higher when he straightened and started for her.

"You think I'm a player, do you?" He tried grabbing her towel.

London jumped out of his reach, letting the towel fly again. It made a slapping sound against his chest. "What would you call it?" she asked, laughing even harder when he lunged at her.

She barely made it out of his grasp and darted out of the kitchen. There wasn't time to twist her towel again and reload before he pounced on her, lifting her off the ground. Her back was pressed against all that steel muscle and his arms were all bulging muscles. London lost her towel and gripped his arms but couldn't budge his grip on her.

"You would attack an unarmed woman?" she asked, barely able to get the words out as she laughed harder than she had in ages.

"You attacked an unarmed man!" he accused, his voice a deadly growl in her ear.

Her heart exploded in her chest. A warmth stretched over her body, causing immediate swelling between her legs and a tingling starting over her flesh. She'd had a few glasses of wine but not enough to make her drunk. As she continued laughing and twisting against his impossible grip, fumes flooded her brain. London might blame it on the wine, but suddenly she wanted to fuck him.

"You're twice my size," she gasped, trying to control her fit of giggles when he hauled her into her dark living room.

"Nonetheless, I'm unarmed so I must use what tactics I can to defend myself."

Her zipper moved down her back, his knuckles brushing over her bare skin. London did her best to flip in his arms. When she did, her breasts smashing against all that roped muscle, her dress slid off her shoulders, no longer hugging her body but now feeling loose and baggy on her.

"That's a crock." She laughed, grabbing his shoulders so she wouldn't slide down him. It was kind of nice being eye to eye with him. Not to mention, his muscular arms securing her against him and his hands cradling her ass was a turn-on she couldn't ignore. "You're using your size and body right now to win," she said, trying to catch her breath.

Suddenly the wall was behind her and Marc was pressed against her. His blue eyes turned dark, like a sky right before a storm explodes. London would drown in those eyes, in his powerful, incredibly handsome face. His grin was as appealing as his serious expression, and she should be scared.

Terrified. She should be more than scared. Marc was a guest, a man staying at the Elk Ski Lodge who would be out of her life as fast as he came in. Once again she would be alone, working day and night to avoid the bitter attack of loneliness. As much as these thoughts hit her hard, it was damn impossible to get them to sink in when his face was so close to hers. His body touched her everywhere. He was so near her she could almost taste him—almost. London could definitely feel him, especially his rock-hard cock that grew by the second and began throbbing against her pelvis.

"Sweetheart," he said, his voice suddenly hoarse, "trust me, your body is a much better weapon than mine."

When his expression turned serious something inside her quickened, causing her to hold her breath when he met her gaze.

"I'm not a player," he said slowly. "I don't like getting hurt and won't hurt anyone else."

"Good to know," she said, her mouth all of a sudden so dry she could barely get the words out.

"If you don't want this, now would be a good time to tell me to stop." His focus dropped to her lips as he spoke.

"That's hardly fair." Again it was hard to get the words out. Her breath caught in her throat. "You're putting the responsibility on me."

"You're definitely the stronger right now," he whispered, dropping his mouth to her collarbone, where he started nibbling.

"I'm not so sure about that."

He was performing some kind of magic. There wasn't any doubt in her mind. London had strict rules. She'd never had a problem sticking to them. Other men at the lodge had asked her out. She'd received gifts before. As she let her head fall back, the hard, smooth wall pressed against the back of her head while Marc continued licking and nipping at the base of her neck. She couldn't get her brain to wrap around why saying no to Marc proved impossible.

His mouth moved to hers and she received him with as much excitement as he offered. It was weird. Kissing Marc was like reuniting with an old friend. London wasn't a virgin, but she had kept her serious admirers at bay for several years now. Once or twice she'd agreed to a date with a local man, spending an evening with him and almost always seeming to come home without having sex. At the moment, though, it didn't make sense to her that she always said no.

Her body screamed for release. The pressure building inside her was almost painful. Her pussy was so soaked she could feel the moisture pooling against her freshly shaved flesh. Her skin tingled, and fireworks kept snapping in her brain.

"Are we going to do this?" Marc moved his lips over hers as he asked.

"It looks that way." She wrapped her arms around his neck and brought one leg up, pulling him closer.

Marc lifted her into his arms, picking her up as if she didn't weigh a thing. "Where is your bedroom?"

She waved a hand in the air, which were the worse directions ever. Marc apparently understood them, though, and walked through her living room to the small hallway that led to her bedroom and bathroom. There wasn't much to her house, but he was still impressed. When he placed her on her bed, her dress slipped down her shoulders, trapping her arms. She wouldn't be able to move until she got out of it.

"Wait," she said when he started crawling over her.

For a second it seemed the moment would turn awkward. But when London went on her knees in the middle of her double bed and started dragging her dress up her thighs, Marc stood and began undressing. She hurried to yank the thing off her, wanting to see all that brawn appear as he stripped.

London didn't mess with her bra and underpants but instead remained on her knees, watching as first his shirt fell to the floor and next his jeans. My God! Her mouth was no longer too dry. Instead she was sure she would start drooling. Muscles rippled and bulged everywhere. There wasn't a man anywhere who could compare with this vision of perfection. Eye candy be damned! Marc King fell into a category of one when it came to ultimate sex appeal.

"You're going to torture me, aren't you?" Marc asked, completely naked when he climbed onto her bed.

London didn't understand the question and wasn't sure she could answer if she did. His cock was thick and long and as hard as the rest of him. It protruded from his body, looking as if it tried stretching to reach her before the rest of him did.

"All of this lace is keeping me from the parts of you I've been fantasizing about all week," he growled, slipping his finger under her bra strap and dragging it down her shoulder.

She understood and grinned, relaxing on her back and stretching her legs, then sliding them up his thighs. "You don't like them?" she asked, running her fingers over each well-defined muscle in his arms. Roped muscle twitched under her fingertips. He was more than aroused and not as in control as he wanted her to think.

"Sweetheart, I love how they look on you." He lowered his mouth to hers, kissing her.

He took his time with the kiss, too. London rubbed his arms, feeling him tremble as he held himself over her. She pressed her legs against his thighs. Body hair tickled her and brought her to a feverish state. The more she touched him, the more her skin became oversensitized.

As she slowly learned his body, he made love to her mouth. Every time they kissed it was even hotter than the time before. She loved his mouth, the skills he possessed, the way his tongue danced around hers. When she was sure he'd push her over the edge just by kissing her, he moved his mouth, placing kisses on her cheek, her jaw, and then down her neck.

Marc eased her bra straps off her shoulders and moved the lace cups from her breasts. He raked his teeth over a nipple. She swelled with eager anticipation as sparks of need shot down her middle until her pussy was just as swollen and hungry for his attention.

London arched into him. She cried out when he latched onto her other nipple. He took her on a ride so exhilarating, so incredibly perfect, she damn near floated off the bed.

In spite of his size, he eased his body over hers, never putting too much weight on her, and shifted his weight without her moving. Marc leaned on one arm, now simply adoring her body, and dragged his fingers down her middle until he cupped her pussy. London jerked, coming off the bed. Her underwear was still on yet he almost made her come, again, with his skilled fingers and meticulous attention.

"I want to learn every inch of you," he said, taking his time easing his fingers under her lace underwear. "I want to know which parts make you moan and which push you over the edge."

London had thought the splurge a good one when she'd bought the matching bra and undies. Now she quietly cursed them because he took his time, enjoying the material and coaxing it down her body. She wanted her underwear gone, wanted him inside her. When she tilted her head, meeting his gaze, her look must have told him as much.

Marc's slow smile simply added more oxygen to the flames already burning fiercely inside her. "The torture will be worth it. I promise. We're going to explode together."

"Who's tortured?" she whispered, her voice raspy. She narrowed her gaze on him when his grin broadened. If he thought he would drag her into a state of erotic bliss where he would control her and make her beg for release, he would soon learn differently.

"My dear," he began.

London rolled to her side, facing him, and reached between them. She couldn't stop herself from hissing in a breath when she wrapped her fingers around his thick, long cock. He was really large. But as well, she also proved he wasn't in as much control as he professed, which gave her odd pleasure.

Marc's eyes rolled as he bit his lower lip. "London," he hissed, dragging her name out and then making a sound in his throat that wasn't quite a growl and was almost as deadly sounding as a male cat purring.

She switched her attention from his face to his cock in her hand, stroking and squeezing. His body stiffened as he grabbed her arm, almost pinching her skin. It was as if he needed to hold on, which was right where she wanted him, where he'd had her a moment before.

There was incredible pleasure in taking control. The pressure inside her continued tormenting her, but it was accompanied with intense satisfaction as she watched him grit his teeth and tilt his head back.

London almost laughed when he damn near pounced off the bed, throwing her to her back and coming over her.

"Hold on," he groaned, leaving her there and sliding off the bed.

She was pretty sure she'd never seen a man make such quick work of pulling a condom out of his pants pocket and sheathing himself with it.

"You're thoughtful," she said.

"As long as you don't think it presumptuous." His sheathed cock danced at her entrance, teasing the crap out of her.

"Not at all," she whispered, wrapping her arms and legs around him.

When Marc slid inside her London swore fireworks exploded. He filled and stretched her, his size a perfect fit. London moved underneath him, allowing him deeper access. Marc hit that spot and it took her over the edge.

"That's it, sweetheart. Perfect," he groaned, running kisses down the side of her face while building momentum.

Marc had skills that added to his growing list of qualities. London took all he had, coming again and again, knowing she'd gone way too long without really good sex. And to think this man had been around her all week. When they finally exploded, both of them coming at the same time, there wasn't any doubt in her mind she would want to do this again, and soon.

* * *

In spite of how sated Marc was, spending the night with London was probably pushing it more than they should. He wanted to see her again, be with her again, and have sex daily with her, if not more. Why the hell did the perfect woman for him have to be halfway across the country from where he lived?

"Want to take a shower?" he asked, keeping her with him when he rolled to his back.

"You can take a shower." She sounded so sated. "You'll see why when you go into my bathroom. I doubt it's big enough for both of us."

Again, he wouldn't push. Although when he entered the bathroom he had to agree with her. Maybe she would have showered with him if she'd had a larger tub and shower. As it was, he had to duck in order to get the shower spray to hit his head.

He reminded himself this was a vacation. He would return to L.A. sooner than he wanted to think. They would be smart to take it slow, not spend so much time together that they'd get too attached. It would be easy to do with this woman. London did something to him. Marc didn't want to hurt her when he left. And he didn't want to get hurt.

Odd, in all the relationships he'd had over the years, Marc had never worried about getting hurt himself.

"Late-night munchies?" London asked when he found her in her kitchen.

Her hair was more tousled than he'd ever seen it and she wore pajama bottom pants and a tank top that hugged her slender body. London shoved hair over her shoulder as she held up a cookie.

"I'm completely satisfied in every way," he told her, bending over to kiss the top of her head. "What are you doing this weekend?"

Marc hadn't planned on asking her out again tonight.

If they weren't going to get too involved, they were better off flirting when they saw each other at the lodge and simply hooking up every now and then for sex. It was a perfect plan except he didn't want to wait until Monday to see her again. And he didn't want to wait that long before he fucked her again.

"Working," she told him, standing and plopping the rest of her cookie into her mouth.

"I thought you said you worked Monday through Friday."

"I do. Technically I have two jobs. It's a separate business that hires me to do the tours. On Saturdays and Sundays I usually do several of them."

"No wonder you're in such incredible shape," he said, pulling her against him and kissing her.

"What's your excuse?" She searched his face as she asked, dragging her fingers over his chest lazily.

"Being an oversized brute runs in the family," he told her, knowing he was still dodging her question as to what he did for a living. It was force of habit, and often smarter if no one knew he was a bounty hunter.

"Your father and brother are as big as you are?" She looked surprised.

"Yup."

"Is your mother really big, too?" she asked.

"Nope. She's about your size." He grinned at her stunned expression. "Believe me, she runs the fort. Size isn't everything, sweetheart."

"It doesn't hurt," she said, grinning, and leaned into him for another kiss.

It sounded like a compliment, so he decided to take it as one and not press the issue by asking her to elaborate. London walked him to the door and didn't say anything when he unlocked the dead bolt.

"Hopefully I'll see you sometime over this weekend," he said, pushing open her screen door and stepping out on her front porch.

"I'm sure you will." She hugged herself when she stepped outside with him.

He would have scolded her for coming out in the frigid cold when she barely wore anything. She'd done it to him. But selfishly, he wanted one more minute with her. More than likely the sooner he got away from her, spent his time doing something else, the quicker the intense feelings plaguing him right now would fade.

Marc glanced down, enjoying how her tank top didn't quite reach her pajama bottoms. Her bare tummy was flat and hard. Her nipples puckered against her tank top. And my God, all that thick black hair toppling over her shoulders and down her back added to a picture of perfection. It was on his lips to tell her how beautiful she was.

"It was a perfect night," he said instead, figuring that summed up about everything. Something on her porch floor caught his eye and he started for it.

London noticed it at the same time and moved faster, squatting down and grabbing a small package.

"I don't remember that being there when I got here," He tried looking at it, but London almost threw it into her house.

"I'm sure it was," she said hastily, again wrapping her arms around her chest but this time scowling at the floor. "I don't have the best mailman in the world."

"Are you sure?" Marc looked around, spotting her mailbox attached to the side of her porch. It was definitely large enough to hold a package that size. He remembered her with a similar package her co-worker Meryl had brought her. "Do you want to see what it is?"

London's gaze was definitely guarded, if not haunted,

when she met his. "I will. You better get going," she added, obviously unwilling to open it with him there. "Please be careful driving back."

"All right." He studied her a moment longer before forcing himself to quit trying to analyze something that was probably nothing. Stepping into her, he kissed her, then hurried down the stairs, waving over his shoulder. "See you soon!" he called out.

Chapter Four

London thought for sure the walking tours would take her mind off the second package that had shown up on her front porch Friday night. Marc didn't seem too concerned by it, which was what she hoped for. Until she figured out who was sending the pictures she wasn't going to talk about them to anyone. Especially not a stranger. She'd known Marc a week, had incredible sex with him, and unfortunately that still qualified him as a stranger. She didn't even know what he did for a living.

At least this was her last tour of the weekend. Heading into the lodge, she hung around with some of the guests and enjoyed small talk or tried to appear like she did. Part of her couldn't wait to get home to a hot bath. The other part of her dreaded returning home, where she knew she would mull over all the pictures sent to her. She had one more activity, dinner at Meryl's family's house, then her obligations would be done. Finally breaking away from the guests and letting them continue to chatter among themselves, London couldn't help glancing around to see if Marc might be nearby. When he wasn't, she grabbed her coat and headed out.

As the week dragged on, London hoped she would think less about the pictures. Instead they seemed to distract her from almost everything she did. Every night when she got off work and drove home, she half-expected to find another package and blew out a sigh of relief when one wasn't there.

This had to stop, she told herself after changing into her pajamas and warming up some soup for her supper. If she wasn't obsessing on the pictures, it was Marc. She slipped the newest silk rose he'd given her in with the others and watered the flowers he'd brought her the previous weekend. Then finishing up her soup, she made quick work of cleaning her kitchen and padded into her bedroom.

Maybe if she could figure out where the pictures came from or who was taking them, she'd quit stressing over them. A different tactic was needed. This whole time she had tried putting the pictures out of her head. It might give her more peace of mind if she gave them her full attention and tried understanding them.

London crawled onto her bed, memories of having sex with Marc flooding her thoughts for a minute. Doing her best to shove him out of her mind, she put the two packages in front of her on the bed and studied them.

"No return address. Same amount of postage," she mused, focusing on the stamps in the corner of each package. "Both large manila envelopes."

She flipped the packages over, noting whoever had mailed them had used clear tape instead of licking the glue to secure them. Nothing odd or unusual about how they were mailed to her, though. Other than the one showing up at her doorstep Friday night instead of with the rest of the mail. Had the first package shown up the same way?

"Crap," London hissed, suddenly wondering if the second package had been delivered while Marc had been there.

It wasn't that she didn't want anyone knowing he was there. There really wasn't anyone to worry about. Other than Meryl, who really was more of a friendly co-worker than a good friend, there wasn't anyone in London's life. She wasn't opposed to having a best friend. There had been times when she'd craved such a person being in her life. Right now would be one of those times. Having someone to talk this over with, brainstorm and try to figure out the meaning behind it all, would be nice.

Her fingers were damp when she dumped the contents of each package out on her bed. The second group of pictures seemed to be more in focus than the first set.

"Why are you doing this?" she wondered, spreading the pictures out on her bed and staring at each one of them.

There were three eight-by-tens in the second package she'd received Friday night. All pictures were in color, one of her mother, one of her father, and the third a picture of the two of them together.

London figured it had been over four years since she'd last seen her mom and dad. She'd been in Chicago, working in a restaurant, and they'd arrived in town for a weekend. Life must have been good for them at the time, because they'd stayed at a nice hotel, taken her out to eat, and not asked for any money. They'd checked out without saying good-bye. London hadn't batted an eye at that. That was how her parents were. The fact that they'd sought her out, in their eyes, was showing their love and affection. She tried remembering if either of them had hugged her during that visit. She didn't think they had.

"What's going on, Mom?" London touched the picture of her mother.

Ruby Brooke was grinning at the camera, as if she knew the picture was being taken. She held a large straw hat to her head, and the small dots of white in each lens of her sunglasses implied a flash had gone off when the shot was taken. Her thick black hair, which London wondered if she dyed, since there wasn't any gray and she was past fifty, was pulled up under the hat, although several long strands blew free past her shoulders. She looked happy, relaxed, maybe even amused at whoever took the shot.

Jonnie Brooke also faced the camera in the picture of him. He had that same cocky, crooked grin he'd always had. London leaned forward, taking her time studying the picture. There really wasn't much to see other than her father, his ornery look and stance the same as it was when she was a child, and the stretch of street behind him.

The third picture was taken inside. Her mother and father were in a restaurant, and there were other people in the picture, too. No one was at the table with them, but all tables around them were filled with people eating. Her parents were enjoying a meal, focused on their food, and possibly not aware the shot was taken.

So who would be taking pictures of her parents without them knowing? If it was the police, London doubted they would send her copies and not include a return address. She couldn't decide if it was better or worse that there wasn't a note with the second package.

"What have you two done?" she asked the pictures, but then laughed dryly at her question. What hadn't her parents done?

Jonnie and Ruby Brooke were criminals. They were thieves. They were con artists. Name it and they'd probably done it. When London did the math and figured they were probably fifty-five and fifty-seven years old by now, she had to give them both credit for never doing time. At least not yet. London was twenty-five years old and her parents had run on the wrong side of the law her entire life. Whether those were good odds or bad would depend on who was asked.

"I don't hate you," she told the pictures, and wondered why she did.

She and her parents had the best relationship possible considering her parents quite possibly didn't understand what love was. She didn't know how many times she'd heard growing up that they probably wouldn't have stayed together if her father hadn't knocked her mother up. London could see him now, rocking up on his heels as he informed her that Jonnie Brooke always did the right thing. He would ruffle her hair and tell her never to spend any length of time with anyone who didn't always do the right thing.

It took her years to understand half of what her father had told her. Probably because it took her a lot fewer years to figure out that her parents were crooks. "I know I held that against you both for a long time."

She continued touching the pictures, staring at them, and letting memories flood her brain. There had been times when she'd scream at her mother and father, threaten to turn them in to the cops. Most of the time it was the threat she'd use just to get them to buy her something she wanted.

"I really was a brat," she mused, remembering some of the hateful things she'd screamed at both of them.

Neither one of them had changed. If these pictures were recent, and London guessed they might be, they looked great, both of them happy, obviously still together. Although it had been four years since she'd seen them, they didn't hold her rebellious growing-up years against her. And neither one of them would qualify as a candidate for Parent of the Year.

There were parents who would come to the lodge, hauling their children along with them, and speak more hatefully to them than her parents ever did to her. Maybe there was a time or two when she'd been left behind, but only because they wouldn't involve her in any of their business deals. London had slept in cars, searched Dumpsters for food, and worn the same clothes for more days than she could remember. Whenever her parents came back for her, and they always did, it was with kind words.

She didn't remember a lot of "I love you" being said. Jonnie and Ruby never blessed her with lots of hugs and kisses. But they didn't yell at her and they always came back. Did that make them better or worse parents than the ones she'd see at the lodge who would bite their kids' heads off, call them names, and stuff a few bills in their hands and tell them to get lost so their parents could have fun?

London looked at the first group of pictures, then the second group again. The note that accompanied the first group sat to the side, and when she noticed it her reminiscing moments ended. A knot formed in her chest and she suddenly hated that note.

Say good-bye to your mother and father. You're never going to see them again.

Someone had a lot of nerve telling her she wouldn't see her parents again.

That was probably the best plan. If she could find her parents, she could talk to them about this. They really needed to know, especially if someone was taking pictures without her mom and dad knowing it. London wouldn't go as far as to think either of them would protect her or assure her everything would be okay. Neither of them had ever done that with her.

"And how in the hell am I going to find them?" London remembered deciding to search for her parents once when she'd been about twelve.

They'd told her to stay put in a motel room. The room

had been paid for through the following few days. She had a six-pack of Coke, several TV dinners, and a bag of cookies to live off of while they were gone. If memory served, London seemed to recall also having some money she'd managed to save up from the times her father had slipped her a dollar bill for some task she'd done. Her parents had told her to stay in the room and not leave. She wasn't supposed to open the curtains, and no way was she to answer the door.

It was the only time she'd decided to go searching for them. The details of the memory blurred in and out of her thoughts, but it was the thunderstorm that stuck clearly in her mind. She'd looked everywhere for them, never found them, and then couldn't get back in her room. It was the only time she'd ever broken into a place, and she endured the scrapes on her knees silently, without her parents ever noticing they were there, after she managed to climb in the bathroom window.

London had learned two things that night. One, finding her parents when they took off was an impossible task. And two, breaking and entering was not for her. She'd been terrified, soaked and shaking miserably, and all she'd done was work an old, dilapidated window open, hoist herself to the windowsill, and fall to the bathroom floor. That was when she'd hurt her knees, not trying to get in but after she was in the motel room, when she'd hit the bathroom floor. A life of crime wasn't for her. She seriously sucked at the very basics.

"And it's not like I can hire a private detective to find them," she decided, speaking to the pictures. "Like I can send someone who makes a living out of chasing down criminals after my parents."

London dragged her fingers through her hair and fell back on her pillows. The pictures remained scattered around her. There was no one to turn to for help with any of this. She couldn't help herself, either. When it came down to it, there wasn't a damn thing she could do other than live without knowing why someone was sending her pictures.

Marc rolled over in bed when the phone in the room rang a second time. He fumbled with the receiver, rubbed his eyes, and propped himself up on an elbow.

"Hello," he grumbled, wondering what time it was.

"You sound good when you first wake up." London's soft, sultry tone in his ear brought his dick to full attention.

"I was just dreaming about you," he said, falling back on his pillows. "And trust me, if it had been anyone else on the other end of the line I probably would have chewed them out for interrupting us."

Her laughter sounded just as good. "Well, I'm sorry to break up the party. You'll have to tell me about it sometime," she added, sounding cheerful and relaxed.

He could see her in his head and knew her well enough after just under two weeks to know no one else was around. Her professional tone was flat, friendly sounding but lacking the sensuality and smooth, sexy sound he was enjoying right now.

"I would love to do more than just tell you about it." It was an invitation, if she would take the bait. The moment of silence that followed encouraged him. She was thinking about it. "So did you miss me so much you had to call? What time is it anyway?"

"It's ten o'clock."

"Oh crap!" Marc sat up and tossed the covers off him.

"I didn't know you slept this late."

"I don't, usually. It was a late night last night."

"Oh really? What did you do?" she asked.

He'd driven around in town a lot longer than he should

have fighting the urge to show up over at her house. "I went out to eat and did a bit of shopping," he told her, which was also all true. Instead of heading back to the lodge afterward, he'd gone by her house.

"Sounds fun," she told him, a bit of her cheerful tone fading.

Had she wanted to see him? Did she need him again as much as he wanted her? Their first time fucking had been so damn intense it hardly qualified as friends with benefits and sure as hell outrated a one-night stand. Marc hated admitting he was in a predicament he hadn't seen coming and wasn't sure how to play it out properly. It would be too easy to get seriously involved with London, and although giving her space seemed the logical answer, doing it was proving harder than he thought.

"I was alone," he added, not sure why he told her that but sensing she wanted to hear it.

"Do you like going out by yourself?" she asked.

He'd guessed right. That cheerful, almost flirtatious tone returned in her voice.

"I'd much rather go out with you." He was at a disadvantage. His brain was still foggy from sleep. If he were more clearheaded he was sure he would give better responses, keep the conversation light, maybe even playful. Instead he was dropping hard-core honesty on her. "I want to see you again," he added, doing it again. Maybe caffeine would help.

"Sounds great." Her professional tone—someone was at the counter. "Oh, and there is a delivery here for you. It's at the front desk and you can pick it up when it's convenient for you."

"You won't bring it up to me?" he asked.

There was a slight pause. They both knew upon request guests could have almost anything brought to their rooms. London had already told him she wouldn't enter his room. Marc knew he'd just put her on the spot and decided to wait out her hesitation to see what she would say.

"Of course," she finally conceded. "I'll bring it up shortly."

"Give me fifteen minutes. I want to be freshly showered when you get here. Unless of course you'd like to join me and scrub my back."

He could have sworn she groaned. Smiling as he pictured her facing another guest and trying her damnedest to retain her professional composure, Marc felt no remorse as he stood next to his bed naked and stretched.

"As you wish. Thank you, Marc." She hung up on him without allowing him time to respond.

He wasn't sure which sounded better, coming up in fifteen minutes or cleaning his back. Not that he cared. Knowing he'd see London soon put him in a better mood than it should have. Marc grabbed clean clothes and headed for the shower fantasizing about having her in there with him before he even turned on the water.

London held the small box that was from some media company in her hand as she knocked on Marc's door. She had no idea what was in it and hadn't heard of the company that had sent it. Maybe it was time to ask Marc again what he did for a living. It seemed he dodged that question whenever she asked. He worked for a family business in L.A. That was all she knew. She'd been tempted to do some snooping, learn more about him. But doing so would suggest she wanted more from Marc than a casual relationship.

Marc smelled like shampoo and soap and a musky aftershave. She itched to feel how smooth his jaw probably was as she smiled at his freshly shaved face. But even more so, thoughts of running her fingers over the tight, still slightly damp curls spread across his muscular chest made her forget what she was going to say.

"Come on in." Marc held the door for her, stepping to the side so she could enter.

"You know I can't come in," she whispered, her heart pattering a mile a minute as a small voice in her head assured her it would be okay to be in his room for just a little bit.

"You're kidding." He really looked disappointed. "Would you really stand in the hallway and wait for your tip from another guest?"

Of course she wouldn't. London walked into his room, taking in his king-sized bed with one side completely crumpled and blankets twisted. There was an indentation in the pillows where his head had been. She bet he'd been all relaxed and warm when she called and woke him up. His rough baritone had sounded so damn good when he'd answered the phone.

"Here is your package," she offered, holding the box out to him. "And you don't have to tip me."

Marc closed the door behind her. He moved faster than she anticipated, wrapping his arms around her waist and lowering his head so his freshly shaved cheek was pressed against hers.

"What do you have for me?" he asked, turning to nibble on her ear before moving one hand in front of her to adjust the box in her hand. " 'Media Corp,' " he said, reading the return address label. "I've never heard of them."

"You didn't order something?" She stiffened and almost dropped the box.

Marc took it from her, letting her go but then pressing his hand against her back and guiding her past his bed. She took a calming breath when he sat down by his laptop and picked up his keys, which were on the desk. Using one of them as a knife, he slit the tape down the middle and along the sides.

He looked up at her several times while opening the box. "I guess it is weird to get something in the mail while you're on vacation when you're not expecting it. Don't let it startle you, though. Are you okay? I swear you're suddenly white as a ghost."

She touched her cheeks and grinned at him, feeling stupid and chastising herself. Marc was perceptive. It should flatter her that he was so in tune to her reactions. She hadn't missed his stressing that he went out alone the other night, as if he wanted to make sure she knew he wasn't spending time with another lady after having fucked her. Some men would, considering it their vacation so no rules applied. Which was why she steered clear of all guests when it came to accepting dates. Marc had made a point of letting her know he was thinking about her, couldn't wait to be with her again, and was alone when they weren't together.

"I guess I just assumed you'd ordered something. You didn't seem surprised when I told you I had a delivery for you."

"You had me at a disadvantage. I'd just woken up," he admitted. "I worried I was too honest and up-front with you on the phone."

"You did? How so?" Her attention shifted to the box, which was now open, although she couldn't see its contents. Although he held it in his hands, his attention was on her.

He wasn't in any hurry to see what was inside. Maybe it was something from his work and it had been sent to him. Possibly he received packages all the time and therefore wouldn't be excited to find out what would show up in the mail. London willed her heart to quit beating. There wasn't anything she could do about it if he didn't want her to know what he did for a living. Marc was smart. She should be, too. They could get involved yet keep their distance. Nothing about their personal lives.

Marc put the box on the desk and took her hands, bringing them to his mouth. "I told you I was dreaming about you, and I was. I really want to see you again and I was out so late last night because I drove by your house at least five times before forcing myself to come back here to my room. Then I couldn't fall asleep because the hard-on I had wouldn't go away. Masturbation loses its appeal when there is one hot, sexy lady nearby."

London laughed, enjoying the hell out of his honesty. It really sucked if he would go away and she wouldn't ever see him again. Marc was nothing more than one huge teddy bear. Although he was far from soft and cuddly. He was hard as steel, with muscles bulging everywhere, and taller than most men. But it was what was inside, a heart of gold and pure as driven snow.

"Sounds like a personal problem," she said, still laughing. London bet anyone who knew this man saw him as nothing more than a really big sweetheart. His size and all that muscle might frighten some, but not anyone who took time to know him. "Why didn't you stop by?" If he had, he would have caught her going through all of those pictures. Or maybe she would have put them away sooner and done something better with her evening than get all soft inside over her parents when she didn't even know where they were.

"You don't mind if I stop by unannounced?"

"I don't mind."

Marc stood and pulled her into his arms, kissing her until she was sure she would melt right there. He would make returning to work pure torture. And that was exactly where she needed to go.

"Aren't you going to see what's in the box?" she asked,

curious if he wasn't opening it because he didn't want her to see what might be inside. "Could it be something from your work?" she pressed.

"I seriously doubt that," he said, letting her go and picking up the box.

Marc opened the flaps and pulled out crinkled paper. A figurine slipped into his hand with the paper. "What's this?" he asked, studying it.

"It's a figurine or doll of some sort." London grabbed a wad of crinkled paper before it fell to the floor.

Marc held up what was actually two figurines, attached to each other—a bride and groom. Except the bride was missing her head.

"What the fuck?" Marc hissed, digging deeper into the small box and pulling out the rest of the packing. He put the box on the desk, stared at the damaged bride-and-groom as his scowl deepened. "Where did this come from?"

Something unpleasant twisted inside London's gut. It rose to her throat in a nasty bile. She stared at the wedding couple that were attached at the foot and hand. It was the type of figurine someone would put on top of a wedding cake, except the bride's head was gone.

"Are you sure you didn't order something to be sent here? Do you know this company?" She reached for the box, trying to get her brain to work. There was a logical explanation here. Marc wouldn't start getting bizarre things in the mail simply because she was.

"I didn't order anything," he said, taking the box before she could see the return address. "Who delivered this?"

"It came with all the mail today. Sometimes guests get mail and we sort through it and contact them, as I did with you."

"So the mailman brought in all the mail and you sorted through it and found this?"

She stared at him. That's what she just said. There was a hard edge to his expression that wasn't usually there. It didn't scare her, although Marc could definitely intimidate someone with his size alone if he wanted. London didn't sense anything like that. What she picked up on were vibes so strong she easily saw his determination to figure this out. Apparently Marc liked a good mystery a bit more than most. His expression hardened as he shifted his attention from her to the box.

"I just told you it came in the mail," she said, suddenly wanting the deformed figurine to disappear. She grabbed the wrapping paper, wadding all of it up in her hands and tossing it in his trash. "If you didn't order it, maybe it can be returned."

"London," he said, his tone softening. "I didn't order it, but someone sent it to me." He tilted the box and pointed to the mailing label he'd sliced through to open the box. "It's got my name on it and this room number. That bothers me. No one knows I'm here other than my family. If you don't mind, humor me. Let's walk through everything that happened from the moment you saw the box."

London sighed, nodding. She understood more than she could let him know. She'd rehashed the moments she'd received both packages of pictures over and over again.

"The mailman brings mail every day," she said, stating the obvious but guessing that was what Marc wanted to hear. "Obviously most of it is for the lodge, management, bills, magazines for the lobby—that sort of thing. Occasionally there are packages or letters for guests. Those are set to the side, sorted through, and the guest is contacted. Sometimes the guests know they're getting mail and they let us know. Either way, we have a special spot on the side counter where this mail goes until one of us contacts the guest and brings their mail to them."

"So you get all this mail, sort through it. Was I the

only one who got mail today? How much mail did you pull out for guests?"

London stared at him. He held the empty box in one hand and the deformed wedding-couple figurine in the other. He was calm, nonthreatening, when he spoke, but there was something different in his eyes, something she hadn't seen before. London accepted there were many layers to this man she didn't know yet, and probably never would. She wasn't sure what made his gaze darken, his blue eyes appear more focused. Looking down so she wouldn't obsess on him, London answered his questions as she stared at his hard abs.

"I didn't sort through the mail today. Jerry is our mailman. I remember him coming and leaving. Meryl talked to him for a minute or two, I think. He's a pretty nice guy."

"The same mailman always delivers the lodge's mail?" Marc put the wedding couple on the desk and started studying the box.

London watched him turn the box over, open it farther to look inside it, then close the flaps and study the mailing addresses. He didn't look up at her when he asked but seemed fascinated with the box.

"Jerry has been bringing our mail as long as I've worked here." She didn't want to look at the figurine. The whole thing was just weird. "Marc, I need to get back downstairs."

He snapped his attention to her. "Of course." Dropping the box on the desk with packing paper and the figurine, Marc reached for her, rubbing her arms until she met his gaze. "Don't worry about this. I'll figure it out."

Her laugh sounded fake even to her. "Right. Someone wants you to marry a headless woman," she offered, taking a stab at trying to make the situation humorous. Maybe it was to Marc. If she freaked out, he might wonder why she'd get so upset about Marc receiving something weird in the mail.

She worried there might be a connection between this package and the pictures she'd received, but until she got out of this room and away from Marc, and after she finished working for the day, she needed to keep her cool about it.

Marc pulled her into his arms. But he didn't kiss her. He held her in a comforting embrace. He held her as a friend or someone more, a lover holding the person he cared about. London relaxed in his arms, resting her cheek against his chest. When he started stroking her hair, she closed her eyes. What would it be like to have someone like him for real? Someone who would stand in her corner and be there for her when times got tough. The thought was so damn appealing she lost herself in it.

She could talk to him about anything, knowing he would hear her and care about what she said. What if she told him about the pictures? Would Marc tell her not to worry about those, too? Would he brainstorm it out with her, weigh all options, and help her figure out why they were being sent to her?

London squeezed her eyes shut, feeling all that steel muscle surrounding her. It would be incredible to have someone in her life who was always there for her. The truth of the matter, though, was that simply wasn't the case. Confiding in him would mean getting closer to him. She couldn't risk losing her heart to someone who would leave and never return.

"I need to get going," she whispered, and forced herself to back out of his arms. "I'm sorry you got a mangled wedding-cake figurine in the mail," she offered, making a face at him when she met his gaze. "Someone has a really sick sense of humor."

"You're right about that." He walked her to the door, turned her, and gave her a quick kiss before escorting her into the hall. "I'll find out who and let you know when I do."

London hurried back to the front desk, grateful to find Meryl flipping through a magazine. She pulled her attention from whatever she'd been reading and offered London a lazy smile.

"So was it good?" Meryl asked, wagging her eyebrows.

London made a face. "You are so bad."

"Well, you were gone long enough I figured you got yourself some. But don't kiss and tell. See if I care." Meryl shrugged and returned her attention to the magazine, an incredibly sheepish look on her face.

"I'm sorry I was gone so long." London walked over to the corner, behind the counter, where items were put for guests. "That package I took upstairs to Marc . . . ," she began.

"He's not Mr. King anymore?" Meryl teased.

London was glad she had her back to Meryl. "He doesn't like to be called Mr. King." It was a good save. "Anyway," she continued, catching Meryl staring at her as she sat on the one stool behind the counter and balanced the magazine on her lap.

She frowned when London stared at her. "Something wrong?"

"Probably not." London forced her expression to relax and smiled. "He said he didn't order it and the item was broken."

"He opened it while you were up there?" Meryl closed the magazine and slid it under the counter, then slipped off the stool. "What was in the box?"

"A bride-and-groom figurine and the bride's head was missing."

Meryl stared at her, the look on her face showing she didn't find anything humorous about what London had just said. "God, that's terrible. Who the hell would send something like that? That's almost scary," she finished, whispering her last sentence.

London agreed. "He asked me all these questions about how the mail arrives and where things are put for guests."

"Did you tell him?"

"Yeah. Jerry brought the mail today and you sorted it." London shrugged.

"I didn't sort any mail today," Meryl said. "There wasn't any to sort."

"But that box," London interrupted, glancing at the corner of the counter where she'd taken the box from before calling Marc. "You put it over here. When I was through checking in that last couple, I saw it and called him."

Meryl frowned at the corner of the counter and started shaking her head slowly. "I didn't put anything over there."

Chapter Five

Marc walked out of the Aspen post office, ducking against a brutal wind and picking up his pace to his car. After he'd received the deformed figurine in the mail, two decisions were easy to make. He needed to secure his phone and touch base with home. Also, it was a smart move to arrange for mail he knew he wanted to be sent to a different address. He'd opened a post office box at the post office first thing that Monday morning, then ordered the necessary scrambler device for his new cell phone and had it shipped there.

Climbing into his car, he cranked on the heat before opening the small package from the place where KFA bought a lot of their equipment. Charging it to the business credit card would cue his parents into the fact that he was taking steps to talk to them. It was time to find out if they had a case that might have had a trickle-over effect on him. He didn't receive that wedding couple in the mail by accident.

Marc disassembled his new phone, pulled the small, flat disk out of the little bag it was shipped in, and slid it alongside the SIM card in his phone. It wasn't a product his cell phone service was thrilled about. The scrambler didn't hinder their ability to track his calls, text messages, or any other use of his phone they would charge him for. There wasn't any legislation outlawing this kind of equipment. What mattered, though, was that once it was installed Marc could use his phone and place calls without worrying about anyone picking up on his frequency and listening in to his phone conversations.

Once he turned his phone back on, Marc pushed the auto-dial to call home and shifted to pull out of his stall.

"KFA," Natasha, Marc's cousin, answered.

"Hey, Natasha. It's Marc."

"Hey, stranger," she said cheerfully. "We figured you were lost in the mountains."

Natasha King was Marc's uncle's daughter. Uncle George was a bum, but his daughter was hot as hell. She was Marc's cousin, though, and they grew up together. There was a time when Natasha was an early teen that Marc had enjoyed a fantasy or two about her. They were short-lived and he'd even felt guilty for having them. She was as much the sister he'd never had as she was his cousin. Today Natasha held a black belt in karate and worked in the office out of his parents' home, answering all calls for KFA and handling all paperwork. She was on top of her act and there wasn't a man on this planet worthy of her time.

"I am lost in the mountains," Marc told her, checking traffic and turning right, in the direction of London's house. "It's gorgeous out here. You can't possibly believe how intense these mountains are until you see them."

"Well then, where in the hell are my pictures?" she demanded.

"Yes, Mom," he said, grinning.

Natasha laughed and a beeping sounded in the phone. "Hold on a minute. I have another call."

She didn't wait for him to answer before putting him on hold. Marc switched the phone to speaker and glanced at the time. It was just after five. If London went straight home after work she would be there soon. She'd said he could stop by unannounced. He continued toward her house, thoughts of attacking her the moment she got out of her car encouraging him to hurry to get there.

"Sorry about that," Natasha said when she came back.

"It's okay. I'm secure now," he told her. "What's going on at the home front?"

"The usual, mainly," she said. "How secure are you?"

"I just installed the scrambler I ordered. There aren't any new cases since I've left?"

Natasha didn't answer right away. There was some background noise and Marc's father came on the line.

"Are you still in Aspen?" Greg King asked, his deep voice vibrating through the speaker on Marc's phone.

"Yup. Figured it was time to touch base. Anything new on the home front?"

"You remember Marty Byrd?" his father asked.

None of them would ever forget The Byrd. It was the case they all worked almost a year ago when Marc's mother returned to them after being in the Witness Protection Program for five years. It was a bittersweet experience. Nothing topped having Mom back in their lives. Yet after they hunted down his mother's boss first, that led them to a hunt to find Marty Byrd, one of the world's most renowned assassins, they'd almost lost their dad in a bloody showdown.

"You know I do," Marc said, feeling his pulse pick up speed, the familiar sensation he always experienced when he tasted a challenging hunt coming on. "What about it?"

"Remember when we learned Byrd was abducting men and women who were the best in their field, private investigators, criminals, people from both sides of the street?"

"Yup."

Marty Byrd had tried abducting Greg King, but Marc's mom prevented them from taking him. Marc had been pissed as hell when his father later allowed Byrd to kidnap him, without Marc or the rest of the family being filled in on the plan. His father almost lost his life just so he could get on the inside and learn Byrd's master plan.

"I remember going to that god-awful hospital for over a week just to stare at your ass lying in a bed when you about got blown to bits," Marc added. "And we never did learn Marty Byrd's sordid secrets."

"Sometimes getting blown to bits is all in a day's work," Greg said casually.

Marc didn't doubt for a minute that if he or Jake decided to take on such a mission just to hunt down a man, Greg King would go ballistic.

"Uh-huh." Arguing with him was almost as much a waste of time as trying to win an argument against Marc's mother. "What about it?" he asked, pressing the conversation forward. "Are people disappearing again?"

"Not quite. Something isn't right in the air, though." Greg was a master at drawing out a discussion about a possible case until Marc wanted to shake the giant brute senseless and force him to speak his mind. "We're receiving some odd messages," he said, apparently sensing Marc would start yelling if he didn't explain what was going on soon.

"What kind of messages?"

"Last week, I guess it was right after you left, we received some pictures in the mail."

"Pictures?"

"Yup."

"Pictures of what?"

"They were shots of your mother and me when we went on our second honeymoon a few months back."

Marc's parents were worse than teenagers in love the first few months after Haley came back home. Giggling like children and whispering secrets, running upstairs to their room in the middle of the day and having sex louder than any parents should be allowed, would have been intolerable and unacceptable if it weren't for the fact that Marc and his brother were just as thrilled to have their mom back home. Marc and Jake were happy for their parents and more than a bit relieved when they decided to take off for a couple weeks for a romantic cruise. His dad needed to take more time off.

Life returned somewhat to normal when they got back. They were still head over heels in love. It was the type of relationship most only dreamed of having, but Marc's parents were proof that true love did exist and could happen if two people were willing to work hard for it.

"I look forward to seeing them. Nothing kinky, though. I'm not sure I could handle that."

Greg laughed. "I don't have a problem showing any of them to you. But you don't get it. They weren't pictures we took. Someone mailed pictures to us. There was no return address on the package and they were taken without us knowing."

"You mean like someone is letting you know they're watching you?" Marc tightened his grip on his steering wheel as he clenched his jaw. There wasn't a worse feeling in the world than believing someone he cared about might be in trouble and he was too far away to do anything about it.

"Exactly," Greg said, his voice tightening.

Marc focused his thoughts. "What's that got to do with the Marty Byrd case? He was killed, in case you've forgotten."

"I'll never forget that." Marc's dad's voice rumbled

through the phone. "Because he died we never learned what game he was playing."

"And he told you he was playing a game," Marc remembered.

"He told me he was lining up his players by abducting people he believed to be the best in their fields. We never learned why, or who he was playing against."

"If he was playing against anyone," Marc reminded Greg. When that case had ended and after he recuperated in the hospital, Greg had been convinced after talking to Marty Byrd that the assassin was taking people to mold into players for some morbid war-type game. As Marc's dad had said at the time, it was like the game of Risk. Byrd had planned on training those he'd abducted from their lives so they would be killers. He had been building an army to take part in some masterminded sick adventure. None of what Marty Byrd had told Greg King could ever be confirmed, though, since Byrd was blown to bits when his house was destroyed.

"If he was playing against anyone," Greg said, although his tone suggested he was simply appeasing his son. "Those pictures pissed me off and scared your mother," Greg continued. "I wouldn't have thought they had anything to do with The Byrd, but then we found another package, this one in the Avalanche."

Marc listened and didn't comment. He imagined his mother was probably out for blood more than scared. It also didn't make sense anything would be found in the Avalanche. His dad bought that truck a couple years ago and treated it like his newborn son. It was never left unlocked. The King men took care of their cars. Marc wanted the rest of the story, though, so remained quiet, silently encouraging his father to continue.

"Jake found the package while he was helping his mother

and your cousin unload bags from a shopping spree they'd gone on. He stopped unloading for a few minutes when one of his girlfriends called."

That explained how something could be put in the Avalanche, although Marc felt the rage his family would have experienced knowing someone was cocky enough to slip something into the truck right under their noses. The Avalanche was always parked on the circular drive by the front door.

"That's the only way we can figure out how anyone slipped it in the truck. Both women swear the truck was locked every time they went into a store." Greg paused, saying something to Natasha when the phone started beeping. "Hold on, Marc," he said, and once again the line went silent.

Marc needed to know what was in the package they found in the Avalanche. Although he would learn in a minute or two, not knowing immediately was hell. Right now it was a stretch matching the figurine he'd received in the mail to anything his father was describing. Marc had made it across town during his conversation and slowed in front of London's house. Her green Jeep wasn't here. It was quarter after five. The drive from her home to the lodge would probably take half an hour. She might not leave the moment she got off work, either. He put his Mustang in park. He would wait it out.

"Okay, I'm back," Greg said, his voice hollow as if he'd switched to speakerphone.

Marc held his phone between his hands, which rested against his steering wheel. "What was in the package?" he asked.

"The one we found in the Avalanche?" Greg made it a rhetorical question, since he continued talking. "You know the movie *The Incredibles,* right?"

"Yeah," Marc answered slowly.

"There were two action figures in the box, Mr. and Mrs. Incredible, or Bob and Helen Parr."

"Were they damaged in any way?"

"Now why would you ask me that?"

"Were they?" Marc pressed.

"Mrs. Incredible's head was torn off."

Marc felt the adrenaline rush surge through his system. Ignoring the cold wind that attacked eagerly the moment he stepped out of his warm car, he stalked up the sidewalk to London's house, needing space, needing to move, as his thoughts started racing in his brain.

"Dad, we have a situation," Marc said, facing the street and glancing up and down it. Someone pulled into a narrow driveway down the block, a husband or wife coming home to their normal family after another day at the office. "I got a package in the mail over the weekend."

"What?" his father asked, his tone unnervingly calm.

"It was the type of bride-and-groom figurine you would find on top of a wedding cake, except the bride's head was ripped off."

"No shit," Greg breathed. "But why a bride and groom?" His brain was processing quickly. "Is there a woman in your life?"

"I've been spending some time with a lady who works at the Elk Ski Lodge, where I'm staying. She works behind the front desk and brought the package to my room."

"What's her name? I'll run a check on her," his father decided.

"Her name is London Brooke. But I'm here to tell you now, Dad, she didn't have a damn thing to do with that package being sent to me." Marc paced back to his car but wasn't ready to climb into the warm confinement of it yet. He retraced his steps up her walk to her front porch, staring at the imprints of his boots in the dusting of snow that had covered her walk since he'd last been here. "She doesn't even know what I do for a living," he added. "And I'll be damned if I let her get mixed up in some case I don't even know about yet."

"I'll run the check anyway," his dad said. "I'm sure she's fine. You've always had good taste in women, just like your old man. But if someone is sending us cryptic messages for some sick game they're concocting, our women might be in danger."

"Run your check and get back with me," Marc grumbled. "I'll keep you posted at this end. Unless you have any more great news to share with me?"

"Your mother misses you."

Marc sighed and watched his breath form a cloud in front of his face. The cold finally hit him and he wrapped his coat around him, stuffing his free hand in his pocket. "Put her on. Let me say hi to her," he said.

He calmed down a bit talking to his mother. It didn't surprise him that she was just as preoccupied with the current events happening to them as Marc's dad was. Haley King had a knack for putting clues together and creating a full picture. When shit hit the fan she didn't panic, and if someone attacked her family, she was planning her counterattack before any of them could start a brainstorming session.

"How much longer are you staying out there?" she asked after going over with Marc all the details he and his father had just discussed.

"I was thinking about staying out here for another week or so. I'm not sure how long. I thought it would do me some good getting away from it all."

"Sometimes it does do you good." His mom was reassuring, her soft, soothing tone always a comfort. "Are you thinking about coming home sooner?"

"I've been out here less than two weeks." Marc knew

his time with London was short-term, but that didn't mean he wanted to leave yet. There wasn't any point, though, in letting anyone know that was the first thought that came to mind when he was asked about heading home. "I've been thinking about booking the room at the ski lodge for another month, but we'll see," he said, hoping that would appease his mother.

"And what's this I hear about a lady?"

Marc studied London's porch stairs, noticing one of them seemed a bit crooked. It would come loose eventually if it wasn't fixed.

"Her name is London and we're just hanging out some," he said, downplaying his current relationship with London for his mother's sake as well as for his. "She works at the Elk Ski Lodge," he added, knowing he had to give his mother something or she would press for more details.

"Is she pretty?" Haley was pressing anyway.

"Yes, Mom. She is very pretty."

That apparently satisfied her. "Maybe you could take a few pictures and send them through your phone. God forbid I forget what my oldest son looks like."

She was teasing and his mother was as close to Superwoman as it got. That didn't mean she wasn't a woman, and he didn't miss her meaning. She missed her oldest son and if there was a woman in his life, she wanted to check her out.

"I'll see what I can do," he said. Then sending his love, and promising to call again soon, he ended the call.

Marc glanced at the time on his phone. It was going on six. Maybe London wasn't coming straight home. It crossed his mind she might be doing one of those walking tours. He hadn't thought to check before leaving the lodge. Glancing at the stairs again, he climbed them, testing the stair that seemed a bit crooked. That's when he noticed the package in front of London's front door.

London walked into the lodge just as large snowflakes started falling. It had been a good group tonight for the walking tour. They were all even more enthusiastic when they made it back to the lobby just as it started snowing.

"We were very impressed with your knowledge of the area." An older woman stood next to her husband, straightening and clasping her hands in front of her as she spoke.

"Thank you. I'm so glad you enjoyed yourself."

"I didn't know skiing didn't start in Aspen until the late thirties and that the sport didn't take off until after World War Two." The husband patted his wife's back and grinned at London. "You not only gave us a good workout; it was educational as well. We were very impressed."

"Again, thank you," London said, and left the couple to visit with some other guests who remained gathered in front of the fireplace in the lobby.

London's boss, Cliff Hampton, the manager of the ski lodge, stood behind the counter talking to several people who were around London's age. They laughed at something he said and she realized he was checking them in as she moved around the counter. She glanced at the clipboard that showed how many had signed up for the tours for the rest of the week. Marc hadn't signed up for any of them. There was still a pang of disappointment that didn't go away even when she scolded herself about getting involved with a guest.

"London," Cliff said when she started around the corner to the break room.

"Yes?" she asked, pausing before the end of the counter.

"I'm hearing how well you're doing with the tours," he said. Cliff didn't hand out compliments. London was convinced he believed himself perfect and assumed everyone else should be, too. He didn't buy into offering praise for anything he thought should be normal behavior. London studied him, waiting for a bomb to drop. "You don't miss a day of work, which is how it should be," he added, holding true to his nature.

"I enjoy my job," she offered, not seeing any reason to tell him anything other than the truth.

"Good." Cliff bobbed his head and not one hair of his dark brown hair moved. "Then maybe you can explain to me why you're fraternizing with one of our guests when you know it violates policy."

The phone rang and Cliff gave her a knowing look, with a gleam in his eye telling her she was busted. He reached to answer it, looking away from her first. London had half a mind to bolt to the break room and dodge out the back door. She didn't need Cliff's lectures. She ran this place as well as he did, if not better. Cliff had been known to allow his mightier-than-thou nature to rub off on a guest or two over the years. London always greeted them with a smile on her face. No way would he belittle her when no one had ever filed a complaint against her.

Running would imply her guilt. As much as she didn't want to, London held her ground and waited for him to get off the phone. Cliff studied her a moment after hanging up.

"I assume you know what I'm talking about," he said finally.

"I know I'm not doing anything wrong, Cliff," she said, seriously doubting he could prove otherwise, not unless he'd stood outside her house and took pictures through her windows. He wouldn't get her to admit she'd had sex with Marc. It was none of his damn business. "If you have a complaint against me, I'm willing to discuss it with you."

Cliff sighed, running his perfectly manicured fingers

through his thick hair. Not too surprisingly, it looked the same when he moved his hand. "You went out in a blizzard to help Mr. King return to the lodge when his car got stuck. The other day you took a package to his room and were gone over thirty minutes."

London couldn't believe either Meryl or Todd, who were the two working during both of those incidents, would go complaining to Cliff about her. Cliff was sniffing around, and what mattered to her more at the moment than his knowing these things was why was he sniffing?

She tilted her head, studying his triumphant smile. He wanted to bust her, really wanted her to admit her guilt. It hit her that possibly Cliff was aggravated with her being the better employee than him. Maybe he felt threatened.

London shook her head, which immediately caused him to narrow his brow and frown. She wasn't going to take a fall so he could assure himself he was still the best there was.

" 'Fraternizing' is a pretty harsh term," she said, taking her time and trying to read him accurately as she spoke. "Now if you were to say I was being nice to a guest who is nice to all of us, I would have to say, 'Guilty as charged.' But you and I both know what 'fraternizing' implies. Are you sure you want to go there, Cliff? That's a pretty harsh charge." And he had no proof.

She wasn't sure if his cheeks flamed red out of embarrassment or anger. He looked away, grumbling something under his breath.

"That's what I thought," she said, smiling and starting to the break room.

"Stay away from him," Cliff grumbled, storming after her but stopping just outside the end of the counter.

London looked in his direction, her hand on the break room door, and was actually surprised. Cliff never raised his voice. For the most part, he never bothered her at all.

Most of their conversations over the past three years since she'd started working here were nothing more than nods and casual greetings. She did her job right, and she did it well. London could live without his praise and gratification, but she wouldn't live with him threatening and raising his voice at her.

At the same time, she wouldn't make a scene by raising her voice down the hall. "I'll treat every guest here the same," she said under her breath, moving slowly in on him until they stood face-to-face. "With a smile and professional attitude," she added, dying to tell him where he could stick that cocky attitude. Cliff wouldn't make her lose her cool, though.

He didn't say anything else and London was still shaking as she drove home. It wasn't the first time she'd gone home from work in the dark, but everything around her being black somehow put her even more on edge. It was bad enough receiving pictures of her parents, which brought back memories and feelings for them she didn't usually dwell on. Marc's receiving the deformed wedding couple probably wasn't related, but it was still really weird. Now Cliff was acting strange. If he really thought she was having sex with Marc, he should have approached it differently. But even more so, London never would have guessed him the type of manager who would have said a thing about it in the first place, unless she was openly fooling around with a guest where other guests could see. Which she was most definitely not doing!

London scowled at the car parked in front of her house. She pulled into her driveway and recognized it. Marc wasn't anywhere in sight, though.

Get a grip, she thought to herself, taking a moment before getting out of her car. It wouldn't help if Marc saw her frazzled. He would want to solve all of her problems, and there wasn't anything he could do about any of this.

An icy breeze blew snow around her when she got out and hurried to her front porch.

"You said I could stop by unannounced," Marc said jovially, trotting up her sidewalk and climbing the porch stairs behind her.

"That's fine," she said, holding her house key and smiling at him when he opened the front screen door for her. "How did you know I worked late tonight?"

"I didn't." He was right behind her when she entered her dark living room. "I came by here shortly after five. When you didn't come home I ran some errands and came back."

London was shocked. What kind of man wasted time and continued coming by just to spend time with her?

"I also called the lodge to find out when you would be off work," he added, following her into her kitchen as she turned on lights.

London couldn't stop herself this time. She stared at him, her jaw dropping. Cliff guessed they were seeing each other on the side because Marc had called and asked about her. Why didn't Cliff say that to her?

She blinked, convincing herself there were many reasons Marc might have asked about her schedule. It still wasn't proof she was having sex with him.

"You look shocked," he said, running his thumb along her jaw.

"Not many men would go to such an effort to see me," she admitted.

"Then they're all fools," he muttered, grabbing her chin and tilting her head back so he could kiss her.

London had an agenda when she came home. There were things she was going to do. For the life of her, as Marc ravished her mouth, she couldn't remember any of what she'd planned for her evening.

"Hungry?" Marc whispered into her mouth.

"Starving."

His deep laughter sent chills rushing over her flesh. Marc ran his hands down her back and cupped her ass. It was such a comfortable spot being wrapped in his arms, with all that packed muscle to lean against. What a life it would be coming home to him, being able to share the good and the bad of her days. It was so incredible, imagining it seemed wrong. Nothing was permanent and this torrid relationship with Marc was definitely proof of that. If she were smart she would listen to Cliff and tell Marc not to come around. She could blame it on a long day or on being exhausted, but she didn't have the strength to tell him to leave. More than anything she wanted him to stay.

"How about a pizza, my treat?" he asked.

It was nicer than she would have imagined cuddling on the couch, the remote on Marc's lap, as they ordered pizza and talked while waiting for it to show up. He didn't bring up the deformed wedding couple and she almost forgot about the pictures.

The last thing Marc wanted to do was leave. Full from pizza and having peeked outside to see his car covered with a thick layer of snow, he thought staying with London was a perfect idea. Not that he searched for an excuse. Something about her made it easy to relax and be himself.

"My mom asked about you," he said, staring at the TV and rubbing his thumb over her shoulder as they cuddled.

Leaning against him on the couch, with his arm draped around her, was cozy and perfect. She shifted, staring at him a moment before saying anything.

"Why would she ask about me?"

He took his time answering and wrinkled his brow, making a show of giving it some thought. "I think it came up when she asked me when I was coming home."

"Doesn't she know you've booked your room at the lodge until the end of the month?"

"She knows."

"Are you a mama's boy?" London teased.

It crossed his mind to tell her more, open up to her a bit. It was terrifying how easy it would be to do. London grinned at him, her black eyes glowing and her hair drifting over her shoulders and tickling his arm. Sexy and a great personality. What the hell was she doing in Colorado and not California, where he might consider taking their relationship to the next level?

"Hardly," he said, scowling.

Her grin broadened. "Sounds like you might be," she continued, twisting against him and facing him instead of the TV. "Mom wants you safe at home where she can make sure you choose a good girl."

"And you aren't a good girl?" He grabbed her, dragging her over his lap.

London laughed out loud, flipping in his arms so she faced him. Her smile faded and she arched one eyebrow while dragging her fingers down his cheek.

"You tell me how good I am," she whispered, moving against his cock.

It leapt to life, eager for the attention. Marc grabbed her waist before she could cause pain. "I swear to God, woman. I'll rip those clothes off your body if you keep that up," he hissed, clenching his teeth and fighting to concentrate.

London showed him no mercy and fought against his grasp to move. When he lifted her, mainly to prevent her from getting him too hard to think straight, she straddled him and lifted her body against him. Her breasts were damn close to his face and her hair shrouded both of them as she began planting soft kisses on his face.

"Is that supposed to scare me?" she whispered.

Marc growled, the rumbling in his chest vibrating between the two of them. She responded with something that sounded like a soft purr as she continued torturing him with her moist lips.

"I warned you," he said, his voice raspy with need.

He grabbed the loose-fitting, soft sweater she wore and dragged it up her body. London responded by arching in front of him. She quit kissing him and straightened, raising her arms and letting her head fall back, making it easy to pull off her. Her hair fanned around her shoulders and fell down past her breasts when she lowered her arms, once again draping them over his shoulders.

"Trying to make me a bad girl?" she asked, lifting herself and pressing her breasts into his face.

She wore a lace bra, this one blue, and her creamy flesh pressed against it, showing off how full and perky her breasts were. He dropped her sweater and ran his hands up her bare arms. London smelled good, making him think she might have dabbed perfume on when she came home without him noticing. Imagining her stealing away for a moment to make herself more appealing to him turned him on even more. He found her nipple through the lace and latched on with his teeth.

"Oh God," she panted, arching further against him and digging her nails into his shoulders. "Maybe your mom wants you home because she knows you're a bad boy."

"I'm not the bad boy. That's my brother," he told her, switching to her other breast.

The sounds she made when he inflicted just the slightest amount of pain to her nipple sent his blood pressure through the roof. Her breasts were soft, the perfect size, so easy to bury his face in and enjoy their smooth roundness. Marc hadn't tried to unclasp a lady's bra without looking since high school, and at that time he'd considered himself a master of the art. A flash of pride rushed through him when he found the clasp in the middle of her back and unhooked it with one try.

Her hair wrapped around his fingers when he pulled the straps down her arms. As the lace fell free from her breasts, London created space between them, looking down at him with lust making her eyes glow.

"We have a serious problem here," she informed him with a sultry whisper.

"What's that?"

"You're still dressed."

She shrieked and laughed at the same time when he leapt off the couch, keeping her wrapped around him. London bounced when he dropped her on the couch. She recovered quickly, stretching out and relaxing one arm over her head as he began stripping.

"That's it, bad boy," she purred. "Give me a show."

"You're asking for it, lady."

"Asking for it?" She cocked an eyebrow. "I thought I was being rather demanding."

Marc made quick work of stripping out of his clothes, taking time to pull a condom out of his pants pocket, where he'd put it while waiting for her to come home, and dropped it on the coffee table. Her gaze shifted to it only for a moment before returning to his face. Her lips were parted and moist and her breath came hard enough that her tight tummy rose and fell. She dragged strands of hair away from her breast, exposing both of them and their hard, brown nipples. As he struggled with his boots, London pressed her hand flat over her stomach and slid her fingers into her jeans.

He'd never get out of his boots at this rate. There wasn't any way he could move to her with his jeans half-off but stuck until he got rid of his shoes. Finally, yanking one off, then the other, Marc finished undressing. It was far from a show, but London's flushed expression and glazed-over look on her face made it apparent she didn't have any complaints.

"I rather like it when you're demanding." He moved around the coffee table and bent over her, grabbing her jeans at the waist and lifting her off the couch.

"Marc!" she squealed, grabbing his arms when he undid her button and pulled the zipper down.

She slapped her hands against the couch as he kept her lower half in the air and pulled her jeans off her. London helped, making scissor motions with her bare legs in the air when he peeled her jeans until they were inside out and tossed with her sweater in a pile. Once again she wore matching lace underwear. The view as he stood over her was enough to render him speechless.

London appeared to be a bit more in control. She licked her lips and slid her hand inside her panties, moving her fingers over her pussy.

"You wouldn't believe how wet I am," she said, and started squeezing her breast with her other hand. "And horny. So damn horny. Think you can help me out with that?"

"Why are you so horny?" he asked.

Her thick lashes hooded her gaze as she licked her lips again. "It might have been because I was thinking about you all the way home," she whispered, shooting him a furtive glance before lowering her gaze to his cock. "I might add my imagination is very accurate."

Marc reached for her, grabbing her legs and pinning them together with one hand. He shoved the coffee table out of the way when he went down on his knees on the side of the couch.

"Tell me, sweetheart," he said, letting her legs rest against his shoulder and reaching for the straps of her panties. "What was it that you imagined?"

"You," she admitted easily, although when she flashed him a smile it seemed almost shy. "And me," she added, whispering.

London wasn't shy. Marc guessed that letting him know she was thinking about him during the day was close enough to telling him this was going further than being friends with benefits.

"What were we doing?" he pressed, removing her underwear and taking her ankles in his hands. He spread her open and damn near forgot what he'd just asked her as he stared at the cream causing her shaved pussy to glisten.

"We were having incredible, mind-blowing sex," she told him, that glimpse of shyness, or hesitation, fading and her cocky, ornery tone returning. "And you were doing this."

When he moved in closer to her she reached for his head and pushed, encouraging him closer. Marc didn't fight her. Her fingers massaged his scalp as he adjusted himself between her legs and breathed in her rich, intoxicating scent. When he kissed her clit she damn near came off the couch.

Marc gripped her legs, holding her down and keeping her from doing him bodily harm as he began licking the cream from her entrance. "How good did you imagine me to be?" he asked, regaining control of his thoughts and his actions when he held her in place and started enjoying her sweet, hot pussy.

"Hum, um," she said, murmuring and whimpering.

The sounds she made were as hot as the rest of her. Marc enjoyed the view, staring up at her full, round breasts and her face. She pressed her teeth into her lower lip and closed her eyes, moaning her approval as her breath came hard and fast. He didn't press the conversation, satisfied to feast and watch her orgasm build inside her.

London's face was flushed. She turned her head from

side to side, groaning as her breath caught more than once in her throat. Her black hair fell in thick strands over her bare shoulders and fanned around her face on the couch. She was gorgeous, beyond beautiful, inside and out. It terrified the crap out of him as thoughts began plaguing him on a more regular basis of making her his woman. There was the distance issue. But at the rate they were going, leaving her after a month would be damn near impossible to do. Already, after just under two weeks, every time he left her he counted the hours until he saw her again.

He didn't want to dwell on their future. It turned playtime with her into something so much more serious. Marc had been with women before who were compelling, intelligent, and sexy, and he knew throughout every minute of their relationship that it would end. Breaking it off with a lady was always a bittersweet experience. He would mourn the loss of a good woman, sometimes get drunk over it, and enjoy the excitement of someone new when she came along. Not once had he ever considered turning anything into something more serious than fun dates and hot sex. And more than one woman had tried convincing him to do otherwise.

"Marc," London said, yanking him out of his thoughts. "God. Marc!" she cried out.

It was enough notice to brace himself and hold her in place. Her dam broke as she lashed from side to side, digging her nails into his bare flesh and probably breaking skin as she cried out. He watched her come, drowned in her cream, and damn near came with her.

"You're so fucking hot," he told her, grabbing the condom and ripping it out of its package. He sheathed himself and climbed over her as she panted and grinned when she stared up at him.

"More," she whispered, her voice hoarse. "Now, Marc. Please. Fuck me really hard and fast. Please."

"I love it when you beg, sweetheart," he said, bracing his arms on either side of her and kissing her tenderly.

She hummed into his mouth as she wrapped her arms and legs around him and pulled him closer. When his cock found her entrance, the heat coming from her entrance burned him alive. His balls tightened painfully. As he entered her, her smooth, soaked flesh constricted around him, dragging him deep inside her.

"Hard, fast," she panted, repeating the words in his ear and dragging her nails down his back.

Marc obliged, taking her and giving her all he had.

"I love it," she said, her voice raspy.

For a moment he thought he heard wrong. Thinking she'd just told him she loved him wasn't half as terrifying as the fact that the words slipped to his tongue and he almost said them out loud. It tripped him up and for a moment he lost his rhythm. His cock didn't go soft, though. The craving he had for her didn't fade. If anything, as he swallowed those three little words he'd almost said out loud his need for her grew tenfold. They wouldn't take this relationship to that level. He wouldn't allow it.

For a moment Marc experienced a light-headedness that bugged the crap out of him. Not because he worried he wasn't giving her what she wanted physically. He picked up the pace quickly. Her gasps grew louder as she came again, soaking his balls and creating even more heat that helped push him to the edge. As he came, releasing and feeling his heart hammer against his chest, he experienced the overwhelming realization that feelings for London existed and they went far beyond lust.

Chapter Six

Marc stepped out of the steamy bathroom, wondering what London might think of him leaving a change of clothes at her house. He'd donned his jeans but opted not to put his shirt back on. Walking barefoot into her living room, he joined her on the couch, where she sat curled in the corner, wearing an extra-large T-shirt, although definitely not big enough for him. It fell past her thighs, and her bare legs and feet were tucked underneath her.

"The snow is coming down really hard," she said, nodding at the weather report on the TV.

"Are you inviting me to stay the night?" He unfolded an afghan that was on the back of her chair as he sat next to her.

London helped spread it open and covered her legs before relaxing against him. "It would probably be a good idea. Knowing you, I'd end up having to get dressed and pull you out of a ditch before you made it to the lodge."

"Are you cool with me staying?" he asked seriously. "If we're discussing safety, I'm sure I could make it to a motel here in town."

She leaned her head against his chest and relaxed further as he pulled her against him and cradled her in his arms. London relaxed her head against his arm and stared up at him.

"I guess you could sleep on the couch," she said slowly.

"Is that where you want me to sleep?"

She studied him with her pretty black eyes. "No," she said after a moment. "I want you in bed with me."

London adjusted herself, shifting to watch TV. A few minutes later her breathing slowed, and when his phone rang she didn't move. Marc managed to get it off the coffee table without waking her.

Glancing at the number, he answered, "Hello."

"I just remembered it's an hour later there as the phone was ringing," Jake said. "I didn't wake you, did I?"

"You didn't wake anyone," Marc said, keeping his voice quiet as he gently stroked London's hair. She moaned softly, stretched under the afghan, and remained relaxed with her head on his lap.

"Dad and Mom told you about the action figures we found in the truck?" his brother asked.

"Yeah, I heard about it."

"I heard you got a similar gift. Is your lady hot?"

He remembered damn near suffocating inside her soaked pussy. "Yeah, she is," he admitted, unable to see enough of her face to tell if her eyes were opened or not. "Did you call to get a rundown?"

"You can fill me in on all of the nasty details later. I need to talk to you. Is this a good time?" The serious edge in Jake's tone made it clear he wasn't calling for girlfriend advice. Not that any of the women Jake saw ever got far enough to rate the label. Jake played them and left them. Maybe Marc should ask how Jake always kept it casual.

"What's wrong?" Marc asked, doubting any advice his

brother might offer on how to enjoy everything a woman offered without losing his heart would sit well with him.

"They told you about the pictures we received of them while they were on that cruise, right?"

"Yeah."

"More pictures came earlier tonight. I was the only one here. They were packaged the same as the others, looked like they came through the mail."

"What do you mean they looked like they came through the mail?" Marc thought of the package he'd found on London's porch floor. There was no return address, yet it had postage on it. Her mailbox was at the top of her porch steps. It didn't make sense that the package wasn't in the mailbox but instead on the porch floor.

"There were stamps and it's gone through the mail, but it wasn't in the mailbox."

"What were the pictures of?" He stared at London's profile, her face tilted toward his jeans and her hair flowing down her back. She didn't move when he ran his hand down the back of her head, but her breathing was quieter than it had been. If she was listening she apparently didn't want to interrupt his conversation.

"Man, they were of Mom and Natasha. Shots of them in parking lots and also in the mall. They were taken while they were out shopping. I remember Mom was wearing the blouse she had on in the pictures. Someone is following her around and it's really starting to piss me off."

Marc lifted his gaze, staring at the wall across the room, and fought for a calming breath. He felt the rage surge to life in him, causing all his muscles to tighten as he fought to remain on the couch and stay cool. He exhaled slowly, pinching the bridge of his nose.

"Okay, let's talk this through," he said, closing his eyes for a moment and forcing the frustration growing inside him to calm. He understood Jake's anger. They'd lost their mom once, and now that she was back no one would ever take her from them again. "Who was it addressed to?" Marc asked, wanting all the details.

"It just says 'Kings' and then our home address. The mailing address is handwritten, kind of a flowing cursive, like a lady wrote it. It's the same handwriting used on the first package."

"They want you to know they're coming from the same person," Marc guessed.

"What I was thinking," Jake agreed. "They're using a black Sharpie, or some kind of pen like that. Both sets of pictures were sent in a large manila envelope, and instead of licking the seal closed they used a piece of clear tape." He spoke as if he was examining the package while describing it.

"So we can conclude they're coming from the same person. What about the stamps?"

"Not much to say. They aren't individual stamps but a postage stamp, as if they mailed it from their post office."

"But no return address?"

"Nope."

Marc's entire body ached as if he'd had his muscles clenched for hours instead of a few minutes. "And all that's in the envelope are the pictures?" He needed to see them. There were other things they could tell, possibly how close whoever took the pictures was to Mom and Natasha, the quality of the shots. The brothers needed to rule out the possibility of Photoshop.

God, maybe he should end his vacation early. It might save his heart if he and London parted ways sooner rather than later. She was getting attached to him, too. They would start something neither of them could finish and it wasn't right, or fair, to either of them. Not to mention, if Mom or any of his family was in danger, he needed to be there to protect them.

"Not this time," Jake said.

"Huh?" Marc blinked, shoving his thoughts out of his head before he made a final decision.

"There was a note. It said: 'Say good-bye to your mother and father. You're never going to see them again.' "

Marc almost leapt off the couch.

"What's wrong?" London murmured, shifting against him and slowly pushing herself to a sitting position. Her eyes looked sleepy and her hair was tousled around her face. She was so damn beautiful and at the moment appeared rather confused. Apparently she had been asleep, which was a good thing.

"Nothing. Sorry," he said, standing and walking around the coffee table.

"You aren't alone?" Jake asked. "Wait. Isn't it almost midnight out there? Damn, Bro, it's not like you to keep them hanging around like that." Jake's usual playful tone was gone. He might have had more time to allow the meaning behind the message sent with the pictures to sink in, but he was obviously upset enough about it to call Marc.

"I'm with London," Marc told Jake.

"Who are you talking to?" London asked.

"My brother, Jake."

"God, she sounds hot as hell," Jake said.

"She is," Marc said. "I'll get back with you on all of this," he added. "Keep me posted and I'll talk to you in the morning."

"Man, you need to come home," Jake said.

"I know." He stared at London, wishing more than anything he could keep her in his life.

"Now is not the right time to get hung up on some chick," his brother snapped.

Marc hung up on him. Anything that came out of his mouth at that moment would let Jake know where Marc's feelings were headed, and he didn't need his brother's shit. Also, London was staring at him, with a confused, adorable sleepy expression on her face. He wouldn't worry or upset her, not when their night had been going so perfectly.

Putting his phone back on the coffee table, he bent down for the rest of his clothes.

"What are you doing?" she asked, combing her hair away from her face with her fingers.

"I'd forgotten," he began. "When I first got here there was a package for you. It was on the floor of your porch, and so I put it in your mailbox. I didn't remember until now and figured I would get it for you."

London almost flew off the couch. "You don't need to go get it," she said, blocking him from grabbing his boots. "Don't worry about it. You don't need to get dressed and go out there where it's freezing. It will still be there in the morning."

He swore she looked frantic and hated that he'd pulled her out of such a relaxed sleep the way he had. Stroking the hair on the side of her head, he leaned into her and kissed her.

"Fine. You win," he said, and kissed her again until she relaxed in his arms. "Let's go to bed."

London rolled over and turned off her alarm at five thirty the next morning. It was strange waking up with such a large body taking over half her bed. When she needed to get up, though, moving away from Marc when he was so relaxed and warm and as snuggly as she'd imagined he would be was almost more than she could do. Rolling into him, she stretched against all that muscle. He immediately rolled into her, wrapping his arms around her and pinning her to his side.

London never slept naked. Living alone for so many years had her in the habit of wearing a nightshirt to sleep in. The shirt didn't last long when she and Marc went to bed, though. Their sex in the living room had been as hot as the slow lovemaking session they'd had before falling asleep.

She stared into his relaxed features, how his mouth formed a straight line; his long, straight nose and dark lashes, fanning just under his eyes, made him so beautiful. His incredible size and all that muscle, yet not an ounce of fat on him anywhere. Then there were the small scars. She'd discovered a few more than just the one on his jaw. There was one on his right bicep that almost looked like a burn. It wasn't new, though. Although she couldn't see it right now, he had a thicker scar on the side of his right thigh. She imagined them war wounds and wondered what kind of warrior Marc King was.

As her mind drifted around thoughts of Marc, their time together, him being at her home when she got off work, it all seemed so comfortable and perfect. But life wasn't comfortable and perfect; at least it never had been. Daring to think that might change scared the crap out of her.

Why couldn't she have a happy, settled life like everyone else? He lay here next to her and he'd wanted to stay. London ran her fingertips over his muscular chest, feeling how soft and warm and incredibly strong he was. Marc was a rock, stability in all that was crazy.

London squeezed her eyes closed, refusing to get lost in a fantasy that probably would never be reality. Marc never suggested he would stay in Colorado. Her thoughts drifted to last night, while lying on his lap and him talking on the phone. She'd drifted off to sleep, but when his tone had changed and his body tensed London lay there awake listening. Not that she understood most of what she heard, other than whatever it was pissed him off.

She knew he was talking to his brother, Jake. Apparently his entire family knew about her. That was a hard one to dissect. Would Marc share with his family information about any woman with whom he was spending time? There were some families who were cozy like that, although it had been her experience that those kinds of families only existed on TV.

When he'd mentioned pictures in a package, London had almost fallen off the couch. There was a noticeable tension in the conversation, although she got the impression Marc got along with his brother. Hell, he came from a perfect family, all of them open and caring about one another. London would never fit into a picture like that.

She remembered Marc telling her he'd found a package at her front doorstep after he got off the phone. His determined nature was hard to fight. She'd damn near panicked when he'd started going after her mail. If he saw the pictures, he'd want to know who they were. It would lead to her having to tell him a really tall tale about her parents or surrender the truth. London didn't want to lie to him, and she couldn't let him know she came from a family of crooks.

Marc tightened his grip around her when she tried sliding out of bed.

"Marc, I need to get ready for work," she whispered, touching his collarbone and feeling the strong, steady beat of his heart. It would be too damn easy to fall back asleep in his arms. She couldn't be late to work, though, especially after Cliff weirding out on her. And she couldn't allow herself to get used to how wonderful this felt.

"Marc, please," she tried again, running her hand over his smooth skin to his neck. "You've got to let me out of bed."

He grunted, lifted his leg, and draped it over both of hers, trapping her further. She was almost crushed under his long, powerful body. Damn! What a way to go.

"Are you going to keep me here all day?" she asked, trying for a teasing tone. "I have ways of making you talk, you know," she whispered, moving her hand down between the two of them.

London gripped his cock, wrapping her fingers around his warm, silky smooth shaft. Immediately it hardened and grew in her hand, lengthening and throbbing as she began a gentle stroke. Marc growled and his lashes fluttered. Her breath caught in her throat when he moved again, this time grabbing her leg, lifting it, and easing himself into place.

There was no way he was that asleep and able to shift into position that easily.

"Marc," she complained, even as her pussy began throbbing with anticipation. "You aren't playing fair."

It was either another grunt or a laugh. London didn't have time to determine which when her sleeping giant came to life, cupping her ass and adjusting her again so he could slip deep inside her.

"Oh God," she moaned, forced to let go of his cock as it filled her completely.

"Good morning, beautiful." Marc's voice was rough with sleep.

"Morning," she said, no longer having the will to fight him as he slowly made love to her.

It was easy. It was perfect. There was a relaxed, comfortable sensation making love to Marc. Every time they fucked each other it was exactly what she needed. This morning there were no demands, no need to speak, just pure satisfaction that left her tingling and in a wonderful mood when she finally crawled out from under the warm blankets.

London stood in the shower when she realized they hadn't used a condom. For a moment her heart froze, creating a tightness in her chest and making it very hard to breathe. She was on the pill. Getting pregnant wasn't the issue.

In all the years she'd been sexually active, London had never had sex without a condom. Although she figured someday, if the right man ever came along, and they settled down into being a couple, they probably wouldn't use condoms. It wasn't a part of her future she thought a lot about though. That would be a time when she knew a man very, very well. Not only did she not know Marc well, she never would. Their relationship had no hope of a future.

Had Marc intentionally made love to her without a condom? Was he letting her know he wanted a commitment?

London climbed out of the shower, having forgotten to wash her hair. Which was the last time she would allow herself to become so distracted.

"How long until you have to leave for work?" Marc asked, handing her coffee when she traipsed into the kitchen after her frustrating shower. One glance at Marc looking so at ease in her kitchen and she knew they'd passed the point of a painless good-bye.

He was back in the clothes he came over in the night before but had managed to clean up pretty good. His easy smile and the way he brushed her hair behind her ear showed he was a morning person. London returned the smile, wishing he would start displaying some kind of trait that didn't appeal to her.

"I get there around seven thirty, so soon," she said, glancing past him at the clock on her microwave.

"Then I guess making you breakfast will have to wait for another day."

"Breakfast, huh?" Maybe she could count that against him. "I don't usually do breakfast," she told him.

Marc cupped her chin, tilting her head and kissing her. He took his time with it, easing her mouth open and then making love to her with his tongue. He was shattering her reserve, making her fall quick and hard for him. There were rules. Most of them she created. London had made it twenty-five years honoring these rules unconditionally. In just under two weeks Marc had caused her to break every one of them. When would the regret kick in? She knew the answer to that one. As soon as he left.

"That's because you haven't ever had one of my breakfasts," he murmured against her mouth.

London shook her head, unable to keep from smiling, and backed up from him. "There's probably time for you to take a quick shower if you want."

Space would help, London decided, as the shower sounded in the other room. She finished dressing, slipped into her boots, and headed out to her front porch. Maybe even the cold weather would do some good. And damn, it was cold. January in Aspen was consistent. There wasn't any getting around it. Resting her hand on the mailbox, knowing what was inside, London gave thought to those consistencies in her life. Things she could rely on, which she took for granted.

The weather really didn't count. And sometimes even it threw her a curveball. Her parents had been consistent. That was an odd irony. Neither one of them would ever win a Parent of the Year award. They didn't call her to make sure she was okay. More than once she'd heard both of them say they were proud that they didn't make the mistake of getting pregnant twice. But in all of their scandalous affairs, they never swayed from their steady pattern. London had grown up knowing they wouldn't be there for her, that she was on her own to find food and quite often a place to sleep at night.

There were other consistencies since her parents. Working was the same. The jobs had varied and so had the towns, but not that much. And since settling here, she could count even more regularities in her life. London reached into the mailbox and took out the package, which looked just like the others. Even this unraveling nightmare was consistent. But the most solid and reliable fact in her world today—guests came to the lodge and they left.

Marc would leave. He came here for a vacation and he was having a wonderful time, she believed. When it was over he would return to his perfect life and his perfect family and have fond memories of his time in Aspen, Colorado. The sooner she accepted that, the easier it would be on her when he left.

Her thoughts dampened her mood as she headed into her bedroom and closed her door. The shower was still going and she wasn't sure if Marc would respect her privacy or not. She moved quickly, sliding her finger under the clear piece of tape and opening the package.

"Just one minute," she told herself, putting it on her dresser and moving to her bed.

When she got home tonight she would wash her bedding, but for now she made her bed, straightened her pillows, and reached for the package. Dumping its contents onto her bed, she stared at the several pictures and at the note accompanying them.

As promised, your parents are gone. Let the game begin!

* * *

London stared at the printer as it took its time printing out the checkouts for the day. She'd slept well last night, in spite of staying up late having sex with Marc. And she'd woken up at her usual time; although they'd fucked again, it hadn't seemed to wear her out at the time. Now she was exhausted.

The note sent with the pictures hadn't made sense. The pictures were more disturbing. There were only two of them this time. Her mom walking toward the camera with two men on either side of her. It almost looked as if she was in handcuffs. The men's heads were down and they weren't in any kind of uniform, but a lot of detectives wore street clothes. The picture of London's father was similar. He glared at the camera, appearing fit to be tied. London knew that look. Johnnie Brooke glared as if he would kill the next person who said the wrong thing to him. His cheeks were flushed and his lips pressed into a straight line. She swore she felt his anger just staring at the picture.

Before Marc got out of the shower she'd shoved the photos with the rest of the pictures in her middle dresser drawer and tried putting them out of her mind. Her parents had been arrested. It really sucked. Not that she had planned on seeing them anytime soon or had a clue where they were when they were arrested, but knowing now that they were gone left an unsettling feeling inside her. Weirder yet, someone wanted her to know her parents were busted, someone who knew it was going to happen before it happened. It sure as hell wasn't standard protocol to mail pictures to the family when a criminal was about to go down. London was more than a bit freaked out thinking whoever took those pictures might approach her soon.

London didn't worry enough that she was in any kind of danger. It still would be nice to talk to someone about it. She'd come real close to saying something to Marc when he got out of the shower. It had been time to leave, though. Marc didn't follow her out to the lodge, which she told herself was for the best. Cliff was never in this early, but she didn't want more crap for being seen with Marc. She was curious where he went, though.

"How many checkouts do we have today?" Sally came around the side of the counter, her brown hair pulled back tight against her head and gray streaks dominating along her temples.

She wore her usual scowl, but Sally was okay. London figured years of frowning had created the permanent expression on Sally's face. In truth, she was usually a pretty cheerful person.

"They're printing right now," London told her, glancing over her shoulder. "I've got coffee made in the break room."

Sally held up her mug. "And it's appreciated," she said. When she grinned, her skin stretched over her gaunt face, as if her face wasn't used to moving that way. She had buck teeth and was anything but pretty. Sally was always on time, though, worked hard, never complained, and never missed work. "Sounds like we're getting more snow today," she said, apparently willing to camp out and kill time until she had her list of rooms.

"Looks like it." London glanced toward the front windows and the heavy gray day looming outside. The walking tour might be canceled again tonight. She needed the money, but getting home early sounded good. If she were smart, she would encourage herself to look forward to an evening alone. Up until Marc sauntering into her life she never gave a thought to her evenings. They were always the same and always spent alone. If she did meet up with anyone it was never at her house.

"Here you go," she said, pulling the list from the printer

and walking over to the counter to separate the copies. One for their paperwork and one for Housekeeping.

Sally picked up her copies as London handed them to her, glancing over each page. "Looks like that sex god checked out. Damn shame. He tipped well."

Her words reached London slowly. When their meaning sunk in, London scanned the list of rooms.

"This is a mistake," she said, staring at Marc's name. "He isn't checking out."

"I don't make the list." Sally grabbed her papers and started around the corner. "I'll get the girls working. Let me know if the list is wrong."

London nodded and grunted but didn't watch Sally walk off. She stared at the list. According to what it said here, he did the self-checkout less than an hour ago. But he hadn't even returned to the lodge yet. Grabbing the phone, she rang his room. There wasn't an answer.

It was a mistake. She would figure it out. Several guests came to the front desk. She helped them, greeted some early arrivals who wanted to know if they could have an early check-in, and even ran towels to several rooms when things got busy. It was a typical morning, and activities she usually didn't mind doing. Today, though, she grumbled at each new task as it came her way. It seemed everything and everyone was against her finding out why the printout said Marc had checked out.

London came down the second-floor hallway shortly after lunch and paused at the Housekeeping cart.

"You knew I was going to clean his room," Sally said, popping out of the room and grabbing clean glasses. She held up a twenty-dollar bill between two bony fingers. "I told you the sex god was a good tipper."

London almost tripped over the cart. She stared past Sally into the empty room. All morning London had believed there was a mistake. Marc didn't check out. Why would he? Now, as she stared at the empty room, her throat swelled closed before she could answer. Emotions hit her so hard she couldn't identify them, let alone deal with them.

"Good," she managed to cough out, and hurried down the hall.

Marc didn't just leave. They'd had the perfect night, the perfect morning, and he was going to see her again. She couldn't accept he would check out and not even say good-bye or at the very least, give some explanation as to why he would leave long before he'd planned.

The rest of the afternoon went by in a blur. Her confusion switched to anger, though, by the time she learned there would be a walking tour tonight. It was snowing again when she drove home. London wouldn't let being here alone bother her; she wouldn't lose sleep or shed a tear over a man she'd known less than two weeks. As she headed into her kitchen and leaned against her counter, knowing she was in there to fix food but doubtful she'd be able to swallow a bite of anything, she told herself Marc King wasn't even worth getting angry over.

"He left without even saying good-bye. He's a shallow, spineless chickenshit. That's why." She glared at her floor, letting her anger release. She'd let it out and then be done with it. "And good riddance, too. Any man who starts something but then is too much of a coward to hang around the moment it goes beyond physical is a coward. And cowards don't turn me on."

Chapter Seven

Marc pulled into his driveway behind his dad's Avalanche later that night. He'd gained an hour but was still beyond exhausted after the fourteen-hour drive. As he turned the car off, the front door opened and Jake stepped outside.

"Hard to believe I left a blizzard and came home to this," Marc said, holding the sweater he'd peeled off several hours ago and walking around to his trunk.

"Man, it's cold as hell tonight," Jake said, scowling at the bags Marc unloaded from his car. "I wouldn't hurry too much to unpack."

"Why? What have you learned?" Marc had gone into auto-drive the second Jake called and told him Mom and Dad were missing. "Do you have a lead on where they might be?"

"Nothing is confirmed. I was just going over those pictures some more."

"Let me see them." Marc grabbed his suitcase and duffel bag and let Jake take the laptop, then followed him inside.

"How was your trip?" Natasha stood in the doorway off the living room leading into KFA's business office.

She looked pale and her eyes were puffy, as if she'd been crying.

"Long," he said, dropping his luggage by the couch, then tousling her hair when he followed Jake into the office. "How long have they been gone now?"

"We got the latest batch of pictures last night. None of us were home, so I couldn't say when they arrived, but they're like all the rest." Jake crossed his arms over his chest as he scowled at Marc. "Dad and Mom went to a movie and didn't come home. The note in the pictures says they're gone."

"Three sets of pictures, huh?" Marc stared at the packages laid out on Natasha's desk. All three packages were handwritten, addressed to the Kings with their personal street address. "And you think Dad and Mom were taken before the last set of pictures arrived?"

"What do you think?" Jake slid one of the packages toward Marc.

He dumped the pictures out and stared at two glossy eight-by-tens. They were in color, taken by a fairly expensive camera if the detail caught in the snapshot was any indication. The first shot was of Mom with two men he didn't recognize walking on either side of her. She glared at the camera, pissed as hell. Both men had their heads down, making it hard to identify them.

Marc lifted the other picture, one of Dad. He also appeared livid. The way his hands were behind his back, it looked as if he might be handcuffed. The hateful stare he gave whoever took the picture would have many men shaking in their boots. There were two men on either side of Marc's father, again with their heads down, and dwarfed with Greg King walking between them. Marc would guess the men to be about six feet tall, since his father was six feet, four inches.

"This is the note that was with those two pictures." Natasha handed him a plain white piece of paper.

" 'As promised, your parents are gone. Let the game begin!' " Marc read out loud, and stared at the simple Comic Sans font with the two-line message typed in the middle of the page. " 'Game begin'? What does that mean?"

"Well, if there is a connection between these pictures and Marty Byrd's game he mentioned to Dad before Byrd died, then someone has picked up where he left off," Jake said, repeating what Greg King had said to Marc on the phone the other night.

"Where's the other note?" Marc asked, moving the pictures around on Natasha's desk. The shots his brother had described were even spookier to stare at in person. Shots of his mother and father on their cruise and pictures of Mom and Natasha shopping went beyond an invasion of privacy. Marc had seen pictures taken by private dicks when they were out to bust a cheating spouse. These weren't intimate shots taken through a window or from the end of some dark alley. They were taken in public settings with Marc's family members happy and enjoying time spent with each other. They weren't doing anything wrong.

A moment of their lives was stolen by some asshole. These pictures were sent to flaunt how close their captors were prior to taking Mom and Dad. It was all Marc could do to maintain the violent rage threatening to rush his insides.

" 'Say good-bye to your mother and father. You're never going to see them again,' " he read out loud, his teeth clenched as he fought to focus and not rip the paper to shreds.

Greg King was a rock, the one solid, impermeable part of their lives growing up. He was also one of the best bounty hunters in the nation, his reputation as solid as his nature. Their mom was just as strong a woman as their father was a man. It scared the crap out of Marc that someone was able to kidnap both of them. Marc remembered his father "letting" himself be captured when they'd been down in Mexico just so he could learn more about what Marty Byrd was up to. He couldn't imagine his father doing the same thing again, especially when Marc and Jake's mother was abducted, too.

"They were threatening us and flaunting how close they were with these pictures," Natasha said, voicing Marc's thoughts. "Uncle Greg was outraged the moment he saw these."

"I can see why. I would have been, too," Marc said. "Hell, I am pissed. Who would take the two of them, and why?"

Marc compared the first and second notes. Same font, typed in the same location on the page. The notes were identical other than the message. "This is fucking insane," he snarled, slapping the first note on top of the other on Natasha's desk.

"No shit," Jake agreed.

"I noticed this," Natasha said, shoving her long, thick black hair over her shoulder as she leaned across her desk and rested her elbows against it. She tapped a fingernail on one of the shots. "Look at this," she said. "See those buildings behind where Aunt Haley is walking with those men?"

"What about them?" Marc leaned forward as well, realizing at that moment how similar Natasha's long black hair was to London's. He needed to call London as soon as possible and should have done so when driving home. He'd been so infuriated and shocked when Jake called after he'd left London's and told him Mom and Dad never came home from their movie the night before and now weren't answering their cells, Marc had headed home without hesitating. If it weren't for the note and new set of pictures saying they were gone, Marc might have believed the two of them simply took off for some alone time. He'd rushed out of there, filling out the quick checkout form and slapping it in the hands of the night auditor before racing out the back door of the lodge.

Maybe Marc had intentionally avoided London when he left, knowing she would have been pissed and hurt. He wasn't done with her. That much held strong in his gut. But he needed to know what was going on with his parents. Marc wouldn't be able to live with himself if he stayed there, falling hard for a beautiful woman, instead of jumping on all clues around his parents' abduction while the clues were fresh.

He refused to believe leaving without saying good-bye had anything to do with how fast his feelings for her were growing. It would do them both good to slow down, and learning what the hell had happened to his parents took precedence over anything else.

"We've been there before. I know we have." Natasha snapped him out of his thoughts as she tapped her finger on the glossy photo paper. "I don't think this is Photoshop. So either whoever took these are willing to give us clues to allow us to go after them or they're idiots."

"Or both," Jake hissed.

"I vote for the latter, and let me see that." Marc reached for the picture and Natasha handed it to him.

His brother and cousin stood on either side of him as Marc stared at the picture. "You're right," he told Natasha without looking at her. He held the picture up so it was in front of all three of them. "We've been there before. Let me think."

Silence grew in the room as the three of them studied the shot. Marc grabbed the picture of his father between the same two men and held both of them up, catching the same buildings at different angles. The background wasn't as obvious in the picture with Greg and his captors, assuming that was who the men were, because the camera had zoomed in closer to the men. They blocked the view behind them but not completely.

"It's cold, wherever they are," Jake said, breaking the silence. "The men are wearing long coats and Mom is hugging herself. Dad is too pissed to be cold," he added, but no one laughed at his comment.

"Where have all of us traveled together?" Marc asked.

"When we were kids we all went camping." Jake started pacing, walking to the entrance to the KFA office facing the street, then back to the desk.

"We did? I went with you?" Natasha scowled and pressed her finger against her lips. "Wait. You're right. God, we were all kids. Where did we go?"

Marc leaned against Natasha's desk, glancing from one picture to the next while his younger brother and cousin brainstormed on all of the vacations they'd taken together over the years. Natasha had been included in almost every family vacation the King family went on. Uncle George would drop her off, Natasha with her suitcase in hand and a book tucked under her arm.

Marc continued studying the pictures, growing angrier by the minute. His dad didn't give him a clue, not any indication something of this magnitude was going down. If he'd been here instead of parading around in the mountains and snow, maybe he would have picked up on something. The goddamn pictures were left practically under their noses. If he'd been here he could have seen something, someone, picked up on a clue. Instead, now all they had were these fucking pictures mocking them.

"Wait! I've got it!" Natasha rushed to Marc's side and almost ripped the picture from his hand.

"What?" he demanded, still feeling the rage boil inside him.

"Remember when we all went to see all those ghost towns? God. Was it in Arizona?"

"Natasha, you're right." Marc faced her desk and spread the pictures out, leaning over and staring at the two where his parents were walking in front of the buildings. "What are the fucking odds?" he whispered under his breath.

"What do you mean?" Jake asked, moving in alongside Natasha's desk and pressing his fists on top of it as he leaned in as well.

"That they'd take our parents to a place we'd all been to before."

"Let me make sure," Natasha said, scooting in around her desk. She sat and started typing. "Is that when we stayed at that bed-and-breakfast?"

Jake snapped his fingers. "That's right! Mom insisted we stay at this huge old house and the owners were all over the three of us."

"They thought because we were teenagers we would be nothing but trouble," Marc remembered. "I swear that old bitch followed me around with a frying pan in her hands, threatening to knock me upside the head with it if I ran through her house or made too much noise."

"Remember when the three of us went outside and she was sure we were out there smoking?"

Jake made a snorting sound. "Yeah. She thought we were smoking those funny cigarettes."

"That was the vacation from hell," Marc grumbled. His parents had fought all the way through it. "I almost became a bookworm just like you in order to hide from everyone."

Natasha made a face at him but shifted her attention back to her computer screen before speaking. "There were advantages to always having my face in a book. Everyone left me alone."

Marc was pretty sure Natasha read all the time to escape from her home life. Her father was more interested in playing the field than raising a daughter, and her mother had taken off on them when Natasha had been really young. Marc knew his parents included Natasha in their family outings as often as they did because Uncle George pushed them to take her off his hands.

Marc wondered if London had been an ugly duckling as a kid the way Natasha had been. It wasn't until his cousin turned sixteen or so that Marc started wishing they weren't related. They had been short-lived fantasies. Natasha was his cousin, had been practically raised as a sister, and thinking of her any way other than that just didn't work in his brain.

London, on the other hand, refused to leave his brain. Even as he stressed out on his parents not being there, she was in his thoughts just as much. He really needed to call her, let her know he didn't walk out on her and definitely planned on seeing her again. At the moment he wasn't sure when, but he knew he didn't want to go too long without seeing her again. With it being less than twenty-four hours since he'd held her in his arms, he already knew he'd go nuts until he had her next to him again. London wouldn't start meaning less to him as time went by as other women in his past had. He accepted there was more with her, but now wasn't the time to figure out what that might be.

"So check out bed-and-breakfasts in Flagstaff," he told Natasha, forcing his thoughts off London.

"I'm already there," Natasha said, chewing her lower lip as she clicked her mouse. "Wait. Here it is. Let me see those pictures."

She grabbed the pictures as Marc and Jake both walked

around her desk so that they were standing behind her. Natasha held the pictures up next to her monitor.

"Bingo," Jake said under his breath.

"What time was this movie they went to yesterday?" Marc studied the pictures. "It's daylight in these shots. Flagstaff is a good seven hours from here."

Jake glanced down at Natasha and she looked up at him.

"I wasn't here," Jake began. "Dad sent me over to Ace Bondsman to pick up a check."

"I was here." Natasha twisted in her chair to face both of them. "Uncle Greg and Aunt Haley left here yesterday afternoon. They had a few errands to run and then were going to the movie."

"And these pictures showed up last night?" They would have had to have driven a hundred miles per hour to get there before dark.

Jake shrugged. "I couldn't say when. They were on the front doorstep first thing this morning. I didn't realize Mom and Dad weren't here until I read the note, then checked if they were in their bedroom." Jake ran his fingers through his mop of curls. Although two years younger than Marc, he stood an inch or two taller. At the moment, his green eyes flared with emotion the way Mom's always did when she was upset. "Of all nights that I went to bed early. If I'd been awake I might have heard someone at the door."

"Dad told me about the pictures of the two of them when they were on their cruise." Marc shook his head, walking around from behind the desk. He needed space and began pacing the way Jake had been a few moments before. "I was so damn set on getting this place out of my system for a while."

"That doesn't matter," Jake interrupted. "I'm the one who dropped the ball."

"If I had been here I would have sensed the seriousness of the matter a lot sooner. I could have made Mom and Dad—"

"Are you saying you would have sensed something I didn't?" Jake countered, turning on Marc.

"Would the two of you cut it out?" Natasha snapped. "Would have, could have, should have. None of it matters now. What happened yesterday, or the day before, or last week isn't as important as right now."

"She's right," Marc cut her off before she continued with her rant. He wasn't in the mood for a lecture anymore than being chewed out by his younger brother. "Okay. So now we act." He pointed at Natasha. "Get me the address of that bed-and-breakfast. Program it into the GPS. Is there gas in the Avalanche? Or do we take my car?"

"Whatever you leave here will be my wheels," Natasha pointed out.

"When are you going to get a car?" Marc was teasing, and the way Natasha rolled her eyes at him let him know she knew that.

"When I get a fucking raise at this place," she said, tilting her head defiantly.

"You drove all day and night," Jake said unnecessarily.

In spite of the adrenaline and anger rushing through him and feeding him with aggressive energy, Marc was more than aware of how stiff his body was and how tired he was.

"You can drive," he told Jake with a wave of his hand. "I don't know how long we'll be down there, but I would pack well either way."

It was after midnight when they loaded into Marc's car and headed out. His eyes burned and every muscle in his body screamed when he climbed into the passenger seat. With any luck he would get some sleep in spite of how cramped he felt.

The way he figured it, whoever took his parents would have a forty-eight-hour lead on them. If they were abducted yesterday afternoon, they could have been in Flagstaff last night. Somehow after the pictures were taken, someone altered them to make them appear as if they were taken in the daylight. The only explanation Marc could figure there was that they lightened the pictures so it would be clear who was in each shot. Now, if he and Jake made good time, they would be exactly where his parents were two days later. Marc hoped that was not too long of a time frame for someone in the area to remember seeing his parents.

It was their only shot. These weren't the kind of odds Marc liked dealing with. As he'd showered and Jake had packed, Natasha had done some more searching online. She found a picture of the bed-and-breakfast, Two Guns Bed-and-Breakfast. It wasn't the most appealing name to entice guests to stay there, but it was under the same ownership. The place was appropriately named.

There was a sporting-goods store two doors down from Two Guns Bed-and-Breakfast that had a Web site. The storefront was on their site and it was a direct match to the building two doors down from the bed-and-breakfast in the picture. The only fact Marc and Jake had at the moment was that they were definitely going to the place where those last pictures were taken. Whether Mom and Dad were still there was another story altogether. His parents' captors would have to be idiots to give away such blatant clues and not think Marc and Jake would be on them immediately. Marc prayed the assholes, who had the nerve to abduct Greg and Haley King, were complete imbeciles. It would make finding his dad and mom a lot easier.

Marc tried several times to stretch out comfortably in the passenger seat. He made sure the seat was all the way back and tilted the seat so he was somewhat reclined. It seemed he was destined not to be comfortable.

"Don't grind the gears," he grumbled, glaring at his brother's hand gripping the gear shift.

"How fast will it go in under a minute?" Jake shot him a crooked grin.

Marc growled and let his head fall back on the seat. Jake would treat his Mustang with kid gloves—or he'd die.

The moment his eyes closed, London appeared in his thoughts. Marc didn't want Jake overhearing his conversation when he called London. He wouldn't text her. That would be insulting, and the last thing Marc wanted was to fight with her. He tried relaxing as he began playing out his reunion with London. He couldn't wait to feel her soft body pressed against his again, her long silky hair brushing over his skin.

"Do you want to stop for anything before we hit the interstate?" Jake asked, yanking Marc out of his daydream with London.

"I'm good." Marc shifted in his seat, reclining it the rest of the way, and did his best to stretch out his legs. "Don't wreck my car," he warned and closed his eyes, willing himself to fall asleep. Once he had a few hours of sleep he would be more coherent. Then he would call London.

To his amazement, sleep hit him hard and fast. As he drifted off, he imagined London tucked up alongside him. He could feel her hair between his fingers. Her soft, warm body pressed against his. And her relaxed expression, her slow, deep breaths as she slept, lulled him into a dream state. Images of her fucking him, standing behind the counter at the lodge, and in her kitchen standing barefoot ransacked his brain. Marc prayed she wouldn't be so pissed at him she wouldn't talk to him.

It was a gut-twisting thought when he realized he was scared to call her. He was a bounty hunter. More times than he could count he'd willingly walked into some terrifying situations. Even now, he and Jake drove into the unknown, ready and eager to take on their parents' abductors. Yet the thought of London screaming at Marc, calling him names and telling him she would never talk to him again, was something he didn't want to face. The longer he put off that phone call, the longer she would remain smiling and willing with her eyes glowing with an emotion stronger than lust.

London stared out the front windows of the lodge at the gray and dismal day outside. For the first time in a couple weeks there wasn't any snow in the forecast. It was supposed to be a dry week. Not that she cared. And it was about the only thing she didn't care about.

She'd hibernated all weekend, turning down Meryl's Sunday dinner with her family for the first time in months. As many times as London analyzed every minute she and Marc were together, she couldn't find justification for him leaving the way he did. Even if he worried they were getting too close too fast, would that have sent him running from her the way he had? It didn't seem his nature.

London had gone from outraged, to crushed, to outright baffled. By the end of the weekend she was numb from the entire experience. It didn't help that those damn pictures in her bedroom kept calling her to them. She'd pulled them out more than once, spreading them out and staring at them. It was hard to say which was the bigger mystery, Marc or those pictures.

"Hello, Miss Brooke." A man stood on the opposite side of the counter extending his hand to her in greeting.

London snapped out of her daydream, her eyes burning from staring at the window as long as she had without blinking. She managed her professional smile at the last minute.

"How may I help you?" she asked, accepting his hand after a moment and shaking it.

"Let's hope that you can." He had a strong grip and gave her hand a hard, firm handshake before letting go and reaching inside his coat. "I'm sorry to bother you at work, but I do need a moment of your time."

London stared at the leather card holder the man placed on the counter between them. He flipped it open, revealing a business card and ID that stated he was a private investigator.

"My name is James Huxtable," he was saying, his crisp, deep voice holding a bit of an accent, as if he was from somewhere back east. "I'm a private investigator working on a case I believe you can help me with."

Her mouth went dry as she grew frantic that Marc was in some kind of trouble. It had never crossed her mind that he might have left as quickly as he had because he'd been in some kind of trouble. He'd never told her what he did for a living. Now that she thought about it, the way he'd maneuvered around the topic every time she'd tried learning what his line of work was might have been because he was a criminal of some kind. Wouldn't that just be her luck? London never would have guessed in a million years that when she finally fell hard and fast for a man he would turn out to be a crook, just like her parents.

She swallowed hard, lifting her attention from Huxtable's ID to his face. London hated that she knew the drill, knew better than anyone how to put the mask on her face and play innocent to protect someone from being arrested.

"I'll help in any way I can," she offered, smiling at him.

"Good. Are your parents Jonnie and Ruby Brooke?"

It was the last question London expected. His words

hit her like a hard wind in a torrential storm with the ferocity to knock her off her feet. She swore she damn near staggered with relief that he wasn't here to ask her about Marc.

The phone rang and she gave silent thanks, holding a finger up to indicate he hold that thought, and picked up the receiver. Someone had called about the rates at the lodge and asked her the usual questions. London rattled off information, answering their questions without having to give it much thought. She was grateful for the moment to regroup, though, and overly aware of James Huxtable watching her like a hawk throughout the entire conversation.

Several guests came to the front desk, asking about times and information on the different activities at the lodge. The investigator stood at the counter, waiting patiently, until he and London were finally alone once again.

"I'm sorry," she said, feeling much more in control of her senses after forcing him to stand there while she worked. "I'm the only one behind the counter this afternoon or I would offer to speak with you privately."

"It's quite all right. It seems this is an impressive lodge, quite the place to get away for a vacation."

"The best in the state," she said, giving him her winning smile.

James Huxtable nodded and his face turned serious. It was obvious he didn't care about the lodge. "Are your parents Jonnie and Ruby Brooke?"

"I'm sorry," she said again. "And yes. Jonnie and Ruby are my parents." She hadn't lied about being the only person working behind the counter. That didn't mean she wanted any of the Housekeeping staff or restaurant staff hearing this conversation. "I seriously doubt I can give you much information about them, though."

"These are your parents?" He lifted a briefcase she

hadn't noticed until now onto the counter and snapped it open. She couldn't see its contents from the angle at which he opened it but stared at the glossy eight-by-ten he pulled out and laid on the counter in front of her. "This is a picture of them?" he asked.

London's mouth went dry as she stared at the picture. All she could do was nod. It was one of the pictures that had been sent to her. "Where did you get that picture?" she asked, her voice suddenly raspy.

London reached for her bottled water. The thing was almost empty and she downed the water, immediately wanting more. She stared again at the shot of her parents in the photograph, a copy of one of the pictures she'd been sent in the second package she'd received.

"Your parents are on the most wanted list," he told her, thankfully having enough discretion to lower his voice so no one heard him but her.

"That doesn't surprise me." She was grateful when he slid the picture off the counter and back into his briefcase.

James snapped it shut and took it off the counter. "Do you know where your parents are?"

"No," she said, shaking her head.

"When did you last talk to them?"

Something told her not to mention receiving the pictures in the mail. "I haven't talked to either of them in well over a year."

Her answer obviously disappointed him. "No contact at all?"

"My parents aren't the kind to keep in touch. It's been quite a while since I've seen, or talked to, them."

James nodded and reached inside his jacket again. He wore a plaid overcoat with patches on the elbows that made her think he looked more like a college professor than a private dick. He was tall and thin, with thick black hair that was short and combed back on his head. She wouldn't go as far to call him a good-looking man, but he wasn't ugly. There was just something about him that made her hesitate in opening up to him. It wasn't that he seemed untrustworthy. She didn't know enough about private investigators to know if his identification was legitimate or not. Her gut told her not to offer any information he didn't ask for, though. Growing up with her parents always on the run taught her to always watch what she said to anyone.

James pulled out another business card and handed it to her. "If they call you, or contact you in any way, would you let me know, please?" He really sounded sincere.

She had to ask the obvious, though, simply to hear how he would answer. "If they were to contact me it would be very out of the ordinary. But if they did and you've just told me they are wanted for something, why would I call and tell you?"

James leaned on the counter, putting his face a lot closer to hers. London fought the urge to back up as she stared into his light brown eyes. She worked hard to keep her expression relaxed and void of any emotion.

"My dear," he said quietly, whatever accent he had coming out a bit stronger when he whispered. "Your parents are wanted because they made the mistake of getting involved with the wrong people. Any contact they make with you will put your life in serious danger. If you hear from them in any way at all, call me immediately. It will mean they've found you, and believe me, you would rather put your trust in me than in the people who will come after you. And they will. I'm surprised they haven't already."

James Huxtable turned and walked away from the counter. The only way she could get more of an explanation was to call after him or run around the counter and stop him. Instead she simply stared at his backside as he left the lobby and disappeared out of her view a moment later.

Monday afternoons weren't usually that busy. London preferred having too much to do over standing around and doing nothing. Today, though, she was grateful for a light workload. Her brain was so frazzled she doubted she'd be able to handle anything too serious. She flipped James Huxtable's card in between her fingers, staring at it while trying to add his conversation into her brain along with all the other insane things that had happened to her in the past couple weeks.

She needed answers. Maybe it wouldn't hurt to walk into the police station and talk to a cop. If she went there she would at least know whoever she talked to would be an unbiased party. James told her if her parents contacted her that would mean her life was in danger from whomever her parents were involved with. If receiving the pictures meant she'd been contacted, then she was in danger. When people were in trouble, they went to the cops.

It might help if she could put all of this into perspective so if she did talk to someone, she'd make sense. At least then if she decided to go to the police she would at least have a plausible story to add to the pictures' being mailed to her without return addresses and a private investigator showing up at her work. Staring at the card, she realized it didn't offer an address. The card said: "James Huxtable, Private Investigator," and had his phone number. That was it. Was it normal for private investigators not to offer a physical address on their business cards?

London dragged the stool over to the computer and decided to do a bit of her own investigating. She typed "James Huxtable" into the search engine and clicked Enter. Plenty of links were listed, but none of them appeared to be anything pertaining to a private investigator.

"Which might simply mean he doesn't have a Web site," she mumbled to herself. But didn't everyone have Web sites these days?

She stared at the screen, her fingers poised over the keyboard, and contemplated her next move. On an impulse she cleared the search bar and typed in "Marc King." Again, quite a few links popped up from her search. She stared at the first few options.

"King Fugitive Apprehension," she read. There were several links for this business, which appeared to be bounty hunters. The third link caught her eye, the partial sentence following the Web site indicating the business was in Los Angeles.

London clicked on it and stared at the article written about the family-run bounty hunter business known for their impeccable reputation for always finding their man, or woman. The article didn't impress her as much as the names mentioned in the paragraph.

Greg King, the father, had started the business after being with LAPD and retiring to start his own business. " 'His sons, Marc and Jake King, have worked with their father and built solid reputations in their own right,' " she read out loud.

Marc had been on the phone with his brother when he'd been at her house. "And he said his name was Jake." London didn't know what to think. Her brain seemed to go into shutdown mode as she reread the few paragraphs singing the company's praises. "So you're a bounty hunter," she mused, trying to get it all to sink in and make sense. "Why did you run out on me?" That was the one question she couldn't find an answer for.

London clicked on a few more links, read some more about KFA, which was what the business went by, and finally found a phone number. Her heart started pounding in her chest when she turned, reached for a pen and realized how sweaty her palms were as she managed to write down the number.

Several guests appeared from the hallway, chatting among themselves as they headed for the front door. London jumped, hating how nervous she was, and glanced over her shoulder at the computer screen. It would really help her peace of mind if she could find something that made sense instead of continually being handed one confusing bit of information after another.

Maybe she could get some answers. London picked up the piece of paper she'd written KFA's phone number on. There wasn't any way she could wait until she got off work to call. And already she knew she would definitely be placing that call.

London blew out an exasperated breath and paced the length behind the counter. Suddenly she felt caged. She didn't dwell on why learning what had happened to Marc mattered more to her than figuring out what the hell was up with her parents. They probably knew they were in trouble long before anyone decided to send her pictures. Neither of them had thought to call and let her know the law was closing in. It probably would never cross their mind to let London know if they were facing arrest.

In less than two weeks, though, Marc sauntered into her life and meant more to her than anyone else in her world ever had. She had fallen so easily into the routine of seeing him every day. It had been so easy to talk to him. Of course, Marc was by far the sexiest man she'd ever laid eyes on. London had never had another man over for dinner, or stay the night. But what bugged her the most was that he was gone, had left without so much as an explanation, or good-bye, and she couldn't quit thinking about him. No man had ever managed to break down her defenses and get under her skin the way Marc had.

"No wonder you're terrified," she muttered under her breath.

The phone rang and she jumped. "Shit," she hissed. She was working herself into a frenzy and over what? If she would just focus on her work, it could be as if none of this had ever happened. As she grabbed the receiver and answered, her voice sounded foreign to her.

"Elk Ski Lodge. May I help you?"

"London?"

Her heart stopped beating, which created a fierce pain in her chest. The deep baritone in her ear spoke her name, and she swore he stood right behind her.

"This is London,"

"London, it's me: Marc. Don't hang up."

So he assumed she would be outraged. Well, she was. And it was grossly unfair of him to call her at work, where she couldn't give him a piece of her mind for not even saying good-bye.

"Why did you leave?" she demanded, her heart refusing to beat until the one question that had plagued her was finally answered.

There was silence on the other end of the line. He'd called her and still didn't have a ready answer to give her, which meant he was considering several possible answers.

"I know who you are," she blurted out, staring at the computer screen.

"What?" Suddenly he wasn't speechless. "London, I didn't want to leave like that. I want to see you again, and soon. I mean that. There was a family crisis and I didn't think. I jumped in my car and raced home as fast as I could."

She wasn't sure what she expected him to say, but that wasn't it. Although family didn't mean much to her, London understood the bond that could exist. Meryl came from a family that was always calling, that cared and sought her out on a regular basis. She was always talking about them. Meryl couldn't hold a conversation without bringing up a brother or sister or parent. London knew what family could mean.

"I hope nothing terrible has happened," she said, and suddenly felt numb.

Marc was gone. He'd left because of his family. He was calling to apologize and to tell her he wanted to see her again. He didn't say when. She struggled with the lump growing in her throat. Her anger toward him faded. He was calling and giving her closure.

"Actually, yes, something has happened to my parents." He cleared his throat. "I don't know how long it will take to clear this up. If you're willing, though, I'd like to have your cell phone number. I'll give you mine if you'll call me."

"So we're going to have some kind of long-distance relationship?" She wasn't sure why she snapped at him. She didn't want him out of her life. But long-distance relationships didn't work and she didn't want to continue missing the hell out of him. "We can exchange numbers, Marc. But you're gone. I think you know as well as I do that you won't be coming back. There's no reason to keep talking and pretend something could come from the few incredible moments we had together when we both know that isn't how life works."

"Why did you say you knew who I was?" he asked instead of commenting on what she just said.

"I googled your name." London didn't see any reason to lie. Even if he had been evasive about his life, it didn't mean she would be vague as well. "I have enough confusing stuff going on in my life right now and didn't want you to be one of them."

"What did you find?"

"I found King Fugitive Apprehension. I know you're a bounty hunter."

"I guess I should have told you. I'm accustomed to not offering details about my life. I find people for a living. That's why I had to come home. My parents have disappeared."

Chapter Eight

Marc leaned against the side of his car, squinting against the bright sun, and waited for his brother to come out of the sporting-goods store. "Are you still there?" Marc asked when a moment of silence seemed to stretch on.

"Give me your cell phone number," London said, her soft, sultry voice dropping to almost a whisper. "I have some issues to deal with, and it might not hurt having an unbiased party to talk to about them."

He didn't think of himself as unbiased when it came to London. "Is something wrong?"

"I'm not sure," she said slowly.

Marc heard the beeping in his cell phone before she added, "There's another call coming in."

"I'll hold," he told her.

"Call me tonight." She rattled off her cell phone number.

Marc reached into his car, scrounged for a pen, and wrote her number on his palm. "I will definitely call you tonight, sweetheart. And London?"

"Yes?"

"I'm going to see you again."

"Good-bye." London hung up without saying anything else.

It hadn't exactly been the phone call he'd imagined, and Marc had worked up so many different scenarios of how London would react to him calling. Glancing up and down the street, he guessed by the angle that he stood approximately right where his parents had been when the last pictures were taken. He and Jake had spent the weekend talking to shop owners along this strip. About all they'd learned so far was that everyone in this town seemed really friendly and willing to talk to them about pretty much anything. But no one had seen anyone who looked like the men in the pictures or their parents.

"Nothing," Jake said as he met up with Marc a few minutes later. "We've hit every shop on this block now."

"I know." Marc clasped his phone to his belt and opened his car door.

"Who were you talking to?" Jake asked, sliding in on the passenger side.

"London."

"Oh yeah? Got something going on there?"

"Kind of hard to do when she's in Colorado and I'm not."

They pulled into a gas station and Marc stopped at the pump, wishing they could pull off some kind of lead. He didn't feel right about returning home, but they'd been here all weekend and they didn't have solid proof their parents had even been here.

"It's really hard to believe no one would have noticed strangers on the street, especially when Dad is six foot, four inches," Jake complained when they stood inside the station staring at the candy bar selection. He grabbed a Snickers candy bar and winked at a young woman when she came out of the back room carrying a bucket of ice.

"Nice ass," he mumbled under his breath when the woman turned her back to them and stretched to dump the ice into the soda fountain machine. "Even if it was dark," he continued, snagging a bag of Doritos, "the men on either side of Dad weren't that much shorter than he was. People notice really large men, just like they notice hot women."

"People notice rude people more," the young woman said, walking past them to the counter.

It didn't surprise Marc that her comment didn't sway Jake.

"Tell me about it," Jake said, placing the junk food he'd selected on the counter, then leaning against it, putting himself eye to eye with the clerk, who couldn't be more than twenty years old at the most. Jake had no scruples. "A job like this would have to make you a tough lady, putting up with bullshit all the time."

She straightened, glancing from Jake to Marc. Mascara was on thick, and when she batted her lashes it appeared a black canopy flashed over her dark eyes. "You're nothing compared to some people who come in here."

"Darling, I'm as harmless as a pussycat. Most guys my size are extremely gentle by nature."

She snorted, proving she was young but not gullible. "That is so not true," she said, grabbing his bag of chips and scanning them, then reaching for the candy bar. "These guys in here a couple days ago were real pigs. Kept going on about some lady that was with them and how hot she was. I could see her out in the car. She was old and didn't look happy at all. They weren't doing anything for her." The girl giggled. "I guess that is proof that size doesn't matter."

"Trust me, size matters," Jake drawled. "Did you see those guys Friday night? Were there two guys? Both wearing long trench coats and kind of seedy looking?"

"There were four guys." She wrinkled her nose, again

shooting Marc a furtive look before returning her attention to Jake and wetting her lips. "Yeah. It was Friday night and they were wearing long coats that went down to their knees. They thought they were all that, worse than you," she added, smiling innocently at Jake.

Marc guessed her anything but innocent.

"Darling, I can trust you, can't I?" Jake changed his tone, dropping it to a deep baritone as he moved his hand across the counter and tapped her wrist with his fingers. "We aren't cops or anything."

The girl's eyes went large.

"My brother and I are here looking for my sister," he continued, pulling his hand away and focusing on his fingernails. He took a moment, allowing some silence to pass and build the moment. Jake was the master; no one who knew him would deny that. He could work a lady any way he wanted. "I won't give you all the details, but let's just say a gambling debt went bad."

"That happened to my uncle Charlie," she said, snapping her fingers and pointing at Jake with stubby nails that were painted green.

Jake nodded. "Then you know," he said quietly.

"So that lady with all those men was your sister? You sure? She really did look kind of old. Maybe it wasn't her."

"These guys were as big as me and my brother?"

She smiled. "No. Not at all. They were big, but not that big." She blushed and messed with Jake's candy bar and bag of chips. "Was there anything else you needed?" she asked without looking at either of them.

"Just peace of mind, darling. You remember which way they went?"

"Yeah. I heard them talking. They were headed down to Canyon Diablo. You're driving into bum-fucked Egypt, though, if you're chasing the wrong guys," she said, and finished ringing up Jake's purchases.

Jake straightened and pulled out his wallet. "It's worth it for my sister. I kill for those I care about," he added, once again using his lazy drawl.

She took his money and rang in the purchase. "I hope you find her. Where you-all from?"

"North of here," Jake lied. "Not too far. We'll catch them."

"I hope these aren't your guys. They were freaks. Kept talking about action figures. What a thing for grown men to talk about!" She shook her head and counted out Jake's change.

Marc's insides hardened. They had their guys. He hadn't dared hope for a lead this strong. It was all he could do not to slap Jake on the back. Instead, Marc pulled out a couple twenties and dropped them on the counter. "Gas on pump one," he told her, and followed his brother outside.

"So what do you think?" Jake asked, looking at Marc over the hood of the Mustang as Marc pumped gas. "Think we should check out of that motel and head down to Canyon Diablo?"

"I think we should head back to the room and check a few things out online." Marc glanced around the gas station parking lot and also at the cars driving up and down the street. "Last I knew, though, Canyon Diablo was a ghost town."

"I know." Jake grinned at him.

" 'Ghost town' meaning there isn't anything there."

None of this sat right with Marc. Granted, it had taken them the weekend to come this far, but it still seemed a bit too easy. They didn't have Mom and Dad back, but Marc couldn't shake the unnerving sensation that he needed to be watching his back more than he was. He stared at the TV in their motel room, not seeing or caring what was on but instead trying to get a grip on their current situation.

"You're right about nothing being there. Apparently there are the remains of a few buildings and some graves. But at one point the town was wilder than Tombstone, according to this article." Jake sat at the table in the corner of the room, hunched over the laptop they'd brought. He stretched his long legs under the table and ripped open his Doritos. "I do still got it, though," he added, rocking the chair back as he popped a Dorito in his mouth and gave Marc a crooked grin.

"Yeah, you still got it." Marc shook his head at Jake. "Just don't give it to me."

"You wouldn't know how to handle my gift with women." Jake dug out a few more Doritos and tossed them in his mouth, then licked his lips with a dramatic flare. "Canyon Diablo isn't too far from here. We might be better off leaving our shit here, though, and just driving down there to see what there is to see."

"Probably." Marc leaned back on the bed, shifting his attention to the ceiling. "That girl at the gas station might have heard them mention Canyon Diablo and it doesn't mean that was where they were headed."

"What are the chances whoever sent us those pictures would have known we would recognize the buildings in the background?"

"I agree," Marc said, focusing on his brother. "I keep trying to wrap my brain around all of it. There's no way they would have known we went on vacation here as kids. The chances are too slim."

"You think we're being set up?" Jake rocked back in his chair.

"Something doesn't feel right."

"A lot of it doesn't feel right. We get pictures and broken action figures?" Jake clasped his hands behind his head, forcing his already-tousled hair to stick out through his fingers.

Another time his appearance might have been worth giving him shit over. Marc was too distracted trying to see the full picture to take time to harass Jake. He couldn't help thinking he was missing something and it was right under his nose.

"We'll drive down there. We'll type in 'Canyon Diablo' in the GPS in the car. I don't know whether we're wasting our time and gas or if we seriously should watch our asses."

"I know. Me, too." Jake leaned forward, causing his chair to bang against the floor. "We are heading down to a place that was once one of the most unlawful towns in the West. Might be a good idea to go armed and loaded."

"You worried about ghosts?" Marc laughed and shook his head.

"Most definitely," Jake grumbled and wasn't smiling.

Their boots crunched over the snow as Marc and Jake walked across the uneven terrain. It was an extreme contrast from the Rocky Mountains although, strangely enough, just as breathtaking. Marc imagined the settlers who helped build the buildings that once made up this town. All that was left were white rocks, remnants of the foundation from a store or post office, long since gone.

"You can almost feel the energy from the derelicts who once stood right here," Jake said, squatting down and staring at the dilapidated ruin in front of them.

"I think you're feeling the harsh north wind," Marc said, squinting and taking in the horizon.

"No way, man. Men stood here and controlled their destiny. There weren't any laws controlling them. Whoever was the better shot, or had more muscle, ruled the land."

"There's something to be said about a life like that," Marc mused, turning slowly and taking in the vast stretch of land. Other than his car parked on the highway, there wasn't anything to see for miles. "Sometimes you run into people who still live that way, too."

"That's what we have here." Jake stood, turning to look in the same direction as Marc. "Someone else has been here recently," he said, pointing to the ground and walking around the ruin.

Marc followed, spotting the footsteps in the snow when Jake pointed to them. An eerie sensation crept over Marc's skin. It could have been anyone here. Tourists probably stopped by from time to time, standing as Marc and Jake were, staring at what once was, then headed on their way.

"I think it's more than one set of footprints. You know it really sucks when you don't have a clue who you're hunting," Jake complained.

"Right now we're hunting our parents. But I agree. We don't know shit about their captors."

"And they know everything about us."

Marc stared at the footprints in the snow. It hadn't snowed since they'd been here, so the accumulation had been on the ground for a while. The prints were pretty clear, the indentations looking as if whoever made them wore boots from the heel and sole imprints. He turned around, staring at their own footprints.

"You know, we make pretty good footprints in the snow, too." Marc retraced his steps, staring at the two sets of prints leading from his car. "It's odd how these other prints start at the ruins and not from the road."

"You're right." Jake met Marc's gaze for a moment, his expression strained, before returning his attention to the ground. "And they don't seem to go anywhere," he added, following them around the rocks that were once a building.

"They're either the ghosts you were feeling or someone attempted to brush away their tracks." Marc walked over the tracks he'd made walking from the road and stared carefully at the snow. "Look. See there. It looks as if someone swept the snow. Look how it's different here than it is over there." He pointed to either side of his tracks.

Jake was right behind him. "You think someone was here and didn't want anyone to know they were?" he asked, lowering his voice although they were very much alone.

Marc got a prickling sensation down the back of his neck and he pressed his hand against his flesh, rubbing his skin as he searched the ground around them. He hated being at a disadvantage. Worse yet, that eerie gut-wrenching feeling that he was overlooking something obvious was starting to get on his nerves. He wasn't one to get panic attacks, but he worried that if he didn't figure out soon what it was he was overlooking that it would be too late.

He jumped, grabbing Jake, when an explosion ripped through the air.

"What the fuck?" Jake howled as Marc tackled him to the ground.

They were big men and Jake was taller. Marc still took him down, instinct taking over to protect his younger brother as another shot sounded. The ground was hard, cold, and uneven. Small rocks stabbed different parts of Marc's body, but he endured it, looking around frantically.

"We've got to make a run for it," Marc said, grabbing Jake's arm and dragging him to his knees. "I don't see a goddamn soul anywhere."

"Let's go!" Jake scrambled to his knees just as someone shot at them again.

They were using a pretty powerful shotgun with damn good range. And they obviously weren't concerned about anyone hearing them fire. Whoever was shooting also had damn good aim.

Marc swore he felt the bullet graze the side of his neck. It was worse than a nasty bug bite and he slapped himself, twisting in the direction of their shooter. Rugged ground covered with snow went on forever. There were groups of boulders sporadically here and there. If someone hid behind any of them they'd been positioned there for a while.

"Crap! Marc!" Jake hissed.

Marc turned and saw blood soaking Jake's shirtsleeve. "Son of a bitch."

He grabbed his brother, wrapping Jake's uninjured arm around his shoulder, and ran, hauling almost all of Jake's weight as he bolted for the car. There was another shot, then another. Reaching his car, he yanked open the passenger door, shoved his brother inside, and raced to the driver's side.

"Man, I'm fucking bleeding worse than it hurts," Jake complained. His face was lined with worry.

Marc wasn't sure whether Jake looked paler or not. But he was bleeding worse than a stuck pig. "Keep your blood off my car," Marc said. "And hold on."

"No problem. You know me. All about bleeding neatly," Jake hissed. "Just give me something to press against this hole in my body."

Marc reached underneath his seat and grabbed his gun, turned on his car, and twisted to search his backseat for something to use as a temporary bandage. Finally yanking a shirt out of his duffel bag, he thrust it at Jake.

"Hold on," Marc repeated, and spun his car around.

"Jesus Christ!" Jake swore, falling into Marc, then slamming against the car door as the tires spun on the highway.

"I told you—"

"I'm fucking holding on," Jake snapped, and pressed the wadded-up shirt against his shoulder. The entire side of Jake's shirt was quickly turning red. Not a good sign.

"We'll put a Band-Aid on you here in a minute," Marc said, gripping the wheel as he shoved it into first and accelerated, giving his car enough gas to make it fly down the road. "But first, turnabout is fair play." He worried

Jake might be more hurt than he at first thought. Giving him shit would keep him alert, though. Marc needed to find out who was shooting at them, and why.

"You know, my mom is pissed at you."

London hit the backspace key on the computer, trying again to type the same thing she'd typed three times now. It was taking twice as long to get her work done this afternoon. What usually took her about fifteen minutes seemed to be taking forever to get done. She realized Meryl was talking to her and looked away from the screen.

"I'm sorry. What did you say?"

"What's wrong with you?" Meryl asked, and tried shoving one of her red curls behind her ear. "I said Mom was mad when you didn't come to dinner yesterday. You never miss Sunday dinner."

"Sorry."

"Have a hot date?"

London shook her head, staring at her computer again. "I got into a cleaning spree and spent the day at home."

"Really." Meryl didn't sound like she believed her. "You weren't with Mr. King, I mean Marc?"

"He checked out." London sucked in a deep breath, refusing to get upset about it again.

"He checked out? He was supposed to be here for the rest of the month."

"He left."

"Why?"

London sighed. Meryl wasn't going to drop it. "I don't know," she said. "I guess he got called back for work, or something. He said it was a family crisis," she added, still perplexed about his comment that his parents were missing. Had he been telling her the truth? And if so, how could it be that both of their parents had disappeared?

"Oh no. But he told you why he had to leave. Do you think he's coming back?"

"I don't know." London backed up from the computer and threw her hands up in the air. "I really don't know."

She wasn't ready for Meryl to walk up and wrap her arms around her. London wasn't sure how to react when Meryl hugged her, holding her for a moment and stroking her back. It would be rude to stiffen and even worse to back out of the embrace. Meryl was the closest thing to a friend London had ever had, and she didn't want to offend her. Fortunately, Meryl put her at arm's length a moment later, smiling warmly.

"We need a chocolate and ice cream party," she said, wrinkling her freckle-covered nose as she made a face. "It's the perfect remedy for a broken heart."

London almost insisted her heart was anything but broken. She'd been damn close, though. Not for the first time that afternoon, she told herself it was a good thing Marc was gone. If they'd spent much more time together, London would have seriously lost her heart to him. She'd been saved from heartache by Marc bailing on her when he did.

"I'm fine. Really, I am," she said, smiling to prove it. "It's just a Monday and I'm ready for the day to be over."

"Uh-huh," Meryl said, giving her a scrutinizing stare. "Go ahead and head on out if you want," she offered, apparently coming to the conclusion that London wasn't fine. "I can finish all of this."

"You're working tonight?" London could have kicked herself for just now realizing Meryl was here instead of Todd.

Meryl gave her a knowing look. "Yes. Todd asked me to cover for him tonight. Can you believe it? He actually has a date. I think he's found a lady who is as big a geek as he is."

"Okay." London turned, walking around Meryl. It was bad enough feeling like a space cadet, but acting like one to the point where it gave her away made matters even worse.

"You are not okay." Meryl crossed her arms over her chest. "If you don't want to be alone you can hang out here with me tonight. Do you have the walking tour tonight?"

"No. I'm on tomorrow and Thursday this week." She glanced at the schedule, not trusting her memory at the moment. "Yeah, that's right."

Meryl shook her head, making a tsking sound. "Hang out here with me tonight," she encouraged. "I bet we can get chocolate and ice cream from the kitchen. What do you think?"

"Meryl, you're a great friend, but you're crazy if you think I want to hang out here any longer than I have to," London stressed, doing her best to make herself sound convincing. "But I will take you up on heading out early. I've got a million things to do."

She didn't have anything to do, but she hurried out of the lodge to her Jeep anyway. London froze, her key in her hand, ready to unlock her car, and stared at the package stuffed underneath her windshield wiper.

"God, no," she whispered. "Why won't you leave me alone?"

There wasn't a lot more she could take. Her hand shook as she reached for it, as if it might come to life and bite her if she wasn't careful. As she freed it from underneath her wiper she glanced around, staring at each car in the parking lot to make sure no one was in any of them. There wasn't anyone around. Even so, London shook like a leaf as she struggled to unlock her car.

Once she started it, London locked her doors, feeling a wave of nausea coming on. Even before she opened the package and the one picture inside slid into her lap, she knew it would be bad news. The picture lay faceup and she stared down at it, shaking so bad she couldn't pick it up. And although it was a clear shot, London couldn't make sense out of it.

"Oh God!" she cried, sucking in a ragged breath as she lifted it to eye level, holding the corner of it with her finger and thumb. "Oh God," she repeated. "It's blood."

London studied the picture, confused although it was a perfect shot of Marc, hovering over another man in the snow, looking as if he was trying to drag him. The dark discoloration saturating the other man's shoulder and also appearing to be on Marc's arm really made it look as if they were bleeding.

"Why are you doing this to me?" she yelled, letting her head fall back against her seat. "Leave me alone. Goddamn it! Leave me alone."

She barely remembered driving home. London hurried up her porch steps, scared to look around her for fear there would be another package waiting for her there. The porch floor was slick and she damn near fell on her face, and racked her entire body when she managed to stay on her feet.

London felt a bit of solace once she was inside her home with the door locked behind her. She took off her boots and left them at the door, then trudged into her kitchen. There wasn't any way she could eat a thing, but a glass of wine sounded good. She pulled out the bottle that she and Marc hadn't finished the night he'd been over for dinner. Although it didn't taste as good as it had the night they'd drunk it together, after she had downed a glass and poured her second the warmth that spread throughout her insides helped calm her down.

"You aren't going to win," she told the picture as she carried it and her full glass of wine to her bedroom. "I'm not going to give you that power."

She stared at the picture some more, studying the rugged terrain around Marc and the other man, then focusing on the two of them. Marc wore the coat he'd bought in Aspen, which didn't make sense if he was in California. The snow on the ground bugged her, too. Last she heard, it didn't snow in L.A. Downing more of her wine, she hurried back to her kitchen, where she'd left her purse.

"I'm done with so many questions." It was time for answers. London pulled out the piece of paper where she'd written down the phone number for KFA, Marc's family business, King Fugitive Apprehension. "Bounty hunters," she mumbled, wondering if the picture was a shot of him working. "Did you have to hunt down and capture some bad guy?"

Returning to her bedroom, London got comfortable on her bed with her wine on her nightstand and the picture of Marc in front of her. Then grabbing her phone, she punched in the number for KFA before she could talk herself out of placing the call.

"KFA." The woman who answered on the second ring sounded cheerful but serious.

London immediately wanted to know who she was. "Is Marc there?" she asked, wondering what she would say to him if he was.

"No, he's not in the office right now. May I take a message?"

London hesitated. Did this woman get calls from ladies all the time for Marc?

"This is London," she began. Her brain went blank and she couldn't figure out what else to say now that she'd spoken. A business like that would probably have caller ID on their phone and he would know she'd called and hung up if she didn't say something else. She needed to sound intelligent, sure of herself. When this woman told

Marc she called, she wouldn't be able to say London sounded like some kind of babbling idiot.

"London?" the woman asked.

"Yes. Do you know when he'll be in?" London asked.

"Marc is out of town right now, on business," the woman added, her tone changing. It softened, the all-business sound leaving, and she was friendlier when she continued. "I don't know when he'll be back, but he told me about you. You're out in Colorado, right?"

Something inside London melted. Maybe it was part of the wall she'd always kept up around her to prevent anyone from hurting her. It could have been hearing a friendly voice and someone who was so far away she couldn't do her any harm. Or possibly it was simply that she was speaking to someone who could enlighten her, London hoped, about Marc.

"Yes, in Aspen," London offered, leaning back on her pillows and sliding the picture to the side of her so she could stretch out her legs. "Where is Marc?"

The woman cleared her throat. "I can't tell you that, but don't take it the wrong way. We don't discuss where the men are when they are out in the field."

London thought she understood, considering his line of work. She glanced down at the eight-by-ten, the glare from her bedroom light making it hard to see from her angle.

"Okay," London said slowly. "Could you tell me if he's okay?"

"Last I heard. Why?"

There was no way she would tell the woman she'd just received a picture on her windshield that suggested otherwise. "Can you reach him?" she asked instead of answering the woman's question. If she could be evasive, then so could London.

"Yes. Is there a problem? I might be able to help you if there is."

London didn't see how she could help when they were hundreds of miles away from each other. "I'd really appreciate knowing he is okay. It would mean a lot to me." London reached for her wine and downed a good swallow. "I'll leave my number unless you already have it."

This time the woman hesitated, although only for a moment. "I have your number." She rattled it off to prove it. "I'll have him call you."

London left her phone on her bed to refill her glass but then hurried back to her bedroom when her phone rang before she had more wine poured. She stared at the unknown area code for only a moment before answering.

"Hello."

"I hear you were worried about me," Marc's deep baritone purred into her ear.

"Marc," she said, sounding breathless.

"I miss you, too."

She hated the damn lump that swelled in her throat. As she considered the possibility that getting a buzz and talking to Marc at the same time might not be her best move, she downed the last swallow in her glass and walked back to the kitchen to refill it.

"Are you okay?" she asked. "I know this sounds weird, but were you hurt today?"

"That does sound weird. I wasn't, but my brother was."

His brother. Crap. Jake. She poured wine quickly and licked her fingers when she spilled some over the glass.

"I got a picture today. It was on my windshield when I got off work. It was a picture of you and another man in the snow and there was blood."

"What?"

He yelled loud enough to startle her and she spilled more wine. London held the glass away from her but then brought it to her lips, drinking and praying she wasn't making a serious mistake as she returned to her bedroom. All of these pictures were making her nuts. She needed to talk to someone about it and suddenly it seemed imperative she tell Marc. After all, he was a bounty hunter and that was really close to being law enforcement. Or at least, she was pretty sure it was.

"I'm getting really tired of getting these pictures," she confessed, and plopped down on the side of her bed, putting her wineglass down before she spilled more of it. "I don't know what to do about them and it's making me nuts. I know this sounds crazy," she added, and tried to laugh to make light of her rambling.

"London," he said, his serious deep voice soothing her with just the sound of her name. "When did you start getting pictures?"

"It hasn't been that long ago, although it seems like it. The first few sets of pictures were of my parents. Do you remember the package you found on my front porch and put in my mailbox for me?"

"Those were pictures."

"Yes. And I knew they would be. That's why I didn't want you bringing them in. I was scared after you opened the package in your room that you would expect me to open my package in front of you."

"I should have." He sounded remorseful. "My God, London. You've been getting pictures of your parents, too?"

"I didn't understand them. I don't understand them. I haven't talked to my parents in years, and to all of a sudden have shots of them sent to me in the mail, and with no return address. It was the notes with them that really made the whole ordeal confusing." Once she started talking about them she didn't seem able to stop. But when she took a deep breath and reached for her wine, she stopped, wrapping her fingers around the damp glass and staring at it. "Marc, what do you mean: 'too'?"

"The entire time I was in Colorado pictures were being sent to my house of my parents. They weren't pictures they took of themselves, though, and neither of them knew anyone had taken pictures of them. There were notes typed on typing paper. Just two sentences."

"That's the same thing that has happened to me." She forgot about her wine as she jumped to her feet, her heart suddenly pounding so hard in her chest she couldn't breathe. "The first note said: 'Say good-bye to your mother and father. You're never going to see them again.' "

"And the second note said: 'As promised, your parents are gone. Let the game begin!' " Marc said, finishing for her.

"How did you know?" she whispered, turning slowly and staring at her dresser where all the pictures were. "You saw my pictures?"

"No. The notes that came with the pictures sent to my house said the exact same thing as your notes did."

"What are you talking about? That doesn't make any sense."

"You're right. It doesn't." Marc was quiet for a moment.

London barely noticed. Her head was spinning. She made the decision to talk to Marc about these pictures and he already knew about them. But he didn't know about her pictures. He knew about his pictures.

"Someone is sending pictures to me and also sending them to your house? I don't understand. You and I didn't even know each other before two weeks ago."

"London, what do your parents do for a living?"

The question took her aback. "Why do you ask?"

"I'm curious. I don't think these pictures are about you and me or whether we knew each other. I think they're about our parents. Are your parents in law enforcement?"

She couldn't help laughing. "No. Hardly," she said, afraid a wave of hysteria would kick in if she didn't put some sense to all of this really soon. "They're as far from law enforcement as you can get."

"Okay. Well, I don't know the connection yet. Do you have any vacation time coming to you?"

If he didn't quit throwing really odd questions out at her, continually changing the subject, she would go nuts. "I'm sure I do. I've never used any of it. Are you suggesting I take a vacation?"

"I don't know how much of a vacation it will be. I want you to call in to work tomorrow. Tell them you're going to be gone for a while. And don't leave your house. I'll be there tomorrow to get you."

Chapter Nine

Staying home just wasn't an option. Marc was serious about coming to get her. There was something incredibly exciting about knowing he was driving to her right now. A rush of butterflies attacked her stomach as she leaned against the counter at the front desk, zoning in on the roaring fire she'd started after getting to work that morning.

Marc called her an hour after hanging up with her last night to let her know he'd be driving up to get her during the night. He was in Arizona, not California, but that was all the detail he'd give her over the phone. When he explained she wasn't secure, London had an image of 007 with all his gadgets and tools of the spy trade. London was probably as far from secure as they came. Up until a couple weeks ago, she liked not having to worry for her safety or look over her shoulder.

London had taken a leap of faith when she decided to talk to Marc about the pictures. She'd honestly believed telling him about them would help clear matters up a bit in her head. Instead she was dragged deeper into a mystery, one that seemed to be wrapped around Marc as tight as it was around her.

"I just got your voice mail." Cliff appeared at the end of the hallway, scowling at her.

London snapped her attention to her manager, dragging her hair over her shoulder and letting it fall behind her back. It took a moment to clear her head from her brooding thoughts.

"Good. I'm sure it sounded rushed," she said, smiling in spite of his continual frown. She hadn't expected Cliff to be thrilled about her requesting immediate time off. "I just got word late last night. I need to leave town for a while."

"You can't just up and leave like this. I'm denying your request," he informed her, sticking his jaw out and glaring at her.

"I haven't missed a day of work in three years," she complained.

"That doesn't give you the right to leave without notice. You'll just have to plan your vacation another time."

"This is hardly a vacation." London had never enjoyed dealing with Cliff. He was egocentric and spoiled. If she avoided any confrontation with him, he was tolerable at best. There wasn't any way she could leave town without discussing it with him. And she'd be damned if she lost her job over this. "I didn't plan this and I've already covered all of my shifts. You won't have to work any more than you do now," she added, knowing she stabbed at him when she implied he didn't do anything around the lodge anyway, other than make his employees' lives miserable. It was a great job if they didn't have to deal with Cliff, and since he seldom came around unless someone famous made reservations or important people held parties, it wasn't hard avoiding him.

"I hardly have time to work the front desk. I have my own workload, you know." The way he tilted his head, looking defiant and superior, showed he completely missed her jab that he didn't work at all.

The phone rang and London spun around to answer it, keeping her back to Cliff when she grabbed it. Losing her cool with him wouldn't help matters. All that mattered was that he approve her time off and leave her alone.

"Elk Lodge," she answered.

"Hey, London. I just got your message. That is so romantic," Meryl said cheerfully. "And yes, of course I'll come in and finish out your shift. I'll be there in a few. How cool is that! Marc King coming in on his white horse to sweep you out of here."

London laughed, all too aware of Cliff glaring at her and really not caring. "Thank you so much for agreeing to work for me, Meryl. I owe you big-time. I was just standing here talking to Cliff and explaining the family crisis."

She'd given Meryl a very abridged version of the story, leaving her a message first thing that morning asking her to help cover her shifts and telling her Marc was on his way to pick her up.

"You told him it was a family crisis?" Meryl asked, lowering her voice.

"I know I haven't missed any work. I wasn't planning on starting now. But you understand. It's an emergency. My parents need me."

"I do understand family. Honestly, I didn't think you had family," Meryl said, buying into London's story with as much compassion as she'd expected her to have.

"Everyone has family. I just never talked about mine much. I spent my time here working and you know I love my job. I think I have all my shifts covered now so there won't be a problem while I'm gone."

"What's wrong with your family? Is someone sick? Or is it just a story you told Cliff?" Meryl pressed.

London squeezed the bridge of her nose, glancing down. There wasn't enough time to explain what was wrong with her family. Although when she didn't talk to anyone about it, she was able to live with how she'd been raised. Maybe her parents hadn't done things the conventional way, but she'd grown up okay.

"They'll be fine, but they've asked for my help and I need to go to them." In a way, she decided, that was true. There was no way of knowing who sent those pictures, but they were sent to get her attention and to let her know her parents were in trouble. Any other child would run to the aid of their mother and father. Why shouldn't she?

"I understand. I'd do the same thing," Meryl said, her tone full of compassion. "I'll be there in a few."

"I'll see you when you get here," she said, and told Meryl good-bye.

Cliff was still scowling when London turned around. "I have everything taken care of," she informed him. "All you need to do is approve my time off."

An older couple walked up to the counter. Cliff's expression transformed and he smiled at them as if they were his best friends.

"London will take care of you," he informed them. "I hope you're both enjoying your stay here."

"Yes, we are. Thank you," the wife of the couple said, grinning back at him.

"Good. Good." Cliff left London, disappearing around the corner without giving her approval to leave.

"Fuck him," she grumbled to herself, and managed her professional smile as she helped the couple at the counter.

It would take Meryl at least half an hour to get to the lodge from her house. The lobby began filling up with guests, their skis and other paraphernalia cluttering the large room as they chatted among themselves cheerfully. They were on vacation, all appearing to not have a care in the world other than hitting the slopes and playing in the snow all day. It was a sight London was very accustomed to seeing, travelers from all walks of life hovering in the warm lobby while waiting for the shuttle to take them to the lifts.

She remembered being in awe of some of them when she first started working here. Her life was so far from anything these people had ever known. After working here a few years, she had grown immune to them. Today she watched the group as they mingled, all wearing their bright ski attire. She'd learned over the years which ones came from way too much money and which guests scrimped and scraped just to enjoy some time here at the lodge.

It was also interesting watching them judge one another. Especially the women, although the men did it, too. They would make a show of being nice to their fellow skiers, but the look in their eyes, the shift of their heads, showed how they sized one another up and judged one another.

London had made a lifetime habit of watching people, learning by their actions who could be trusted and who couldn't. For the most part she'd determined very few could be trusted. It created a sinking feeling inside her when she wondered for the tenth time, at least, why she'd confided in Marc. Worse yet, she'd known him two weeks. She was uprooting her life and had agreed to leave the state with him. Maybe once in her life running on a moment's notice had been par for the course. But today she had order. It amazed her, and scared the crap out of her, when she realized how quickly she conformed to her old habits, making decisions on the spur of the moment and packing hastily, leaving everything she had and taking on the unknown.

The shuttle bus pulled up out front and the large group seemed to talk louder as they filed out the front door. One man didn't leave them but remained standing with his back to her, facing the fire. London noticed the patches on the elbows of his jacket and her gut twisted painfully.

She moved around the counter, refusing to let the PI unnerve her. "You're here again," she said when she came up behind him.

"I heard in town this lodge was once a millionaire's home, and that he built it so he and his wife could enjoy a reclusive lifestyle in the mountains," he said without turning around.

James Huxtable's hands were clasped behind his back and he didn't change his position as he glanced at the large painting over the mantle of the couple who had once lived here. Since he was right, London didn't see the need to comment. Nor was she in the mood to elaborate and offer a history lesson.

"Do you know where my parents are?" she asked.

That grabbed his attention. His expression was somewhat amused when he turned around and faced her. "Now if I did, why would I be here?"

He hadn't answered her question. "If you were a good detective, you would have known I've had no contact with them," she pointed out.

"You're right. Sometimes family members seek each other out in a time of crisis. It's been known to happen."

Maybe normal families, she thought to herself. "You never answered my question."

He shook his head, his dark hair remaining in place as he looked down at her, his gaze drifting before meeting hers. "I don't usually spend my time focusing on con artists who drift from town to town. They're a dime a dozen."

He would have to do better than that to insult her when it came to her parents. She'd heard it all before. "So if that's a 'no,' " she began, again thinking he didn't look at all what she would expect a private investigator to look like. "Where do you think they are?"

James smiled at her, his lips smooth and moist as if he'd applied a thick layer of lip balm to them recently. At least when she learned Marc was a bounty hunter he looked the part, so tall and muscular and with that blunt side to him that made it easy to imagine him diving to the ground and pulling a gun from his hip at the same time. This man facing her looked as if he would get upset if he got dirty at all.

"You must have some idea. I can't imagine you didn't research them before approaching me."

"I did," he consented. "They were in Chicago last year and I do believe they headed west when winter set in." Whether he was telling the truth or not she couldn't tell. His expression never changed, and that smile on his face was growing more and more annoying. "My guess is they're with one of the game players. I just don't know which one yet."

"What does that mean?" she asked as the phone at the front desk began ringing.

London left him without a word, hurrying around the counter to answer it.

"Wait!" she called out when James walked out the front door. "Shit," she hissed to herself, and answered the phone.

What the hell did he mean by "game players"? God. Was it possible for all of this to get any more confusing?

She headed back to her house less than an hour later. Maybe she'd be smart to grab her packed bags and head out on her own, leave Aspen for new territory, and put all of this strangeness behind her. It was something she knew how to do. Take off and leave all problems behind, forgetting about them completely before the new town and new adventure came upon her.

Wasn't that the one thing her parents taught her how to do better than anything else? When shit got too deep, run. Don't hang around and try to solve it. If her parents heard she was in trouble, would they run to her aid?

Although that thought left a bitter taste in her mouth,

London wouldn't run. She wouldn't ignore the growing mystery surrounding her or the dangerous implications coming with it. It made it easier to accept her decision when she pulled into her driveway and Marc was already there.

"Got to love all this snow," he announced, getting out of his car and looking larger than life when he walked up to her, his long legs helping him clear the distance between them within seconds.

Marc didn't hesitate. He didn't ask. He wrapped his arms around her, lifting her off the ground and damn near squeezing all air out of her lungs. "I'm sorry I left without saying anything," he whispered in her ear.

He smelled so good. All that muscle and the warmth of his body had her melting against him before she could think of anything to say. His greeting confirmed what she'd come to believe during the time he'd been here. There was something growing between them.

"We'll discuss that later," she informed him instead of saying what came to mind first, which was that she was used to it.

Marc let her slide down his virile body and brushed her hair away from her face. When he lowered his mouth to hers, greeting her further with a kiss hot enough to make her insides melt, she prayed she would get through all of this without losing her heart. The pictures arriving in the mail didn't terrify her half as much as the fact that she might have already lost it. As she gripped his shoulders, leaning in and deepening the kiss, London moved her hands under his coat, soaking in his warmth and feeling his heartbeat just above his collarbone. The solid throbbing under her fingertips matched the hard beating of her own heart.

"Where were you?" he asked when he finally let her up for air.

Marc ran his hand down her back and escorted her up her porch stairs. London wondered if any of her neighbors were home to witness that public display of affection. It was really the least of her worries, though, and she slid her key into her lock and let her and Marc into the house.

"I had to tie up a few ends at work before I could leave," she explained.

Marc nodded, glancing around her living room and noticing her luggage stacked against the wall. "How long did you say you'd be gone?" he asked, and picked up her suitcase and overnight bag.

"A week."

"What if you're gone longer?"

He started to the door and she stared at his broad back, her insides throbbing with need after that incredible kiss. "My boss wasn't thrilled I was leaving for a week."

Marc didn't comment but let the screen door close behind him as he took her luggage to his car. She was really going through with this. He had all her clothes and was putting them in his car. As her insides twisted, she admitted to some excitement in being with Marc nonstop over the next few days.

"Where are those pictures?" he asked when he came back inside. "Did you pack them? I want to see them."

"They're in here."

"Were you not going to bring them?" he asked.

London glanced over her shoulder when he followed her into her bedroom. His expression was harder than it had been when he greeted her. The bounty hunter she imagined him being stood before her in the flesh, strong, powerful, and focused.

"Honestly, I didn't want them in with my clothes. I have all of them here." There was something creepy about them she didn't like.

London picked up the stack of large envelopes off her dresser and handed them to him, then walked around him and turned on her bedroom light. "Have you heard of a James Huxtable?" she asked when Marc sat on her bed and let the first group of pictures slip into his hand.

"No. Why?" He looked up at her for a moment before returning his attention to the pictures.

"He's a private detective who showed up at the lodge the other day and asked me about my parents."

That got Marc's attention. "When did he come talk to you?" he asked, looking at her instead of the pictures.

"The first time was the day you left." Which was a good thing. The look on Marc's face was enough to let her know Marc would have bullied the PI and possibly even made a scene if he felt London's honor needed to be defended. "He showed up again this morning," she continued. "It was strange. The first day he showed up he told me my parents were on the most wanted list and wanted to know if I knew where they were."

"The most wanted list? Which one?" Marc asked.

"I didn't know there was more than one," she said, shaking her head and pulling her gaze from Marc's. "But this morning when he showed up again I decided I didn't want him harassing me at work, even if I am leaving. I confronted him and asked if he knew where my parents were. He told me he guessed one of the game players had taken them, but he didn't know which one. What kind of answer is that?"

"One of the game players?" Marc asked, suddenly sounding angry. "What is this guy's name?"

"James Huxtable. His card is in my purse. Not that it says much. Just a name and his number." She hadn't meant to blurt out the bit about her parents being on the most wanted list. Marc had picked up on it, commented on it, and would ask her about her parents again. He wasn't the kind of man to ignore a detail, under any circumstances. Oddly enough, she wanted him to know everything. She didn't want to shoulder all of this by herself anymore. For now, though, London was cool with the conversation swaying away from the subject of her parents.

"Let me see his business card."

London left him in her room with the pictures and went to the living room, where she'd left her purse. When she returned with the business card in hand, Marc was holding up two of the pictures, comparing them to each other.

"Do you know this place?" he asked, glancing at her over the eight-by-tens.

London sat down next to him and he made room on the side of the bed for her, then held up the two pictures she'd received with the note saying her parents were gone.

"What place?" she asked.

"Look at the buildings in the background. Have you ever been there?"

London frowned. She'd focused on her parents in each of the shots, comparing how they looked to the last time she'd seen them. She hadn't given a lot of attention to the background in the shots. Both her mom and dad in each picture stood in between two men who had their heads down. They were walking toward the camera, or so it appeared. London narrowed her gaze on each shot, studying the street they were on and the row of businesses partially visible behind them in each shot.

"I don't think so. Why?"

"Just curious." He put the pictures back in their envelope and took the business card out of her hand. "Jake and I recognized the buildings in the background, which is what took us to Arizona and then, curiously enough, got us shot at and Jake injured. I'm searching for similarities between our situation and yours and wondered if you'd by chance been there, too."

He flipped the business card over in his hand, stared at the blank back side, and flipped it again. "It's just his name and a phone number."

"I found that odd, too. I don't even know where he's from."

Marc shook his head and grunted, handing the card back to her. "Let's get going. I'll drive for a while and let you take the helm once I run out of juice."

London worked to calm her nerves by talking. She assured herself again and again she'd worked her way out of worse ordeals in her lifetime. Marc could be trusted. She'd seen the Web site advertising his family business and had called the number on it to reach him. None of that knowledge helped soothe her nerves when she sat next to him in his vintage Mustang and drove out of Aspen.

"So were the pictures you received similar to mine?" she asked once they were on the interstate heading south.

"Identical. Especially the notes. Down to the same font. I'd bet good, hard money they were sent from the same source."

"God. Weird," she whispered, studying her fingers in her lap. "What would your parents possibly have in common with mine?"

"That's what I want to find out." He looked over at her, studying her for a moment.

London didn't look back at him. Instead, sighing, she stared out the window so she wouldn't see him at all, not even through her peripheral vision. "Are your parents good people?" she asked, deciding if they were going to compare notes, he would start.

"The best." He didn't hesitate. "Dad was a cop with LAPD for twenty years. When he retired he started his own business. Jake and I jumped on the bandwagon almost at the same time. We're licensed bounty hunters in the state of California."

"So you can't be a bounty hunter anywhere else?" she asked.

"We don't usually have to cross the state line. We go after those who skip out on their court dates or violate their probations. Most of them don't get out of the city before we bring them down. I can count only a couple times when we've had to leave the state."

"Then what do you do?" She looked back at him, curious about his work. If she could keep the topic off her parents, everything would be okay. London really didn't want to lie to him. But at the same time, telling anyone, especially Marc, what kind of people her parents were would cut her to the core. Admitting they could be on the most wanted list spoke volumes, and she hoped would satisfy him for now.

"We've been known to work with the local law. It hasn't happened too many times." He leaned back in his seat, yawning. "I've got a thermos of coffee behind the seat. Would you mind?"

"I can drive." She twisted against her seat belt and found the thermos.

"Do you know how to drive a stick?"

London laughed, thinking of the many different cars she had driven before being old enough to have a driver's license. "I can drive anything," she promised.

They pulled into a roadside rest stop and London stood on her side of the car, stretching and squinting against the sunny sky. The air was crisp, and snow covered the ground in patches. There were a few other travelers, none parked too close and all going about their business, ignoring her and Marc. It was a quick, hard rush she hadn't anticipated, being on the road, no one around her giving her a thought. Every time they'd taken off when she was a kid, London had listened to her parents as they grew eager for the next town, discussed the golden opportunities awaiting them there. London had shared their excitement, not knowing any better or any different. The same rush of excitement attacked her now.

"God, you're sexy." Marc wrapped his arms around her from behind before she finished stretching.

London jumped but smiled when she tried twisting in his arms. "I admit I've enjoyed the view you've been offering, too," she said.

His blue eyes matched the color of the sky. "Have you, now?" he said, his voice dropping to a husky drawl. "You were a thousand miles away just now. What's on your mind, London?"

"Oh gee. I don't know. Maybe that I just left my job and home to travel to another state with a man I just met, all because I've received pictures in the mail of my parents whom I haven't seen in years."

His expression grew solemn as he searched her face. When he touched her cheek, there was something so incredibly gentle and comforting about it, London closed her eyes, unwilling to let herself drown in his gaze. Marc would sweep her off her feet without even trying; then she'd have no one to blame but herself.

"As intense as all of that sounds, there's more to it than that," he said, continuing to stroke her cheek with his fingers.

"Oh, lovely," she said, wrinkling her nose and making a face when she opened her eyes and looked up at him. "Do tell. I love a good mystery."

He smiled and she saw how tired he was when the sun highlighted the dark shadows under his eyes.

"First, let's do that bathroom run," she added, thinking the sooner he got some sleep in the car the better it would be. Not to mention, standing so close to him with his hands on her as they were made her ache to have sex with him. She didn't know when that would happen so she didn't want to get herself worked up about it.

They were back in the car and Marc finally accepted that she wouldn't wreck his car and relaxed in the passenger seat when London's cell phone rang. He jerked his head up, looking around the car as she gestured behind her seat.

"My purse," she indicated, pointing behind her seat. "My phone is in my purse."

Marc pulled her purse into his lap and opened it, finding her phone and glancing at the screen before handing it to her. "Can you talk hands free?" he asked.

"If I put it on speaker." She saw Meryl's name on the screen and took the call. "Hi, Meryl. Hold on; I need to put you on speaker."

Marc turned down the heater in the car and returned to his reclined position, although London doubted he was trying to fall asleep.

"Hey, girl, how are you doing?" Meryl sounded cheerful as usual. "I figured I would check up on you, make sure everything is okay."

London couldn't help smiling. She hadn't elaborated on anything before leaving. Meryl was insightful enough to know this was a unique type of adventure and wanted to make sure London was all right. It felt good having a friend, knowing someone out there cared about her.

"You're such a sweetheart," she said, grinning at her phone, which she held in between her fingers while holding on to the steering wheel. "And I'm doing fine. We stopped at a roadside stop and now I'm driving."

"Okay. I won't keep you. This guy asked about you after you left. He seemed surprised you left work."

Marc rolled his head on his seat, glancing at her and then the phone.

"Who was it?" London asked.

"He said his name was James Huxtable. He said you two were friends, but I'd never seen him before."

"We're not friends and don't tell him I left town. If he asks about me again tell him I'm home sick, or something," London said.

"You've got it. I figured he wasn't telling me the truth. There was something about him I didn't trust. You know I'm good at reading people."

"The best," London said, and couldn't help agreeing with her. There was something strange about James Huxtable. "Feel free to call again if you need to," she added before saying good-bye.

"You don't want a private detective knowing you're out of town?" Marc asked when she'd dropped her phone into her purse, which was still on his lap.

She took her purse from him and slipped it behind her seat. "I agree with Meryl. I don't trust him."

"Why not?"

"He was very evasive, wouldn't answer my questions, and when he did he spoke in riddles. Worse yet, he knew he was talking in riddles and seemed to get off on how it frustrated me."

"Sounds like a creep." Marc didn't elaborate but closed his eyes.

Eventually London started exploring Marc's car, learning how to work the radio and then finding his CD collection and popping a classic rock compilation into the CD player. Marc's breathing slowed and grew raspy. He never started snoring, but his heavy breathing let her know he was finally sound asleep. She kept the volume low and sang under her breath to Eric Clapton while enjoying the drive and beautiful day. The peaceful surroundings didn't completely relax her thoughts, though. London couldn't help wondering what more there was to the story that Marc had mentioned at the roadside stop.

By the time they reached Arizona, London had become familiar with the GPS, and even found Marc's atlas stuffed between the seats. She was glad to see that even though he used modern technology, he hadn't turned his back on the classic reliability of a good atlas. London compared notes, made sure the GPS understood where they were going, and was proud of herself when she pulled into the motel late that night where Marc had told her he and his brother were staying.

"Wake up, Sleeping Beauty," she whispered, nudging Marc after she'd parked and turned off his car.

"What?" He jerked awake, looking around and appearing confused for a moment.

"We're here."

"We're here?" he repeated. "Why didn't you wake me?"

"I didn't need you to be awake." She'd never understood why every man believed no woman could navigate from town to town without his assistance. "I just figured I'd wake you up before I went to get a room." She ran her hand over his soft hair that was flat on one side of his head from sleeping. "I wouldn't want you waking up in the dark all alone and getting scared," she teased.

Marc cleared his throat as he straightened and opened the passenger door, letting the cold night air flood the nicely warmed car. "You're not getting a room. Jake can get a room."

"I thought he got shot."

Marc wagged his finger at her over the hood when she stood on the driver's side. "Don't you dare baby him. He'll milk it until you're exhausted."

London didn't say anything else, deciding she would have to meet this brother and draw her own conclusions. Marc pulled her luggage out and carried it, walking ahead of her after they locked up the car. She stared at their surroundings as they hurried across the practically empty parking lot. Everything was so dark and so quiet, but she couldn't shake an unnerving sensation that someone was watching them. It wasn't a feeling most people probably understood. But, growing up, quite often the local police were watching them. London grew to understand the difference between knowing when she was safe and when she wasn't.

"The key is in my front pocket," Marc told her when he stopped in front of a motel room door and faced her with her luggage in his hands. "You have to get it out."

"I do?" She didn't miss his satisfied grin when she slid her hand into his pocket and felt a plastic card. She also felt his cock jump to life and snapped her attention to his face. His smile had changed into an incredibly innocent expression. London almost laughed out loud and possibly would have if the prickles weren't going down her neck. "I swear someone is watching us," she whispered, easing the card out of Marc's pocket and sliding it into the lock by the doorknob. "I know it sounds weird, but it's a sensation I get from time to time and usually I'm right."

"I believe you." Marc didn't say anything else as he looked over her head into their dark surroundings. "We'll be inside in a moment."

London followed Marc into his room but stopped just inside the door and let her eyes focus in the dark room. A large man, a very large man, lay on one of the beds damn near naked, wearing just boxers. He had a mop of curls fanned around his head and dark hair across a very muscular chest. His long bare legs were slightly spread and his feet were bare. She would have gawked at what were probably size 14s if it weren't for the hard-on that created a tent in his boxers.

Marc put her luggage down and flipped on one of the lamps. "Good God, man," he snapped, slapping the man's foot hard enough to make him leap to a sitting position. "Put some fucking clothes on. You knew I was bringing London here."

She noticed then that Jake's shoulder was bandaged and part of the gauze wrapped around under his arm was stained with something dark. She guessed blood.

"Jake!" Marc barked, raising his hand to strike his brother's foot again when Jake simply sat in the middle of the bed, tousled hair that almost fell to his shoulders giving him a very bad-boy appearance. "Wake up," Marc ordered.

"Hey," Jake said, giving her a crooked grin and an appraising once-over. "I'm Jake, Marc's better half."

Marc grunted and walked to the other side of the second bed to turn on the rest of the lamps. "Get dressed," he ordered again.

"He's always this grumpy. I'm the nice one." Jake slid his long bare legs off the side of the bed and reached for jeans with one hand. "Welcome to our home away from home."

"Thank you. It's nice to meet you," she said, diverting her eyes when he stood.

Jake gave her another crooked grin when he carried his crumpled clothes and moved past her to the bathroom. London didn't turn to watch him leave.

"There's blood on his bandage," she said after the bathroom door closed.

"I'll take a look at it here in a few," Marc said, walking up to her. "Are you okay? Jake is a terrible flirt, but he's harmless. I promise. If he gets too annoying just clobber him, or tell me and I'll do it for you."

London didn't doubt for a moment that he would. She remembered the picture she'd been sent of the two of them and knew Marc would defend his brother to the death as well. In spite of how he talked about Jake, Marc cared for his brother and it showed.

"How was your trip?" Jake asked when he came back out of the bathroom. He wore faded jeans but no shirt and was still barefoot. He'd dampened his hair and straightened it, although loose curls fell around his face. The day-old growth on his jaw and thick, muscular torso were enough to make any woman drool. It was quite clear Jake knew this about himself, which somehow diminished his sex appeal. "You two hungry? I'm starved. Let's order pizza and get acquainted."

Marc took London's hand and pulled her to him when he sat, encouraging her onto his lap. He was staking his claim. London wondered if they'd spent a lifetime competing for ladies. She could only imagine how lucky any woman would be having these two hot on her trail.

"Are you hungry?" Marc asked, his warm breath tickling the side of her face.

"Order food if you want." She wasn't convinced letting anyone come to the room was a good idea but forced herself to trust these two. "I'm not that hungry."

"You've hardly eaten anything today."

"Maybe she'll change her mind when it gets here. I'm ordering pizza."

London listened as they decided on their order and Jake placed the call. After he relaxed again on the bed where he'd been sleeping, London excused herself to go to the bathroom. When she came out they were discussing the pictures London had shown Marc.

"Let me see them," Jake said. "They sound identical to the ones that came to the house. Did you get action figures in the mail, too?" he asked her.

"Action figures?" London sat on the edge of the bed closest to Marc.

"Marc got the wedding couple with her head chopped off and we got Mr. and Mrs. Incredible and she was beheaded, too," Jake explained.

London gawked at him. "You got a woman without her head in the mail, too?"

Jake looked serious for the first time since she'd met him, which helped her see a strong family resemblance. "When Marc told Dad about the figurines he was sent, Dad knew you were in trouble."

"Jake," Marc began.

"It wasn't until you told Marc about getting the pictures that it sunk into his thick head and he raced up to get you. Now we just need to figure out why you're involved in this mess, too."

"Slow down," Marc ordered. "You're scaring her."

"I never thought this was about me. It's about my parents, and apparently yours, too." She'd show Marc she could handle this, and more if it was sent her way. They didn't know each other really well yet, but Marc would see she knew how to take care of herself and had for quite a while now, as in most of her life. "It's our parents that brought us together."

He gave her a knowing look and she simply smiled, unwilling to let him sway the conversation into something more personal. Exhaustion would kick in soon enough after all the driving she'd done, but until it did she would discuss this with both of them.

"Do you have the pictures that your family received?" she asked.

"Get yours out, too," Marc said, standing both of them up, then moving around her to their luggage.

A few minutes later London stood in between both men, feeling incredibly short, and stared at all of the pictures they'd spread out on the bed.

"Good Lord, they really are all identical," she said

under her breath, and tried studying them as a detective would.

"Tell us again what that private dick said to you," Marc said.

"Huh?" She looked up at him, tearing herself away from the pictures and glimpses into Marc's happy home life.

Marc ran his hand down her arm. "That James Huxtable guy."

"Who?" Jake asked.

"A private investigator came to my work," she began.

They were both so tall. London moved to the chair at the desk, sat and put a bit of distance between her and the two of them. She could see how anyone would feel safe with both of them nearby. They were damn near giants, and both of them incredibly sexy at that. As much as they looked alike, there was something incredibly different about the two of them, too. Marc moved with a silent confidence, his expression hard and commanding when he was focused on something.

Jake, on the other hand, had a slow, almost lazy drawl about him in his speech and his mannerisms. His longer hair and crooked smile made him appear the bad boy out of the two. At the moment, though, his expression was as serious as Marc's. Both of them were taking in all information, processing it, and working to solve a mystery.

"What was his name?" Jake asked.

"James Huxtable. He gave me his card, but it didn't say anything on it other than his name and a phone number."

"Did you ever call it?" Jake asked.

When she told him no, he simply nodded. Both of them sat, each of them taking a separate bed, and watched her, waiting for her to continue.

"The first time he showed up he gave me his card. I was at work at the lodge. I work at the front desk," she added for Jake's benefit. "He asked if Jonnie and Ruby Brooke were my parents."

"Jonnie and Ruby," Marc repeated. "I don't think I knew their names."

"They're my parents and I told him that." London glanced down at her hands, knowing the time had arrived. Marc would find out sooner or later, and it might as well be from her. She shot him a furtive look. "Have you heard of them?"

He shook his head. "Should I have?" he asked. "What do they do?"

London sucked in a breath. "My parents are fairly well known in their own circles," she said, then decided not to beat around the bush. "I guess you could say they are a modern-day Bonnie and Clyde."

Chapter Ten

It was the last thing Marc expected her to say. He realized he must have appeared stunned when London lowered her gaze, fiddling with her fingers in her lap. Jake let out a hoot, shaking his head as he leaned forward.

"Your parents are bank robbers?" he asked, just as stunned and started laughing.

"They don't limit it to banks," she said, her soft tone hard to hear as her hair sifted over her shoulder and covered part of her face.

Her shame was obvious and suddenly Marc felt sorry for her. "Go on," he told her, shooting Jake a hard look and shaking his head once as he mouthed to him to shut up. "Tell us the rest of what the PI said."

London cleared her throat and sucked in a breath, shoving her long, silky black hair behind her shoulder as she looked from Jake to him. "He told me they were on the most wanted list, which didn't surprise me, and he wanted to know if I knew where they were."

"What did you tell him?" Marc wanted to slide off the bed and pull her into his arms but worried she didn't want that at the moment.

London sat with her back straight and her expression pinched when she continued. "I haven't seen or heard from my parents in at least a few years, maybe more, which isn't unusual," she continued. "He acted like he didn't believe me, though. When he showed up this morning I confronted him before he could me. I asked if he knew where they were and he didn't. But then he speculated that probably one of the game players had them, and that he just didn't know which one."

"One of the game players?" Jake looked at Marc and it was clear he was thinking the same thing as Marc.

"Does that mean something to the two of you?" London asked.

"It might." Marc leaned forward and slid his legs off the edge of the bed. "London, I—"

A firm knock on the door saved him from fumbling for reassuring words. He hated seeing her so distraught. He turned to the motel room door as Jake stood behind him. Marc was aware of how stiffly his brother moved.

After paying for the pizza, Marc and Jake convinced London to have a slice. The conversation shifted as the three of them ate and chatted about anything not related to why they were here.

Jake was relaxed around London and flirted with her shamelessly. Marc would have been irritated if London didn't so skillfully dodge every one of his brother's advances. He imagined her avoiding many men coming on to her as she worked at the lodge, just as he had. The fact that she'd succumbed to his advances made him want to protect her even more, and do whatever it took to keep the smile on her face that was there right now. "Jake, you should see about getting another room before it gets much later," Marc said as he placed the empty pizza box by the trash can.

"You're kicking me out?" Jake looked mortally wounded.

"I told London I'd protect her. You think I'm going to let her sleep in the same room with you?" Marc glared at Jake, wanting a moment alone with London before they laid much more on her. He already guessed she needed reassurance that his learning her parents ran on the wrong side of the law didn't change his feelings toward her. It was obvious just from knowing London for a couple weeks how law-abiding she was.

"Damn, kicked out of my own bed," Jake mumbled, reaching for his shirt and taking his time easing into it.

"Seriously, guys," London said, standing and looking concerned as she watched Jake struggle with his shirt. "I can get my own room."

"No!" Marc and Jake said at the same time.

Marc stood as well and helped his brother finish dressing. "I know how to dress myself," Jake muttered, his speech somewhat slurred.

"I know you can," Marc said quietly, seeing how little fight his brother had in him. "Can I trust you to keep your paws off my girl while I go get a room for you?"

Jake met Marc's gaze with a look of relief, although he managed one of his ridiculous-looking, crooked smiles. "I don't know, man. She's really hot."

Marc pushed Jake's uninjured shoulder and his brother fell helplessly onto the bed behind him, and sat without moving. He studied Jake for a moment.

"You got into the meds Mom stashed in the first-aid kit," he accused, taking in his brother's glazed-over expression.

"Getting shot hurts," Jake said, scooting back on the bed and lying down. "Sorry, London darling, my big brother told me to keep my hands to myself. You're going to have to make the first move."

Marc rolled his eyes and turned to find London watching the two of them, her head tilted and a curious expression on her face.

"He probably won't move," Marc told her, then, because he couldn't stop himself, moved over to kiss her. "I'll be right back."

After Marc helped Jake into his room, content his brother would sleep off the pain meds which were left over from when his father had been shot, he returned to London. He caught her standing in the middle of their motel room, scowling at the floor. In spite of her tormented expression, London was breathtakingly beautiful. Marc moved across the room, captivated by how her sweater hugged and showed off her full round breasts, and pulled her into his arms.

"It wasn't easy to tell us about your parents," he began.

"Would it have been for you?" She stiffened, pursing her lips when she looked up at him and searched his face.

"Were they crooks when you were growing up?" he asked, trying to keep his tone gentle.

"Yes. They have been all my life. And I don't need sympathy over it."

He imagined how hard it must have been for her. The more he ached to pull her into his arms, the more she seemed to resist.

"I've never told anyone about my parents. *No one,*" she stressed when a moment of silence had passed between them. "I'm sure I never would have told you if I didn't have to. But as you can see from when you asked me earlier, our parents have nothing in common."

"I'm not so sure about that."

"What?" she gasped, her tone disbelieving.

"There's got to be a common link," he murmured, giving it some thought.

London looked up at him, studying his face with haunted dark eyes. Every move she made dripped with sensuality, yet he saw now how disparaged she looked. He fought the urge to pull her into his arms and whisper anything it took to relax her and assure her he didn't think any less of her. Then he'd make love to her, taking his time to learn every detail of her hot sexy body.

"Why do you think our parents have something in common?" she asked. "Is it because your parents are so wonderful and mine were never around?" She sounded bitter.

Marc wouldn't press about her childhood but ached to know more about her. He would soon with time. Patience would work in his favor more than pressing her to open up to him all at once.

"Have your parents ever been arrested?"

"Not that I know of, although apparently they're on the most wanted list now."

"I'm not so sure about that either, but we can check if you like." He ran his hand down the sides of her hair, aching to take her to bed right now and make love to her until she cried out his name as she came harder than she ever had before. "But if they've been breaking the law all of your life and have never been caught, they are quite possibly the best in their field, just like my parents."

London's entire expression transformed as she looked up at him wide-eyed and broke out in laughter. She shook her head, holding her gut, and walked away from him. He had her trapped on that side of the bed so she walked the length of it, continuing to laugh and shake her head. When she faced him, her face was flushed.

"You're really stretching it, aren't you?" she asked, and again noticeably jumped when a clicking sound came from the door.

Jake opened the door with his key and walked in. "I left the first-aid kit in here," he said, letting the door close on its own and headed to the bathroom. "Don't mind me. Continue with your foreplay."

Marc ignored him, giving London all of his attention

when he walked into her and gave her a hug. "You're beautiful when you laugh," he whispered into her hair.

Jake came out of the bathroom fidgeting with the contents of the first-aid kit. Marc glanced Jake's way, wishing his brother would go away. Jake looked like a giant five-year-old, pathetic, and not wanting to be alone.

"Marc thinks your parents and mine have something in common," London said, leaving Marc's arms and sitting on the end of the bed. "Can you guess what it is?"

"I'd say maybe they are both the best in their fields." Jake was focused, his expression tight as he spoke. His eyes still looked doped, but he was obviously feeling the pain.

"Oh my God, you're kidding me." She started laughing again, and Marc caught Jake looking at her with appreciation.

Jake could drool over London all he wanted as long as that was all he did. When Marc told Jake as much with a look, Jake simply cocked an eyebrow at him. Marc would wipe that cocky stare right off Jake's face if necessary, regardless of how much pain he was in.

"We're serious," Marc told her, sitting next to her and stroking her hair until she gave him her attention. "When we were down in Mexico last year chasing the son of a bitch who killed Mom's boss, we ran into one of these game players."

"What are you talking about?" London scowled at Marc, looked over at Jake, then heaved a sigh and stared in the mirror at both of them, possibly believing it was a way to appease both of them. "I don't know if my parents were in Mexico, or not."

She had no clue how damn sexy she looked.

"We don't know if they were either. Mom's boss disappeared, which started the hunt," Marc explained, focusing on London's finger when she tapped it against her lips. "We tracked him into Mexico."

"Isn't bounty hunting against the law in Mexico?"

"It's illegal in every country in the world except here and the Philippines," Jake offered.

London looked across the motel room at him, nodding.

"We were very careful," Marc said, shooting Jake a hard look before London returned her attention to him. There wasn't any reason to let her know they'd ended up in jail while down there because they were bounty hunters. The charges were dropped and they were behind bars less than twenty-four hours. He wasn't going to let what he did for a living scare her away. "Some other people disappeared and while we were down there Dad was taken, too."

"Taken?" She looked at Marc wide-eyed. "What do you mean, 'taken'?"

"We were in this small village south of Tijuana in a dump of a motel room." Jake jumped in to tell the story, his expression sobering as his tone dropped to a whispered drawl. "Marc and I were there first, scoping out the place. We were pretty sure we knew where our guy was, a well-known assassin named Marty Byrd."

"Assassin?" London gasped, then began shaking her head. "You hunt down people like assassins?"

"One sadistic son of a bitch," Jake said, nodding. "He was gathering up men that he felt were the best in their field to join him in a game of murder," he continued. "We all knew he wanted Dad. When they came to our room, armed and dangerous, Dad let them capture him so he could get on the inside. We had to take the entire place down to get Dad back out of there. Marty Byrd was killed and so were almost all of his men."

London let out a loud breath, giving herself a fierce shake that caused her long black hair to tumble over her shoulders and past her breasts. She arched her back while sitting cross-legged on the bed, grabbed her hair, and held it in a ponytail with her hands for a moment as she closed her eyes, letting it all sink in. Her breasts pressed against the pale pink knit sweater she had on. Marc watched her nipples harden enough to see them perfectly through the material. He shot a quick glance at Jake, knowing he was enjoying the view, too. Marc was more than ready for his brother to go call it a night in his own room. If London needed assurance that being a bounty hunter wasn't a bad thing, Marc could handle it without help.

"So if this guy was killed, what does any of it have to do with what is going on now?" London turned to Marc, her confusion apparent when she frowned.

"Before he died he told our father he was gathering people to serve as players in a game he was playing."

"I don't understand. What kind of game? And you said he's dead."

"Dad compared it to a game of Risk," Marc told her, watching her expression as he gave her a peek into his life. "He said Byrd, or The Bird, spelled B-I-R-D, as he was known in his circles, wanted Dad to become part of his team. He was building his players and preparing for an attack against other players in the game. We never found out more than that because he was killed."

"Okay, let me see if I understand all of this." London shifted on the bed, and her leg brushed against his. When he put his hand on her thigh, keeping her close, London shot him a look that for a moment didn't look confused. Her eyes were bright with unleashed passion. "Some really bad guy decides he wants to play a board game, but instead of using game pieces, he decided to use people."

"Exactly. As with any board game, there is more than one player. We suspected this all along, but everything got quiet after The Bird was killed. So now we think the rest of the players are organizing their game pieces once again."

She snapped her fingers, smiling at him. "So that is what James Huxtable meant when he said he didn't know which game player had my parents." She looked down, rubbing her face with her hands.

"This is terrible. What kind of mess are my parents mixed up in?" she whispered, for a moment, her defenses down. London probably had years of training appearing strong for the world.

"I don't know," he told her honestly. "But we're going to find out." He caught her gaze and saw her unadulterated fear. Marc's insides boiled to a rage that he fought to suppress for London's sake.

He imagined her childhood might have been anything but normal. Regardless, she seemed to love her parents very much and their disappearance was affecting her more than she wanted him to see. Jake cleared his throat when a moment's silence passed.

London jumped, then exhaled, diverting her gaze and turning as Jake spoke.

"I'm heading to bed." He winked at London. "We'll get our parents out of this mess," he told her. "Don't worry."

Marc came up behind London and put his hands on her shoulders, feeling how tense she was. She slipped behind him when he walked his brother out of the motel room.

"Get a good night's sleep," Marc said, standing outside the door with London leaning against their motel room door watching him. He noticed she kept shooting wary glances at the dark parking lot, and was anxious to get her inside and take that worried look off her face.

"If I didn't feel like I'd just been shot," Jake said, his lazy drawl worse than usual, "I'd be damn jealous of you, having such a hot chick with you and me all alone."

"I'm sure you'll make up for lost time as soon as you're up to it." Marc sensed Jake was in more pain than he let on. The flesh wound looked clean when he'd cleaned it and Marc didn't see any infection, but he knew a flesh wound like that could hurt like hell for days. "Holler at us when you wake up and we'll do the same."

"Night, Bro," Jake mumbled, backing into his room and closing the door.

Marc walked into London when he entered their motel room. She latched her hands behind his neck when he wrapped his arms around her and pulled her to him.

"Are you sure he's okay?" she whispered, her complexion looking exceptionally creamy next to her black eyes and black hair.

"I'm more concerned about you," Marc admitted. "Jake has pain meds and I'd say they're kicking in pretty good right about now. He'll be fine," he told her, continuing to walk her backward until her legs pressed against the bed Jake hadn't been sleeping on when they first arrived. "But if it makes you feel better, I have a key to his room. We can check on him if he doesn't wake up when we do."

She nodded once, chewing her lower lip. "Why are you worried about me? I'm fine."

"You're more than fine, sweetheart," he drawled, hating how he sounded like his brother but wanting to reassure London that she was safe and always would be with him.

"I'm surprised you would say that after hearing about my parents." London's shame over her parents was eating her alive.

"You haven't met my parents yet. I'm nothing like either one of them."

"What? Are they both short and fat?" she teased, making a face at him.

"Mom is short but not fat. Dad is the same size as Jake and I."

"Jake is taller than you are."

"The bigger they are, the harder they fall."

She smiled, although her eyes didn't glow as they usually did when she grinned. He knew she was tired. She had driven most of the way down here. But there was fear and pain lodged deep inside London that he'd never seen before today. Something told him it had been there a long time. Before telling him about her parents, Marc might have mistaken the dull haze that occasionally appeared in her eyes as wariness or uncertainty. London had left her life to join him in retrieving her parents. She wasn't wary or uncertain, and her fear wasn't of her surroundings, but of what he, or anyone, would think of her once they knew her history. Marc intended to do a background check on her parents as soon as he could. In spite of what he learned, he also intended to do what it took to gain London's trust.

When she edged around him, Marc let her go and moved to pull back the blankets on the bed, then arranged the pillows. More than anything he wanted to make love to London but wouldn't push, at least not too much. It was more important that she learn with him she was safe.

"Take whichever side you want." London waved at the bed as if the subject had been an issue.

She disappeared into the bathroom and came out wearing a long T-shirt that fell almost to her knees. She wasn't wearing a bra and he'd bet there were no undies, either. Her choice of pajamas didn't exactly say no sex, but he would still tread those waters carefully. He remained where he was, in between the two beds, and made little ceremony out of undressing. Although London paused and watched him, when Marc glanced up after stepping out of his jeans, she directed her gaze and moved to the head of her side of the bed.

Marc climbed into bed, opting to leave his boxers on, and held out his arm for her to crawl in next to him.

"It's kind of interesting when you think about it," she

mused, sliding under the covers and leaning on her side, staring at him with her head resting against her pillow.

He assumed the same position, leaving the remote on the nightstand and rolled to his side so he faced her. "What's that?" he asked, taking a strand of her hair and playing with it between his fingers.

"You grew up being the son of a cop and I grew up being the daughter of a crook."

He moved his leg over hers, dragging her closer with the lower half of his body, and continued stroking her hair as he lifted his gaze to hers. "I can't imagine what it would have been like," he admitted, wanting her to open up to him and at the same time not completely sure what to say.

"Sometimes it really sucked." She shrugged and stifled a yawn. "I never knew any different, though. There were times when I wished we would stay somewhere long enough for me to make friends and other times when I didn't care."

Marc moved his arm under her neck and pulled her closer. Her soft, warm body fit perfectly against his. She relaxed her head on his forearm and rested her hand on his chest. A powerful tug rose from his gut, the raging desire to protect and care for her overwhelming him so much, for a moment he couldn't speak. It had rubbed him wrong, leaving her the way he did, and now, knowing how displaced her childhood had been and the abandonment issues she must have known, it bit at him fiercely. He wouldn't leave her again, but blurting that out would more than likely scare her back behind her protective shield.

Although it terrified the crap out of him that quite possibly he'd found the woman for him, London just admitted to not having many friends. It explained why such a hot, sexy lady, working at a ski lodge, was single and unattached. The hard shell she'd built around her prevented her from having friends, and also boyfriends.

But Marc had made it through that shell. Now all he had to do was convince her he'd never hurt her.

"I'm not going to leave you again," he whispered, and kissed her forehead.

"Okay," she agreed, her lashes fluttering over her eyes as she relaxed next to him.

London answered so quickly, without hesitating, that it not only did a number on his ego, it also stabbed at his heart. She hadn't batted an eye at his promise—as if she'd heard the same words many times before. How many times had London been left alone while her parents were out breaking the law?

Or was it that her parents dragged her on one heist after another, ordering her to stay hidden and promising to return in a few minutes, but then leaving her for hours, or God forbid, days? Marc's brain wrapped around all different kinds of scenarios, none of them pleasant, and all of them resulting in creating a person gun-shy to commitment, or to a promise never to leave.

Marc doubted London grasped the intensity of his promise. He held her as her breathing slowed until she was asleep, then managed to drift off to sleep with her.

A loud pounding woke him with a start and he jumped to a sitting position, disoriented for a moment. London looked frantically around them, the panicked look on her face waking him up even more.

"What was that?" she asked, her long black hair in disarray around her shoulders and down her back.

"I'm not sure." Marc climbed out of bed, hurrying to his luggage and pulled sweats free from clothes he'd had with him in Colorado.

"It's almost 7:00 A.M.," he said as he donned his

sweatpants, meaning they'd both slept soundly for seven hours. Everything in the room appeared in order.

"Was it someone at the door?" London asked, moving her bare legs off the side of the bed.

"I'm not sure." Marc didn't see anyone through the peephole. When he opened the door, though, there was a package on the ground at his feet. "Stay here!" he ordered, barely turning around to look at London before hurrying out the door.

There wasn't anyone along the sidewalk from one end of the building to the other. A few cars were parked in stalls along the motel and a few more were parked in the parking lot, including Marc's car. He walked toward it as London opened her motel room door.

"What are you doing?" she called out, then, "Oh crap!"

Marc didn't have to turn around to know she'd spotted the package at the door. He wished she would stay in the room, but what mattered more at the moment was searching outside. Whoever knocked on their door did it minutes ago. They couldn't have gotten that far.

"Well hell," Marc complained a few minutes later, and stared at cars driving on the road. He'd been disoriented just long enough after waking up to allow whoever it was who banged on their door enough time to escape. There wasn't anyone outside at all, except him, freezing his balls off standing outside in sweats, barefoot, with no shirt, in the frosty, early morning dawn.

"Marc!" London called across the parking lot, sticking her head out of the door but having enough sense herself not to come outside in the frigid morning air half-naked.

The door next to her opened and a confused-looking Jake stepped outside still wearing the jeans he'd put on the night before. He said something to London and she answered. Before Marc could get across the parking lot to them, Jake had picked up the package off the cement sidewalk outside their doors and was walking into Marc and London's room.

"What the fuck time is it?" Jake scowled, scrubbing his curls into a torrential mess around his head.

Marc took the package out of his brother's hand and walked past him to the desk, sitting down and searching for his pocketknife he usually kept in his pants pocket. "Too goddamned early," he muttered, finding his knife and sliding it under the clear tape that secured the flap on the envelope closed.

"I'll fucking say. Where is the coffee?" Jake was always a prick first thing in the morning and even worse when he was forced awake before he was ready to crawl out of bed. "I'm sound asleep and wake up to you two screaming like the world had come to a fucking end."

"At least you weren't woken up by someone pounding on your door." London put her hands on her hips, looking ready to take him on.

Marc glanced up at both of them but returned his attention to opening the package. London might be able to knock Jake down a size or two, which would be very interesting to watch. Either way, at the moment she looked anything but pleased with him. Marc hated feeling jealous, but he preferred her behaving that way toward his brother to her grinning and falling for his half-assed cheesy lines.

"And if you want coffee you can make it yourself," she added, her expression relaxed but her black eyes sharp. She probably didn't have a clue how sexy she looked with her black hair tumbling around her and her oversized T-shirt showing off her perky breasts and her long, slender legs. "You don't have to come in here grumbling. We were just woken up out of a deep sleep, too."

Jake gave her an appraising once-over, not saying anything for a minute. The silence grew in the room and

Marc paused from opening the package, not sure he was in any hurry to see what wonderful surprise they'd been sent this time. From the feel of it, they were more pictures, but he waited to make sure Jake behaved before adding to the pleasantness of the morning.

"Sorry. I'll be back to my usual charming self once I have coffee." Jake moved closer to Marc, placing his hand over his bandage. It probably hurt like hell now that his pain meds had worn off. "What is it?" he asked, nodding at the package in Marc's hands as he again fingered his bandage and grimaced.

"We're about to find out." Marc slid the pictures out of the envelope. Several glossy eight-by-tens fell free. "Son of a bitch," he hissed, staring at the shot on top.

"What?" London and Jake said at the same time.

Both moved around him and London turned on the lamp that was fixed to the wall above the desk. She let out a cry, covering her mouth with her hand when she got a glimpse of the first picture.

"I knew someone was watching us," she whispered, her voice wavering.

Marc spread three eight-by-tens out on the desk, his anger threatening to boil over as he stared at them. There was a picture of London getting out of his car. The shot made it appear to be daytime, but the motel was in the background and from what she was wearing it was obvious the picture was taken last night when they first arrived here.

The next picture was of London following Marc to the hotel. He carried her luggage. It was the last shot that made him want to hit something—hard. The photographer had narrowed in and taken a picture of London's ass. Marc put his hand over the picture, ready to wad it up and send it flying. London pressed her hands into his shoulders and leaned forward so her cheek brushed against his.

"They took that picture to piss you off," she said.

"They did a damn good job." He wanted to tear it to shreds, howl as loudly as he could while heaving something very heavy and throwing it as far as he could. "They're toying with us. That's what these pictures are about, to get under our skin so we can't think straight."

"That, or to lure you into a trap." London stared at Marc and Jake when both of them looked at her. "I mean, think about it. Why send these pictures? Why even bother? If they kidnapped our parents and wanted money they would send a ransom note. But they aren't doing that. I can't for the life of me think why they would want me, but I'm willing to bet whoever took your parents, and mine, wants the two of you, too."

"I can imagine why they would want you," Jake drawled.

Marc stood quickly, forcing London to jump backward when he sent his chair flying in Jake's direction. "Now isn't a good time for comments like that," he warned Jake.

"Man, I'm not flirting with her. Just chill out. She's all yours." Jake sounded disgusted. In Jake's own way, though, he just accepted Marc and London being a couple, which was high praise. Jake never liked admitting something was all Marc's. "All I'm doing is pointing out the obvious."

"I know how hot she is," Marc said under his breath and gave in to his anger and frustration. He crumpled the picture of London's ass with his fist.

"Marc," London began.

He stood, moving around Jake.

"It's bad enough knowing these assholes managed to take our parents," he began when he faced London. Marc gripped either side of her head, tangling his fingers in her tousled hair. "I can't bear the thought of them wanting you, too, for any reason."

"I'm not completely incapable of taking care of myself," she informed him.

She was serious. Imagining London defending herself against the men in the pictures they'd already received curdled his blood. If any of them so much as tried laying a hand on her . . .

"Okay then," Jake said, clearing his throat and slapping Marc on the back. I'm going to try and shower and get dressed. I'll be back in a few and we can head out." He opened the motel room door, waving over his shoulder.

"We're heading back down to Canyon Diablo," Marc told him, letting go of London and returning to the desk and the crumpled picture.

"I already know that." Jake let the door shut behind him.

"Canyon Diablo?" London asked.

She was shifting from one foot to the other, her hair streaming down her front as she stared down at her hands. Sensing Marc was studying her, she straightened, meeting his gaze with her own determined look. The pictures upset her and she was trying really hard not to let it show.

"Yes. That's where Jake got shot."

Her eyes widened. "Why do you want to go back there?"

"Because they don't want us there."

"Are you so sure about that?"

Marc combed his fingers into her hair until they snagged, causing London to tilt back her head and look up at him as he explained his hunch.

"Whoever was shooting at us had damn good aim. Most can't come close to a target when they're firing from the distance our attacker was. I never saw a soul. And it was an open area. Even after I got Jake in the car, I drove to the only cluster of rocks where someone could have been hiding. There wasn't anyone there. No one could have run to a new hiding place without me seeing them. There just weren't that many places to take cover."

"So what are you saying?" she asked, wrinkling her brow but relaxing her face in his hands.

"I can't be one hundred percent sure about anything. This isn't a line of work with any hard-core guarantees. My father often claimed he was working from a hunch," he tried explaining. Marc hoped his gut would lead them as well as his father's always had. "I think they were testing us, seeing how we would react to being shot."

"To see if you'd make good soldiers for their game?" London pushed away from him, backing up as she crossed her arms over her chest, and continued frowning. "So you think whoever sent those pictures, took our parents, and sent broken dolls in the mail is also testing you two by shooting at you?"

"More than likely to see if we'll come back. London, it's a ghost town. There's nothing there but some rocks and old graves. It's not around any buildings or anything, just out there in the middle of nowhere by itself. There's no reason anyone would have shot at us. We weren't trespassing or disturbing anything."

"Obviously whoever is behind this isn't sane." London pushed past Marc and went to her suitcase, bending over and teasing him with a glimpse of her ass. She pulled clean clothes out of her bag, then headed for the bathroom but paused in the doorway and looked at him. "Which would make whoever is doing this dangerous, and unpredictable."

London soaked in the shower a lot longer than she normally would. She was so distracted by their conversation, she'd forgotten to grab her shampoo and conditioner. The small bottles the motel offered were barely enough to cover her hair. Without conditioner, her hair would be frizzy all day. Not that she should care. It wasn't as if she needed to look her best to visit a ghost town where there might, or might not be, a killer. There was only one reason why she cared how she looked. And she needed to give that reason some good hard thought. Maybe it would be best to slow things down with Marc, work with him and Jake to find both of their parents, but then call it quits. Why did she have to fall for a guy who risked his life on a daily basis?

She would go nuts, be absolutely insane. London pressed her hands against the shower wall and lowered her head, letting the water spray over her. She'd led a nice, quiet, peaceful life for the past three years. It was the life she'd always dreamed of: no guns, no violence. Sure, there were times when she was lonely, times when she wished the perfect man was in bed with her, the two of them sharing a life together. Today she had a nice home that was the same every night when she came back to it. She didn't have to worry about it being yanked away from her. No one was going to shoot her and no one she loved would be shot.

Images of Jake's bandaged shoulder made her cringe. That could just as easily have been Marc. Next time it might be. And there would always be a next time. Marc hunted bad guys. And apparently some bad guys hunted him as well. The pictures at their motel room door this morning were proof of that. They weren't the same as the pictures before, which she believed were intended to inform her and Marc that their parents were in trouble. These were sent to piss them off. London hated letting someone she didn't know affect her life like this. Not to mention, the man she was just getting to know who was affecting her life even more.

This was definitely pissing her off.

It had been bad enough when she was growing up and was old enough to figure out what her parents were up to and know every time they left her they might not come back. She saw the guns, understood the dangers of her parents' line of work. And she'd hated it. London had vowed over and over again not to live her life like that once she was old enough to be on her own. The second she came of age, she'd done just that. She was a law-abiding citizen who didn't do anything to bring trouble upon herself. Apparently she forgot to add to that list of rules not to fall for a bounty hunter, which would bring on the same amount of pain and anguish as living with two criminals.

"Damn it to hell and back," she hissed, hitting the shower wall with her fist. That was exactly what she'd done, too. It was too late. She'd already fallen true and hard for Marc King; otherwise she wouldn't be so pissed off right now. If she didn't care about him as much as she did, it wouldn't bother her so desperately that he was headed right back to the exact same spot where he and Jake were almost killed the day before.

London straightened, shoving wet hair over her shoulder, when the bathroom door opened.

"Are you okay?" Marc asked.

She must have hit the shower wall harder than she realized. "Yes," she told him. "No. I don't know." She was most definitely not okay.

"Care if I join you?" he asked.

Immediately her insides soared. A pressure built inside her, her pussy started throbbing, and the quickening in her gut almost made her stagger. Regardless of what her brain thought, her body very much wanted him to join her. She'd fallen asleep last night and missed an opportunity to make love to him. Now her body screamed—demanded—let him in and fuck him now.

"That's fine," she heard herself say, even as her brain and body continued arguing.

Obviously, her body was bigger than her brain.

Marc took almost all of the space when he came around the shower curtain, his large body barely fitting in the average-sized bathtub and shower. His hands were on her immediately, holding her by the waist as he helped her move to the back of the shower. When he let her go and turned his back to her, ducking into the shower spray, London got an eyeful of his well-defined muscles bulging along either side of his spine. She also discovered a few new scars. War wounds. Proof he was a lifer, as her dad used to say whenever London cuddled next to him, or her mom, found a new scar, and traced it with her finger.

"Think of them as trophies." Her father's voice was as clear in her head as if he stood next to her. London had later found out "lifer" didn't mean someone sentenced to life in prison. It meant someone committed to a life of crime. A "lifer" was a person who knew from their first heist that they'd be a criminal for life.

London shivered and forced the old memory to go away. Her hands were on Marc's back and she yanked them away. She wasn't sure when she'd started touching him.

Marc's chuckle was a deep baritone. "Feel free to scrub my back while you're at it."

She glared at the back of his head but didn't trust herself to speak.

When her gaze travelled down him, his ass looked hard as steel. She itched to touch it, run her fingers down it, and grab him from behind. Forcing her attention higher, watching roped muscle twitch and flex in his biceps and triceps, didn't help her any. London's mouth watered, heat rushed over her, and the steam trapped in the bathroom suddenly made her light-headed. When soap started flowing down Marc's body she thought she might swoon from the need to have him. It didn't matter how many scars she counted. She wanted to fuck him so desperately it washed all of her anger away. Later she would worry about him killing his sexy ass. Right now she just wanted him inside her.

"Something occurred to me just now," Marc said, breaking the silence when he turned his back to the shower and started scrubbing his front side.

"What's that?" She could barely speak. His cock was fully erect. Soapy water streamed around it, getting caught in the dark, tight curls at the base of it. But Marc's smooth, thick, hard cock called her name loud enough to make her ears ring and blood pump through her veins faster than it should.

"The package the pictures showed up in today wasn't addressed to anyone. The pictures sent to your home, and to my family, were addressed and posted. They'd gone through the mail. These this morning were hand-delivered."

It took everything she had to focus on his face and not that virile body of his. She heard what he said and tried to guess his meaning.

"They would have had to mail them to the motel. Whoever it was wanted to make sure we received the pictures and so pounded on the door, dropped the package, and ran." London watched his gaze drop down her body when he nodded his agreement. She swore her flesh singed with energy wherever he focused.

"It means they are here, somewhere in Flagstaff." He turned sideways, letting the water rinse off the soap." Dad would have my ass for not spotting the obvious sooner."

"You've been a bit distracted."

"Don't ever defend me to my father, please." Marc chuckled sardonically as he wiped his fingers down her cheek. "A good bounty hunter doesn't allow distractions."

"I'll do my best not to become one," she said, her tummy twisting into knots from the meaning behind his words.

This time Marc's laughter was more sincere. "You'd distract a blind man," he told her, grinning, then tweaked her nipple.

Sparks exploded inside her and shot straight down her middle to her pussy. London gasped and felt the heat grow inside her as his grin turned into an enticing smirk.

"The pictures taken of your parents and mine when they were captured offer a clear view of the buildings in the background. Jake and I recognized one of those buildings as a bed-and-breakfast we all stayed at on one of our family vacations when we were kids. That's why we came here. All of our parents were here in town and might still be here." His gaze travelled hungrily over her even as he continued brainstorming.

"It would explain why they shot at us," he muttered more to himself. But when he met her gaze, his light blue eyes darkened a magnificent shade. "Maybe they weren't testing us. We were just getting too close."

Marc's theory made sense and he looked rather satisfied with himself for thinking it through. She imagined him piecing together clues all of the time. With a father as a cop, Marc probably grew up learning how to solve crimes. London grew up hearing how to commit them. Her parents didn't raise her to be a criminal. And she wasn't any worse or better of a person than Marc. London could only imagine what her father would think of him, though.

"Then I guess we'd better hurry with this shower so you can go get them." Her voice sounded flat, but she wouldn't cry. Marc was damn near perfect. But the look on his face reminded her of her father's right before he raced out the door into some perilous, life-threatening situation. She'd hated it then and refused to let herself live through it again.

It sucked mourning the loss of someone before she ever had the chance to truly love them.

Chapter Eleven

London wrapped fresh gauze around Jake's shoulder. It amazed her how clean the wound looked and how quickly it was healing.

"I take really good care of myself," Jake explained, glancing over his shoulder at her with that crooked grin planted on his face.

A couple cups of coffee sure did transform his personality.

"It sucks we can't take more time to plan this out and bring in the big guns," Marc said, pacing the length of the bed and pausing, staring at the piece of typing paper they'd used to draw a map of the ruins at Canyon Diablo. "There's not time, though, to get what we need to do this any other way than what we're going to do. Dad's never going to let me live this down if it takes too long to rescue them."

He looked at her and London swore there was an apology in his eyes. She wouldn't let him see how all of this bothered her. They were going in after their parents. London pictured the shot of her father, looking pissed as hell. Where were her parents right now? Were they in some jail cell, being tortured, coerced into joining some kind of militia? Were both of their parents together? That would be interesting.

"You got him wrapped up?" Marc asked.

"Yeah. It's hard to believe it's a gunshot wound."

"How many gunshot wounds have you seen?" Marc asked.

She hesitated. "A few."

"Can you shoot?" Jake stood, rolled his shoulder, and twisted to get a look at her handiwork.

The times her father had taken her target practicing when they'd lived in Indiana were some of her better childhood memories. They'd shot tin cans until London could hit her target almost every time. The pride in her dad's eyes made her look forward to any time he would take her out there.

"I can shoot," she said, glancing at the guns the two of them had already cleaned and loaded.

"We should use her, too," Jake suggested, reaching for his shirt and pulling it over his head.

"No," Marc said, slicing his hand through the air.

"Wait a minute," she said, studying him as his frown deepened. "Do you think I can't shoot?"

"I'm sure you can," he said, dismissing her comment and walking over to the laptop. "We're going to drive down there. I want to drive past the ruins to those rocks before we park. This time we'll have daylight in our favor."

"We've got our guns, mom and dad's, and binoculars," Jake said, then nudged a black bag on the edge of the bed." There's bottles of water in there and a few snack bars."

"It's not a lot." Marc shook his head and sighed, then shut down the laptop. "Hopefully Dad and Mom, and her parents, have been fed. We've got the rooms reserved for another day?"

"Yup," Jake said.

London watched them meticulously continue through their checkoff sheet as they armed themselves. She suddenly felt very naked going with them and being unarmed.

"Marc." She stepped in front of him when Jake started to the door. "I want a gun, too."

It wasn't something she ever thought she'd hear herself say. Up until very recently, London would have laughed at anyone who told her she'd be running with bounty hunters, carrying a gun, and chasing after someone who'd kidnapped her parents.

"London, I'm not sure," he began.

She put her hands on his chest. "Since I first met you, I begged for you to display some kind of trait that would turn me off. I really didn't want any kind of relationship with you at all," she told him, whispering.

Marc's mouth opened, but he didn't say anything. She took advantage of his stunned reaction and continued before she chickened out and didn't say what needed to be said.

"Learning you were a bounty hunter didn't turn me off. I tried to convince myself that someone who knew more about breaking the law would never make it with someone sworn to uphold it."

"Actually, I'm not sworn," he began.

She placed her finger on his lips. "Let me say this," she pressed, a sense of urgency hitting her. "Then this morning, listening to the two of you plan to return to where Jake was shot, and knowing you did this all the time, was the first time I wavered. I panicked. This was the reaction to you I wanted. I'd prayed for something about you that I wouldn't be able to stomach, so I could walk away. Because if I don't walk away from you I'm going to fall in love with you," she said, speaking faster and managing a breath.

This time Marc didn't say anything. He stared down at

her, his blue eyes darkening, her only indication that emotions were climaxing inside him. He didn't interrupt, though, so she gulped in another breath and got the rest of it out.

"The more you talked about guns, seeking out this bad guy, rescuing our parents, the more real it became. Jake has already been shot. You might get shot. This is how your life is. How can I live every day with you knowing that you could be shot at any time? I was convinced I'd found my out."

"You were convinced?" he asked, searching her face. "What changed your mind?"

"Nothing," she insisted. "But today, when we leave this room, we're going after our parents. You have no idea how many times I've been left behind, believed I'd been forgotten, or finally the day had arrived when my parents would never come back." She let out a choked laugh. "It made me nauseous every time they walked out the door."

London dropped her hand and focused on his chest, unsure if she could get the rest of what needed to be said out if he started looking like he felt sorry for her.

"I've sat here listening to both of you all morning and came to a decision."

"What's that?" His tone sounded guarded.

"I'm going to rescue my parents."

Marc nodded once, reached inside his coat pocket, and pulled out a small handgun. It would protect her against anyone trying to attack her, but that was about it. He'd saved the good stuff for himself. More than likely he believed he would be rescuing both of their parents and covering her ass at the same time. It would fit his nature and arguing over it would waste more time. She wouldn't bother telling him she would cover his ass, too.

"Thank you," she said, taking the gun and checking the safety, then confirmed it was loaded.

"Here," he said, reaching for his leather holster.

"No." She smiled up at him, trying not to dwell on how incredibly gorgeous and concerned he looked as he focused on her. "This is a secret my dad taught me when I was a kid," she said, sliding the gun inside her coat and into the pocket next to her chest. "If you're frisked, the first thing they will do is pat down your body, especially if you're a woman." She couldn't help grinning when every inch of him tightened at her comment. "After they pat down your front, they turn you around, pat down your backside. That is when you pull your gun and ensure your freedom."

"Your father taught you how to escape if you were arrested?" Marc's look of disbelief was classic.

"Are you two about done?" Jake stood by the motel room door. "Let's get out of here."

"On our way," Marc said over his shoulder, but then grabbed her, his actions rougher than usual. She stumbled against him as he held on to the side of her head, twisting his fingers through her hair. "Did he also tell you that long hair could work against you? There's very few men on this planet who don't get off yanking a woman by her hair," he whispered, pulling her closer until he gripped her jaw and pulled her face to his. "Now it's my turn to tell you something, London. Be scared all you want. Be terrified. I'm not letting you go, though. Put your hair up. The only man who is ever going to pull it will be me. Understand?"

She nodded, her heart suddenly throbbing so hard in her chest she could hardly breathe. Marc lowered his mouth to hers, his kiss hot and demanding. When someone pounded on the motel room door, she yelped, her heart exploding in her chest.

"Who the hell is that?" Jake had his back to them, blocking the door.

Whoever it was knocked again, the repetitive rap sounding how it did when someone woke them up that morning. Instinctively she leapt out of Marc's arms, backing as far from the door as she could. The weight of the gun in her coat brought more comfort than she expected. London patted it, and kept her hand over the gun, feeling the hard metal, and the shape of it, press against her body as she moved behind Marc. With both men in front of her now, their large frames making it impossible to see the door, she should have felt a bit of comfort when the impatient knocking sounded again. Instead her world turned into a surreal experience, with first her instincts kicking into high gear, then reality shoving in right beside it.

She wasn't sure what compelled her to dive to the ground when Jake opened the door. Most likely old habits die hard. London scrambled alongside the bed farthest from the door. It had been a lot easier to scurry under beds when she'd been a child. She didn't remember her heart going off like a jackhammer when she'd been younger and rushed to a safe hiding place. But it did. It beat so hard against her ribs the pain was excruciating. Not as painful, though, as when she'd bashed her knee and forehead simultaneously against the pedestal under the bed.

"Hello, gentlemen. Welcome to Flagstaff," a deep, smooth-sounding male voice said, his tone a bit too friendly.

There wasn't anywhere to hide. A panic attack worse than any she'd ever had as a kid ransacked her system. London rolled toward the bed, trying to scoot under the blankets hanging off the side and knowing if she tugged on them to cover herself someone would see them move off the bed.

"Who the hell are you?" Marc demanded, his bellowing baritone sounding pissed off and dangerous.

"Your escort into the game." The humor in the man's

tone was terrifying. "The two of you should be honored. Marty Byrd underestimated your skills and talents, unlike me. Shall we go?"

"We're not going anywhere with you," Jake growled.

Something crashed and London was sure she screamed. She bit her lip and her heart pounded so hard in her chest it hurt. Her eyes watered so furiously she couldn't see, and the floor shaking from large men slamming into one another was making her sick to her stomach. There was no way to know if moving or staying put would be smarter.

The skirmish that followed ended in seconds. London remained flat on the floor, staring at the ceiling and breathing so hard everyone probably heard her. There wasn't any slowing her heart down, though. Every muscle in her body clenched with terrified anticipation. She hurt from head to toe. It was all she could do to catch her breath. The worst part was, London had learned many years before that trying not to move, not to breathe, not to be seen, was easily as painful as being part of a brawl in the middle of a motel room.

And why was it that fights always happened in motel rooms? There were no good hiding places. There was even less room to fight.

This was the life she vowed to give up. What the hell was she doing here? Whether it be a good or bad guy, the life for London would be the same. It meant continual fear for her life, and for those she loved.

She strained her eyes until they burned, frantically trying to see as far over the top of the bed as she could, knowing someone would appear any moment and snatch her up. Every time someone moved it was as if he jumped as hard as he could, making the floor move. Her stomach continued churning, motion sickness and panic making for a terrible combination.

The grunts and profanity continued as large bodies

knocked into furniture and one another. There wasn't any way everyone in the entire motel wouldn't be able to hear the fighting. Someone would call the police. Someone would come running.

London was afraid to breathe as she waited for the first gunshot to go off. She didn't know who was winning the fight. In her frantic state a clear thought actually slid through. She needed to protect herself. Marc and Jake were incredibly tall men and probably very skilled in their line of work. That didn't mean they could dodge a bullet or stop these men from winning by sheer force. The good guys didn't always win. Her parents were proof of that.

She shook, desperately trying to slide her hand inside her coat. If she looked down to see what she was doing she would miss the first glimpse of anyone moving to this side of the bed. She had to be ready.

As she wrapped her fingers around the cold metal of the gun inside her pocket, the room grew silent. She prayed for the ringing in her head to go away so she could hear everything. But it was quiet, too damn quiet.

"Where is your pretty girlfriend?" That cocky, rich tone made her jump.

"She went to her room," Marc said, sounding winded.

"What is her room number?"

"Go to hell." Marc grunted loudly when someone hit him.

London fought the urge to squeeze her eyes closed. She wanted to disappear until this entire ugly nightmare was over. She would do anything to back time up, even just a few minutes, to when she was standing with Marc, in his arms once again. She couldn't close her eyes, though. Her life depended on them staying open. Instead she slipped the gun out of her pocket, held on to it, and moved her finger to the trigger as she slid it down her body. She would have to shoot whoever appeared at the end of the bed. And she had to aim to kill or seriously injure. It was her life or his.

"Find his bitch," the man ordered, still sounding way too amused. "Bring her straight to me."

She jumped when the motel room door closed and was terrified that she yelped again. When it grew unbearably quiet London didn't know whether to jump up and chase after them or stay where she was. Was she alone in the room? Her eyes burned from trying to see over the top of the bed without moving her head.

Oh God. There was a footstep. Someone was in the room. London held the gun with both hands, feeling sweat bead over her flesh as terror continued to hold her in a death grip. When a man appeared over her, London raised her gun, pointed at his face, and fired.

Marc couldn't get the nauseous feeling out of his gut. London was on her own, left unprotected shy of the small handgun he'd given her that wouldn't do much damage unless she shot at close range. God. He wouldn't have given her a gun at all. She'd insisted and that was the only reason she had any protection right now. What the hell was wrong with him? He wasn't some chauvinistic pig. He'd seen how his father protected his mother, when she was perfectly capable of covering her ass.

The urge to protect London had overwhelmed him. When she'd spoken to him right before the men showed up at the door, everything inside him had seized up. Marc didn't know the details of her upbringing. He wanted to know. He wanted to know everything about her. But from the bits and pieces she'd shared with him it was clear it was a life she wanted no part of. All she'd seen of him so far was a life of running and violence. London didn't want any part of it.

Marc stared out the window of the backseat of the black

Ford Explorer where he sat, handcuffed, with Jake next to him. The driver and the man who had done all the talking in the motel room were up front. Marc glanced over his shoulder and saw their goons following in a pickup. His attention shot forward, though, when they slowed.

Where the hell were they going?

He stared at the ruins of Canyon Diablo where Jake was shot the other night. There wasn't anything here. If they were going to pull him and Jake out of the SUV out here in the middle of nowhere, they might have a chance. A very slim chance. He and Jake were handcuffed, but one of these bastards would have a key on him. It would be a tough fight, but Marc prepared himself for it, feeling his muscles bulge and the handcuffs tighten at his wrists. One glance at Jake told Marc he was just as eager for the chance to regain his freedom.

Son of a bitch, Marc thought to himself when they came to a stop at the group of rocks just past the ruins. He'd driven past these when Jake was shot, certain their shooter had been hiding behind the rocks. He hadn't been; he'd been hiding underneath them. The SUV went off the road and came to a stop. Marc stared in disbelief when the ground ahead of them caved in and a cloud of dust blew up into the cold morning air. When it cleared there was a road going into the ground. Darkness surrounded them as they descended into the underground tunnel, but Marc met Jake's gaze. He shook his head, frowning. How would anyone ever find them down here?

The driver flipped on his headlights and a loud banging noise, metal against metal, sounded behind them. Marc jumped, twisting in the seat fast enough to see a flat door secured into place, concealing them from the world above. His anger spiked all over again when he met the man's gaze in the rearview mirror and saw him smiling. The driver stopped the SUV and turned it off as a series of lights flipped on around them. That's when Marc realized the goons in the pickup truck didn't follow them down here.

"Shall we, gentlemen?" The tall black-haired man smiled at him and Jake, stepping out of the front seat of the black SUV.

The driver got out as well. The two men opened Jake's and Marc's doors for them. Marc slid out on his side, glaring down at the sharp-dressed man who was too smooth of a talker. If the man really believed handcuffs rendered Marc useless, Marc would enjoy showing him otherwise. He stepped into the man, standing easily five or six inches taller than the asshole.

"You are seriously going to regret this," Marc promised, whispering so only the jerk heard him.

"We'll have London with us safe and sound in no time." The bastard smiled at Marc, fool enough not to even look nervous. "There's no reason for you to worry about her."

The fact that he would comment on London when Marc implied he would regret his actions warned Marc the man was hot on the pursuit of capturing her, if he hadn't already.

"Touch one head on her hair and I swear to God I'll kill you myself," Marc hissed under his breath.

"Your devotion to her is commendable, but I don't think being obsessed with her will be an asset to your role. You haven't known her long enough to create an unbreakable bond. I'm sure it will fade with time." The man laughed as he walked away from Marc.

Marc leapt in the air, kicking the man square in the back and enjoying immense satisfaction when the pompous jerk screamed and slid forward across the cement floor. Marc landed on his feet, grounding himself and ready to take on whoever came at him next. This would end here, while there were vehicles, when he was close to the exit. No way in hell would he become captive to some arrogant little runt who wouldn't quit smiling like some annoying pretty boy.

Something zapped Marc in the shoulder, sending a fierce pain down his back.

"Son of a bitch," he howled, damn near falling to his knees.

"Get them both out of here!" the man yelled, struggling to his feet and dusting off his overcoat. He wasn't smiling anymore and the humorous gleam in his eyes was gone. "Lock them up good and tight, but don't beat them senseless." This time his laughter bordered on demonic instead of defiant. "We don't want to break that raw King spirit, now do we?"

The man walked over to the wall and pressed a large button that buzzed loudly, echoing off the garage walls. Marc turned on the driver and eyeballed a long metal stick he held in his hand. It had shocked the living crap out of Marc. His muscles still twitched painfully, making it hard to move. The guy had a large gun in his other hand, large enough to blow a hole clean through a man. Marc shifted his attention to Jake, who came around the back of the SUV, the fire in his eyes showing how furious he was.

"You want to knock the pretty stick out of his hand, or the gun?" Jake asked, glaring at the man.

This guy didn't appear as confident as his leader did and took a step backward, raising the gun and pointing it from one of them to the other.

"I wouldn't advise either," the man behind them said, his cocky attitude returning.

Marc turned when a door opened and five men, easily as tall as he and Jake were, entered the garage and surrounded the two of them.

"Sure you brought enough of your goons?" Jake asked.

The man laughed. "You get your cockiness from your

father. This really is going to be fun." His grin broadened as he rubbed his hands together. "I will definitely be the victor. Let's go, men."

Marc had seen insanity before. It came in variations, the symptoms appearing in different ways in different people. A psychiatrist might have different labels, but the way Marc saw it, people were right in the head or they weren't. Whoever this captor of theirs was, he was definitely certifiably insane. The man whistled, almost skipping, as he led the way down a long, narrow ramp to another door where once again he pushed a large button on the wall. When the door opened, a flood of fluorescent light was almost blinding.

They weren't on cement anymore but plush carpeting, and a high ceiling overhead arched above them. The walls were painted a pale pink, probably something Marc's mother or Natasha would refer to as mauve. There were large pictures hanging around them, adding color to the very large room. The man walked over to an expensive-looking desk, moving behind it and sitting. He appeared very satisfied with himself when he leaned back, steepled his fingers, and rested his elbows on the armrests of the high-back leather chair he graced as if it were a throne.

"Lock them up for now and meet me back here," he instructed, dismissing them with a wave of his hand and turning to his computer.

Marc growled at the man who nudged him in the back but saw no other option at the moment but to walk with them across the room to another door. This one didn't require a button to be pushed but opened when one of them turned the handle. Apparently security diminished once they were inside this underground office building. Marc wondered how long it had been here.

They entered what easily could be defined as a jail. The hallway was narrow and bars were on the other side. One of the men moved ahead of them, stopping and unlocking the jail cell. Marc walked in front of Jake but stopped when he spotted his parents.

"Dad," he said as his mother jumped up from where she'd been sitting and ran to the bars.

"My God, Jake! Marc!" She grabbed the bars, her eyes welling with tears. Their dad was behind her in seconds, grabbing her shoulders and pulling her back as he eyed the men surrounding his sons warily. "Are you two okay?" she demanded.

"Pissed, but fine. How about you two?" Marc faced them, ignoring the man when he held the cell open that was directly across from Marc's parents. "Any clue what this place is?"

Greg nodded his head, a gesture barely noticeable toward the man who held open the cell door. Jake reacted first. Bulldozing into the man with the keys, Jake rammed him into the prison cell, sending the keys in his hands flying across the floor.

Marc turned on the men behind them, not having as much room this time but managing to jump in the air and attack with his legs again. The metal around his wrists rubbed fiercely against bone, causing just enough pain to fuel his anger even further. He'd picked up on his father's suggestion quickly, knowing this might be their last chance for escape before they were all locked behind bars. Marc had been surprised to see his parents. It pissed him off further that he hadn't seen this opportunity to attack.

Marc swore he heard bones snap as the man he made contact with howled and fell backward into the men behind him. It was like a domino effect, their large captors toppling backward into one another with Marc damn near falling on top of them. He'd left his brother on his own to take on the guy with the keys and prayed Jake could handle it. Marc did his best to regain his balance in time to attack again, needing to keep the three men he was attacking distracted long enough for Jake to get the keys and slide them across the floor to his parents.

"Over here!" Marc heard his father yell.

"Jake!" his mother screamed. "Watch out!"

Marc leapt again, hearing the men yelling and not paying attention to anything they were saying. Tunnel vision seemed to take over, his only focus taking down each of the men as effectively as possible. Being handcuffed seriously sucked and hindered his efforts, but he gave it hell, determined not to let them take him down.

He kicked higher the second time and watched blood splatter across the face of the man he'd attacked. Jake screamed behind him, howling at the same time an alarm sounded. Its repetitive piercing sound was deafening and made it impossible to hear when his father yelled.

Marc staggered backward and felt his mother's hands on him. Whether she was trying to grab him or help to push him back at the guards he couldn't tell. He used his brother's tactics with his third attack, lowering his head and bulldozing into the two remaining guards standing. They were giant men, built of steel, and he swore his neck snapped in two as he drove into them with everything he had.

It was that damn black stick. He saw it for only a second as his vision cleared. The electric charge that surged through him sizzled his flesh and racked every muscle in his body. Marc howled, hearing his own voice and his throat burn when he screamed from the pain that tore his body in two. He flew backward, losing control of his own actions as the voltage ripping him apart sent him flying into the jail cell bars behind him.

He hit the ground hard, aware of his mother crying out in fear as his vision blurred. No matter how hard he tried to overcome the electricity that was paralyzing him, he couldn't regain control fast enough to defend himself. He saw the gun aimed at him, heard a popping sound, and everything went black.

London sat in a parking lot, gripping the steering wheel of Marc's car, and tried to remember how to breathe. She'd just killed a man. His blood was splattered on her clothes. The police would be called. They would find the body. It was probably a matter of minutes before they would find her and take her to jail. No one would believe her story. She wasn't in her own car. She didn't live in this town. At the moment she didn't even have ID on her. She'd left her purse in the motel room.

She dropped her head against the steering wheel. "Damn, damn, damn," she cursed, rolling her forehead against the bumps on the steering wheel and moaning over her stupidity and foolishness. She might as well have left a calling card for the cops to come find her. "I have to go back. God. Crap. I can't go back."

Life as she knew it was over. The years she'd managed to pull off being a law-abiding citizen, swearing she would never be like her parents, were nothing but a joke, existing to taunt her. In a matter of seconds she'd ended all of that. She could still hear the gunfire in her head. It was all worse than a nightmare and she didn't have a clue how to fix any of it. The only things she had on her right now were the murder weapon, her cell phone, and the key card to the motel room.

Like there was anyone she could call for help. Marc was gone. No one at her work had a clue why she was here. There wasn't anyone to turn to. She was on her own to figure her way out of the worst disaster imaginable. Not to mention, not only were her parents still missing, but now Marc and Jake were gone, too. She hadn't caught a glimpse of the men who took them.

"It's all too incredible for anyone to even believe."

Leaning back in the seat, she tried for a few calming breaths, staring at the parking lot where she'd stopped driving after fleeing from the motel. Cars drove up and down the road; more than one pulled into the parking lot and parked. People walked in and out of the large grocery store at the other end of the lot. No one noticed her.

"Okay, maybe you have a few minutes. Think, girl. Think this through." Being a criminal was in her blood whether she liked it or not. She wasn't sure either of her parents had ever murdered anyone, though. Her parents might have been good enough at what they did never to have been caught, but it wasn't as if they'd spent time trying to teach her the trade. Which up until now she'd believed had been the one good thing they'd done for her.

She should go to the cops. London straightened, glancing down at her clothes. The dark splotches staining her coat and jeans taunted her, and they stunk. Would the cops believe her if she walked into the police station looking the way she did now and told them the entire story? There was proof. She could argue self-defense, show them the pictures and the notes that were with them. Then she would tell the police how she came down here with Marc. He was part of a reputable business. Maybe the cops would have heard of KFA. They would know she was with the good guys. She would explain how she was trying to find her parents when men showed up and took Marc and Jake. She hid and thought she was alone, but then she wasn't alone. All she did was pull the trigger. Cops shot guns all the time. They would know how easy it was to pull that little trigger. The damage done was irreversible.

"Holy crap! I've shot a man," she wailed, letting her head fall against the steering wheel again. "I can't believe I've shot a man."

If she went into the police station right now, they would

have her committed before they even took time to hear her story. Suddenly the car seemed too small. She needed to get out, to breathe fresh air, to walk off this insanity surrounding her until she could think clearly.

London shed her coat, struggling until she could throw it in the backseat. Her legs were wobbly when she climbed out of Marc's car, then leaned against the open door, gulping in the cold air as she stared at her surroundings. She would take a short, quick walk and figure her way out of this mess. It was cold outside but not intolerable. Her heart was pounding so hard in her chest that her blood pressure would keep her from freezing. Right now it had to be off the charts. If she didn't wear her coat, there wasn't as much dried blood on her.

She squatted next to the door, glancing around her again to make sure no one was watching, then tried getting a look at herself in the side mirror. London barely recognized the wild-eyed look that stared back at her. There wasn't any blood on her face, though; that was good enough for now. Straightening, her legs seemed to turn into wet noodles for a moment. She braced herself, pressing her hand against the cold metal of the car. Then making sure she had the keys and that it was locked, she patted her cell phone in her jeans pocket before closing the car door and taking slow, careful steps across the parking lot.

London wondered if insane people felt more sane when they walked among other sane people. No one seemed to pay any attention to her. It was a good sign. At least on the outside she appeared normal. That was other than the drying blood on her jeans that made them feel tight and stiff. But walking was good. She fingered her hair, working to comb it and look presentable.

After a few minutes she decided she'd mastered walking. And appearing normal. Lord. She was going insane. She was walking up and down aisles in a grocery store, commending herself every time she passed someone and they didn't look at her. This was accomplishing a hell of a lot.

Maybe it was, though. Her head was clearer and now she could pragmatically create options of what to do next. The obvious solution was to tell someone what had happened. She didn't have a clue where Marc and Jake were. She hadn't even seen the vehicle they'd taken off in. It crossed her mind to try calling Marc, but she wasn't sure at the moment if he even had his cell phone on him and she didn't know Jake's number. Not to mention, they might be able to locate her if she tried calling. She wasn't sure what all could be done with a cell phone.

By the time she was back out in the parking lot, she'd created a list of several options. Go to the police. Go back to the motel room. Take Marc's car and return to Aspen and pretend none of this ever happened.

"Like you would do that," she said to herself, ignoring the first person who did look at her when she spoke to herself. There was one incredibly strong possibility she couldn't ignore. Whoever took Marc and Jake were probably still looking for her, too.

"God, they're probably combing this town right now trying to find me." She stopped at the door to the Mustang, staring frantically around her, this new realization hitting her hard enough to rob her of her next breath. London started hyperventilating and bent over, worried she might puke. "You've got to hide. But if you hide, then what good will you be?"

She made one hell of a lousy criminal. She was an even worse bounty hunter. It was up to her to find Marc, his brother, her parents, and his parents and she didn't have a clue how to do any of that.

London gripped her hips, straightening slowly as a thought occurred to her. Maybe she didn't know how to hunt people. But she knew someone who did. Pulling her phone out of her pocket, she searched through the numbers she'd recently called. When she found the number she needed, she unlocked the car and climbed in, pushing the button on her phone to place the call.

"KFA," the pleasant female voice on the other end of the line said.

Chapter Twelve

"Hold on a minute," Natasha silenced London after a few minutes of listening as London shared the horrific events that had just transpired. "Where are you?"

London took a deep breath. Everything she'd just told Natasha sounded insane even to her and she'd just lived through it. "I'm sitting in Marc's car in a parking lot." She glanced over at the grocery store and the people hurrying in and out of it, business as usual. At least for the rest of the world. "I'm next to a grocery store," she added.

"The first thing we need to do is secure your safety. And you don't have any idea where Marc and Jake were taken?"

"None." She thought of Canyon Diablo, where they were headed that morning. Maybe driving out there would give her some answers. She stared at the GPS on the dash, which displayed her current location, and wondered if she could program it to direct her to the ghost town.

"I just tried calling both of their cell phones and they are going straight to voice mail. Either they've been turned off or wherever they are doesn't have a signal."

"We were headed out the door, so I'm guessing they

had their phones on them. But honestly, I don't remember watching them do anything with their phones." She'd been too distracted trying to sort through her feelings for Marc. That wasn't something she would share with Natasha though. "I'm not too sure where to go to be safe. I don't even have my purse or driver's license."

"They're both still in the motel room?" Natasha asked.

"Yes."

"We've got choices." Natasha's strong, commanding tone had a soft edge to it. She didn't quite whisper, but there was a husky sound to her voice. "I need to do some checking at my end, see if there's any way I can track their cell phones and secure a location. That is, assuming they have them on them. In the meantime, you can stay put, go to the police, or try going back to the room to get your things."

London gave it some thought. Somehow talking over everything that had happened with Natasha had helped London regain control of her senses. She leaned back in the driver's seat, turning the car on to start the heat, and chewed her lower lip, weighing her options.

"I'm not accomplishing anything sitting here, and six people are in serious trouble. I'm the only one who can help them. No one else knows anything about this," she began, thinking out loud as Natasha remained silent on the other end of the line. "I don't know that the police will be as compassionate to this situation as you and I are. The only solid proof I can give them right now is a dead body and a murder weapon. The pictures and messages with them could imply a hostage situation except we don't have a ransom note."

"True," Natasha said, but didn't elaborate.

London continued breaking her options down. "If I go back to the motel and the police have been called, they will probably be there right now. It would be obvious and

I would keep going." Like a bat out of hell, she thought to herself. "If the police aren't there, then probably they aren't going to be called. I've been sitting here a good thirty minutes at least."

"Hold on a second," Natasha said, listening or not but obviously doing her job as well.

London continued anyway. "I'm going to drive by the motel. If there isn't anyone there, I'm going to try and get our stuff out of there."

"Call me back as soon as you get there. If I don't hear from you in fifteen minutes I'm calling you back." Natasha said good-bye and hung up.

London shifted the car and accelerated slowly out of the parking lot. When she started trembling, London bit her lip until it hurt. No way would she back out. The time for hiding and being scared was over. Maybe she'd spent her entire life doing both and fearing any adventure of any kind. She sucked in a breath, remembering how she'd heard Marc and Jake fight the men who came into the room before they were abducted. Other than size and a hell of a lot more muscle, what did either of them have that she didn't have?

When she blew out a loud breath it was with new resolve. She couldn't quite stop from trembling, but she would be brave. After all, she hadn't done anything wrong. There wasn't any reason to hide and cower. She was in the right. And now, for whatever warped reasons, it was all up to her to free six people who'd been taken. Natasha never mentioned contacting the police on her end. So until London knew otherwise, there wasn't any backup. No one else would run to the rescue of her parents, Marc, or his family.

"God. It's all up to me." Saying it out loud didn't help it sink in any better. She tried again, though. "I'm in charge of rescuing six people." That didn't help, either. She did manage to grind the gears a bit when shifting down, though. The engine rumbled underneath her in protest. For the first time, London wished Marc had a little less of a conspicuous car. She'd enjoyed the hell out of driving it from Colorado to Arizona. But now, as she pulled out into the street, London swore everyone she passed stared at the car in appreciation. There was no hiding in this classic, red with black stripes, street rod.

Managing to make a face and telling herself it was a good thing Marc wasn't here to see how she was treating his Mustang, she continued convincing herself she could see this through, and with the pristine muscle car as her sidekick.

"You're never going to hide under beds again." That statement made her laugh, but her smile faded quickly as the true meaning of what she'd just said hit her.

That's what she'd been doing, for years. Maybe as a child she'd mastered diving under beds or into closets or making herself invisible some way or another when trouble came to their door. But as an adult, over the years she'd been working, never missing a day, being the perfect employee, she'd still been hiding under a bed.

She never made any friends, wouldn't get serious with any guy who asked her out, and worked way too many hours. Granted, she could justify the hours worked. She had a new car and lived in a nice house. But at twenty-five she'd never been with the same guy longer than a month or so, and there wasn't anyone on the planet she would consider a best friend.

"No more hiding." Her words almost got stuck in her throat, her strong convictions she'd just talked herself into accepting threatening to waver when the sign for the motel came into view.

London gripped the gearshift, white-knuckling it, and managed to keep her leg from trembling when she pushed on the clutch. She neared the parking lot, stared at where

Marc's Mustang had been parked before she took off in it and then at the door to their room. It was closed. There were a few cars in the parking lot. Other than that, everything seemed normal.

It certainly didn't look the way a crime scene would look, or how she imagined it looking. Her heart pounded in her chest, and her palms were almost too damp to shift. Turning into the parking lot, she pulled into a stall. The car jerked and turned off when she let up on the clutch too soon.

"Everything looks normal." Now all she had to do was get out of the car and walk up to the motel room. "You're in charge, girl," she reminded herself. Enough of the talk, now for the walk.

London automatically reached for her purse and sighed. She had her cell phone and the card key and the only reason she had either was because she'd already put them on her when she was going to leave with Marc and Jake. Opening the car door, she shot a wary look around the parking lot, her nerves so frazzled a car appearing in her peripheral vision on the road caused her to jump.

There was no way she would be able to rescue a fly at this rate. She'd already endured escaping a potential captor by killing him; anything else should be child's play in comparison. London forced herself into a confident walk to the motel room door and slid her key into the notch by the doorknob. The light turned green and she pushed open the door.

It smelled like cleaning supplies. Crap! Had Housekeeping cleaned their room?

In the next instant she realized how insane of a thought that was. Someone had definitely been in the room. They'd spent a fair amount of time here, too. Either that or London had seriously hallucinated a lot of what happened earlier today. Although the room smelled clean and there was no sign of a dead body, the bed she and Marc slept in the night before was unmade.

She walked past the two beds and stood where the man had stood when she'd shot him. There should be blood on the carpet, a lot of blood. London looked down at her jeans and turned, staring at herself in the mirror. There were dark, dried blotches covering her pants. Looking again at the carpet, she kept her focus on it as she walked around the bed, now standing where she'd been lying on the floor.

London squatted, pressing her fingers into the carpet. She pulled them back with a shriek. The carpet was wet. Her stomach turned as she brought her fingers to her nose and smelled them. They smelled like cleaning supplies.

"Someone came in here after I left, pulled a dead body out of here, and cleaned the carpet." London stared across the motel room, her mind spinning. What kind of people was she dealing with here?

Her cell phone rang and London yelped again, reaching behind her and bracing herself when she fell in a crab-like position.

"Good God," she moaned, pushing herself to her feet and pulling her phone out of her pocket. She was off to a damn good start at playing sleuth when cleaning supplies and ringing cell phones scared the crap out of her.

It was Natasha calling her. "Hello," she said, praying her voice didn't sound too shaky.

"Just checking in."

"Everything's fine." She didn't even know where to begin in explaining how not fine it was.

"Good. Perfect. Hey, do you have enough gas in Marc's 'stang to come pick me up from the airport?"

"Huh?" London was taken off guard. She'd expected Natasha to laugh at her sarcastic response instead of accepting it. "The airport? What airport?"

"I'm getting ready to board now." There was a burst of static through the phone and what sounded like a loudspeaker in the background when Natasha continued. "LAX sucks big-time, but I managed a quick flight. I'm landing at Pulliam Airport an hour and a half from now. You shouldn't be too far from the airport."

"What flight are you coming in on?" London hurried to the desk, using the pen and paper supplied by the motel, and wrote down the details of Natasha's flight. "Why are you coming here?" she asked, writing the name of the airport next to the flight schedule.

"We're boarding now. See you soon," Natasha said, sounding way too cheerful.

London hung up and stared at the notepad. She didn't get it, but it looked like within the next couple hours she'd have help finding her parents and Marc and his family.

Natasha King was too damn pretty for her own good. Her long black hair wasn't thick like London's but silky and glossy. It looked so controllable and was twisted loosely behind her head with two long, Oriental-looking sticks. She wore faded, loose-fitting blue jeans that had to be incredibly comfortable and at the same time showed off how slim she was. Even with the black leather coat covering most of her torso, it was impossible not to notice how her bright red sweater clung to really large breasts. Natasha was one of those women you just had to hate because of their incredible sex appeal. London swore every man they passed, leaving the airport, tripped over himself trying to get a better view.

"This way." London nodded as she led the way to Marc's car. "So how did you know it was me?"

Natasha had grinned broadly and walked right up to London when she made her way through the passengers in the airport. London had a physical description of Natasha but wasn't positive it was her until Natasha said her name.

"I could say you describe yourself well." She had such a soft-spoken voice, but there was something dynamic about this woman, who London guessed was around her age. "And you really did. But I have a few advantages," she added, and walked up to Marc's car without being told which one it was. "I ran a trace on you."

Natasha laughed when London looked at her, shocked. "What does that mean? And what did you find?"

"Nothing bad. I promise," Natasha told her, heaving her large suitcase into Marc's trunk when London popped it open. "It was kind of like a background check, but all I really searched for was a picture of you."

"And you found one?"

Natasha finished putting her luggage in the trunk and closed it, then went to the passenger door as London opened the driver's side. She hadn't been sure if she should offer to let Natasha drive, since after all, they were in her cousin's car. Natasha didn't mention it, though, and secured her seat belt as London started the car.

"Yes. Your driver's license picture. Not many people take good pictures for the DMV. You got lucky."

"And now I know you're a liar." London wrinkled her nose and Natasha laughed again, the sound almost melodic. It was hard hating her when she was so friendly and smiling all the time. "You know, you've got a real knack for this business. I was really impressed when you told me everything was fine when I knew you'd arrived at the motel."

"How did you know I'd arrived at the motel?" London couldn't bring herself to tell Natasha she'd told her everything was fine because she was being sarcastic. She'd been thrown off guard with news of Natasha flying in so hadn't elaborated on the truth. "And trust me, everything was far from fine."

"But you knew you weren't on a secure line. I didn't know if Marc had told you about it or not. But I was impressed. Cell phones are so easy to tap into. You don't have to be a professional to eavesdrop on conversations."

London made a show of focusing on traffic as they left the airport. It had been the last thing on her mind to think about how safe her phone was when she'd walked into the motel room. She couldn't say at the moment what she'd been thinking or if she'd had a rational thought in her head at all. It was incomprehensible that someone could enter a motel, remove a body and all indication someone had been shot without anyone knowing what they were doing. If the motel management had any clue what had happened, they would have been all over that room, along with the cops.

With the skills these people had to get such a disgusting job done in such little time, London didn't doubt for a moment they'd be able to listen in on any phone conversation they wanted.

"The body is gone." This time London had the satisfaction of watching Natasha's jaw drop as she gawked at her.

"You're kidding," she whispered.

"When I entered the room I didn't understand the thick smell of cleaning supplies. But someone came into the room during the time I was gone, removed that body and all blood from the carpet. It was damp where his body had been, but it smelled of carpet cleaner, not blood."

"Holy crap. They have one hell of an impressive housecleaning system."

"I don't think the motel cleaned up the body. They didn't make the bed."

Natasha laughed, shaking her head. "No, that's not what I meant. Criminals refer to housecleaning when they send someone in to remove all evidence that a crime was just committed. I bet you there isn't a single fingerprint in that entire motel room."

"Now that I didn't check for," London said dryly, feeling foolish for not understanding Natasha the first time.

"We're not dealing with kidnappers or terrorists or anyone holding a grudge against any of them." Natasha stared ahead of her, her lips pursed and her expression serious. "I think Uncle Greg was right with his hunch after the action figures showed up." She glanced at London, giving her an appraising look. "I don't know if Marc told you how livid he was when Marc told him about the wedding couple he got in the mail. Uncle Greg is a master. You'll find that out when you meet him. Nothing gets past him and there isn't a case yet he hasn't solved. I'm sure you've noticed how Marc is always trying to outdo him."

London didn't bother mentioning that at the moment Marc's father was missing, along with his wife, so someone had obviously pulled one over on him. It was Marc who'd gone in after his father. "I'm sure he's amazing," she said easily, believing he probably was.

"Uncle Greg knew right then and there that Marc had found someone he cared about very much. In fact, he cared about you enough that whoever these people are knew sending that wedding couple with the wife beheaded would kick Marc's protector mode into full effect. He wouldn't want anything to happen to you."

"To happen to me?" Now London laughed, shaking her head, ready to deny Natasha's implication in spite of how her tummy suddenly filled with butterflies. "Marc and I have only known each other a couple weeks. He's a great guy, but there isn't that kind of bond between us."

"Yet," Natasha finished for her.

And London hated that the word was on the tip of her tongue. She focused on traffic, her thoughts frazzled all over again. Marc's blue eyes burned with emotions when she'd tried telling him before they were attacked that she didn't want this kind of life. He'd made it clear with a few words he didn't want to let her go.

"Uncle Greg worked a case down in Mexico almost a year ago. One of the world's most infamous assassins was killed when they were down there hunting him. Before he died, he suggested to Uncle Greg that he was part of a sordid game. It was like a board game, but instead of plastic pieces they were using human beings."

"Marc told me something about that." London slowed at the next intersection, trying to remember if this was her turn or if it was the next block. "Marty Byrd, right?"

Natasha gave her an odd look.

"What?" London demanded when Natasha was quiet for a longer period of time than she'd been since they met at the airport.

"Marc doesn't talk to anyone about his cases. None of them do," she said quietly.

London hated how her cheeks burned. She stopped almost too fast at the red light ahead of them and turned to stare at Natasha head-on.

"I didn't even know what he did for a living until he decided to come get me and bring me down here. And then I went on a leap of faith. Honestly, if I hadn't found the KFA Web site and called and talked to you, which helped me believe the legitimacy of all of this, I don't know if I would have agreed to come down here."

"I'm glad you did." Natasha sounded serious for the first time. "The action figures really spooked my uncle. He took it as a personal stab and believed the same jab was directed toward Marc. Whoever sent those pictures and action figures was sending a very cryptic message. But they made one thing very clear. You and Aunt Haley were in serious trouble, or you two both would be if Uncle Greg and Marc didn't cooperate or see out some agenda.

The person who sent everything was telling us you both would be hurt, or worse," she added, lowering her voice, "if we don't do what they want."

"This is all just so fucked up," London said, blowing out an exasperated sigh. "These people are dangerous and seriously sick in the head. If they went to all the work they did to clean up that motel room, who is to say they also didn't go to the effort to booby-trap the room somehow?"

"I wouldn't be surprised. But we have a few traps of our own we can set."

London wasn't sure what to think of Natasha when she looked at her smug grin. Her light brown eyes were almost golden, and they glowed when the corner of her mouth curved. She gave London a crooked smile that reminded her of how Jake looked when he was pleased with himself.

"I'm going to teach you all about this line of work," Natasha said, pulling her attention from London and reaching for her purse, which was on the floor by her feet. "The King family all use scramblers in their cell phones. Let me see yours."

"You mean so no one can listen in when you talk?"

"Exactly."

London pulled into a busy convenience store lot and parked alongside the building. They could see the motel across the street. She pulled her phone out and handed it over, then watched as Natasha disassembled it, installed a flat disk underneath the SIM card, and put the phone back together.

She handed London's phone back to her. "Not only do these awesome little gizmos scramble our calls so no one can eavesdrop; they also have a tracking device in them."

"Like a GPS?" London asked, flipping her phone in her hand and glancing up when several teenagers hurried around their car and into the store.

"Yes. Something like that."

"So do you know where Marc and Jake are?" London's heart skipped a beat as she shot an anxious look at Natasha.

Natasha was so beautiful. When she smiled it made her appear classy and graceful. It was hard picturing this woman hunting criminals. Maybe what she was doing right now was her part of the job in this business. It sounded exciting playing with gadgets and searching on the computer to track down criminals.

"Their tracking devices are still operating." She suddenly looked really excited as she hugged her purse to her chest. "This isn't the safest place and I really don't want to check into a hotel just yet. We'd be making ourselves the bait instead of the hunters. Let's find a park, or somewhere a bit more secluded. I'll show you how this works and we should be able to track down their exact location."

"I won't promise you I won't get lost," London said as she began backing out of the stall. "This is a pretty good-sized city."

"That's why we have our handy GPS navigator here," Natasha said, and began pushing buttons on the GPS fixed to the dash. "And in case you're curious, I've got a scrambler installed in this baby, too. No one can pick up on any course we plot and learn where we're going."

London was more than a little impressed. She was backing out of the stall just as a pickup truck turned into the parking lot.

"Crap," she hissed, slamming on the brake to avoid hitting the truck.

She looked over her shoulder, her heartbeat accelerating as a cold sweat broke out over her flesh. They'd just missed hitting that truck, which would have meant calling the police if they'd been in an accident. Not to mention, she wouldn't want to have to tell Marc she'd wrecked his perfect Mustang.

Another car pulled away from one of the gas pumps and the crashing sound was like an explosion in London's head.

"Wow," Natasha said, staring at the pickup truck they'd just missed and the car from the gas pump with their front ends attached.

"No shit," London breathed, watching as several college-aged boys piled out of the car, ranting and raving as they started at the pickup truck.

London looked over her shoulder carefully, not sure her nerves could handle much more today but something was telling her she needed to toughen up quickly in order to handle what lay ahead. She backed out of the stall, avoiding the rear end of the truck, and turned to leave the parking lot. Two large men got out of the truck, both of them mean-looking and ugly. Instead of focusing on the college kids who were making a big deal out of a fender bender, both men were staring at her as she headed out of the lot.

"God, blame us for your accident," Natasha sneered, and fastened her seat belt.

Something crawled over London's flesh as they left the convenience store and took off down the street. There were jerks on the street all the time. Just because that truck came flying into the parking lot just as she was trying to back out of her stall didn't mean anything. The men glared at her as if they were pissed she was leaving. That didn't necessarily mean anything either.

What if they were the men trying to find her ever since she ran from the motel room? And if they were trying to find her, why hadn't they been at the motel room when she'd gone back for her purse and her and all of their luggage?

"There is a school-crossing sign," Natasha said, pointing out her window.

London was all for cutting off the main road as quickly as possible and getting lost on side streets. An unsettling feeling continued brewing inside her that she didn't like.

"This might work," London said, forcing her grip to relax on the steering wheel as she slowed to the speed limit and checked out a quiet park to their right.

She didn't wait for Natasha's consent but pulled into the park and stopped the car alongside a row of trees that offered a fair bit of privacy. She was out of the car and stretching before Natasha released her seat belt.

"Are you okay?" Natasha hugged herself against a brisk wind as she walked around the front of the idling Mustang. "Almost hitting that truck rattled your nerves, didn't it?"

"I don't know if it was that as much as it was how they glared at us when we left."

"As if they were pissed we were getting away?" Natasha asked.

London shot Natasha a quick look and stared at her a moment until Natasha's expression relaxed and she grinned, knowing she'd figured it out.

"Yeah," London admitted. "What if those were the men who have been trying to find me ever since I ran from the motel room?"

"Then I'd say you got away from them."

London nodded, rubbing her arms and taking in her surroundings. Swings swayed back and forth against the gusts of wind that caused tree branches to make creaking noises around them. The sun was gone and a gray, overcast sky hung low overhead. There wasn't that feeling in the air of a storm coming in like she would sense back home. She couldn't tell if it was going to snow or just get cold and dismal.

"For now," she said finally, continuing to watch her surroundings. "These people went to a lot of effort to take my parents and make me aware of their efforts along the way." The fact that whoever plotted this ordeal had gone to the effort to find out Jonnie and Ruby Brooke had a daughter, and then to learn where London lived, showed all the effort they'd put into pulling this fiasco off. She paraphrased for Natasha, though. "They plotted and planned. Those aren't the kind of people who are going to let a loose end like me simply slip away. They're going to keep chasing me."

"You can handle it," Natasha said quietly, sounding like she believed London was that strong.

London didn't want comfort. When she sensed Natasha might reach out and touch her, she walked around her, facing the street through the trees and watched the cars drive up and down it.

"You'd be surprised what I can handle," London said, having no desire to paint a picture of any kind for Natasha. At the same time, though, London couldn't stomach sympathy. "This is a different world for me. I'm going to freak out about it, but that doesn't mean I'm not strong enough to handle it."

"I'm the same way," Natasha said.

She didn't elaborate when London turned around. Instead, Natasha held up her purse and nodded. "I'm going to set this up and I'll show you how it works."

London ended up standing outside the passenger side door, watching as Natasha set up a small laptop and plugged it into the cigarette lighter.

"I love these things," she said, looking up at London and grinning. "Every time I learn of a new toy that performs some amazing feat, I go nuts until I can get my hands on it. I'm really quite the geek. Don't tell anyone."

"I won't." London had a feeling those who knew Natasha well probably already knew that about her.

In a matter of minutes she had the small laptop up and running and was typing so fast her fingers were almost a blur. "Okay. It really is quite simple," she began.

London always grew wary when anyone started out an explanation with those words. She knelt outside the car, though, leaning in and watching the screen as Natasha explained how it worked.

"Every scrambler comes with its own code. I simply load them on here," she explained, pointing to the screen as she spoke. "And once I activate the scrambler and link it to this program, it goes live. See?"

To her amazement, London did see. "Wait a minute," she said, leaning in closer and pointing to a small red blinking circle on the screen. "Is that me?"

Natasha laughed. "Well, technically it's your cell phone. But assuming your phone is on you or very nearby, then yes, that is you."

"So where are Marc and Jake?" she asked.

"Well," Natasha began, and began tapping on the keyboard. "I'm pulling the screen out, making the perimeter larger. Now, you and I are still right here. This is Flagstaff, and as we continue to move out we see the surrounding land around the city. And this," she said, pausing and then pointing to the bottom of the screen when a red circle began beating. "This would be Jake's cell phone."

"Oh . . . my . . . God," London breathed, drawing out the words as she stared at the small circle. It was a paler red than her circle and occasionally disappeared. "Does that mean his signal is weak?"

"Yes, which is the part I don't understand. There is incredible interference around him. The only other explanation would be that his scrambler is wearing out or somehow malfunctioning, but Jake's scrambler isn't that old." She looked up at London and made a face. "He ran over his phone a few weeks ago in the driveway, crunched it beyond recognition," she added, rolling her eyes.

"Then Marc's should be even stronger, since it's brand-new."

"Those two go through cell phones faster than they do women." She slapped her hand over her mouth the moment the words were out and looked at London wide-eyed. "Shit. I'm sorry. It really was just an expression. Marc doesn't date that many women. Now, Jake, on the other hand." She shook her head. "But anyway."

London really didn't want to touch the topic of how many women Marc had, or had not been with prior to them meeting. "So where is Marc's signal?" London asked, staring at the screen. "And where exactly is that signal coming from?"

"Hold on; hold on," Natasha said, and continued tapping her fingers against the keys, hitting the up and down arrow keys, then the side-to-side keys as she navigated and worked her way closer into the location where Jake's signal had first appeared.

"There's another signal," London announced, speaking too loud as she thrust her finger at the small laptop.

"Yup. Give me a minute." Natasha didn't comment on London's sudden excitement over the second signal appearing.

"Where are they?" London tried reading the screen and figuring out for herself when Natasha didn't say anything.

"It doesn't make sense," she said finally.

"What doesn't?"

"Well, they aren't anywhere." Natasha shook her head, taking her hands off the laptop and crossing her arms. She balanced the screen on her knees and scowled at it.

"I'm starting to think their phones might have been dumped somewhere. We can drive down there and make sure, but these signals are coming from south of town. There's nothing there."

"Are you sure there is nothing there?"

"I'm sure. The signals and map don't lie." Natasha suddenly sounded irritated and thrust her hands into her hair, messing with the two sticks that held it in place. "According to this, Marc and Jake are out in the middle of nowhere. There isn't even a road there."

London straightened, glancing around her again when the wind picked up. She grabbed her hair, pulling it behind her head to prevent it from slapping her in her face as she hurried around the car. Then sliding into the seat, she cranked up the heat.

"God, it's freezing," Natasha complained, pulling her door closed and continuing to balance her laptop on her lap.

"Is there any chance those signals are coming from around Canyon Diablo?" London asked, shifting into gear and turning around in the parking lot.

"Canyon Diablo?" Natasha glanced at her before trying to type with one hand and hold on to the laptop with the other to keep it from sliding off her legs as London left the park and accelerated.

"This morning we were headed down there. Marc and Jake were there the other day, and that's where Jake was shot."

"Interesting." She typed faster and stared at the screen. "That is exactly where the signals are coming from. But according to this, Canyon Diablo is nothing more than crumbling foundations from old buildings and a few grave markers."

"Apparently there is more there than it appears," London

said, accelerating into traffic and trying to program the GPS on the dash at the same time.

"Here, I'll do it," Natasha offered, taking over and typing in the information the GPS needed. "You drive. Sounds like we're going to go explore some old ruins."

Chapter Thirteen

Marc rubbed his wrists, the swelling and chafing irritating the crap out of him. His skin was on fire and felt tight against his bones. The cold, hard cement underneath him didn't help matters. When he turned his head he swore there were several large bumps on the back of his head. His vision was blurred and the metallic taste in his mouth pretty much convinced him that whoever it was he had taken on, Marc got the raw end of the deal.

As he searched through the cloud in his brain trying to remember whom he'd gotten in a fight with, Marc continued trying to focus. He didn't have a clue where he was. It appeared to be a jail cell, but for the life of him he couldn't remember what he'd done to get here.

Maybe it was because he got in a fight.

"I think he's waking up," a woman said, her voice crisp, which helped slice through the fog in his brain.

Marc turned his head in the direction of her voice.

"Good. I'll come back in an hour or so once his head is clear." The voice of the man who spoke sounded familiar. "Keep an eye on his vitals."

"They're fine now, although that doesn't surprise me. Would you look at him?"

The man laughed. Marc knew that laugh. Anger spiked inside him and he knew he hated that man. But why? Marc's brain wasn't cooperating. For the life of him, he couldn't find any memories of why he was here or who that man was.

"He's not my type," the man said. "And he's not your type, either," he added, his tone darkening. "Just do your job."

"Aye, aye, boss," she said, and giggled.

Marc heard both of them as if they were right next to him, and couldn't figure out why he couldn't see them. The room grew quiet, if it was a room he was in. He lifted his hands and rubbed his eyes. His fingers were like sandpaper. When he tried licking his lips his tongue seemed swollen. Even clearing his voice seemed a task too complicated to perform. These weren't side effects to losing a fight. There was something else wrong with him.

"Don't worry, darling." The woman was right next to him, standing over him. Her fingers were cold when she touched his forehead. "You'll be back to your usual Neanderthal self in an hour or so. Although it's a shame. I think I like you docile like this."

"Where am I?" Marc struggled to get the words out. His mouth was too dry. "Water," he added, managing to make himself more audible.

"Very impressive," she purred. "You really shouldn't be able to speak yet."

She rewarded him with something wet against his lips. Marc opened his mouth, sucking greedily on what felt like a wet washcloth.

"Not too fast, my dear," the woman told him, and started pulling the washcloth out of his mouth. "Don't fight recuperating. Your body will take some time to recover and we want you up to full speed again, now don't we?"

"Where am I?" he asked again, and focused on the blur hovering over him. He wouldn't have known she was a woman if it weren't for her voice.

"Recuperating," she said, which didn't answer the question.

She patted his forehead with the cold washcloth and Marc was certain nothing had ever felt better. With every passing minute, his skin smoothed over his bones and began to fit right on his body again. Talk about a strange sensation.

"Open your eyes, good-looking," she whispered, sounding as if her face was inches from his.

Marc blinked, obeying, and his surroundings came into focus.

"Look at me, sweetheart," she whispered, leaning over him. "I'm not bad to look at, right?"

"No," he said automatically. Marc tried swallowing and his tongue seemed stuck to the roof of his mouth.

"I think you've slept long enough. Do you want to try sitting up? Maybe a drink of water?"

"Yes." Marc pushed himself to a sitting position and damn near fell over.

"Hold on. Take it easy, sexy," she drawled. "It's going to take a while for your muscles to be your own again." She laughed and started whistling when she walked away from his side.

Marc closed his eyes, but that didn't help much, either. So keeping them open, he endured the room spinning until slowly it seemed to stay in place. He was leaning on one elbow, lying on what appeared to be a cement slab raised several feet off the ground. The floor, walls, ceiling were all gray and there were bars ahead of him. He was in some kind of cage that opened up into a larger room.

That's when it all came back to him. He studied the woman when she returned. She left the cell door open behind her when she entered his small, nondescript prison. Apparently Marc wasn't considered a flight risk at the moment.

"Here you go, hon. Drink this." She held a small paper cup up to his mouth.

He wanted to down it more than he wanted to breathe. It really sucked. He didn't trust his senses at the moment. When he tried sniffing the contents as she put the side of the cup to his mouth, it smelled too sweet to be water. But he might be smelling her perfume. Marc wasn't sure.

"Come on. It's time to get all that brute strength of yours back in order. Boss says so," she added, snickering as she wrapped her arm around the back of his neck and held him against her breasts while tipping the contents of the cup into his mouth.

If it was water, he was more out of it than he thought. It tasted like really sweet Kool-Aid. Marc let some of it dribble out of his mouth and spit out what hit his tongue before he could swallow it.

"Oh crap," she hissed, that sweet tone of hers fading when she jumped back.

"Sorry about that," he breathed, lying back on his cement bed when she let go of him. There were some nasty bruises on the back of his head. He could feel them.

"You know, if you're going to be difficult about this, the boss is going to do this to you again." The woman had bleached-blonde hair pulled into a ponytail that fell past the collar of the flowery shirt she wore tucked into comfortable-looking jeans. She put her hands on her hips, looking rather exasperated with him, but then wagged a finger, as if she were reprimanding a child and threatening him with his father coming home and not being pleased. "You need to trust me and cooperate. Trust me, gorgeous, it's your only option."

"It's hard to trust anyone who put me in a cage after beating the crap out of me," Marc grumbled, not trying to lift his head this time and closing his eyes while trying to do a mental survey of the damage done to him.

The woman walked away from him and he turned his head, opening his eyes far enough to watch her leave his cell. He wasn't in any shape to try to escape at the moment and she knew that. Marc didn't doubt for a moment that when he could stand and move around, that cage door would be locked securely every time he was left alone.

"I remember kicking someone in the face. How is he doing?" Marc called out, closing his eyes again and managing to swallow this time.

"His nose is broken, but he'll live. I'll let him know you asked about him."

Marc couldn't see her but could hear her easily enough. He tried moving to a sitting position again, taking his time and handling the intense pounding in his head when he didn't fall over.

"Is my Neanderthal back?" she asked, grinning broadly at him when she entered his cell, but she stopped in the doorway without approaching. She held another paper cup in her hand.

"I won't hurt you." He noticed her amused look that she'd been giving him since he woke up was gone.

"What makes you say that?" She walked to him with the cup in her hand.

"Because you needed to hear it," he said, staring at the cup. "What is that stuff?"

"It helps clear the brain and aids in your recuperation."

"Water does the trick, too."

"Point taken." She held the cup out to him. "Drink this and I'll get you some water."

Marc took the cup and looked down at the clear liquid inside. It had a really sweet smell to it, but he didn't know enough about chemicals or medicines to identify what it might be by scent. He put it to his lips and tipped the cup. When she turned from him and headed back out of the cell, Marc crushed the cup in his hand, letting the contents soak his hand.

As he stared at his hand and made a fist, it appeared his mind was once again in charge of controlling his actions. There was a bruise alongside his palm, which possibly he got falling after kicking one of the guards in the face. Marc took a moment to replay his and Jake's attack on the men who'd brought them down here. Obviously, he and Jake had lost. Marc wondered where Jake and his parents were as he slowly inspected his body, searching for more bruises and any cuts.

He still wore his clothes. Blondie out there apparently hadn't had too much fun with him while he'd been out cold. Which led to his next question. Exactly how long had be been unconscious? As he ran his hands down his body, it didn't take more than a second to confirm his next suspicion. He no longer had his cell phone or his gun on him.

"How is our patient doing?"

Marc shot his attention to the cell door, which was still slightly ajar, recognizing the male voice. It was the man who'd brought them in and dismissed them to his goons to be caged up like animals.

"He's perfect in every way," Blondie purred, almost sounding as if she wanted to make the man jealous with her praise of Marc.

"Has he fully recovered?" The man's voice did sound a bit sterner.

"He should be ready to go."

Marc decided standing would be to his advantage. He'd have company soon enough, and for some reason he wanted to appear ready for whatever plans were in store for him. The sooner he learned what the hell was going on here, the easier it would be to plot their way out of here.

His legs were wobbly and for a moment Marc worried he would hit the ground. The cement floor didn't look too appealing. He braced himself, putting one foot in front of the other until he was pretty sure he wouldn't crash and make a fool out of himself.

"Would you look at you?" Blondie grinned at him when she led the way into his cell.

The man who brought him here wasn't smiling when he followed her in but stopped dead in his tracks in the doorway to the cell and stared at Marc, his lips parting as if he was shocked to see Marc standing there.

"What dosage did you use?" the man whispered, his astonishment apparent as he continued gawking at Marc.

Blondie walked up to Marc, searching his face and letting her gaze travel down him before taking the crushed cup out of his hand. She frowned when she touched it, noticing how sticky it was from its contents having been squeezed out of it.

"How are you feeling, Marc?" she asked, looking at him warily while holding the crushed cup gingerly between her fingers. She held another cup in her other hand and held it out to him. "As promised, your water."

Marc gave her a gallant nod, accepting the cup and bringing it to his lips. It was water this time and he downed it with one gulp, crushed the cup, and handed it to her.

"Never felt better," he told her, winking but hardening his expression when he focused on the man still using her as a guard as he remained behind her. "Why am I here?"

"Because you started a fight." The man straightened, some of his cockiness reappearing, although he didn't enter the cement cage. "Although your skills are commendable, you'll need to learn to attack only when I tell you to."

"Is that so?" Marc tilted his head, wondering if the man really believed he could train Marc to attack on command. "I tend to attack when someone tries putting me in a cage."

The man shrugged as if what Marc said didn't matter. "Your quarters will improve once you've mastered some of the basic rules."

"You're going to learn King men don't take orders very well." Marc shifted his attention to Blondie, who seemed fascinated by the crushed cups in her hands. She looked up at him the moment he glanced down at her, and her eyes grew large when he winked.

"You still seem on edge," she said, narrowing her gaze on him. "Maybe it's taking longer for your medicine to take effect than usual."

"Maybe you need to increase his dosage." The man walked away from the doorway, leaving her alone in the cell with Marc. "Don't waste my time by calling me down here until he's properly prepared."

A door opened and slammed closed, causing an echo around them.

"I can't imagine you find these quarters that appealing." Blondie walked out of the cement cage as well, this time closing the cage door and twisting a lock on the outside of it. "Next time you see Claude you'd be smart to be a bit more hospitable. Or I could increase your dosage."

She knew he hadn't taken whatever was in that first cup. He guessed its contents were supposed to make him behave in a certain way. Blondie had just given him an option–be hospitable or be given a higher dosage. That told him two things. The sweet-smelling drink he'd been given would make him nicer, agreeable, if that's what Blondie meant by hospitable. Also, Blondie wasn't completely loyal to Claude, her boss. Maybe she thought he was a prick, too. Both were small bits of information Marc filed away for the time being.

Marc walked up to the bars and stared into a large room beyond his cell. It looked like a laboratory. There were cages similar to the one he was in surrounding the room. All of them appeared to be empty.

"What is this place?" He hung his arms over the crossbar and watched Blondie as she sat at a large worktable and worked at a computer.

"There really aren't any options for you if you don't cooperate," she said, ignoring his question. "Right now, your dosage levels are really low. If you continue refusing to go with the program they'll be upped until you're nothing but a walking zombie. Is that what you want?" She glanced over at him, raising one eyebrow.

"You led him to believe I'd taken whatever it was in that cup you wanted me to have. You did that for a reason."

Blondie was damn good at flirting but equally good at looking seriously pissed. "It's my job," she hissed, glaring at him. Letting out a puff of air, she stood and ran her fingers down her ponytail. Blondie came around the table and faced him. "I don't need drugs to know what to do. Behave and do what you're told and maybe you won't, either. But believe me, if I double the dosage you supposedly just took, you'll become so compliant you would lick the drops of that dose off the floor of your cell if I asked you to." She gave him a hard stare, which under the bright fluorescent lights that weren't in his jail cell, made her look a lot older. Maybe not quite as old as his mother, although his mom was a much better-looking woman. "Do you really want the rest of your family seeing you like that?" she asked.

"Your compassion is touching." Marc wasn't offended when she turned her back on him and returned to her computer. He took a moment to run his hand over the outside bars, trying to reach for the door handle but realizing his wrist was too thick to pass between the bars.

"Remember, blondie. I refused to take the drug you gave me. If I don't take one dose, how am I going to take two?"

She slipped her hand under the table and pulled out a gun, pointing it at his face. Marc froze, focusing on her face and not the weapon aimed between his eyes.

"There are other ways to administer drugs than in a cup, Neanderthal," she informed him. "I could give you a lethal dose this very second with a twitch of my finger. It wouldn't matter whether you decided to take it, or not."

"Point taken." Marc raised his hands in surrender. He decided not to breach the point that she didn't turn him in for not taking the drug. Blondie had some compassion but apparently valued her job. "So is there any harm in telling me why I'm here?"

She sighed, looking at him over her shoulder. Blondie wasn't bad looking. She was working for the wrong side, though, and her loyalty to her boss was apparent. That took away any appeal whatsoever.

"You'll find out when Claude decides you're ready to know." She continued studying Marc over her shoulder for another moment. "You're wrong, though. Claude isn't an idiot. If you continue mocking him every time you see him you'll lose credibility in his eyes. Trust me, Neanderthal. You don't want that to happen."

Marc didn't see Claude for the rest of the day, or what he assumed to be a day. Blondie left the lab for a while and returned after quite a bit of time had passed, carrying a tray with food, which she left for Marc. She also left a bucket for him in the corner of the cell. He didn't need to ask what that was for. The next time she entered the lab she ignored his questions altogether or dodged answering them. When she left she turned out the lights, leaving him in the dark. Marc drifted off to sleep, and dreamed about London.

"Neanderthal, wake up." Blondie stood over his cement

bunk staring down at him, holding a Styrofoam cup. "I've got a drug I bet you would love to have."

He smelled the coffee and pulled himself up, reaching for the cup and taking it as he grunted his response. Blondie left the cell and locked the door, not saying anything and disappearing from his sight. The humming of computers and start-up music as she brought the room to life removed the death-like silence he'd endured all night, making it seem as if he'd slept in a tomb. Since he was in an underground cell, he figured his analogy to be damn close. Marc picked up the bucket she'd left the night before, ignoring its contents, and placed it in the corner of his cell so he could have his back to her when he relieved himself.

"I'm going to give you a choice." Blondie didn't wait for him to finish his personal business before she started talking. "You won't get many of these, so you might want to enjoy the moment and take your time considering before answering."

Marc finished his business, left the bucket where it was, and turned to face her as he zipped his pants. Her gaze dropped to his hands and she took her time returning her attention to his face before continuing.

He kept his expression bland, waiting for her to continue. He hadn't considered yesterday how well set up Blondie's lab was. Marc wondered how long it had been down here.

"You're leaving here this morning. Claude's reviewed your file and has decided you're ready."

Since nothing had changed since Marc had last seen the man, he could only imagine what Blondie had fabricated in his file to convince Claude that Marc was where they wanted him. He walked over to his coffee that he'd left on his cement bed, anxious for her to continue. He didn't like this solitary confinement. He was bored out of his mind. He needed to know his family was okay. And being moved might give him a chance to escape.

"Before you join the others he wants you cleaned up. Honestly, I can't say I blame him." She wrinkled her nose and Marc noticed freckles he hadn't seen before. "There is a small bathroom over there," she continued, nodding in the direction she indicated. "I can handcuff you and lock you in there and you can shower."

"With handcuffs on?" he asked, sipping his coffee.

"Yes. With handcuffs on." Blondie walked from the computer over to a cabinet on the wall and used a small key on her key chain to open it. "Or," she said, pulling several things out of the cabinet and closing it with her foot, "you can stay in there and I can give you sponges to wash yourself down."

She placed what looked like folded clothes on the large table and held up handcuffs in one hand and a large yellow sponge in the other.

"You're going to handcuff me?"

"I can call for reinforcements if I need them." She didn't bat an eye.

"I'll take the shower."

Blondie nodded and put the sponge next to the clothes. She walked up to the cell and unlocked his cage door, stepped aside to let him walk out, then reached for his hand. It would be too easy to knock her off balance and take her keys. Almost too easy.

"How many people are watching and listening right now?" he asked, whispering. After pulling off his shirt, he held out his hands so she could cuff him.

She didn't look up as she put the cuffs on him, but he saw her smile. "One that I know of," she said, also keeping her voice down.

"How many will watch me shower?"

"One." This time she did grin at him.

He wouldn't say it was the best shower he ever had, but Marc felt incredibly rejuvenated when he was led up a narrow flight of dark gray stairs later. The door at the top of the flight opened before he reached it, and Marc stepped out into the plush office he and Jake had entered the day before when they'd first arrived. Marc immediately spotted the door that led to where his parents and brother might still be.

Marc had hoped his family would be wherever he was being sent. He'd be a lot less distracted if he knew they were all right. He hid his disappointment when Blondie escorted him into the large room they'd first seen when they arrived, and they weren't in the pretentious office. Claude sat behind his desk, giving Marc only a moment's attention. There were three other men in the room all dressed identically to Marc. Apparently the black slacks and shirt he'd been given to wear, which to his surprise fit him perfectly, was some kind of uniform. The other men in the room didn't bat an eye or glance at Marc when he joined them.

"Now that we're all here, we'll begin." Claude didn't stand up but rested his elbows on his desk and pressed his fingers together, looking almost as if he might start their meeting with a prayer.

It was an odd thought and Marc had a hard time not smiling over the image of Claude blessing their meeting before beginning.

"Take your seats, gentlemen," Blondie told them, walking over to Claude's desk and leaning against the front of it.

The other men in the room found chairs and sat. Marc started toward the chair that was still empty and forced himself to stop. For a moment the sensation gripped him that he needed to sit. Blondie told him to sit and he had to sit.

He forced himself not to move. It took more effort than it should to listen to his own thoughts and not Blondie's instructions. Suddenly his mind raced back. She'd given him coffee and the meal last night. She'd drugged him. Snapping his attention to her, then to Claude sitting behind her at his desk, Marc caught both of them watching him curiously. A moment ago he'd found it humorous that Claude appeared to be praying. Those weren't normal thoughts. That wasn't how a man behaved when he'd been abducted. They were thoughts of a passive person, indifferent to the world around him and simply existing until given instruction.

What the hell was going on here?

"You need to take your seat, Marc." Blondie spoke quietly, almost too quietly, and watched him as if waiting to see if he'd perform the trick she'd just taught him.

"I think I'll stand." He really wanted to sit.

Blondie looked down at the floor, scowling, at the same time Claude's attention shot from his computer to Marc. Claude stood slowly, tugging on his pullover shirt, and walked around his computer.

"Does it matter to you that much if you sit, or stand?" he asked. "We're simply offering a courtesy by offering chairs. If you wish to stand, by all means, stand."

Marc didn't know what to do, sit or stand. He looked at Blondie and she straightened, then nodded to the chair. Marc looked away first, still struggling with the decision. Some odd sensation pushed forward from the back of his brain. He focused on it and felt a headache coming on. All of his thoughts were trained on whether to sit or stand. It hadn't crossed his mind to determine if anyone else in the room was armed or where the nearest exits were. He wasn't even thinking about escaping but simply whether he should sit or stand.

"Today is the beginning of the rest of your life," Claude said, straightening and sobering as he studied each man before him. "It can be a long and prosperous life." He looked pointedly at Marc. "Or it can be a very short, painful life."

Marc looked away first, doing his best to ignore the growing headache as he forced himself to take in the layout of the room. Other than paintings hanging on the walls, the plush carpet under their shoes, and several bookshelves that appeared to be stocked with a variety of fiction and nonfiction books, there wasn't a lot to give away the nature of the man in this room.

"The four of you are here because you are the best in your field." Claude rocked up on his heels. "I guess I could say the best of the best."

Blondie rolled her eyes behind him and winked at one of the men sitting.

"You've all proved yourself as bounty hunters and, I will say, your reputations are impeccable and very impressive." Claude grinned as if his praise would mean something to them.

Marc took in the three men sitting in the folding chairs alongside him. They didn't look at him but continued focusing on Claude. Marc didn't recognize any of them and he knew quite a few of the bounty hunters in the country. Some whom he would dub as the best weren't in the room, his father being one of them. What Marc did find interesting was these men's blank stares.

"We need top-of-the-line here. And I'm proud to say that is what I now have. Over the next few weeks you'll be trained to perform."

"Perform what?" Marc asked, wanting Claude to cut to the chase.

Blondie chewed her nails, looking at the backside of Claude warily. Claude studied Marc as if he'd just grown a third eye. When Claude looked over his shoulder at Blondie, his expression disgusted, if not pissed, she shrugged.

"He's been prepared just like the rest of them," she said, arguing with Claude before he said anything.

"Then why is he behaving like this?" Claude whispered, although Marc heard him easily.

"A man performs better if he knows his motivation," Marc offered, and did his best to master an innocent expression when both stared at him. He was also acutely aware how the other three men continued staring ahead, as if they weren't interested in this side conversation.

"A man performs better when he behaves and follows orders," Claude hissed at Marc through clenched teeth. "You are part of the winning team now. You'll do as you're told, when you're told, and how you're told to do it."

Marc stared at him, waiting for him to continue. His headache seemed to fade as he continued watching Claude. The moment Marc diverted his attention, glancing at the door that he supposed led to his family, the headache returned.

Claude exhaled slowly, staring at the ground, "We'll start with the basics, making sure the four of you know everything there is to know about being a soldier. Once I believe you've reached my level of expectation, we'll see how you do out on the field." Claude glanced at Marc as if he was ready for him to interject some comment. "All that matters is we win. We conquer and win and we're triumphant." Claude walked over to Blondie, gripping her shoulder. "We're going to do it, Evelyn," he said quietly. "I can feel it. These are the best of the best. We'll show the rest of those bastards who can play war games, and win the game, better than any of them. We're going to win."

Chapter Fourteen

Marc spent the rest of the afternoon in a gym. It amazed the crap out of him how elaborate of a facility Claude and Evelyn had underground. And under a ghost town that was once known as one of the most ruthless and lawless towns in the U.S. How was that for warped irony?

Jake and his parents were nowhere to be seen. Something told Marc that was intentional. The King family had proved that the moment they were together they could plan an escape with minimal discussion. He was also acutely aware of how compelled he was to obey Claude's orders. Although all Claude told Marc and the other men to do, once they entered the gym, was run. If he did another lap around this godforsaken gym he would collapse.

Claude's words to Blondie, or Evelyn, before they were escorted out of the office to this gym bothered Marc. "War games" was an oxymoron in itself. When men like Claude, who showed signs of an unstable personality, started boasting about such activities, Marc got scared.

By "war games" did Claude mean they would practice attacking before they participated as part of the game? And if so, what, or whom, was their target during practice?

Marc would kill Claude before killing an innocent person. But they hadn't ended the game when Marty Byrd was killed a year ago. Marc needed to keep Claude alive long enough to learn who the other players in the game were. His father wasn't going to blow the whole damn place up this time.

Marc had his work cut out for him. He hoped London would give him a chance once all of this was over with.

Blondie entered the gym, pausing just inside the door and letting it close behind her with a bang that echoed throughout the gym. She crossed her arms across her chest and smiled. Marc had been determined at first to not let the other three men show him up. None of them wanted to talk to him. He'd tried several times to start conversations with each of them and been ignored. Blondie smiled at each man as he passed her and didn't seem bothered when they continued running without acknowledging her.

Marc had never considered himself much of a conformist. He'd had enough of running around in circles anyway. Slowing, Marc stopped in front of Blondie. He rested his hands against his thighs, leaned forward, and caught his breath.

"Are you trying to kill me?" he asked, remaining bent over but cocking his head and looking at her.

She'd changed clothes and wore a business suit, with a skirt cut straight and ending just above her knees. Her suit jacket matched her skirt and was unbuttoned to reveal a silky-looking blouse, tailored to show off her decent-sized breasts. Her bleached-blonde hair was down and fell in soft curls just past her shoulders. The makeup she'd put on seemed to highlight the lines at the edges of her eyes, though, instead of hide them. Blondie was older than she wanted the world to know.

"Do you realize these men will run laps until I tell them

to stop?" Her soft voice was full of awe as she watched the three men run alongside one another as they came around once again. "They will run until their hearts quit beating."

"How nice for them," Marc grumbled, feeling his own heart pound in his chest.

"Nice?" Her tone hardened as she stared at him with cold eyes. Flirtatious Blondie was nowhere in sight. "Try more like Pulitzer Prize, darling. And do you think I'll get any credit for it?" Already she was shaking her head.

Marc straightened slowly. He'd kill for a bottle of water but had a feeling changing the subject would piss her off. Instead he studied her aggravated expression, trying to piece together what she'd just said to him. That damnable headache got in the way any time he tried focusing on anything other than what he was told to do.

"That sucks," he said slowly, watching her expression. Blondie, or Evelyn as Claude had called her, might give him more information if he worked her right. Say the wrong thing, though, and she would clam up on him in a second.

"I've been conducting experiments for years." She dropped her arms to her sides and looked at him, her eyes narrowing. "My results have been published time and time again. I'm going to get credit for this. Mark my words. I'll see to it."

She turned to storm out of the gym before he could think of what to say next, but then she spun back around. "Take five, gentlemen!" she yelled, her voice echoing off the gym walls. "You're all doing fabulous. Cool off and we'll get you some refreshments."

Marc didn't doubt the refreshments would contain more of whatever drug it was she and Claude were using to turn them all into spineless, submissive robots. He watched the men stop running, all of them breathing so hard they looked ready to collapse. He'd dodged two doses of whatever drug Blondie was using to make them submissive. But apparently that was all it took to wipe out the part of their brains where common sense would tell them to stop before hurting themselves. They responded only to orders.

"You should get credit for this." Marc decided to pick up the conversation again when Evelyn led the four of them out of the gym.

"Not right now," she said under her breath, and pushed open double doors, which brought them into the laboratory with the cement cells around it.

It took Marc a moment to notice this wasn't the same lab and they weren't the same cement cells where he'd been since arriving. Not only was this place a fucking maze, but it was a lot larger than he first thought.

"There you are!" Claude came in through another door, barely giving Marc and the other men around him a second glance. He focused on Evelyn. "I've exhausted all names off all of the cell phones," he began.

She held up a hand, and he snapped his mouth shut, looking more than a little annoyed that she would silence him.

"Gentlemen, please head to the showers."

When Marc didn't move along with the others, she took his arm and guided him into one of the cells, then closed the door behind him. He heard the lock click and turned to watch her secure the locks on the other cell doors, too.

"Is he still not cooperating?" Claude demanded.

"Actually, he's improved immensely. They are all working above my expectations. Now, you were saying?" she asked, leaning against the large lab table so she faced Marc. Claude faced her with his back to Marc.

Marc took in his cement prison, everything looking identical to the one he'd been in earlier. That's when he noticed the narrow door in the corner. When he opened it, there was a full bathroom, complete with toilet, sink, and shower stall. He'd just moved up in the world.

"I went through everyone's cell phone," Claude said.

Marc entered the bathroom and stood just inside the door, not closing it but listening.

"I needed to know who some of these names are."

"I'm sure a lot of them are friends."

"You know as well as I do they're going to have access to some prominent names in California. Hell, he was a goddamn cop for years before becoming a bounty hunter."

Marc didn't dare move as he strained to listen and ignore the dull headache that throbbed at his temples.

"While I was trying to go through their phones, suddenly all of them went blank. Everything on them erased as if there was nothing ever loaded on them," he continued, growing excited and raising his voice loud enough that Marc probably could have heard him if he'd gotten in the shower.

"All of the phones cleared at the same time?" Evelyn asked. "They've got them booby-trapped. Damn it. I should have known or at least thought through that they'd have some kind of setup like that."

Marc peered around the door. Evelyn began pacing and tapping her lips with her finger. Claude scowled, not watching her but staring at the ground in front of him.

"You might be right," he said, but then glanced around them. "We had some visitors up above last night."

"Who? Why didn't you tell me?"

"I don't answer to you," Claude informed her, his tone turning cruel.

Marc dared move enough to see out the bathroom door better. Evelyn came into his view, her back now to him as she stood in front of Claude.

"Maybe not. But if you want these men to be submissive and do whatever the hell you say, then you better keep me informed. I won't risk all my work here falling into the wrong hands."

"This isn't just about your work."

"Of course not. The game. It's all about the game," Sarcasm dripped from her voice.

"You still don't get it, Evelyn. It's not about your work. It's not about the game. It is about winning. Winning, damn it! Once we blow everyone else off the map the entire world will respect us. You'll have people begging to kiss your feet, do whatever you say. It's all about winning," he emphasized.

"So who were our visitors?" she asked, not commenting on what he'd just said.

"Two women."

"Two women? Were they up there to see the ruins?"

"I don't think so." Claude moved around her to the door.

"What do you mean, you don't think so?" Evelyn followed him.

Marc worried they'd take their conversation out of earshot and really needed to know who those two women were.

"They took off after I sent a couple of the men up there to investigate. But we found something."

"What?"

"Some kind of device. I didn't want to bother you with it until our meeting was over today."

"Show it to me."

The door slammed closed behind them and Marc was left alone with the drugged men nearby as his only companions.

London could barely hold on to the steering wheel. Her palms were soaked as her nerves twisted in a frenzy.

"Slow down. We're almost there." Natasha was focused on the screen in front of her, as always. The woman had some kind of contraption in her hands at all times.

London could appreciate a good computer geek as well

as the next person, but Natasha was in a class all by herself. There didn't seem to be anything she couldn't figure out.

"I see the ruins." London hit the brake, slowing on the dark highway. There weren't any stars out tonight. It was as overcast as it had been all day. The headlights offered a narrow view of everything in front of them. "Tell me again what we're going to do?"

"We're going to get our families out of there." Natasha flashed her a grin before focusing again at the screen on the small laptop. "Okay. It's at those rocks."

"An entrance." London refused to feel foolish for asking the same questions over and over again. None of this made any sense. "You're sure there is an entrance that goes underground at those rocks?"

"Positive." Natasha finally looked out the front windshield. "Pull off the road here. The only thing I'm not positive about is how to open it, but I have a hunch."

"Hunches are always good," London mumbled, praying they wouldn't end up dead tonight, or worse.

Marc's Mustang wasn't designed to drive off-road. Fortunately, the ground was frozen and there wasn't too much ice. She cranked the wheel, watching until the rocks came into view, then straightened and drove forward.

"What do I do now?" she asked, glancing up and down the highway, nervous someone would come along and stop, thinking they were in trouble. She didn't have a clue what they would say if someone confronted them.

"Pull forward slowly." Natasha wasn't watching her screen any longer. She stared ahead, her eyes wide and her mouth pressed into a thin line. She looked as terrified as London felt.

It occurred to London that Natasha might work in this business and was a master at gadgets and anything computer-related, but that didn't mean she'd willingly walked into what had to be a deadly situation before.

Natasha was as terrified as she was. When Natasha looked at London it showed in her eyes. London reached for her hand, oddly enough finding strength in Natasha's fear.

"We can do this," London whispered.

Natasha's laughter was strained and she sobered quickly. "We're going to do this," she said with determination.

London nodded, focusing ahead as they pulled up alongside the wall of rocks and stared at a field of nothing ahead of them. They hadn't driven off the road when they'd come here the night before. Instead they'd walked around the rocks. There wasn't anything to see and there was no one for miles. Natasha had spent all day poring over her laptop and jotting down notes. London wished Natasha had brainstormed out loud, but as it was, Natasha was positive she'd figured out where Marc, Jake and her parents were and was incredibly excited about driving back out to the ruins.

The car jerked. London wasn't the only one who screamed.

"What the hell was that?" she whispered, looking around them frantically before staring at Natasha.

Natasha looked at London wild-eyed, damn near panting as she fingered her hair, making a show of trying to make sure it was in place. London instinctively patted her head, having twisted her hair into a bun before they'd left to drive to the ghost town. Her hair was suddenly no longer a concern when the car jerked again.

"We're sinking!" London grabbed the gearshift, shooting panicked looks at the mirrors and over her shoulder as she tried to figure out what to do.

"Wait!" Natasha grabbed London's shoulder.

"What do you mean?" She held on to the steering wheel

hard enough to hurt her hand yet still felt it turn against her grip. Dirt flooded the beam from the headlights. "Natasha!" she yelled, unable to see a thing outside and panicking as the car was being moved by some force other than her. "What's happening? The car is driving itself."

"I'm not sure." Natasha was breathing hard when she stared ahead of her while gripping the dash. "I think we've found the entrance."

"The entrance?" London did her best to see through the cloud of dirt flooding her headlights. "Oh my God!" she whispered when the dirt started clearing.

"Drive," Natasha ordered, gripping London's arm but letting go of her just as quickly. Natasha grabbed her laptop before it slid to the floor. "Okay. This is it. We're going to get them out."

London tried blocking Natasha out as she spoke to herself under her breath. "It's okay. You can do this."

She could barely see when the headlights beamed on a dark entrance into some kind of underground tunnel. The car was on a steep incline and her seat belt dug into her chest painfully.

"We can do this. The guns are loaded. Where are the guns?" The laptop fell to the floor at Natasha's feet when she twisted to reach for the weapons they'd loaded and packed in the backseat under blankets and every emergency supply they could think of. "Oh shit!" she cried out, flinging to the floor of the front seat to save her computer. The seat belt prevented her from grabbing it. "We need the guns. We've got to do this!"

"Natasha!" London cried out, no longer able to maintain her cool as they descended into the darkness. And it *was* dark, too. She could barely see the cement walls that loomed up on either side of the car. "God. Please!" she wailed.

"Sorry. Shit." Natasha managed to grab her laptop and

slapped it closed as she blew out a loud breath. Letting it slide again to her feet, she rubbed her face with her hands. "I'm sorry," she said again.

This wasn't the time for either of them to fall apart. There wasn't any turning back. London doubted she could make the car back up the steep decline onto the ground if she tried.

"Get the guns." London strained to see ahead of her, riding the brake as they continued descending into darkness. Marc, her parents, and his family were down there somewhere. It couldn't all be pitch-black in this underground hideout. "We need to be armed now."

"Right." Natasha managed to grab the handguns from the backseat and checked each one before handing one to London. "Have we hit bottom?"

London strained to see when the car leveled and suddenly moved on a flat surface. She hit the brake and stared at what looked like a warehouse. From what she could see through the headlight beams, they were in a very large garage with another car parked ahead of them. It was some kind of SUV.

"Well, we're here." Her heart hurt in her chest and claustrophobia kicked in as the darkness seemed to close in around them. "I don't think I can handle sitting here waiting for whoever to come find us."

"Okay." Natasha took off her seat belt. "We're getting out. There's a door over there. If my equipment will work down here I can figure out what kind of security system they have."

London sucked in a breath, nodding, and shut off the car. "I don't know how long we can leave the headlights on without draining the battery."

"Turn them off. We have a flashlight and we need the car to get out of here."

"I'll leave them on long enough for you to search for

any kind of alarm." London held her gun up in her hand, checking the safety. "I'll watch your back."

Natasha nodded and blew out a breath. It was a nervous release of energy. "Scared?" she whispered.

"Terrified," London admitted.

"Me, too." Natasha reached between her legs, putting her laptop on the floor and picking up a small black box that looked like a walkie-talkie. "We've got to do this," she muttered under her breath.

"There's no turning back," London said, trying to look everywhere at once. "Let's get our families."

She held her gun in her free hand like a lifeline. And in truth that was exactly what it was. There wasn't any doubt she and Natasha would need to shoot to kill. London hadn't had time before to consider how she would aim her gun when the men showed up at the motel and took Marc and Jake. Everything had happened so quickly. Now, though, time seemed to move at a snail's pace. Natasha was taking forever getting out of the car and holding up the black gadget in her hand that scanned their surroundings and told her what kind of alarm system was being used. She'd explained how it worked earlier when they had prepared to leave, but London only understood half of what Natasha told her. The small box picked up on different types of signals being used within a certain parameter and would tell Natasha what type of security system or any other type of machinery was activated around them.

Natasha moved around the SUV and London stepped out of the car when she lost sight of her. "I can't see you," London whispered. "Should I turn off the headlights and join you?"

"There's a panel on the wall over here." Natasha didn't answer her but instead was quiet for a moment. "I think this button pad needs a code to open this door. The rest is a security system. They've got to know we're here. I don't see any cameras in here, though, do you?"

London turned, staring at the walls and ceilings. There weren't any obvious cameras fixed to the walls like someone would find in grocery or department stores. The ceiling was high and the entrance was a deep incline. The ceiling angled into the entrance and London was surprised to see the steep road disappearing into the ceiling. She hadn't heard it close.

"You might want to learn how to open the door so we can get out of here when we want to," London said, daring to speak a bit louder, although looking around again nervously when she finished talking, especially when there was a slight echo.

"This is the only panel I see in this garage. Anything that can be controlled in here has to be done from here."

"I'm shutting off the headlights and joining you." London reached into the car, gripping her gun as she shut off the headlights.

The darkness quickly closed in around her, increasing her claustrophobia and making it hard to breathe. London straightened, jumping at the sound of her car door closing when she pushed it shut gently. Her nerves were so shot she'd be lucky if they made it out of here alive, let alone rescued anyone else.

"Hurry up," Natasha ordered, waving the beam of the flashlight.

London moved around the cars, coming up behind Natasha.

"How do we get out of here?" she whispered.

Natasha put her hand on the doorknob. It clicked when she turned it, confirming they were locked in the garage. "Hopefully this won't take too long. Be quiet." She didn't elaborate as she held up the black box in front of the panel and began pushing each button on the panel.

Something sounded on the other side of the door and both women stared at it, wide-eyed.

"I don't think I need to figure out how to open the door," Natasha whispered, putting her arm out in front of London as she backed away from the door.

London backed up with Natasha, moving her finger closer to the trigger as she gripped her gun. Sweat broke out over her body, making her itch, and her eyes burned as it seemed to take forever for whoever was on other side of the door to open it.

The doorknob turned. The moment had arrived. London stepped to the side suddenly, trying to figure out whether the door would open toward them or not. Natasha followed her lead, also moving so she stood alongside the wall and out of view from whoever would step into the garage. When the door opened, the flashlight turned off.

London was momentarily confused when light flooded the garage from the other side of the door. More than one man entered the garage and gunshots burned her ears as they echoed off the walls and high ceiling. She jumped when the first man crashed to the floor.

"Son of a bitch!" the man behind him howled, almost falling over the first guy.

London raised her gun, fighting not to close her eyes as she fired. She and Natasha had more bullets on them, but London wasn't sure she fired repeatedly with that in mind. Her body and mind went on auto-drive, the only thought in her head being that if she continued firing the men wouldn't be able to capture her.

"Come on." Natasha stepped over a man lying on the ground, the metallic smell of blood growing thick in the air. "Let's go."

"We need to reload," London argued, but ran into the hallway behind Natasha.

They didn't have a clue where they were going and she

couldn't run into more trouble without knowing her gun was loaded.

"Get the bullets out." Natasha looked over her shoulder at London for only a moment before focusing ahead of them.

Following Natasha and struggling with the box of bullets in her pocket, London looked behind them. The bodies in the doorway, just inside the garage, lay lifeless and tangled over one another. It was a sickening view and one London was positive she'd never get out of her head.

"This is insane," she muttered, unable to accept how many deaths she'd caused in the past couple days. Everything she'd vowed never to be involved in she was now in so deep it was overwhelming.

"Dealing with criminals often is," Natasha agreed. "Okay. Next door. Something tells me they won't come barging in after us this time."

"They're going to wait until we enter and start shooting at us?" London froze, feeling trapped in the hallway with dead bodies at one end and a closed door at the other.

"Load the guns." Natasha shoved her handgun at London.

She took it, struggling with both weapons and the box of bullets. It took all her focus to slide bullets into each chamber and not drop either gun, or the bullets. Her hands shook so hard and were so sweaty she could barely finish her task. All the while she was positive she and Natasha would be fired at before she finished. Natasha stood with her back to London, not saying anything.

"What are you doing?" She finished loading Natasha's gun, shoved it at Natasha, then hurried to load hers. Her hands wouldn't quit shaking and perspiration dripped down her body. It was too hot. They were too closed in.

"We're in luck."

London didn't understand but looked up, searching

Natasha's backside, as a glimmer of hope made her light-headed. She would grab any amount of luck thrown their way. If she could get to Marc and he wasn't hurt, he would help find her parents. It was an odd thought to pop into her head but one she held on to. Having a particular goal in all of this madness helped her keep her thoughts straight.

"There isn't anyone on the other side of this door," Natasha explained.

London fought to close the box of remaining bullets. A few fell loose and she stuffed bullets into her pocket, then gripped her gun with both hands as Natasha turned the doorknob.

"The door isn't locked," she whispered.

It was as if they entered a different world when they walked through the doorway and it closed silently behind them. Soft, thick carpet muffled their footsteps. London stared at the beautiful oil paintings hanging on the walls and the many bookshelves housing books of all kinds. Each wall was painted a glossy pale pink, which offset the dark, bloodred carpet. There was a large, heavy-looking wooden desk to her left, with two chairs facing it. There were more chairs to the right of her on the other side of the room. Although there weren't windows, which of course there wouldn't be since they were well underground, the paintings gave the illusion of a bright, sunny room. She didn't know a lot about art but these paintings just looked like they should be hanging in museums.

"What is this place?" she muttered, staring in disbelief at the office someone had put effort, and money, into decorating, and not something recently thrown together.

"I don't know, but we're going to find out." Natasha walked around the large desk and began opening drawers. "We just seriously scored," she added a moment later.

London edged closer to her, but there were two more

doors to the office other than the one they just came through. She doubted anyone would come after them through the garage, and if they did, they would have to get around all those bodies, which would create some noise. Just thinking about that made London cringe. Telling herself not to dwell on the fact that she'd killed at least one more person now didn't make the images go away. There was no way she could leave her parents here. And in spite of worrying she and Marc might not be compatible, she ached to be in his arms again, to know he was all right, to have him with her so they could get through this nightmare together. London glanced repeatedly at the two closed doors on the opposite side of the office from where they entered. Her hand was starting to cramp from holding the gun alert and ready, but she couldn't lower her defenses for a moment. And Natasha grew more excited as she continued looking through the desk.

"We've hit the mother lode. Someone was just on this computer. I bet they ran when they heard the commotion in the garage." Natasha looked up at her, grinning. "I don't need to worry about passwords."

"Will it tell us where everyone is?" She prayed this office was an indication that Marc and her family were at least comfortable. "Can we figure out what this place is and what they planned on doing with Marc, and everyone else?"

"We're going to find out." Natasha glanced around the office. "Make sure you're covering me, London."

"I am." She gripped her gun, fighting panic with each slight sound she thought she heard.

Natasha started typing, grunting to herself every few seconds. London glanced at the screen, but Natasha flew through pages too fast for London to keep up. She focused on her surroundings instead. There could be something to learn about this place by what was around her.

The few items on the desk didn't help her much. She

lifted the top page of notes on a legal pad only to find the rest of the notebook blank. London kept her eye on both doors and both doorknobs, watching and listening while trying to fight off a panic attack. The words on the notepad kept drawing her back to it, though.

"I wonder who Evelyn is," London mused, staring at the printed name that was underlined several times. "Looks like whoever sits here doesn't trust her."

"Huh?" Natasha glanced at the notepad.

Someone had written: "*Follow up on Evelyn*'s *work. There are obvious discrepancies. It makes no sense one pawn resists.*"

"Look here." Natasha pointed at the screen. "Here are Marc's and Jake's names. Uncle Greg and Aunt Haley," she continued, and ran her finger down the screen at what appeared to be some kind of schedule and checkoff sheet. "It seems they're being run through some kind of boot camp. See this legend?" she asked, pointing to the corner of the screen. "These marks indicate if they're meeting the requirements."

"Requirements for what?"

Natasha didn't answer right away. She clicked the mouse, moving around on the computer as if she used the programs on it every day. "It appears they're being trained to be some kind of army. But along with the amount of calisthenics and combat exercises they're putting them through, there is also this side chart."

"What's it for?"

"Apparently they're documenting how much drugs they're administering to each of them."

"Drugs?" London stared at the screen. "What kind of drugs?"

Both of them looked up at the same time when there was a sound on the other side of the door. Footsteps sounded quickly, as if someone was running. They stopped without notice, just as they'd begun and London watched the doorknob turn. She was frozen in place, watching in horror when the door opened. Even if she'd had time to think it through, there wasn't anywhere to hide. Other than the desk, there were the bookshelves flush against the wall. There weren't any windows. Going back the way they came wouldn't help them. They were trapped.

A tall, thin man with black hair hurried into the room, coming to a halt and looking at London and Natasha. His shocked expression turned to one of disdain as he narrowed his beady gaze on them.

"You're not going to ruin everything I've worked so hard to accomplish," he informed them, his cold, sinister tone enough to chill London's blood. "I'm going to win and no one will stop me." The man raised a gun he'd been holding out of sight, aimed, and fired.

Chapter Fifteen

Marc stepped out of the shower and swore he heard gunfire. He shot a worried look at the bathroom door, which was still slightly ajar. There it was again. Someone had just fired a gun, and it was nearby.

"Crap," Marc hissed, rubbing the one rough towel that had been folded on the back of the toilet—there were no towel racks—over his body too fast to dry himself off. Not that the thing would have been able to dry him thoroughly if he'd tried. He shoved his damp body into the clothes he'd had on before showering.

He twisted and yanked until he heard threads pop in his issued clothing. Marc was struggling to zip and button them when the third shot went off, this one louder, closer, and leaving no doubt as to what he'd heard.

"What the fuck?" Marc grabbed the door, peering around at his cell and the bars that kept him prisoner from the lab.

He wasn't armed. There wasn't any way to hide or sneak out and see better without exposing himself. He'd heard three gunshots, but no one had cried out in pain. As he listened, someone walked across the lab, their footsteps sounding determined and rushed. Marc couldn't see a damn thing from where he stood, but walking into the cell could be his death sentence.

"Come on out, Marc," Evelyn said, her tone sounding accusatory.

Marc left the bathroom, walking into the cell.

"Fucking figures. Now you listen to me." She rolled her eyes but didn't give him any more attention as she hurried from filing cabinet to computer and over to the large lab table. "There isn't much time. Are you dressed?"

"As dressed as I can be." He slipped the loafers on that were part of his prison uniform and moved to the cell door, wrapping his hands around two of the bars as he frowned at Evelyn. She almost seemed to be in a panic and appeared to be packing. "I heard gunshots," he said.

"Yup." She didn't slow down.

"Why were there gunshots?"

"A good scientist never invents something without having a backup to delete everything. I doubt I'll ever get credit for any of this, anyway."

"That would depend on who you work for."

She paused in her tracks, staring at him, as if his comment didn't make sense to her. "That wouldn't matter," she drawled, her tone soft, almost remorseful.

Evelyn jumped back into high gear and continued rushing around the lab, gathering notes and files and stuffing them into a large duffel bag. Marc was surprised there were that many documents when the bag was so stuffed she could hardly zip it closed. She then slid on to the stool at her computer and began clicking the mouse furiously as her eyes darted across the screen.

"Mind telling me why I heard gunshots?" he asked.

"Actually, right now I do mind." She never looked up from her computer but continued whatever it was she was doing, typing frantically as she scowled at the screen.

"Something's wrong, isn't it?"

When she shot him a look to kill but then continued typing, his heart skipped a beat. Last night Claude and Evelyn worried about two women aboveground. Now, after gunfire, Evelyn was cleaning house as if her life depended on it, which it very well might. Had they been infiltrated? And if so, were they good or bad guys?

His thoughts raced to London. God, he prayed she was far away from this place. Somewhere safe and protected. Because if she wasn't, there was little he could do to help her. Marc gripped the bars so hard they rattled.

Evelyn turned, ignoring him, and yanked open a drawer, then pulled out a flash drive. She slid it into the computer. Clicking the mouse again, she stood there, chewing her nails and staring at the screen. When her system beeped she replaced the flash drive with another one, then went through the process again, each time sliding the full flash drive into the side pocket of her duffel bag.

There was a muffled boom from somewhere else in the facility. Evelyn shrieked and ducked, gripping the side of the table as she started coughing, or crying. Maybe both. He couldn't tell.

"Evelyn, let me out of here," Marc insisted, shaking the bars to get her attention. "This place is being attacked, damn it! You've got a hell of a better chance of escaping with me than without me. Let me out."

He strained to see into the other cells but didn't see anyone in any of them. If the other men were in there, possibly sitting on their beds, they were drugged worse than he imagined. There was another muffled boom and the floor and walls shook.

"Damn it, Blondie!" Marc yelled, moving his hands down the metal poles and shaking them with all his strength. They didn't budge.

"Shut up!" she snapped, slowly straightening and looking around her frantically. "Crap. Crap," she hissed, ignoring him and staring at her computer. "There isn't time. There isn't goddamn time."

"Time for what?"

"I told you to shut up!"

Evelyn checked the zippers on her duffel as she slid the strap over her shoulder. It was obviously a strain on her when one side of her slumped over as she fought to carry the weight of the bag. She backed up and reached behind her, pulling out a black Glock and holding it with both hands.

"Evelyn," Marc warned, backing away from the steps. "Murder one, my dear."

She pulled the trigger and the computer exploded into hundreds of pieces, the plastic flying everywhere. Marc ducked, covering his head with his arms, and dared glance in her direction a moment later when the plastic settled. She hurried to his cell, shoving the Glock behind her and yanking keys out of her pocket. Evelyn didn't say anything when she unlocked his cell.

"Let's go," she ordered, turning and hurrying to the door that led to the gym.

Marc followed her, deciding he wouldn't argue with her choice of direction at the moment. As he passed the other cells, he stared at the three men lying flat on the ground in each one of them. Were those the shots he'd heard? Had Evelyn shot the other three men?

"Would you mind telling me what the hell is going on?" he asked when they reached the door leading into the gym. Marc reached over her head and pushed it open for her.

She didn't complain about his chivalry, nor did she try pushing it open herself. Evelyn wasn't appreciative, though. "You really don't follow orders well, do you?" she accused, snapping him a deadly look over her shoulder as she adjusted her duffel and started across the gym. "Remember, I can still drug you. Now shut the fuck up and stick close. See if you can handle those simple instructions."

He seriously considered grabbing her and showing her what he thought of bossy women. Marc didn't have a clue how to get aboveground and wasn't going to try until he knew where his family was. He would tolerate bossy Blondie until he found them, then they would get the hell out of there together.

Evelyn struggled with the door at the other end of the gym. Marc didn't help her until she'd managed to open it. No one bit his head off, then expected him to submit. He wouldn't let being snapped at keep them from making a timely escape either. Once he knew the way out, he'd go back for everyone else, regardless of what Blondie wanted.

Following her, he looked at her rear end and the duffel bag bouncing against it. Her Glock was stuffed inside her jeans. Marc wouldn't be surprised if it wasn't the only weapon she carried. Blondie took care of herself. Her actions right now—escaping and taking all of her work she could carry and destroying the rest—followed suit with her personality as he'd come to know it. He bet she'd killed the other men so no one could tell how lobotomized they were.

There was a reason why she hadn't drugged him like the others. Marc doubted it was simply because he resisted. There were other ways she could have made sure he ended up with as much of whatever that drug was the other men had. Blondie had risked being discovered by telling Claude that Marc was ready and praying he wouldn't be too defiant to blow her cover. Yet for some reason, she'd decided to let Marc keep his brain functioning in his head. He was grateful yet more than a little curious what her motivation was.

They left the gym and hurried down a long hallway. There weren't any doors and the walls were rough and not painted. Either she and Claude hadn't gotten around to modernizing this end of their underground haven or whatever they used this section for, it didn't need to look nice.

"Okay, push that door open." Evelyn stood to the side and gestured at a metal door.

Marc cocked an eyebrow at her. If she thought he would run after her, obediently quiet, then handle her grunt work when she ordered it, she could think again.

"*Please,*" she stressed.

"We're getting there." He placed his palm against the door. It was really cold, as if possibly the other side wasn't as temperature controlled as it was on this side. "Tell me what's going on."

She sighed, her expression turning annoyed. "We've been compromised. Satisfied?"

Hardly. He told her as much with a look.

"Fine. Move." Evelyn tried shoving past him and pushing against the door.

Marc grabbed her, pushing her back. When she tried reaching for her gun, he took her arm, twisting it around her duffel bag until she bent over and squealed.

"Don't think for a second you're being armed and me not will enable you to control me," he whispered over her. Then pulling her upright, Marc let go of her and crossed his arms. "I've gone along with this insane charade to try and learn what the hell is going on here. We've gone far enough. If you want to leave, you better start talking."

"You've gone along with?" When she grinned, there was a bit too much confidence making her eyes glow. "Look here, Neanderthal, I'm not an idiot. I know I can't control you without having a card up my sleeve."

She had an obsession with controlling someone over trying to work with him. But the way she continued grinning, her expression relaxing when she should have been the one watching him warily, kept him alert.

"It better be one hell of a good card," he informed her.

"Feel under your left arm." Evelyn adjusted the duffel on her back once again. The thing looked really heavy. She shot a furtive glance down the hall where they'd just come before returning her attention to him. "Find it?" she asked casually.

Marc ran his fingers up his left arm, frowning at her. "Feel what?"

She sighed again but maintained her pleasant expression. "Just before your armpit. I put it in the flesh under your arm. It's not in your armpit. I didn't have time to shave you. But its location is sufficient. Find it?" she asked sweetly.

He didn't like the look on her face or her tone. Where she'd been short and way too bossy since leaving her lab, Evelyn now talked to him as if he were a child, speaking calmly and slowly, with a sweet, almost motherly tone to her voice. He couldn't tell if she was patronizing him or if possibly Blondie suffered from a severe personality disorder. It was almost as if she'd changed completely from one person to another. Evelyn, on the one hand, was the cutthroat scientist with little patience for anyone who couldn't keep up with her analytical brain. Blondie, on the other hand, was flirtatious, almost precious, soft-spoken, patient, and calm, as if she didn't have a care in the world. It was when the two women mixed that he became nervous. When she met his gaze with a triumphant gleam in her eyes while her smile remained friendly and patient, a cold sweat broke out over Marc's flesh. He rubbed the hard, cylindrical bump under his flesh.

"What is it?"

"I guess you could say I have my trump card up your sleeve instead of mine." She giggled, grinning broadly at him like she'd just told one hell of a good joke. "To answer your question, there are two cylinders under your flesh. The remote for them is in my mouth." She poked her index finger into her mouth toward one of her molars. "I clench my teeth hard enough and I turn on the remote, which sends a signal to your arm, and voilà!" She waved her hand in the air between them. "You become my personal slave, willing to do whatever I tell you to do without giving a thought to your own safety or well-being."

"Why, you fucking little bitch!" he sneered, grabbing her before she could move out of his reach. She almost toppled to the side from the weight of her duffel bag as he dragged her up against him. The urge to throw her as far as he could damn near overwhelmed him.

"Marc!" she whined. She dragged her fingers down his chest, her look frantic for a moment when he looked down at her. "Neither one of us will make it out of here if you don't calm down," she pleaded. "Not to mention, you can throw me, hit me, or drag me out of here by my hair. I can clench my teeth together through any of that. Almost without giving it any thought."

Marc glared at her, not sure he'd ever felt hatred as strongly as he did now. "You're going to take that thing out of your mouth. And if you're feeding me a line, you'll seriously regret the moment you came up with such an asinine idea. Because I'll yank it out of your mouth myself if I have to."

"It's not asinine. If you ask me, it's more insane to rob a man of his free will and ability to think. I'd rather a man have his own thoughts and do as I say of his own free will."

He let go of her, barely able to resist tossing her regardless of what she'd just said. Something told him if she wanted him to be a fucking zombie she would have turned him into one already.

"Run from me or turn on me and I'll cause one of those capsules in your arm to explode. If I make both of them explode at the same time you'll become a functioning human being without a single thought in your head, permanently." She used her hands to shove the duffel into place in the middle of her back and nodded at the door. "Open the door, Marc, please."

The black pants and pullover V-neck shirt he wore weren't much to protect him from the cold, winter wind blowing outside. He wasn't sure why it surprised him that it was nighttime outside. The sky was dark, overcast, without a single star visible. It was the icy wind that damn near did him in and helped soothe his outrage somewhat. He was too damn cold and his blood too thin from living most of his life in a warm climate to focus on anything other than doing whatever it took to get back inside or at least somewhere a hell of a lot warmer.

Evelyn didn't run but hurried with a quick pace across the uneven frozen desert-like field. She kept her head ducked, her arms crossed over her chest, and didn't once look behind her to ensure he followed. The only light they had was the small handheld-flashlight beam that raced over the rough, snow-covered ground just ahead of them. Evelyn held it in her hand, next to her chest, and pointed into the darkness in front of her.

Marc didn't see the ruins anywhere or the group of rocks just south of them where the underground garage was. To the best he could figure, all of that was at least a mile or two east of them. They'd surfaced on the far west side of the underground facility and were heading farther west as quickly as Evelyn could walk. He could take the pack from her, help them pick up their pace, but although he was half-frozen, he wasn't sure he should be in a hurry to get wherever they were going.

One thing held steadfast in his mind. They were leaving his parents and Jake behind. If London tried finding him, if she figured out where the underground prison was, he would no longer be there.

Somehow he'd have to figure out a way to let all of them know where he was. And even more importantly, where he was going. He didn't trust Evelyn as far as he could throw her, although with the rage inside him right now, he could probably hurl her a fair distance. At least until he had a clue where he was, or had means to escape, find a phone, Evelyn was his unwanted partner.

Marc glanced back in the direction they'd come, but it was barren desert all around them. Who had compromised Evelyn and Claude's underground haven? Was London anywhere nearby? His parents and Jake had better be okay. Returning his attention to Evelyn, he watched her continue to flash the light across the ground.

Lord! She was a madwoman. He'd give her a few more minutes to prove to him she hadn't lost it, or he was going back to find his family. The capsules in his arm be damned.

London crawled out from under the desk using one hand to brace herself, as she aimed her gun with the other, finger on the trigger, ready to save her life.

"Come on out, bitch," the man sneered from the other side of the room.

London did as she was told, leaping into sight and pulling the trigger at the same time.

"Son of a bitch!" the man screamed, crashing to the ground and making the floor shake under her feet. "Crap. Damn you! You shot me. You fucking bitch. God, bitch!"

London wanted to shoot him again just to make him shut up. Blood quickly soaked one of his pants legs and he hunched over, falling to the floor, gripping his thigh, as he continued wailing loud profanities.

"I can probably make the bleeding stop if you tell me where Marc and the others are," she told him, not at all sure she could help him and more than a bit amazed at how calm she sounded. "You better hurry, though. You're bleeding pretty fast."

"Through that door. Down the stairs and turn right. Now make it stop. Make it stop now!" he screamed.

She wasn't a nurse and didn't know if all the doctor shows she watched on TV were accurate or not. London didn't watch a lot of TV, though, and although she searched her mind for a similar scene from any show at all that might help her know what to do right now, she drew a blank. All she could think of was that a person stopped bleeding by applying pressure.

Glancing around the room, she didn't see anything she could use to put pressure on his leg. Natasha wasn't screaming in pain, which meant her gunshot wound was more serious. The longer London stood there trying to figure out how to shut up the jerk writhing on the floor, the more time she was wasting.

There was a thick tapestry draped over a side table. She grabbed the vase off it and dropped it to the floor, then pulled the tapestry off and started wringing it into a rope.

"Stupid bitch," the man howled. "That vase is a fucking original!"

"So is your leg!" she yelled at him, and threw the tapestry in his face. "Wrap that around your leg and stop your own bleeding."

London wouldn't waste any more time seeing to the needs of a rude bastard who quite possibly was the man behind abducting her parents and Marc. She ran through the door and almost fell down the stairs. There was another door across a large room to her right. London didn't bother looking around her but raced to the door. She yanked on the doorknob and it opened easier than she'd anticipated, causing her almost to fall backward.

"Drop your weapons or die!" she yelled, holding her gun in front of her and ready to shoot anything that moved.

She slid to a stop when two people, a very tall, large man and a woman clinging to him, stared at her wide-eyed behind bars. They were in a cage.

"London?" someone asked, sounding shocked, or disbelieving. Maybe both.

There were more cages, three of the walls made of cement and the bars facing her looking really solid as they disappeared into the floor. She spotted Jake in the cell across from the couple. He gripped the bars, looking at her with shocked amazement, and that stupid crooked grin.

"There aren't any guards in here," he told her. "You aren't alone, are you?"

London glanced up and down the short hallway between the jail cells. There wasn't anyone else in there. Nor did she see a large ring of keys hanging on the wall as there would be in an old Western.

"London?" It sounded like London's mom, her voice hesitant and surprised.

London moved down the hall, past the jail cells holding the couple and Jake. There was another cement cage next to the one where the couple was. London stared at her mother and father.

"London," her father said, rushing to the bars.

She lowered her gun, taking her father's hand and grinning at him and her mom. "Fancy finding you two here," London said.

Ruby Brooke laughed, the sound rough and husky from years of smoking cigarettes and probably other stuff, too. "What in the world are you doing here?" she asked, reaching through the bars and stroking her daughter's face.

"I'm here to rescue you." London felt an overwhelming urge to laugh, too.

She stared at her parents, at the two people who were always on top of their act and calm and cool during a crisis while she had been the child freaking out and panicking. It amazed her how suddenly she felt incredibly calm and in control of her senses.

"Honestly, though, I never thought I'd be staring at the two of you behind bars."

Her father looked grayer than he had the last time she saw him, but his confident bellow of a laugh hadn't changed. "There's a big difference between being caught and being captured, my dear," he said, speaking under his breath so Jake and the other couple wouldn't hear him. "See if you can get that panel open that's on the wall over there. The keys to open these jail cells are in there."

She hurried to the cabinet in the wall at the end of the hallway near the door. There didn't appear to be anyone racing down here to prevent her from freeing their prisoners and she could still hear the man upstairs wailing and complaining. At least he was still alive. No one was helping him, either. If they were, he'd be screaming even louder at them or be silent by now from their knocking his ass out in frustration. Maybe she and Natasha had eliminated all the guards when they were first ambushed in the garage.

London held on to that belief. It helped keep her calm. She closed the door she'd entered and faced the cabinet that was flush in the wall. It didn't surprise her that it was locked.

"Aim your gun at the door handle," the large man in the cage nearest her suggested.

London glanced at him. The man's short brown hair and blue eyes, not to mention his incredible height and muscular stance, reminded her of Marc.

"London, these are my parents, Greg and Haley King," Jake said from his jail cell. "Mom, Dad, this is London. She's Marc's girl."

"You've got yourself a guy?" Ruby asked from the cell at the end of the hall.

"We'll talk about it later," London announced, turning

her back on all of them, holding her gun in both hands, and aiming. Odd how she'd pulled the trigger without giving it a thought when men lunged at her. But standing in front of the cabinet and staring at the handle, she suddenly wondered the best way to shoot it.

"Aim and fire, baby girl," her father instructed.

"I know how to shoot, Dad," she said. Then, needing her parents to see that she wasn't the scared child anymore, she added, "I got down here past all the guards, didn't I?"

"You shot all the guards?" her mother asked, her disbelief almost annoying, if it hadn't been so comical.

"Every single one of them," she said, aimed and fired, jumping at the loud sound when the bullet slammed into the metal handle. The door flew open and flew shut, making even more of a racket.

London reached inside the small closet built into the wall and pulled out a ring of keys that did in fact look just like they did in old Westerns. Everyone behind her cheered and sang her praises. Maybe the adrenaline that got her this far was suddenly crashing inside her. London almost swooned when she turned, reaching and grabbing the bars to Marc's parents' jail cell. She didn't fight Greg King when he reached through the bars and took the keys from her, then unlocked his own jail cell.

There wasn't any doubt at all that she'd faint when all of them were around her, both her mother and father pulling her into their arms, hugging her fiercely, and saying all the words she'd ached to hear all her life. At the moment, though, too many other thoughts started plaguing her and ruined her ability to enjoy her parents' praise.

"Where is Marc?" she asked, turning in her mother's arms and facing Jake and his parents.

"They took him the night we arrived," Jake said.

"Natasha is upstairs in a really nice office. She's been shot."

Jake's mother shrieked and covered her mouth with her hands.

"Oh God! Where is she?" Haley asked, looking frantic but breathing deeply as if she was searching for some inner calm.

London glanced at her parents, who were watching the Kings. They both looked at her when she focused on them and smiled at the same time.

"Pretty impressive, baby girl," her father said, stroking her arm. "I should have known it was in your blood. Now who is this Natasha?"

"She's someone I recently met," London said, moving when Greg, Jake, and Haley headed to the door. "She found this place, but when this tall, dark-haired man shot at us and she got hit."

"And you didn't?" London's mother asked, moving in alongside her and studying her, looking concerned when she tried running her hands down London's side.

"No. I shot him."

Greg King stopped at the closet in the wall and pulled out several black poles, handing one to Jake and another to her father.

"They're better than having nothing," he said, then focused on her with eyes that were just like Marc's. "How many men did you shoot? Did you shoot a woman?"

"I don't know," she said, shaking her head. "I think three in the garage and one in the office and no, no women." She frowned at the black sticks. "What are those?" They were like small broom handles without the brooms on the ends of them.

"They send out electric charges," Jake explained, indicating a button that was barely visible at one end of the pole. "They've got enough juice in them to knock a man clear out."

"We've got to go to Natasha." Haley sounded worried

as she tried pushing around her husband to the door. "And we need to find Marc. He's in here somewhere. They wouldn't have killed him."

"Why did they separate you?" London felt as if she was pushed out the door and turned to study Jake's brooding expression when he stared at the large empty room they walked into.

"What is that noise?" Ruby grabbed London's arm, sounding shocked and causing everyone to pause and stand and listen to the wailing and moaning coming from upstairs. "Is that your man?"

Already Haley was hurrying to the door leading to the stairs. Her husband was right behind her.

"No. That is the man I shot. I got him in the leg and he told me where all of you were when I agreed to give him something to hold against his leg to stop the bleeding," London admitted, following the Kings up the stairs with Jake and her parents behind her. "He charged into the office upstairs when Natasha and I were on the computer."

The man on the floor, who was curled in a ball hugging his leg and covered in blood, looked up at all of them, terrified. "Help me. Please, I need help."

"You'll get help. Trust me," Greg told him, stepping over him and hurrying to the desk.

Haley slid to the floor where Natasha lay, not moving, although she wasn't covered in as much blood as the man was.

"We've got to get her to a hospital," Haley announced, looking up at the rest of them.

"Marc's car is in the garage," London announced, pointing to the door where they'd first entered but staring at Natasha, who looked grossly pale and very still. London couldn't look away from her new friend even when she ordered herself to do so. Natasha had been as scared as London was when they entered the office, unsure of what they would find. Her stomach twisted and the room started spinning when Haley clutched Natasha against her chest. Natasha's head fell limp off the side of Haley's arm, looking very lifeless.

Greg lifted his niece into his arms and Jake hurried to the door. London found the flashlight Natasha had used when they left the car and climbed the stairs behind the men and in front of her parents. They weren't all going to fit into the car, but they hadn't found Marc yet. As desperately as London wanted this nightmare to end and to be back in safe and comfortable surroundings, she knew someone had to remain behind and find Marc.

She turned on the flashlight, but her father found a light switch on the wall, turning it on and flooding the large, almost warehouse-sized garage with light.

"Does anyone else think Evelyn and your other son, Marc, aren't here anymore?" London's father asked, running his hand along the black SUV that was parked in front of Marc's car.

"We need to confirm that." Jake took the keys from London when she offered them to him and hurried to help get Natasha into the car. "I'll remain behind. We need to search this entire facility."

"You two take her to a hospital," Jonnie decided, facing Greg. "Come back for us. We'll find your boy if he's here."

Greg nodded, giving Jonnie an appraising once-over and glancing at London before turning to his wife. Haley was climbing into the backseat and reaching for Natasha when they eased her into the car. Jake and Jonnie moved around the garage until they figured out how to open the door in the ground. A rush of fierce, cold air filled the garage as the runway heading up to the outside appeared. Greg climbed into the driver's seat and the Mustang roared to life. London backed up and stood between her parents, wrapping her arms around herself and trying to ward off the cold as she watched Greg skillfully back the car up the incline until he disappeared into the night outside. They were left there without transportation other than the black SUV. God only knew where the keys were. She glanced around at the cold underground facility where all the terror that so recently entered her life began. If Marc was here, she worried he was in worse shape than Natasha.

There was no way all of this could end with him being dead. London knew how unfair and cruel real life could be, but she refused to accept that he was dead. Turning, she walked away from her parents and Jake, gripping the gun she still held in one hand and the flashlight in the other. She was going to find Marc.

Chapter Sixteen

Marc couldn't feel his hands, ears, or nose. The soft loafers he wore didn't do shit against the rocky, hard snow-covered ground. His feet burned so badly he started worrying frostbite might kick in and make it hard for him to keep walking across the frozen desert. Evelyn pressed on alongside him, though, keeping a hard, determined pace with her duffel bag bouncing against her back. They hadn't said anything to each other for a while now. He'd worry she was leading them into a frozen world of nowhere if it weren't for the cell phone she held with some kind of navigation program on it. She glanced down at it from time to time and continued walking without a word through the pitch-black, frozen night.

More than once it crossed his mind to knock Evelyn out, hitting her just right to render her unconscious. She wouldn't grind her teeth, if there was in fact some kind of remote that would activate whatever was under his skin. He considered it again when Evelyn glanced at her phone, holding the glowing device up in her hands and studying it as she slowed her pace.

"Over here," she broke the silence between them, grinning up at him as if she'd just accomplished some feat and was proud of herself. "We'll be enjoying a hot shower and hot meal here soon enough."

Her amiable nature didn't relax him or end his thoughts of knocking her out cold. Especially when she hurried forward but stopped suddenly, looking around as she began walking in circles. Marc stopped, watching her while worrying he was slowly freezing to death.

"You really need to learn to trust me." She grinned as she stomped her foot on the ground. Then squatting down, she reached for something on the ground.

He was amazed when she picked up what looked like a remote and began pushing buttons on it. Evelyn hurried toward him, turning around before she reached him and backing into him as she held the remote out and looked as if she were trying to find a channel to watch while aiming at a TV that wasn't there.

He took a step or two backward when the ground parted, just as it had when he and Jake had been taken to their underground prison in the black SUV. Evelyn didn't reach for Marc or gesture for him to follow her when she hurried toward the dark hole appearing in the ground. There wasn't any hiding his surprise when a platform rose out of the ground with a car parked on it.

"The escapemobile," she announced, laughing. "I told him it would come in handy," she mumbled, not elaborating as to who "him" was.

Marc walked around to the passenger side after Evelyn jumped into the car and started it. The platform it was on stopped when it was flush with the ground. He felt the ground give way slightly when he stepped next to the car. There was a hollow thud as his weight caused the platform the car was on to rock. He chanced it, climbing into the passenger seat. She had the car running but didn't try putting it into drive until Marc adjusted the seat backward so he could fit inside alongside her.

Evelyn laughed, driving the car off the platform and holding the remote up between them, pointing it backward and pushing a button on it. "No reason to give away my secret garage," she said, still chuckling when she dropped the remote between them. "Don't worry, Neanderthal. The heat works fine and you'll thaw out soon enough."

He turned to make a comment but didn't react quickly enough. Evelyn had a syringe in her hand that must have been in the car. She stabbed Marc in the side of the neck with it and the sharp pinch was the last thing he felt before everything around him went black.

"Wake up, sweetheart."

Marc blinked, thinking for a second London rubbed his arm. He wanted to pull her into his arms. Cuddling with her would keep him warm and at the moment he was cold as hell.

"Come on, Neanderthal," Evelyn whispered, leaning close enough that her breath prickled his flesh.

Marc blinked and leaned forward, resting his head against his hand for a moment before rubbing his face and squinting at his surroundings. Bright lights glowed against the black night, which illuminated the parking lot and curved drive in front of a large hotel.

"The valet will park the car," Evelyn told Marc, nudging his arm until he looked at her. "Wake up. Now. Come on. We're going up to our room now." Her words were choppy and didn't make sense.

She got out on her side of the car. Marc reached for his door, ignoring the young college kid who held on to the passenger door as he climbed out. Evelyn said something about him being a sound sleeper as she passed over keys and a bill for the tip. Marc didn't care what she told the kid but instead focused on the fancy hotel, searching for some indication of where they were.

Evelyn was already at the front desk when Marc walked through the revolving doors. She laughed easily with the lady behind the counter. Marc pictured London behind the counter at the lodge, her friendly, relaxed nature making it easy for anyone to approach her with any question or just to check in or out. He didn't bother looking at the woman talking to Evelyn but instead stared at the sign next to the front desk.

WELCOME TO PHOENIX.

Crap. Evelyn had done some driving. Marc rubbed his neck, remembering when she'd injected him with something strong enough to knock his ass out as she drove across the state of Arizona. She accepted the card keys and walked across the lobby, apparently feeling she didn't need to tell Marc to follow her or look over her shoulder to see if he was.

He waited until they were in the elevator before grabbing her wrist and lifting her hand. Then removing the card keys from her hand, he released her and read the room number on the cards.

"Why are we in Phoenix, Blondie?" he asked, pocketing one of the cards and flipping the other one between his fingers while staring down at her.

"Because I got tired of driving." She pressed her lips into a straight line, narrowing her gaze on him. Apparently, studying his face told her that he wasn't in the mood to be bullied by one of her drugs being used on him. She relaxed her expression and focused on the elevator doors. "I'm not taking the rap for any of this," she said under her breath, then stormed out ahead of him when the elevator doors opened.

Marc took his time walking down the plush-looking

hallway, partially because he was still groggy from whatever she'd shot him with. He also needed to make his brain work. Evelyn had driven all night and he got a good night's sleep. That would work to his advantage if he could get the fog out of his brain. Evelyn stopped in front of one of the doors, not looking at him. Marc double-checked the room number against the number on the cardholder, slid the plastic card out, then reached around her and opened the door.

"What are you doing?" she asked when he walked into the room and collapsed on the king-sized bed.

He thought of asking her the same thing when he noticed there was only one bed in the room. Marc stretched out, lying from corner to corner and rolling over, easing a pillow under his head while his feet almost reached the end of the opposite corner.

"You're not sleeping while I shower." She didn't comment on him being sprawled out on the entire bed. "Until I know I'm clear of this mess you're my insurance policy, and that means we're both going to have to live with a few rules."

"I'm not your insurance for anything and I think we've already established what I think of following your rules." He clasped his hands behind his head and stared at her.

Evelyn stood at the end of the bed, scowling at him. There were dark shadows under her eyes, and in the lighting from the lamps already on when they entered the room it was obvious she was much older than she wanted the world to know.

It wasn't her physical appearance that mattered to him, though. Evelyn did nothing for him. Her physical beauty was superficial at best and faded quickly when the cold-hearted bitch inside her came forward. What grabbed his attention was the way she looked at him. Marc knew when a woman wanted him, and there was absolutely no interest in Evelyn's eyes at all. Instead, the way she focused on him, forcing her gaze to travel down his body slowly before returning to his face, revealed even more about her. Evelyn would try seducing him if she believed it would be to her advantage. Not that this revelation surprised him. It was the flash of fear in her eyes when she returned her gaze to his that he focused on. Evelyn was afraid of him, terrified in fact.

"Whether you like it or not," she said, cocking one eyebrow. They were one-on-one now and it was obvious Evelyn planned on ensuring her title as captor and his as the prisoner. "You're not free to do as you wish. I would prefer you honor my wishes of your own free will, but if you force my hand I'll make sure you do what I tell you to do regardless of the means necessary."

"Whether you like it or not, you've broken quite a few laws. Take your shower, order food, or go to sleep. Your next move won't change the fact that I'm going to see you arrested and behind bars."

Evelyn shook her head, walking away from him and into the bathroom. Marc didn't move. He suspected she didn't want to leave him alone and believed he would try doing something, either escaping or calling someone the first chance he had. The shower didn't turn on. No other sounds came from the bathroom. Marc didn't move, either. Instead he worked to sharpen his thoughts while replaying everything in his mind he could remember prior to leaving the underground facility.

There had been shots, although he was pretty sure what he heard was Evelyn shooting the men in the other cells. He could only speculate as to why she'd shot them but hauled him along with her. He was not an insurance policy. She'd been frantic to clean out her lab, packing files and deleting files from her hard drive to flash drive. When she'd thought she'd run out of time she'd blown up her computer, which annoyed her to do. Obviously, she would rather destroy whatever work was on her computer than allow anyone else to find it.

She'd repeatedly mentioned that she wouldn't take the blame for any of this, which seemed to be her motivation for running. Marc had to conclude someone had found the facility. Evelyn told him they'd been compromised. If London somehow figured out where he was, she must have pulled off some kind of impressive show to send Evelyn scooting out the back door. But did that mean she was at the facility when he left with Evelyn? Had she searched and found her parents and Marc's family?

He prayed that was the case. It would mean that she got past the men who had taken him and Jake out of the hotel room. It would also mean Marc's sexy dark-haired seductress had some hidden talents he hadn't initially seen in her. Maybe growing up as the only child of two habitual criminals made her despise anything to do with guns or law enforcement or criminal investigation. Did London know of her skills and simply not want to put them to use? Was she forced to use them, then put on one hell of a show that he'd missed? A show so spectacular it sent Evelyn running?

Evelyn popped out of the bathroom, almost jumping around the corner but then frowning when he was lying in the same position she'd left him. "You can try all you want to make me think you're not going to try to escape, I won't believe you."

He turned his head to look at her. "That would make you a smart woman."

She seemed surprised he so openly admitted he would try to escape. "Which I am," she said. "Therefore, you're not staying out here alone. I want to take a shower. You're coming in here with me."

"Do you have luck with many men seducing them like

that?" He rolled off the side of the bed, taking his time standing and moving around the bed until he stood in front of her. "Or is that why you're so obsessed with controlling men?"

"You're not going to say anything I haven't heard before." She stepped to the side and pointed to the bathroom.

Marc walked into the large fancy bathroom, turning when he stood in front of a large sunken bathtub complete with jets to turn it into a Jacuzzi. Evelyn paused in the doorway but entered as well, closing the door behind her.

"I know what you think." She moved to the counter, staring at him through the mirror as she pulled the ponytail holder out of her hair. "You think I'm crazy, some kind of mad scientist."

"I've never thought of you as a scientist."

Evelyn was one of those people blessed with a very nondescript appearance. She wasn't ugly, far from it. In fact, she was thin, with large breasts, clear skin and long blonde hair. That generic description would imply she was hot, sexy, stunning, and she was none of those. His insult hit a nerve, and eyes he wouldn't have been able to describe once he was away from her suddenly glowed with raw rage.

She turned on him slowly. "Displaying your ignorance only makes you even more of a Neanderthal," she hissed.

He watched her teeth, remembering her accusation that clenching them would erupt the capsules under his skin. "Actually, I find it interesting that you claim to know what I think when, since I've met you, it seems to be your intention to make me not think."

"If I didn't want you to think, you would have been running laps until you collapsed," she pointed out, and ran her fingers through her hair once it was loose, fluffing it out until it hung past her shoulders, looking wild and untamed. Again, it transformed her appearance, and she actually looked better than she had when it was pulled back tightly against her head in a ponytail. "You were an experiment of one, an attempt for me to show in my work that soldiers can perform and meet exceptional standards without being drained of all cognitive thought."

"And apparently I was an experiment that no one but you wanted done," he added, putting it together as he spoke to her. "Claude didn't want you working with any of the men abducted unless they were drugged. Why is that, I wonder?"

"Claude is an idiot."

"If he's an idiot, then why did he choose such a successful scientist as yourself?"

She straightened, accepting Marc's praise with a nod. Her anger drained out of her as quickly as it had spiked. Evelyn walked around him and turned on the tub, bending over to adjust the water while the silence between them grew. The last thing he wanted to do was sit there and watch her bathe. Closing the lid, he sat on the toilet and waited for her answer. Once she was soaking in her bath he would make his move.

"Claude wouldn't have chosen anyone else to work with him when he decided to enter the game," she said, satisfied with the water and pulling off her shirt. She faced him in her jeans and bra, putting her hands on her hips and showing off round breasts that filled her lace cups perfectly. "I'm his wife and in most cases that means I can't testify against him. But it's not just that. I know how to work with him. Claude doesn't get along well with many people."

Marc didn't find that as surprising as he did the fact that the two of them were married. It explained their banter that he had overheard while in the facility. The way she taunted Claude, suggesting she enjoyed her prisoners possibly more than she actually did. He was jealous of her working with the men and Evelyn fed off that jealousy, believing he cared for her because he insisted she not be too impressed with any of the men in her care.

"Why did you leave him there if he's your husband?" Marc's gaze fell to her hands when she unzipped her jeans. Evelyn was possibly twenty years older than London. She looked forty years older.

"He knows where I am." She waved her hand in the air, dismissing Marc's question. "He'll come crawling to me when he realizes I was right. I told him from the beginning he wouldn't be able to set up his players by himself. When he insisted on choosing all the wrong kinds of people for his pawns, I knew I would have to step in and help. And it was the perfect opportunity to show how well my new drug worked."

There were so many questions. He needed to stay on topic, though, going with the flow of their conversation, to keep her talking. Since Marc and his family were the pawns chosen to play his game, Marc was curious if Claude had wanted them on board, or Evelyn. "Why didn't you like the idea that Claude chose my family?"

"Because Neanderthals don't train well." She slipped out of her bra and her jeans. "I lined you up with the dummies we'd chosen, intending to prove to him that you wouldn't conform simply because you were told the men around you were conforming."

"Who were those men you killed?"

Evelyn pushed her underwear down her legs and stepped out of it while laughing. "I didn't kill them. They are all still alive. I injected them with a neutralizing drug so if anyone found them they wouldn't be able to detect my drug in them. I'm not ready to announce it to the world yet. But I will be soon, very soon."

Marc would have to find out more about this drug she

was so proud of, but there were other questions he needed answered first. He ignored her as she pranced around him naked, moving to the counter and gathering her shampoo and conditioner. Marc rested his head on his hand and stared at the water filling the tub.

"What do you mean by 'dummies'? You knew before I showed up I wouldn't follow orders just because the men already there were? They were high on your drug, though, and I wasn't."

" 'High' hardly describes what this drug does to you. 'High' implies you're enjoying the sensations stimulated around you. My drug renders you blank, steals your free will. Claude wanted to take some of the most stubborn, bullheaded men who were known for upholding our laws by breaking them and turn them into his pawns. I do love my husband, whether you believe it or not." Her words might have been more convincing if she weren't standing in front of Marc naked. "But he's not man enough to control pawns of that magnitude. I needed to show him if he wanted in on the game he would need pawns he could control, and not ones who would inevitably destroy him."

"You set him up to fail so he would choose pawns that were more submissive from the beginning?" Marc searched her face and knew he was right. Now that he understood her motivation, he needed to learn more about this game and, most important, who the other players in the game were. Others would be abducted to play this war game. Marc needed names and locations. But, at the least, names.

"Claude believed the other men were also bounty hunters. I brought them in. All I had to do was find large, muscular men who were full of themselves and he believed me. Claude lured you and your family in. It was my idea to send the little slut in Colorado pictures of her parents once I knew you were sniffing around her. My theory was correct that you would insist on protecting her. She was the perfect distraction, for both you and her parents, which made it easier to capture both of you."

"Her parents were sent pictures, too?" Snapping at Evelyn for calling London a slut would distract her from the conversation. He was pretty sure she'd insulted London to test him anyway, and he was done being Evelyn's personal guinea pig for whatever hypothesis she wanted to explore at that moment.

"Jonnie Brooke knows his line of work well. When I sent the Brookes pictures of their daughter with a famous bounty hunter sniffing around her, they immediately grew suspicious. They panicked, thinking you were going through her to find them." Evelyn smiled. "Which I might have suggested you were doing."

"What about the private investigator who came to the lodge questioning London about her parents?"

Evelyn frowned. "I don't know anything about a private investigator." She snorted. "More than likely he was legitimate. The Brookes are crooks, scam artists, and I'm sure on quite a few hit lists."

Marc wasn't a strong advocate of coincidence. He made a mental note to learn more about the PI who'd been sniffing around London. "So why abduct bounty hunters and thieves? What kind of game is this?"

"Enough questions for now, Neanderthal. We'll continue with your education after my bath." She placed her shampoo and conditioner on the edge of the tub. "Get undressed."

Marc raised one eyebrow. "Why would I get undressed?"

She gestured at the bathwater. "I thought you could scrub my back. After all, I'm the one who drove all night, not you."

Marc looked at the items she'd scattered across the counter. Picking up one of those round, rough balls he remembered seeing in London's shower, he tossed it and caught it in his hand. "I tell you what. I'm not getting in the water with you and I think you know you can't force me. I'll kneel next to the tub and scrub your back." He looked at the other items on the counter, focusing on tweezers and spotting fingernail clippers. Far from surgical equipment, but his options were limited. He returned his attention to Evelyn, pulling off his shirt. "Climb in," he encouraged.

"Now you know I'm not going to relax in a hot bath so you can leave." She seemed to forgot she was naked. Wagging her finger in the air, she made a tsking sound. "Don't ever treat me as if I were stupid."

"I'm not getting in the tub. Better start grinding your teeth. Don't lose a filling over it," he mumbled, turning his back to her and picking up the fingernail clippers.

Marc moved fast, not only because he knew it would hurt like hell but also because he might not hit his mark if she jumped on him.

"What are you doing?" she shrieked when he raised his arm over his head, faced the mirror, and brought the clippers to the soft flesh under his arm.

Marc ignored her, pressing the clippers into the foreign objects just under his skin and grabbing them between the metal. He clenched his own teeth when he squeezed, feeling the pain ransack his body as he closed his eyes and focused on yanking the small cylindrical objects out of his body.

"God! Stop it!" She did jump at him, grabbing his arm that held the clippers and hanging on when she couldn't make him lower his arm.

He braced himself, using her attack to distract the pain and instead focused on remaining still when she lunged at him.

"You're nuts. God, you idiot. You're bleeding everywhere."

"You're not helping matters." Marc threw her off him. It was more instinct when he was unable to prevent his body from reacting to the pain consuming his body.

He didn't pay attention when Evelyn fell backward. There was blood everywhere, making it damn hard to make sure he had the small objects out of his arm. Holding his arm high, he forced himself to keep the small silver fingernail clippers in his arm until he thought he had both small, cylindrical bloody tubes. Marc dropped the clippers, which were drenched with blood, into a small glass cup next to the sink and grabbed one of the towels folded on a rack on the wall. It wasn't until then that he noticed he'd hurled Evelyn into the tub.

The way she was splashing around, fighting to get out and cussing him out at the same time, was enough proof she wasn't hurt.

"I'm not going to be your insurance policy," he growled, wrapping the towel around his arm and enduring the pain as he struggled to put his shirt back on. "In fact, it would help me if you stayed in there. Enjoy your bath, Blondie."

She probably had more clothes somewhere, but it bought him a couple minutes when he grabbed her clothes with his uninjured arm and threw them in the tub with her.

"Marc, you don't understand," she wailed. "You can't leave me. This isn't about you, or me. You don't understand."

She was destroying the bathroom, splashing water everywhere. She began cussing him out worse than before when he tossed the towels in with her as well. It would probably be the last time she ever asked for a room with a sunken tub. Marc grabbed her arm, feeling the pain streak through him and ransack his body. He swore getting shot didn't hurt this bad.

"I don't think *you* understand," he said, trying to stay patient when he wanted to knock her out and insure her silence. "*I'm . . . not . . . staying . . . with . . . you,*" he said, stressing each word slowly as he forced her down into the water.

"You're not leaving, damn it!" She dug her nails into his arm, inflicting even more pain.

Marc was raised not to hurt a lady, no matter how evil or demented she might be. His upbringing on treating women with respect didn't leave him even now. But he did manage to shake her free of him, which caused her to lose her balance and fall into the water again. Her rear end hit the bottom of the tub and her arms flew up in the air while her pretty-much-soaked hair slapped against her face. Water flew out of the tub as if someone had tossed a small bomb into the tub.

He ignored her and grabbed the small drinking glass with the fingernail clippers and the capsules in it, soaking in a small pool of his blood. Taking the plastic that had been wrapped over the top of the glass, he secured the contents, left the bathroom, then pulled the hotel room door closed behind him. Marc was grateful the nice hotel had thick walls. The moment he took off down the hallway he no longer heard Blondie yelling. Marc took the stairs instead of the elevator, pausing in the stairwell and yanking the drenched hand towel out from under his shirt. It was completely soaked with blood. He would be ruining someone's night when they found the towel, but he wasn't about to take it with him.

It was time to endure the pain and pray he wouldn't bleed up a storm before he reached the lobby. He smiled at the lady who'd just checked him and Evelyn into their room when he reached the front desk.

"Have the valet bring our car around, please," he drawled, grinning at her.

"Of course, Mr. VanCooper," she said, reaching for her phone.

Marc nodded, walking out the front door to wait for

the car. As long as Blondie didn't fly into the lobby in a mad rage, all he would have to deal with was the pain in his arm. He glanced up and down the curved drive, staring into a dark parking garage and praying the valet service wasn't backed up.

There wasn't anyone else around and Marc knew the kid probably hoped for a good tip when he pulled up in the small dark green Honda Evelyn had stashed underground as her getaway car.

"Nice evening, isn't it, Mr. VanCooper?" the valet asked when he strutted around the Honda and handed Marc the keys.

"It just got a lot nicer," Marc said, grinning at the kid as he hurried around him and slid into the car. The pain was so bad he prayed he'd be able to navigate his way out of Phoenix. One thing, though, he was sure he'd remember a name as odd as VanCooper. Marc wondered if it was Claude and Evelyn's real last name.

Chapter Seventeen

London squinted against the morning sun and hugged herself against the cold. She went from wanting to help to feeling as if she wasn't wanted or needed there. Men and women scoured the area, walking over the frozen desert with equipment they were using to search for Marc. Apparently Evelyn VanCooper, Claude's wife, who was the man London had shot in the office, was also missing. As the sun slowly climbed against the flat, gray sky, more and more police and other officials who weren't in uniform continued showing up until there was a line of cars parked up and down the two-lane highway.

"We're heading out," her father said, coming up behind her and touching her shoulder. "Your mother has a headache and it's too cold to stand out here."

London nodded, facing both of them. "It was good seeing both of you." She knew her parents were getting the hell out of Dodge. More than likely they'd answered a few questions, promised to stay in the area to assist with the investigation, and would now disappear while everyone was too busy to notice.

"You too, baby girl," her father said, ruffling her hair.

"Maybe we can get to Aspen sometime soon." Her mother smiled at London and actually looked like she was serious.

London nodded, refusing to get her hopes up that she would see either of them again anytime soon. "Take care of yourselves," she said, her voice cracking. She hugged both of them and pulled away before she made a scene.

Her parents hurried to a nearby car. London didn't have a clue who was giving them a ride or where they were taking her parents. She sucked in a ragged breath, filling her lungs with the frigid cold morning air. The two of them climbed into a backseat. She couldn't see them anymore and was pretty sure neither of them looked back to see her. They were probably busy plotting how they could put all of this behind them and prevent any investigator from digging too deep into their backgrounds. London returned her attention to everyone working around her. She needed to focus on what she should do now, too. Her parents would be fine. That much of her life, at least, was back to normal.

Marc's father, Greg King, walked across the field with Jake alongside him. Haley hadn't returned when her husband did, and London had been told she remained at the hospital in Flagstaff with Natasha. There wasn't any report on Natasha's condition.

"We're going back into town," Jake announced, cutting across the field.

"Okay." London prayed she didn't look too lost when Jake's father moved to stand next to his son. The two men were so big, so tall, their presence overwhelming. She tried to think of something to say.

"Come on," Jake said, gesturing with his head. "You're not staying out here by yourself with no one to give you a ride."

She'd come to Flagstaff with Marc and drove down here

with Natasha. It hadn't occurred to London until this moment that she didn't have a ride. Not that she had anywhere to go. Returning to Aspen didn't feel like an option.

"So you're leaving?" She scanned the field. It wasn't right leaving without Marc, but this was his family. London wanted to say they should stay put until he was found.

"London," Greg said, speaking her name slowly and with a deep, commanding baritone. "Marc isn't here."

She nodded quickly, biting her lower lip. She didn't lose it when her parents walked away from her; she wouldn't lose it in front of these two men she barely knew.

"Let's get coffee, warm up," Jake said, holding his arm out and dropping it when she walked alongside him to the line of cars. "We're going to find him," he whispered, looking down at her and searching her face when she glanced at him.

There was dirt stained across his face. His clothes hung on him wrong and were wrinkled as if he'd slept in them for days. Jake had endured an underground jail cell and he was reassuring her.

She smiled, determined to be strong. "More than likely he'll find us."

"They've got Claude VanCooper in the same hospital where Natasha is," Greg offered when they reached Marc's Mustang. It was dirty with highway grunge plastered to both sides of it. Greg and Jake didn't say anything about it, and it was too cold to go to a car wash. London knew Marc would find a way to clean his car. In Aspen, the Mustang had always been immaculately clean. Greg walked around to the driver's seat, looking over the hood at both of them. "Apparently, when he isn't throwing a fit demanding to be flown to a hospital suitable for a man of his station, he's singing like a canary."

Jake opened the passenger door and she pushed the front seat forward, climbing into the backseat.

"He's blaming the whole thing on his wife," Greg continued, turning on the car and adjusting heat vents, although between him and Jake the two men were so large not much heat blew back to her. "Claude is denying any knowledge of a game, or abducting any of us with intentions of forcing us into some kind of war activity."

"He's lying." Jake stared straight ahead, leaning back in his seat and looking exhausted. He sounded mad, though. "We all heard him and the guards. We can testify."

"This won't go to court," Greg stated, shooting a hard glance at his son. "You can bet my word on that. I'm willing to wager it will all disappear, without any of us being contacted for any further questioning."

London wanted to ask why, but she felt she was eavesdropping on a private conversation. Neither one of them glanced back at her, but they continued discussing what had happened to them while they were underground and what they'd seen. They'd been through a horrendous experience.

"You're going to document everything you remember," Greg told Jake. "Write all of it down. Your mother and I are going to do the same. This is the second time we've been pulled into this game, and I'm going to find out what it's all about."

"Do you think someone will come after us again?" Jake didn't sound scared but more curious when he leaned his head back on the seat, closing his eyes.

"We're high profile." Greg relaxed one hand on the steering wheel and stared ahead of him at the two-lane highway they were taking back into Flagstaff. "Natasha did the right thing closing down the office to come out here and I'm not going to hold it against her. But word will spread quickly that we shut down at the same time Claude VanCooper went down. It might take a while to get back to us, but in the right circle word will spread and put us even more in the spotlight."

"Sounds like we need to figure out where that right circle is," Jake said.

London wondered if Marc was already in that circle.

They checked into the Embassy Suites, and although Greg started to get London her own room, she refused. Jake backed her quickly.

"London doesn't want, or need, to be alone right now. Get two rooms for now, Dad." Jake looked at her, the flirt she'd met now completely gone. Either he was behaving in front of his father or Jake was too exhausted to remember he was a player. "I promise to behave," he added, winking at her, although he looked more harmless than she'd ever seen any man his size ever look.

"I can't see you ever doing anything behind your brother's back," she told him, although if he tried London would kick his ass, no matter how big he was.

Greg signed for the rooms and handed a room card key to her. "You know my boys pretty well. I'll have to give my son hell for not letting us know about you."

"We haven't known each other that long," she admitted.

"Two weeks for Marc is a long time," Jake muttered.

"Very true," Greg agreed.

Her thoughts were torn as they rode the elevator in silence. Greg muttered something about a shower before disappearing into the suite across the hall from theirs. There wasn't any luggage and Jake paused at the bathroom door when they entered long enough to ask if she needed to use it.

"Go shower." She waved her hand at him, walking farther into the room.

Standing and staring out the window at the city of Flagstaff, she wondered again if she should be here. Maybe she needed to return to Aspen. It seemed wrong, if not impossible, to twist her brain around, returning to the life she'd been so in love with up until meeting Marc.

He'd not only swept her off her feet but also forced her to take a good look at how she was leading her life. Where once she would have sworn she was making all the right choices and living her life to the fullest, now as she pictured her home and a job where she worked well over forty hours a week, it all seemed empty and meaningless.

She'd told Marc his life wasn't for her. London didn't want to think about having a gun in her hand or worrying about when someone would come along and create full chaos in her life. That was until he disappeared. She'd wrapped her fingers around a gun as if she'd done it every day. All the chaos thrown at her she'd stormed through, not giving a thought to losing her own life or what insane monster might be around the next corner. It was all about doing the right thing. Not only did she risk her life, but London also stood in the middle of a hotel room feeling antsy and anxious to hurry out the door and run to where Marc might be. The danger surrounding all of it no longer seemed to matter.

So what happened to change her mind? Was she falling in love with Marc? Or was it something less glamorous and more realistic, like the urge for adventure had been simmering in her blood all along and she'd spent years trying to ignore it?

Her father had beamed with pride once she'd rescued all of them. London wouldn't have been able to do it without Natasha but her father hadn't seemed to care when she'd told him that. Jonnie Brooke bragged that she had it in her blood. Her mother had been harder to read. Was it that Ruby never could connect with her daughter? Or possibly Ruby knew how hard her life was, always running and never being able to stay anywhere long enough to lay down roots and make a house into a home. She might not want that for her daughter.

London wasn't breaking the law when she gripped that gun and rushed into that underground jail cell, though. She knew she was doing the right thing and would do it again in a second. Would she do it again for someone else if they were in trouble? Because that was what Marc did all the time.

Someone knocked on the door and London stared at it, hearing the shower running and knowing Jake would probably be in there awhile. There wasn't anything to worry about, though. For her, the nightmare was over. Marc was still out there somewhere, but he wouldn't be knocking on her hotel room door. Nor would whoever had him. She walked to the door calmly, taking time to look through the peephole.

"Natasha is fine," Haley announced when London opened the door, grinning broadly as she passed London, letting herself into the room. "She's in stable condition and resting. It will take her a while with physical therapy. She took a bullet in the shoulder. But she's going to be fine."

There was enough relief in Haley's voice to show how much she cared about her niece. London had liked Natasha immediately. The news took a large weight off her shoulders. She could have taken that bullet instead of Natasha.

"That's such good news." London grinned at Haley, although she must not have been able to hide the emotional roller coaster she'd been enduring while standing in the room alone.

"We're going to find Marc," Haley told her, putting down a couple shopping bags and grabbing London's arms. Then, without asking, Haley pulled her into a hug. "You're making yourself nuts pacing in here alone worrying about him. Come on over and hang out with me. Jake paced that cell the entire time he was in there like a caged animal.

He'll shower and probably crash." Haley let go of London but held her hands in hers. "I bought him some clothes. He won't want to put the clothes he was wearing back on."

Haley dumped jeans, socks, boxers, and a T-shirt out of the bag. "I spotted a Large-And-Tall store after leaving the hospital and stopped and grabbed clothes for the men. Fortunately, it was close to a Walmart, and I bought new clothes for me, too. Greg and I thought we were going out to a movie, not being hauled across the state line and dumped in an underground cage. We've been in the same clothes for the past couple days," she told London as she walked to the bathroom door and looked at her, grinning, as if it were all in a day's work, before opening the bathroom door without knocking and announcing to her son he had clean clothes.

"Come on, sweetheart." Haley gestured for London to follow her when she walked to the door. "Let's get to know each other. Natasha had all kinds of good things to say about you."

"She did?"

London followed Haley into the hallway but stopped when two men paused, looking at the hotel room doors and then at both of them.

"Haley King?" one of the men asked. He wore a brown suit, and his gray hair added to his official appearance.

"Yes," Haley said. "I'm Haley."

"I'm Detective Torrance. This is Detective Murray. We'd like to speak to you and your husband if you have a minute?"

"Yes," Haley said, sounding excited. "Of course." She hurried to her hotel room door and fumbled with her card key until she opened the door. "Greg is in the shower, but please, come in. Do you have news of Marc?" she demanded the moment the door was closed.

The detectives entered the room and London brought

up the rear, her stomach twisting in knots. Detectives didn't show up at someone's door with good news. Haley seemed so excited to see them and faced them now, her eyes wide and her expression flushed as she stared at the two men expectantly. She didn't look as if she expected them to give her bad news.

"Ma'am," Detective Torrance began, glancing around the hotel room that looked just like London's except everything was opposite. "We were down at Canyon Diablo this morning." He glanced at London. "I'm sorry we didn't get to introduce ourselves."

Haley took the hint. "This is London Brooke. She's Marc's girlfriend. And I'm Marc's mother. His father, Greg King, is in the shower. I'll introduce you as soon as he comes out."

The detective nodded. "We've also been over to the hospital and have interviewed Claude VanCooper. Natasha King didn't have a lot to share with us, but she was also very tired. We'll visit with her further when she is feeling better."

"I'm sure she'll be very willing to speak with you once she's recuperated more," Haley said, gesturing to the round table in the kitchenette part of the suite. "Please come sit down. I just came from the hospital myself or I'd have coffee made, but it won't take but a minute." She hurried around the table, patting the backs of the chairs indicating that they all sit, before moving to the small counter and sink in the corner of the suite. "Please, tell us why you're here," she insisted, filling the small coffeepot with water and ripping open a package of coffee.

"Claude VanCooper told us about a car that was hidden half a mile from the facility under Canyon Diablo." Torrance sat at one of the chairs and pulled out a small spiral notebook that he flipped open so he could refer to his notes. "He informed us it was a green Honda Civic that he remembered being an early-2000s model."

London slid into the seat opposite the detective, staring at his stern expression as he referred to his notebook. She wanted to yell at him, demand he say why he was here. If he had news of Marc, she'd waited long enough to hear it.

"We investigated his allegations and found a ramp that had little to no dirt or snow on it, as if it had recently been raised from the ground."

"Does this have something to do with Marc?" Haley demanded, obviously as anxious to know the truth as London was.

Torrance held his hand up. "We're not sure, ma'am. After investigating the ramp, we established that it did lower into the ground and could have held a car and kept it hidden from view."

"So Marc took the car and escaped?" London asked.

"We're not sure," Torrance said again. "There is still a lot we don't know yet. It takes time to piece an investigation like this together. And this one is a doozy; I don't have to tell either of you that."

Haley sighed, coming to the table. "You're right. And I do know that all too well. So we now know how Marc got away. But how would he have found that car? It was under the ground a mile from the facility? Do you think Evelyn VanCooper took him to the car?"

"We don't know yet," Torrance said, changing the variation of his answer but not its meaning. "Before we left the hospital we got a call from highway patrol. We'd already put out an APB on the green Honda, which we also knew was registered in the state of New York."

"Highway patrol?" Haley pressed, leaning forward with her elbows on the table. She looked ready to leap over the table and grab the detective so he'd spill what he knew faster.

"A late-model green Honda with New York tags was found out on Interstate Seventeen." He paused, looking over his notes.

Haley jumped from her seat. London couldn't stay seated, either. What were the odds? Sure, Hondas were a dime a dozen, but one with New York tags in Arizona? How many could there be?

"A man was in the car. Apparently he had pulled over and passed out," Torrance said, not looking up but staring at his notebook. "There wasn't any identification on the man, but the reports state he was covered with blood."

"Oh my God," London gasped, covering her hands over her mouth.

Haley was around the table, putting her arms around London. "Where is he now? Do you have pictures? I can identify my son."

Detective Murray leaned back, reaching inside his suit and pulling out a manila folder. London had a flashback to the large envelopes that were delivered to her house with pictures of her parents in them as she stared at the envelope in the detective's hand.

"I need to warn you," Detective Murray said, his voice very soft-spoken as he glanced from Haley to London.

"You might be surprised at some of the pictures I've seen," Haley assured him, stepping forward. "Not to mention what I've seen in real life."

"It's often different when you're staring at someone you know," Detective Torrance said.

"Or someone you're related to," Murray added.

"Show me the pictures." The sudden stern edge in Haley's voice was enough.

Detective Murray slid eight-by-tens out of the envelope. These weren't glossy, colored shots. They were black and white and looked as if they'd been faxed or sent via the computer somehow. They were printed on regular typing paper.

Haley blocked London's view. Either intentional or not, London wasn't sure. But Haley picked up one of the shots, then another. After staring at them for only a moment, she dropped them on the table, letting them fall as she almost ran to the bathroom, yelling for her husband.

"Greg! Greg!" she demanded, opening the door and flying into the bathroom. She was out of view but easily heard. "They've found Marc. Get out here. They know where he is."

Greg King appeared immediately, his tall, large frame filling the bathroom doorway before he stepped into the hotel room, giving each detective an intense once-over before moving toward them. He wore dark blue new-looking jeans, probably the pair Haley had bought for him before returning from the hospital. He still held a white towel, and water beaded across his bare chest as he approached, barefoot and solemn.

"Detectives," he said quietly, using the towel to dry his hand and then extending it to shake hands with both men.

"It's an honor to meet you, Mr. King." Detective Torrance was probably a good ten years older than Greg but seemed in awe when the large man shook his hand. "I regret it's under such circumstances."

After shaking hands with both detectives, Greg picked up one of the pictures Haley had tossed on the table. He looked at it for a second, his expression hardening as he stared over it at the detectives.

"Is my boy alive?" he demanded.

"He's been flown to Phoenix Baptist Hospital," Torrance said, once again looking at his notebook. "The car was about twenty miles outside of Phoenix."

"What would he have been doing down there?" Haley asked, although she didn't direct the question at anyone.

"He was headed north. If he's your son, it appears he might have been taken down there and was trying to come back here."

London listened to the detectives and the Kings speculate. It was obvious both detectives had heard of Greg King and treated him with a reverence that showed his reputation had preceded him. London was impressed and watched as Greg spoke with them, slipping into their language and using a lot of slang whose meaning she wasn't sure of. She remembered Marc telling her his father had been a cop for years before becoming a bounty hunter. Maybe he did what many cops dreamed of doing. Something told her the detectives came to the hotel with this new information as quickly as they did because they suspected they'd found Greg King's son. She'd always heard law enforcement took care of their own, treating them better than they would anyone else reporting a crime. Whether there was truth to that or not, the detectives listened and didn't interrupt when Greg shared his opinion of the underground facility, their abductions, and everything they'd learned so far. The detectives didn't deny his accusation when he predicted this investigation would be shelved before they had all their answers.

London stayed out of the conversation, not having anything to say and still so very new to being included among the good guys. She'd had a lifetime of listening to criminals plot and scheme. Hearing the detectives and bounty hunters plot and predict outcomes didn't seem all that different from hearing it from the other side.

No one paid attention to her when she stepped up to the table and glanced down at the pictures. She didn't pick them up at first but took her time looking at the first picture that was facing her on the table. Although printed and not an original, the image of a man sitting in a small car, his head reclined against the back of the seat and one hand resting on the steering wheel, was clear enough to pick up on details.

London grabbed the second picture, staring at it up close before she realized she'd picked it up. Someone had leaned into the car, placing the camera in front of the man to take the picture. She stared at Marc, his eyes closed and his head tilted with his mouth opened. He looked like he was sleeping. There were dark smudges going down his cheek, but it didn't look as if he'd been beaten.

The picture of him taken from outside the car, with the door opened, was more revealing. They'd taken the pictures with the morning sun behind them, making it easy to see details in spite of the picture being black and white and a copy. The dark stain covering the front of Marc's shirt and sleeve looked like it could be dried blood. He'd been driving back here, possibly having escaped from Evelyn VanCooper, or whoever took him from the underground facility. He was injured and the pain had overtaken him until he'd pulled over and apparently passed out.

London looked up when something one of the detectives said grabbed her attention.

"I'll head down there. I can leave right now. How far are we from Phoenix?"

It was awkward riding for over two hours to Phoenix with Greg and Haley King. After London had been watching how the detectives treated Greg, he seemed almost larger than life to her. She reminded herself more than once that he was just a man. He'd been a cop, had probably done well with his career, and now was a bit more glamorous leading the life of the bounty hunter. But he was just a man. And she'd never done anything to make herself less than his equal.

In spite of her private lectures, it was still hard driving

in Marc's car with Greg and Haley, sitting in the backseat and for the most part not being part of their conversation. Although after they'd been on the road a bit, the three of them drove in silence. Jake had grumbled a bit about not going but resigned himself to the fact that crashing for the day while his family drove to and from Phoenix would make him rested when the rest of them returned exhausted.

London was feeling the weight of a rough couple of days as she followed the Kings into the Phoenix hospital later that afternoon. Her eyes burned and her muscles ached when they walked down the large hallway and breathed in the familiar hospital smell.

"It's about goddamn time you two got here." Marc turned from where he stood, staring out a window, and looked more relieved than grouchy when his parents walked up to him. "I've been climbing the walls. Do you know how hard it is to exist in this world when you don't have ID? They wouldn't release me."

"Marc!" Haley ignored every word he said, hurrying into him and wrapping her arms around her son. "Thank God you're okay."

"Hi, Mom." Marc hugged his mother, his tone softening drastically when he buried his head on top of hers for a moment. They whispered to each other while Greg stood facing the two of them, seemingly content to give the two of them their moment without intruding. When Marc lifted his head, looking at his father, his expression was hard and focused. "Did they find her? No one here would tell me a fucking thing."

"Find who?" Greg asked.

"Evelyn VanCooper," Marc said.

London was growing used to being on the outside of the conversation with this family and stood quietly, just inside the doorway, glancing at another patient Marc shared his room with, who was sleeping on his side with a curtain pulled halfway the length of the room, giving a bit of privacy.

"She took you from the underground prison?" Greg asked, and lowered his voice, which made him sound harsh and cold. "That pompous weasel, Claude, is her husband."

"I know." Marc shifted his weight and moved his mother to one side of him.

Greg didn't comment on how his son appeared to be nursing his left side. "Claude spilled his guts to the cops but didn't indicate he knew where she was. Thanks to our London here, it's not too surprising he doesn't handle pain as well as he dishes it out. She shot him and he's been singing like a canary ever since. There were a few topics, though, he got real closemouthed about. One of them being his wife. I can't help but think he really doesn't know a lot about her affairs. If you hadn't pulled over on the interstate we might not have found you as soon as we did."

Marc seemed to notice London for the first time when his father mentioned her. He let go of his mother, moving around his parents. Marc wasn't in the same clothes he'd been in when they had thought they were leaving the motel to check out Canyon Diablo.

The black pants and shirt he wore made him look even more dangerous. They fitted him perfectly. Whoever had provided his outfit had shopped specifically for him. Marc's height and incredibly muscular physique would make it hard to pick clothes up for him just anywhere. Haley had shown her excitement over finding a clothing store suited for her men. Marc's captor would have had to do the same thing. The VanCoopers had singled Marc and his family out and had made all preparations to keep them prisoners.

When she caught a glimpse of a bandage barely visible at the edge of his collar, she started to reach for it. Something in the way he looked at her made her hesitate. Marc offered a small, polite smile and touched her cheek with his fingertips before dropping his hand to his side.

"You came with my parents," he said, almost whispering as he smiled down at her. "It's good to see you."

He turned before she could respond, once again speaking to his parents. "Where's Jake? Is he okay? And Natasha?"

"Everyone's fine," Haley said, hurrying back to her son's side. She was glowing with happiness, but then she had a wonderful family and now had them all back together. "Let's get you discharged and get out of here."

"Best thing I've heard all day," Marc said, hugging his mother as he kept her on his good side.

The men sat up front and Haley and London in the back on the drive back to Flagstaff. Haley leaned forward, resting her hand on her husband's shoulder while talking to him and Marc. London could have done the same, making herself part of the conversation, but Marc's rather formal greeting when he saw her confused her. Greg and Haley had welcomed London into their world on the assumption that she was seeing their son. What would they think of her now when Marc was barely giving her any attention?

Worse yet, there was no backing away from them so she could be alone. They all stayed together when they returned to the hotel, rehashing the events each of them had endured. Even when they traveled to the hospital to see Natasha, a shuttle was provided, so they could all ride together. Marc told Natasha how he'd yanked capsules out from under his skin near his armpit, and although it was now the third time London had heard the story, it still made her sick.

"Where are the capsules now?" Natasha asked. She looked pale and her pretty long black hair was stringy as it fanned around her on her hospital pillow. "If they really were what Evelyn said they were, we could run tests on them and possibly learn what this drug is that she was using on everyone."

"Everyone but Marc." Jake sneered at his brother. "The woman was obviously insane if she had the hots for you and not me."

"You can have her," Marc grunted as his father punched Jake in his noninjured arm. "And the last I saw them, the capsules and fingernail clippers were in a small glass I took from the hotel room. I wrapped the glass in plastic and had it in the passenger seat of the car I was driving back up here."

"God only knows where that glass is now," Haley said, leaning on her fist as her gaze shifted from one of them to the other.

"My guess is the car would have been impounded. I'll contact Torrance and Murray and see if they can help us narrow down which wrecker service would have picked up the car." Greg stood at the end of the bed, his thick arms crossed over his large chest.

"Who are Torrance and Murray?" Natasha asked, and pulled her hand that had the IV in it out from under her blankets to cover her mouth when she yawned.

"Your cousin might have mad scientists who have the hots for him," Haley offered, causing Jake to snicker. "But your uncle has detectives drooling over him."

Everyone laughed and the conversation lightened after that. London was even pulled into their easy bantering until it became obvious Natasha was exhausted. They each took turns hugging her, with promises to return first thing in the morning, when they hoped they would be able to arrange to have her transferred to an L.A. hospital so they could all go home. No one suggested any of them leave without all of them heading home together.

It was an odd feeling and one London enjoyed as well

as disliked. Marc's family was tight, all of them so open with one another and relaxed in one another's company. In a world where she'd never had a best friend, let alone another person who knew that much about her, spending the entire day with the King family left her overwhelmed.

"Should we eat in the restaurant or order up for room service?" Haley asked when they all stood close to one another on the elevator ride up to their rooms.

"I think London and I are going to bow out on dinner," Marc said, not even looking at her when they stepped into the hallway and started to their rooms. "We'll catch a bite on our own."

Jake was the only one to glance from her to Marc. "I'll head into Mom and Dad's room," he offered, winking at London but then turning his back to her when he stopped behind his parents at their room.

The three of them disappeared into the hotel room across from London's and she pulled out the card key. Marc took it from her and opened the door, holding it with his good hand so she could enter ahead of him. Suddenly she was incredibly nervous.

Marc let the door close behind him and grabbed London's jaw, walking into her and backing her up against the wall as his mouth captured hers. It wasn't a soft, hesitant kiss. The unleashed hunger, aggression, and possessive way in which he devoured her mouth left no doubts why he wanted to be alone with her.

He pressed his body against hers, keeping her pinned where she was, and deepened the kiss. Raw, untamed hunger roared to life between them. All uncertainty, hesitation, and worries dissipated in moments when passion ignited and burned furiously inside her.

London wrapped her hand around his waist, running her fingers over solid, hard-as-steel muscle, and ached to touch him everywhere. She didn't understand his reserved nature earlier, but his behavior right now was very clear. Marc made a feast of her mouth, making it clear his intentions and that stopping to discuss them wouldn't be an option.

Not that she could think of a word to say. Pressure spread throughout her insides. She was immediately soaked. Her pussy pulsed and swelled, anxious for him to touch her there and fill her with his swollen cock. She could feel it growing between them, pulsing and jerking against her hip.

When Marc finally released her from the wall, it was to pull her along with him to the bed. He didn't speak but stared into her eyes with blue orbs the color of a dark sky before a thunderstorm erupted and exploded. In a way, that was exactly how it was. There was a storm building between them. Any moment it would release its wild and torrential passion and knowing that moment was close stole London's breath. She couldn't look away from him when he yanked on her shirt, dragging her to the bed.

All day he'd gingerly used his left side. London was very careful not to touch him anywhere near his injury, since it obviously seemed to be bothering him. There was no sign now that any part of him wasn't in perfect working order, however.

"God, woman," he growled, his voice rough as he almost ripped her shirt off her.

She willingly lifted her arms when he undressed her, his hands all over her and almost rough when he unzipped her jeans and dragged them down her legs. When she lost her balance, Marc pushed her backward, causing her to fall on the bed.

"You have no clue," he rumbled, every word thick with emotion.

London slipped out of her bra, sensing if she let him remove her underwear she might not be able to wear it again. "Clue about what?" she asked, leaning back on her elbows, completely naked and staring up at him.

Marc's expression was dark, intense, and so incredibly sexy as he stared down at her, not answering her right away but instead taking his time letting his gaze travel down her body. Her flesh sizzled. It was the worst kind of torture. He stood over her, adoring her, while need ransacked every inch of her body until she wanted to leap at him and demand he fuck her.

"I missed you," he said simply, and started removing his shirt.

London couldn't remain on the bed any longer. She felt as if she jumped to her knees like some eager child, unwilling to wait any longer before unwrapping her present. As anxious as she was, when she touched him she wasn't rough as he was with her.

The moment her fingers brushed along his waist his gaze sharpened. Marc stilled when she slowly lifted his shirt. The way he looked at her would make her melt, turning her into a puddle at his feet. No one had ever made her feel so beautiful, so incredibly wanted, as he did.

Marc raised his arms, letting her take off his shirt. The moment she dropped it to the floor she focused on the bandage neatly taped under his left arm. Roped muscle twitched under his taut flesh when she brushed her fingertips across his chest, coming closer to the bandage. She wanted to investigate, see what damage had been done to this perfect body. London wanted to see for herself exactly how badly he was injured and redress the wound, tending to it herself.

It was an odd sensation and an untimely urge. Her body surged with an overwhelming need to fuck him. Now wasn't the time to remove the gauze and inspect the cut he'd described to all of them earlier.

"Later," he hissed, moving her hand away from the

bandage and dragging her fingers down his chest as his gaze locked onto hers. He was reading her mind, but she swore she knew his thoughts, too. Marc didn't tell her to leave the injury alone. He understood her need to know in her heart how badly he'd been hurt. He didn't deny her desires but prioritized them for her. "This needs to be taken care of first."

He placed her hand on his swollen cock, which immediately danced against her palm when she pressed her hand over his jeans. Marc let go of her wrist and cupped her pussy.

"Oh God," she gasped, grabbing his uninjured arm with her free hand.

"The pain is worse there. I promise," he whispered, lowering his head and nipping at her lips.

"Then we should take care of that." London experienced a wave of confidence stronger than she'd known all day. Suddenly the world seemed right again. She was comfortable in her existence and knew exactly what she wanted and just how to go about having it. No matter that her rough-and-ready man would make her life hell when he disappeared to stalk some insane criminal. Marc would return to her, his war wounds fresh and needing to be tended to. But the raw passion he released on her let her know nothing hurt him more than being away from her. "I missed you, too," she admitted.

He pulled away from her just far enough to focus on her face. "You never ached to run home?" The way he asked let her know it was something that had bothered him, and he searched her face as if trying to learn her answer before she spoke.

London thought of the times she'd imagined returning to Aspen. She didn't look away from him as she unzipped his black pants and pushed them down his thighs. "It would have meant running further from you," she whispered.

Chapter Eighteen

"I want to be with you." Marc grabbed her when he stepped out of his jeans.

The way she knelt on the edge of the bed, helping him undress, was fucking hot as hell. But hearing her say she didn't want to be away from him did something to his insides too intense to fight.

"Okay." She didn't fight him when he pushed her back onto the bed.

But she thought he meant he wanted to fuck her. Marc needed her to understand this was for real. He wanted her to know how hard it had been being away from her, especially when he hadn't had a choice of returning to her. All he'd thought about when he'd left that Phoenix hotel was driving back to London.

"I considered driving to L.A. when I left that hotel." The throbbing in his shoulder annoyed him and made it impossible to hold himself up over London. As he knelt between her legs, running his hands over her soft flesh, making her understand his thoughts seemed as important to him as fucking her.

She lay on the bed, her legs spread around him, and grinned up at him. "You wouldn't have made it that far."

He'd been damn lucky to pass out from the pain when he'd pulled over on that interstate. When he couldn't see straight any longer and knew driving wasn't an option, he'd managed to pull the car over and fought to stay conscious as long as possible. Passing out had been a godsend. Being found as quickly as he had been and rushed to a hospital was a blessing.

"I wanted to find you," he stressed. Staring down at the glowing wonder in her onyx-colored eyes let him know he'd made the right move. London had built a wall of security around herself all her life, Letting it down, letting him in, took some effort on her part, but the look on her face showed him she wanted him with her.

"I'm glad we found you." She held a small foil package in her hand. "Do you want me to put this on you?"

"More than anything." Lifting her legs, he moved closer, the heat between her legs drawing him in. His cock burned with need, the pressure overwhelming.

London's fingers on his cock, her efforts to protect them, were an erotic torture almost too intense for him to handle. She tried sitting up, running her hands up his body, then tugging on him.

"Lay down. Let me . . ."

"I want you like this." He didn't want to be too rough with her, but making love to her with London looking up at him, being able to see every emotion that hit her as it appeared on her face, would make uniting with her all the more complete.

Marc pressed her flat on her back and grabbed her legs. Her hair fanned around her, away from her face so he could see her watching him. His cock found home, and as he slid into her—the overwhelming heat wrapping around him like a protective glove—the anxiety, frustrations, and aggravations from the past couple days faded away. The throbbing pain in his shoulder was no longer at the forefront of his thoughts. All that mattered was London, that she was here, with him, part of him.

"I want to make this permanent," he told her, and thrust deep into her pussy, feeling her constrict around him and drag him even deeper.

London's eyes widened and that uncertainty he saw on her face earlier when they'd picked him up in Phoenix reappeared.

"I love you," he stressed, needing that glow to come back into her pretty eyes. He wanted her expression flushed with emotions that were so easy for him to read.

Marc thrust again, watching her mouth form a small circle and her hands rise, reaching for him. He impaled her and she cried out. Marc fucked her with all he could give her, loving how she moaned, her eyes closing as she shook her head until long, black strands clung to her cheeks.

"You're mine, London." He wanted her acknowledgment, her words of understanding and commitment.

"Marc," she gasped, blinking and staring up at him with fogged-over lust clouding her gaze. "God! Yes!"

As she reached up, dragging her nails down his chest, London came so hard she damn near suffocated him. Her body shook, vibrating with orgasm after orgasm. She was a vision of beauty, so incredibly perfect. For the life of him, he wouldn't give her up. And he didn't want to fuck this up. No woman ever came so hard for him, released everything she had so willingly, yet wouldn't open up completely. He wanted her submission, her complete and undying love. He wanted her adoring him, assuring him she would never leave him and that no matter how dangerous any case might be, she'd be there with open arms when he returned to her.

The moment she sighed, caught her breath, and blinked, staring up at him with a small smile, Marc went at it again. The hell with the pain in his shoulder. Nothing mattered more than showing London how serious he was. She might not know yet that he'd never spoken like this to another lady, but she would understand before he was done. If it killed him, London would believe in her heart and her soul that they were meant to be together.

He increased momentum the moment she looked up at him, once again riding her and giving her everything. There was no holding back, no hesitancy, as he drove deep inside her soaked pussy, feeling her come soak his balls and thighs. It was the most incredible sex in the world, and there wasn't any doubt London offered him all she had—physically.

It was that pang of knowledge, somewhere far in the back of his head, that warned him there was still a barrier inside her she hadn't released for him. Somewhere in that beautiful brain of hers, London held back. Marc didn't claim to be an expert on relationships. He'd never paid much attention to what might make it work or not work with his friends or his parents. Not that anything they might use to stay together mattered to him. What mattered was London, knowing her heart and soul were his. He would make her see he was offering her everything, and he'd be damned if she turned him away because of emotional damage done long before he met her.

"London," he gasped, feeling his dam of determination waver. He would come at this rate, and she hadn't spoken the words that would bond them together. She hadn't shown him on her face with that special glow he'd seen on her once or twice that she didn't want to live without him. "You want me," he uttered, barely able to get the words out as pressure built inside him.

"Yes," she whispered, and she ran her hands up his arms, trying to reach for his uninjured shoulder but unable to with him not coming down over her. "Fuck me, darling. Fuck me harder."

She was keeping it physical, holding back.

Marc damn near burned alive inside, every inch of him so tense his entire body shook. Yet he slowed the pace, enduring pain more intense than any wound could ever inflict, and stared down into her clouded, dark eyes. They were like a midnight storm, the imminent eruption of emotions so damn close yet swirling, rotating with hesitancy and fear. As he stared at her, feeling himself drawn deeper inside her, and not just his cock, when he sunk into her scalding, soaked heat, Marc saw, when that swarming storm of reluctance broke inside her, London's commitment to him would be stronger than possibly anything he'd ever known. She didn't halfheartedly give herself to anyone or to anything.

When London took on something, she gave it all she had, performing and meticulously ensuring the job was done perfectly. She'd abhorred guns yet had embraced one and attacked with fury when her world was jeopardized. Her parents were in trouble and she'd dived into the terror of a bizarre situation, not stopping until they were safe.

This was the woman for him. She gave her all to something when it mattered to her. He had to know that what she felt, what he saw warring inside her, were the same overwhelming emotions that consumed him.

"Do you love me?" He couldn't wait any longer to know.

London licked her lips and slick, drenched muscles

tightened around his cock at the same time. As much as her hesitancy to answer him tore him in two, the heat of her pussy engulfing him and encouraging him deeper had him teetering on the edge, ready to explode in spite of his efforts to control the moment.

"I'm scared," she whispered, her words so soft he almost didn't hear them over the roaring in his brain as he fought not to come.

"London." His brain was in turmoil.

Marc could control and manipulate a situation no matter its intensity. He was positive being with London was the right thing. It was more than physical, more than feeling her hot, tight pussy clinging to him and threatening to milk all life out of him. It sure as hell wasn't convenience that had him positive, beyond any doubt, she was meant to be his woman. Their worlds were far apart. There would be matters to work out that many couples didn't have to worry about. Yet no matter what it took, Marc wasn't going to let her go.

"Don't be frightened, sweetheart." He dared lower himself over her, holding his weight with his good arm, "We're here, together. We're meant to be together," he stressed, searching her eyes for understanding and acceptance of what seemed so clear to him.

"I do love you. I think you're right." She spoke the words clearly but then closed her eyes, wrapping her arms and legs around him, shutting him off from the warring emotions tumbling around inside her, and inching him deeper into heat he couldn't fight off.

Marc sunk deep inside her, taking her hard and fast again in moments before he gave thought to it. He rode her, impaling her as his cock thrust inside her with enough energy to singe him alive. Fire tore at his groins, erupting inside him with a ferocity that split him in two.

He roared when he came, giving London everything he had and knowing without any doubt he wouldn't ever get it back. As much as he didn't care, pain stabbed at his heart with the realization she hadn't done the same.

Flying home was a hell of a lot nicer than driving. And it was good to be home. His underarm throbbed, the annoying pain that would shoot down his arm any time he lifted anything starting to make him grouchy.

"I just got a phone call." His father walked into the kitchen the same time Marc did. "They found the car you were driving when you left Phoenix," Greg offered, heading to the refrigerator.

Marc watched his brother down a large sandwich as he sat at the table. Jake stared at his mom, who followed their dad into the room. His cheek bulged from the bite he'd just taken.

"That glass was still in the passenger seat," his mom announced, grinning at Marc and then rolling her eyes at Jake. "Why don't you just put the whole sandwich in your mouth next time and save time?" she teased.

Greg popped open a bottle of juice and pulled Haley against him, resting his arm over her shoulder as he focused on Marc. He knew that look in his father's eyes all too well, that rush of satisfaction when it all finally started to pull together.

"Detective Torrance just told me the glass and its contents are being overnighted to his station. He's going to personally oversee the tests run on its contents. We're going to know what that drug was that bitch threatened all of us with," Greg offered triumphantly.

"There better be something in those tiny vials I yanked out from underneath my flesh," Marc grumbled, sliding into the seat across from his brother and stealing a potato chip off his plate. "If I'm enduring this annoying pain for nothing, I'll hunt that bitch down until she regrets the day she laid eyes on me."

"I'll let you know," his father said.

Marc's mother chuckled, ruffling his hair when she left the room, his father in tow.

"Get your own damn food," Jake complained, swatting his hand when Marc stole another chip. "And you probably wouldn't be in so much pain if you'd quit moping around here like a fucking lost dog."

Marc glared at Jake, the thought of punching him in the head a rather gratifying one.

"Christ, man. Go get her ass," Jake snapped, giving him a hard stare that was a dare if Marc ever saw one. "You're annoying as hell wallowing in your pity over that woman."

"We have an agreement. And I'm not feeling sorry for myself." He fought not to stand up quickly and send the chair underneath him flying. Pounding that smug look off his brother's face sounded better than anything he'd done all day.

"We've all heard your agreement." Jake waved a potato chip in the air between them and rolled his eyes. "Sounds to me like you just don't have the balls to go get her. Now if it were me and a hot, sexy piece of ass like that—"

"Shut up!" Marc roared, sending the chair underneath him sliding backward into the wall when he stood and loomed over his brother. "Don't you ever call her that," he threatened, hissing at Jake.

"If she were more than that to you, you wouldn't be here in California and her out in Colorado." Jake looked away from him, taking another bite of his sandwich then raising his eyes to Marc, maintaining that silent challenge.

Marc had hated the arrangement London proposed before they'd left the hotel in Flagstaff. She would return to Aspen. He'd come home to L.A. They would sort out their feelings and talk to each other in a week. After three days, there weren't any more feelings to sort out. He loved her and didn't want to live without her.

"I don't know, man. If it were me, I'd go get my woman." Jake popped the last bite of his sandwich into his mouth and stood to take his plate to the sink. "That is, unless you don't think you can live without your mommy."

Marc lunged at him, aiming a hard knuckle sandwich directly at the side of his head. Jake flew out of range, letting the back door slam behind him as he laughed and disappeared around the corner of the house.

Marc and London had had a long talk before they'd checked out of the hotel. She was trying to be practical, she'd explained to him. There wasn't a job waiting for her in L.A., and she'd never lived relying on anyone else to support her. She'd told him she loved him, more than once, but that cloud of doubt never lifted from her eyes. Marc had stood with her at the airport, waiting with her until her flight was ready to board. When he'd joined his family and boarded their plane, which was flying in the opposite direction as London's, he'd hated the concerned looks all of them gave him.

His little brother made a point, though, and Marc hated that as much as he hated the truth stinging at his insides when he realized it. She was his woman and he couldn't let her get away.

"Do you two have a minute?" Marc paused in the doorway to his father's office, meeting his parents' gazes when they both looked up at him.

Haley gave her husband a knowing look before putting paperwork she'd been holding on the desk and turning to face Marc. "Come on in, Marc. And of course we do," she said, turning a chair that faced his father's desk so Marc could sit.

"I need to talk to you two." He rested his arms on the back of the chair instead of sitting in it. His father studied him and his mother searched his face, the worry in her eyes making him believe she already suspected what he would say. "I think I'm going to move out," he announced, and blew out a sigh of relief so overwhelming it almost made him stagger. He straightened, feeling a weight of worry lift off him. "Actually, I know I am. I'm moving out. I'm moving to Colorado."

"Oh, baby!" His mother wasn't at all upset, as he'd imagined she would be. Haley leapt around the chair, throwing herself into his arms and hugging him as she laughed and cried at the same time.

His father stood, a small smile on his face as he watched his wife wrap herself around their son. Greg held out his hand, nodding once. "Go get your woman," he instructed, and shook Marc's hand.

It all fell together so quickly Marc swore his family had plotted the whole thing behind his back and had just waited for him to come to his senses to put the plan into action. He would just take a couple suitcases; once he and London knew where they would live, he could get the rest of his things. There was a nonstop flight into Colorado leaving later that day, and after he had booked a seat on it, his parents drove him to the airport, both of them chattering cheerfully. He was starting to think they were happy to get rid of him.

He was still overwhelmed when he landed later that evening, grateful that this time he'd thought ahead to dress warmly before leaving L.A. It was the end of January and the bitter cold winds blew around him fiercely when he stuck the key into the door of his rental car. By the time he pulled up in front of London's house, it was dark.

Too dark. There wasn't a light on in her home.

Maybe he should have called first. From the moment

he told his parents his decision to when he landed at the airport in Aspen, his brain had been in such a whirlwind he wasn't sure he would have made a damn bit of sense if he had called her. Besides, he'd managed to come up with something resembling a plan. He would arrive at her home, climb her porch steps, and knock on her door. She would answer it, wearing her long T-shirt and her long, flowing black hair tumbling down her sides. She would be barefoot, surprised, and possibly even cry when he told her he was here to be with her. They would cuddle together, dreaming of their future, and then lay out a solid game plan together.

Marc got out of the warm car and ducked against the bitter wind as he hurried up her walk. He stomped his feet on her porch, making enough noise that it would be impossible for anyone inside not to know he was here. As he knocked soundly on her front door, the sinking feeling inside him began churning, making him forget he was freezing. London wasn't here.

His frustration over his idea of cuddling with her not panning out turned to worry when he drove out to the lodge and received even more upsetting news.

"London quit," the college boy behind the counter at the lodge told Marc, frowning as he gave him a sympathetic look. "Sorry, man. I don't know where she went."

London should have called first. It was such a leap of faith for her, though. Marc said he loved her and he wanted to be with her. She'd stared at her parents just the other day, wishing them well and watching them walk out of her life, again. They were supposed to love her. People who loved each other weren't supposed to leave each other. But Marc had let her go. She'd told herself again and again since coming home he hadn't let her go, she'd pushed him away. It was in his eyes, in his expression when he stared down at her. The pain she'd seen wasn't from the cut under his arm; it was from his heart breaking when she told him to go home and she would do the same.

Returning to work, trying to fit back into her busy schedule, proved impossible after only a couple days. London was forcing one foot in front of the other, pushing against a brick wall, trying to make her life work when half of her was missing. She wanted Marc. It would take sacrifice. It would be scary. But she'd pulled a trigger and lived through that; the fear of giving herself to him wouldn't be half as bad as the happiness she knew would come with it.

She sat in her car, most of her possessions piled in behind her, and tapped her steering wheel with her fingertips, staring at the incredibly nice house on the beach. All she needed to do was get out of the car and go up to the door. There wasn't any doubt she was at the right place. The KFA sign over a door at the side of the house, probably the business entrance, confirmed all suspicion she'd found Marc's home.

Her cell phone rang and she jumped, then shook her head at her jitteriness. "You're being silly," she told herself, pulling her phone out of her purse and staring at the number. Her worries melted and she grinned when she answered. "Hello," she said, a flush of nervous energy creating butterflies in her stomach.

"Where are you?" Marc bellowed into her ear, sounding mad.

She laughed, suddenly giddy. "Umm, well, actually, I'm outside," she explained.

"What the hell do you mean, outside?" He sounded pissed.

Nerves spiked to life inside her and suddenly her palms were too damp. "I sent you away. I realize that now. But it wasn't you; it was me. Anyone I've ever loved has taken off on me. They don't even look back as they walk away." She pictured her parents leaving her at Canyon Diablo and squeezed her eyes shut. Pinching the bridge of her nose, she kept going, knowing she needed to get this out and Marc had a right to hear it. "I know you won't do that. I believe you love me. I love you, too. And I'm not so dysfunctional that I don't believe everyone will do that to me."

"London," he said, his deep baritone sending shivers over her flesh. "Where are you?"

"I told you, I'm right outside." She opened her eyes and shot furtive glances at the windows, the front door. No one was peering out of any of them and the door remained closed. "I'm here," she explained.

"Where . . . is . . . here?" he asked, saying each word slowly, as if he were losing his patience.

"Look outside." Her heart started thumping in her chest and she opened her car door, stepping out into the cool, salty-smelling air.

"I am outside," he stressed.

"You are?" London swung around and shrugged out of her coat, then dropped it in the driver's seat. "Where are you? I don't see you," she added, laughing.

"I'm standing in front of your house."

London's smile disappeared. She froze. "You're where?" she whispered.

"Where exactly are you?" he demanded.

He sounded rather upset and she shouldn't start laughing, but she did. Her nerves shattered inside her, making it impossible not to laugh. When the front door opened she spun around and grinned at the shocked expression on Marc's father's face. Then she laughed even harder.

"Where the hell are you?" Marc roared through the phone.

"You're not going to believe this!" Greg called out,

disappearing into the house and leaving the front door open.

"You're not going to believe this," she repeated, shaking her head as she started understanding what had happened. "Apparently you and I had the same idea at the same time."

"Oh my God!" Haley clasped her hands over her mouth as she started out the front door behind her husband.

"London, I'm freezing my ass off." Marc was losing his patience.

"I'm standing in front of your house," London explained, staring at the amused expressions on Greg's and Haley's faces.

"You're where?" Marc roared through the phone.

London bit her lip so as not to start laughing again when Greg slapped his leg and then threw his head back, letting out a roar of laughter. His wife joined in, her eyes sparkling with amusement as she walked up and placed her hand on London's shoulder.

"I decided to come after you," she confessed, lowering her voice and looking at the ground when Marc's mother's beaming expression became too much.

Marc walked along the beach, feeling extreme jet lag after flying out to Colorado, then racing back to the airport and catching the first available flight to L.A. When he learned London had packed up everything she could fit into her Jeep, quit her job, and told her landlord she was leaving, Marc had insisted she stay with his parents until he returned. He dropped his luggage on the floor the moment he entered the house, and began searching for London. As he left his backyard, staring at her as she hugged herself and faced the ocean, her beautiful long black hair flowing out behind her, Marc almost stumbled in awe.

Even in the dark, Marc saw her face light up when she saw him. London turned, starting toward him and breaking into a run as they drew nearer. Marc opened his arms, catching her when she leapt into them, and hugged her fiercely as she wrapped her arms and legs around him.

"Call me next time before you leave," he whispered into her hair, burying his face in her and breathing in her intoxicating scent.

She laughed, the melodic, happy sound making his heart swell.

"You better promise to do the same," she said, lifting her face from his shoulder and then instigating their kiss.

London had come to him. He'd let her go, given in to her wishes, and she'd come running to him.

"I'm never letting you go again," he swore, breaking off the kiss and staring down into her flushed expression. It was the look of pure happiness and satisfaction he'd tried so hard to make appear when they'd made love.

"You better promise that, too," she said, her voice cracking.

London slid down his body but cuddled next to him when she turned her head to stare out at the ocean. "As many places as I've been in my life, this is the first time I've ever seen the ocean."

"What do you think?" he asked, stroking her hair and admiring how the moonlight glowed against it.

"It looks dangerous and powerful, kind of like you," she added, smiling up at him.

"I'll never be a danger to you. I swear it, London."

"I know." She stretched against him, grabbing the sides of his head, and brought his mouth to hers for another kiss. "I love you, Marc King," she whispered into his mouth. "I love you so much it scared the crap out of me."

"Love is scary. But we're going to experience it together."

"I hope I'm not making a terrible mistake." She frowned, pressing her hand against his chest and studying his face, her expression suddenly very serious. "Your family has an incredible reputation as bounty hunters. I saw how those detectives adored your dad in Flagstaff. My parents are famous crooks, and there might be times when that comes around to haunt us."

Marc thought about the private investigator who'd harassed London about her parents. He dared the motherfucker to give London grief now.

"I have a feeling the ghosts who have crept into your life in the past will think twice before trying to do it now." He didn't like the worried look on her face. "Are you scared you won't see your parents now that you're with me?"

She laughed, shaking her head and making her hair float over her shoulders. "My parents chose not to be a part of my life many years ago." She tried hiding the sadness in her tone when she shared this with him, but the trace of resentment couldn't be missed. "I'm sure they'll find out through the grapevine that I'm with you. All I can do is hope they are happy for me that I've found true love, if they even know what that is."

"I hope you know what that is," he whispered.

"I think I do. It's knowing you can't live without someone. It's the most powerful feeling in the world. When you truly love someone you're willing to go to all odds to be with him." She cupped his face again, her soft smile melting his heart when she continued. "You're willing to pick up a gun when you swore you'd never touch one. You're willing to walk into danger to make sure he's safe. And you're willing to finally start living, knowing you've found your soul mate. I never thought I would get this lucky."

He couldn't believe it. London stood in his arms, her long black hair lifted by the evening breeze off the ocean, and explained to him all the emotions he'd been dealing with since leaving her in Arizona.

"I'm the luckiest man in the world," he told her, and kissed her, knowing he truly had found his soul mate. The daughter of crooks, a woman afraid to love, had stolen his heart, and he was so grateful she had.

"My mighty hunter," she whispered against his mouth. "I'm so glad I hunted you down."

Read on for an excerpt from Lorie O' Clare's next book

STAY HUNGRY

Coming soon from St. Martin's Paperbacks

Jake glanced up from the couch when someone knocked gently on his hotel room door. She'd said half an hour but it had been forty-five minutes. Did Angela primp and prepare herself to come see him?

He stood, stretched, then tugged his shirt and smoothed it out as he headed to the door. Patting his gun, which he'd tucked into the back of his jeans, he leaned forward and looked through the peephole. He stared at Angela's profile, distorted through the small circular glass. She looked both ways up and down the hallway as if the chance existed she might be followed. It was one of the negative aspects of their line of work: being more cautious than most.

He unlocked and turned the handle, then opened the hotel room door. Angela Torres stared up at him with defiant green eyes. Her long, thick black hair was damp and the light was reflected in it. He breathed in a hint of roses. Angela had showered and cleaned up before coming to see him. Something tightened inside him, and not just his dick. It wasn't a familiar sensation, but he wasn't staring at just another pretty lady. Something about Angela made her stand out, caused her beauty to be more unique and compelling, and created a radiant glow around her that worked like a magnet in drawing him to her. It also had the strength to keep her in his thoughts for a year.

Angela entered his suite without a word, managing not to touch him as she glided past him while he stood holding the door. She paused in the middle of his room and turned to face him, not bothering to check out her surroundings but instantly snaring him with a hot and determined stare.

"Come on in," he drawled, taking his time closing the door and securing the dead bolt.

"What are you doing here, Jake?"

"Your dad didn't tell you? He hired me. I'm your backup, darling," he informed her and enjoyed the hell out of her stunned expression. He took advantage of her shock to move closer. "Your father flew out to L.A. and personally hired me to help you out with the game," he added, lowering his voice as he studied her thick black hair.

It fell to the middle of her back and the sleeveless pink blouse she wore helped offset its color. Her tan skin, green eyes, and slender figure with curves in all the right places made her a vision of beauty. But the hard, focused glare she gave him, beaming with intelligence and her willful nature created an image of perfection he ached to know better—a lot better.

Angela didn't balk when he stopped close enough to reach out and grab a strand of her hair.

"My father hired you?" She didn't change her pose but continued staring at him, hands on her hips as she pressed her lips together in a thin line.

Jake let go of her hair and tried gripping her shoulders. Angela turned, walking to the window that faced the street below.

"Sit, Angela," he suggested, pulling out the chair he was

going to guide her into before she slipped out of his grasp. "Bring me up to speed on what you've been doing here."

Angela wore blue jean shorts that hugged her tight, round ass and ended just as that perfect curve met leg. It was one of his favorite parts of a woman's body, the tender flesh on the backside and inner thighs, right at the top of her legs. They were legs he bet would squeeze the life out of a man as she came. He might have to fuck her just so he could work with her. Just standing in the same room, watching her ass in those short shorts, was proving to be one hell of a distraction.

She turned, staring warily at the chair he'd pulled out from the desk. "You sit," she instructed, her voice clipped. She continued flexing her hands into fists, then relaxing them.

Angela no longer looked him in the face. Her gaze would slip down his body, then as soon as he focused on her, she'd shoot her attention across the room. As if he wouldn't notice her checking him out. Hell, he would know how closely she scrutinized him with his eyes closed. The charge of energy in the air hadn't been there before she'd entered his suite.

Jake had guessed it when he'd captured her attention in the lobby. Neither of them had expected to see the other at that moment. What they got from each other wasn't guarded, or covered up, but raw, unleashed carnal desire. Sexual tension between two people wasn't usually so strong it charged the air between them at such a distance. Now, however, with not even a few paces between them, and the smell of her perfume and clean body wrapping around him and proving to be the strongest aphrodisiac he'd ever experienced, it was nice knowing he didn't suffer alone. Angela was fighting to maintain control.

"I don't mind sitting." Jake relaxed in the chair, straightening his legs, as he crossed one socked foot over the other.

He would put her at ease, although he seriously doubted he'd be able to relieve the sexual tension. Jake wasn't a rapist, though. Not that she appeared overly worried about him attacking her without her consent. Angela wanted to fuck him.

"My father hired you to be my backup," she muttered, uttering the words aloud more to make their meaning sink in than to ask a question. She sliced her hand through the air, finally meeting his gaze. "We can't work together, Jake."

He held her stare captive, probing into her milky green eyes, seeing emotions tumble over each other behind her mask of indifference. It was on the tip of his tongue to ask why, but he wouldn't insult her. The reason why was incredibly obvious. It was charging the entire damned room, and making his cock ache to stretch and swell.

"I think we can make it work." He spoke slowly, still staring into her eyes.

When she inhaled, the bra underneath her sleeveless sweater pressed against her breasts. Her V-neck collar allowed a glimpse of her cleavage. He let his attention drop to the view. Her skin color was as appealing as the rest of her, tanned but not quite caramel. She wasn't dressed to show off her features, but nonetheless they were easy to notice. It would be damn hard for Angela to be completely inconspicuous.

"We'll see." She took her time looking away from him. Angela wasn't shy. Her straightforwardness was as appealing as her bedroom eyes and every last soft curve on her incredibly enticing body. "First things first." She walked behind his chair, then came around him on the other side. "You said my dad sent you here. He hasn't mentioned you to me. Tell me what he said to you, and what you think you're going to be doing while you're here."

Jake dropped his attention to the slender curves that

rounded into her narrow waist. "Bossy bitch," he grumbled, and fought a smile when her jaw dropped.

"How dare you," she hissed. "Good grief!" She threw her hands in the air and spun around, causing her thick long hair to fan across her back. "I knew it. This isn't going to work. There's no point in even trying. I'll explain to my dad. I don't need, or want, the type of backup you would offer. Someone lingering in the shadows, or available on cell if things get tricky, that would work. But I seriously doubt you'd be able to do that."

"The type of backup I would offer?" Jake understood her meaning. "This is your show, sweetheart. I'll do what you want." And he'd protect her. Again, he wouldn't insult her by stating the obvious. Angela knew he'd guard her with his life, as her dad had obviously known as well. He held his arms out, palms up, as he looked up at her, keeping his expression relaxed. "I'm offering my services. Use me as you see fit."

"I know damn good and well what you're offering," she sneered.

Jake watched her, deciding he would let her form her own conclusions and not sway them with responses she would choose to believe, or not, no matter how truthful they might be. And the facts were, if she didn't want to fuck him, he wouldn't press the matter. That had never been his style. Jake knew women, though. Angela was making a scene to cover up her own desire. Raging need damn near burned her alive. He saw the flush slowly spread across her face as she shot him fiery glances.

"Are you going to deny you're undressing me with your eyes?" She stopped in front of him, pressing her hands into her hips and glared at him.

If he stood, he'd be head and shoulders taller than Angela. She was already on the defensive and he wasn't going to push her into a corner. So instead, checking his slight irritation, he stretched out his legs, forcing her to jump to the side so she wouldn't trip over them.

"You say I'm hands-on. I'm sure you know all there is to know about me, darling." He didn't speak too slowly, kept his voice flat, and only stared at her face as he spoke. Already, from what he knew of this case, Angela needed him. Jake doubted even her father would have been her best backup. Possibly Huxtable had reasoned that one out, too. "According to your father, you were very aware of me, and my reputation, when we danced the night away in Tijuana."

"I gave you critical information and you proceeded to blow all evidence to hell and back," she accused.

"The FBI blew our evidence up, sweetheart. Our hands were rather tied with that matter."

She stared at him, her expression remaining chilled and tense. "And if things get out of control here, would you call the FBI once again?"

Jake stood, forgetting his effort to help Angela relax. She tilted her head back, staring up at him when he spoke.

"If a madman who prefers his women doped up on slave juice captured you, put your life in serious danger, and I wasn't able to get you out, you're damn fucking straight I would call in whatever authorities can help."

She searched his face, pressing her lips into an adorable pout before slowly looking down. Her gaze traveled down his chest and fire erupted inside him. She'd just pissed him off and he still wanted her. Angela might be right. Maybe they wouldn't be able to work together.

"I heard your father was abducted in Mexico, but rumors suggest he allowed himself to be captured to get on the inside." She began pacing the length of the hotel room, and continued shooting him hesitant looks. "That's what I've done, Jake. I'm on the inside, but not at the risk of slave juice being stabbed into my arm."

"Because you're getting cozy with some Italian warlord, you think you're exempt from his slave juice?" Jake was having more and more trouble keeping his emotions in check around her, which bugged him.

"I don't know what you know about Mario Mandela, but let me tell you, he's not an idiot. Right now, my cover is secure. Mario knows I'm high profile because of the circles he believes I move in. He is under the impression my schedule is very full and I'm often in the public eye. If I stray from my hectic schedule for even an hour, I would be missed. He won't risk the game and all it means to him just for me. Women don't mean that much to him. He is smart, though, and I'm covering my ass."

"I'm going to help cover that ass of yours." He didn't smile this time and she didn't appear as insulted with his crude comment.

When she tilted her head slightly and pierced him with those sexy eyes of her, several strands of hair fell over her shoulder and drifted across her arm and breast. "I'm not sure you're the best man for the job," she mused, her voice suddenly soft-spoken, gentle, as if she were contemplating something pleasant, instead of deciding if she could handle having him up close and personal without getting too close.

"Why would your father think otherwise?" he asked. His fingers itched to pet her thick black hair. It would be so smooth and silky. Her probing stare captivated him just as much as the rest of her did. When Angela met his gaze, staring hard and straight into his eyes, it was as if she saw past the surface and analyzed and discovered everything about him. As unnerving as the thought was that she might be able to see more of him than he wanted her to see, at the same time it was somehow erotic that Angela wanted to dig and learn more about him.

"I'm not sure." Her hard lines of anger began fading. "Sounds like he and I need to talk about this."

"Tell me about Mario." He wanted her talking, opening

up to him. They weren't going to throw in the towel on this until they were sure as to whether they would work well together, or not. Already he thought they would make a good team. "How close have you gotten to him?"

"He took me shopping today." She looked mighty proud of herself.

"You move fast, sweetheart," he drawled. "When did you two meet for the first time?"

Her grin was wicked. "We met over the weekend at his private club I managed to get myself into, then seated myself conveniently under his nose."

"Sounds like I missed the good stuff."

"There isn't any good stuff with this case," she added quickly, her smile fading.

Angela had a point there.

"So tell me about Mario Mandela. What makes the man tick?"

"He's an evil bastard." She shivered and hugged herself, wrinkling her nose as she shook her head. "I've never been this close to someone so evil, so heartless, and so sure of himself that he is doing the right thing. He has no conscience."

"He couldn't to be part of the game."

"Point taken," she said easily, shaking her finger at him. "I have successfully bugged the back of his limosine."

Jake was impressed. When she studied his face for a moment, then grinned, her expression lit up. "I've already got track running upstairs in my room," she offered, looking really proud of herself.

"You've got the ball rolling beautifully, darling," he praised her. "I'm seriously impressed."

Angela must have realized she'd relaxed too much, was actually enjoying having a conversation with him, and apparently decided she wouldn't allow her guard down even that far. That warm look disappeared and she pressed her lips together.

Angela stared at Jake, not saying a word. She took him in from head to toe. He was acutely aware of wherever she looked. When she lifted her attention to his face, he swore he witnessed her mind switch gears.

"I'm going to head upstairs to talk to my dad," she announced, starting toward the door. "Mario is supposed to send his car for me early this evening. I'll be in contact with you before I leave and let you know what we've decided at that time."

"You aren't leaving yet." Jake was right behind her, reaching for her and dragging his fingers down her smooth, thick hair before she spun around, yanking the strands from his fingers.

"Rule number one is this is my case. You answer to me, not the other way around. I'll give the orders." She held her index finger up toward his face and straightened to her full height, which was probably somewhere around five and a half feet tall. "That is, if I decide we can work together. I need to call my dad and debrief." When she took a step backward, her hands were facing him, palms out, as if she warded off some dangerous animal. "You aren't going to stop me and you aren't going to touch me."

"I'm not the bad guy here, Angela," he said, holding his own hands out in a gesture of surrender. He had no problem with Angela running the show. If she remained this skittish, though, he would have to work even harder to protect her.

When she let out a loud breath, her body deflated. "You're right. I'm sorry. This case means a lot to me. I've come so far on it. And I'm really curious why Dad doesn't want to do backup and asked you instead," she mumbled, pushing hair behind her shoulder.

"Because of his missing persons case."

Her eyes opened wide when she stared up at him. "My dad doesn't have a missing persons case."

"How often do you two discuss each other's cases?" Jake didn't know Huxtable and his daughter's relationship well enough to know if he'd tell her everything, or not. Angela's tone suggested she believed she knew about every case he had, though.

Angela tugged at her sleeveless sweater, stretching the knitted material over her breasts, then crossed her arms, showing off her cleavage as she leaned against the door instead of opening it.

"Lately all we've talked about is this case." She dropped her attention to her hands, unfolding her arms and staring at her fingernails, which were nicely filed and painted a bright pink. "I guess he could be working other cases right now without me knowing it." She didn't look up when she tucked her hair behind her ear. "I'm used to knowing everything he does," she added, sighing and shaking her head.

Jake sensed her sincerity. Angela was proud of her father, loved him, and more than likely believed she took care of him. Huxtable might be a hard-ass, but he wouldn't weigh her shoulders down with anything else while she worked this case. That meant he loved his daughter as much as she loved him. Maybe it was that tight bond that sent him flying out to California, stuffing his pride the best he could, and asking for help on his daughter's behalf, because he knew she was going in way over her head.

"What are your plans tonight?" he asked.

"To end the game," she said without hesitating.

"Nothing wrong with optimism." He noticed her hand on the doorknob again, but she wasn't turning it. He really didn't want her leaving. If she did, he'd probably boot up his laptop and start researching her. It would be a lot easier, and more enjoyable, learning about Angela from

Angela. "Call your dad here," he decided, moving into her space and taking her hand off his doorknob. "It would be a good idea to hear your debriefing. I need to be brought up on everything."

Her hand was soft, her fingers long, slender, and warm. Jake gripped her smaller hand in his, turning her as he did, and guided her back into his suite. When he ran his fingers down her back, he swore she shivered. Her silky black hair was thick, very straight, and had an enticing aroma to it he'd love to breathe in deeper, fill his lungs with it. Holding her hand and escorting her, his fingers and palm barely moving across her slender, perfectly arched back, damn near hardened every inch of him to stone. Jake needed to figure out how to work with this woman without sporting a hard-on every time he got close enough to smell her, feel the sexually charged energy she emanated, or touch her. Maybe it was the Chicago humidity affecting him. Jake didn't lose control around women, no matter how hot they were.

Angela slid her hand out of his when she once again stood near the chair where he'd sat. She stared at her hands, rubbing them together. Jake wondered if he affected her the way she did him. That was one hell of a scary thought. If it were the case, knowing both of them were defenseless around the other, would either prove incredibly deadly, or wear both of them out trying to fight it.

"And if you're in charge," he added, trying to relax her, especially if she were fighting to douse the fire burning alive inside her, "you're going to have to tell me what you want me to do."

Don't miss the first HOT novel in Lorie O'Clare's
Bounty Hunter series

PLAY DIRTY
ISBN: 978-0-312-37215-6

And look for the novels in her dangerous and sexy
FBI series

STRONG, SLEEK AND SINFUL
ISBN: 978-0-312-94344-8

LONG, LEAN AND LETHAL
ISBN: 978-0-312-94343-1

TALL, DARK AND DEADLY
ISBN: 978-0-312-94341-7

Available from St. Martin's Paperbacks